THE

BLUE

NATURE

THE
BLUE
NATURE

Suzanne
Hamilton
Free

ST. MARTIN'S PRESS
NEW YORK

DESIGN BY JUDITH A. STAGNITTO

Library of Congress Cataloging-in-Publication Data

Free, Suzanne Hamilton.
   The blue nature.

   I. Title.
PS3556.R38285B5   1989   813'.54   88-29894
ISBN 0-312-02549-1

First Edition
10 9 8 7 6 5 4 3 2 1

The author is indebted to the following:

Excerpt from "Dream Song #1" from 77 *Dream Songs* by
John Berryman. Copyright © 1959, 1963, 1964 by John
Berryman. Reprinted by permission of Farrar, Straus &
Giroux, Inc.

Barry Lopez, excerpted from *Arctic Dreams*. Copyright ©
1986 Barry Holstun Lopez. Reprinted with the permission
of Charles Scribner's Sons, an imprint of Macmillan
Publishing Company.

Excerpt from *Arctic Mood* by Eva Richards. Copyright ©
1949 by Eva Richards. Reprinted by permission of The
Caxton Printers, Ltd.

Excerpts from *The White Dawn: An Eskimo Saga* by James
Houston. Copyright © 1983 by James Houston.
Reprinted by permission of Harcourt Brace Jovanovich,
Inc; in the U.K. and British Commonwealth, reprinted by
permission of William Heinemann, Ltd.

Permissions continue on page 419

for Bob

CONTENTS

PART 1

PART 2

"Then came a departure.
Thereafter nothing fell out as it might or ought."

THE DREAM SONGS
by John Berryman

PART I

"Winter darkness brings on the extreme winter
depression the Polar Eskimo call perlerorneq....
the word means to feel 'the weight of life.' To look
ahead to all that must be accomplished and to
retreat to the present feeling defeated, weary before
starting, a core of anger, a miserable sadness....
The victim tears fitfully at his clothing. A woman
begins aimlessly slashing at things in the iglu with
her knife. A person runs half naked into the bitter
freezing night.... Eventually the person is calmed
by others in the family, with great compassion,
and helped to sleep. Perlerorneq. Winter."

ARCTIC DREAMS
by Barry Lopez, 1986

1

PROLOGUE:
THE APHELION
OF THE COMET

This warm spring night, the second Friday in Lent, 1982, Maddie Cameron took deep breaths to keep herself awake. Her husband Nate was late again. This time the Presbytery meeting was in Cincinnati, and he had a carful of Elders to drop off before he'd get home—around midnight, she guessed. Her third night alone this week.

Was it reducing the dosage of her medicine that made her feel so sleepy tonight, or just plain tiredness? It was hard to tell. Today she'd actually felt better than usual—had measured the progress of the daffodil shoots in the backyard with pleasure. (Once she planted bulbs on church property, which this latest old barn of a house in southwestern Ohio was, the ground became more hers.) She had cleaned out her son's drawers, made a chicken dinner, and all day long looked forward to now, when the kids would be in bed and she could read her Uncle Deane's old astronomy books.

She'd been thinking about her uncle a lot lately for no reason, going over and over the old photograph albums of Alaska as her grandmother Bert used to do. She still looked for clues to the family mystery—which perhaps wasn't a mystery at all. Deane had disappeared into the Arctic thirty-two years ago, in spring. When Maddie was ten, the sudden, peculiarly inconclusive loss of him had weighed on the family like ice accumulating on the wings of his single-engine plane, slowly bringing it down in the middle of a vast, sublimely hostile wasteland—lost forever. (*Sublime.* She pondered the word now, reaching for her grandmother's worn, coverless dictionary: "Exalted, extreme, lofty—like that of a person who does not fear the consequences; threatening but irresistible.") How long had it been since anyone in the family had done anything without fear of the consequences? Her turning down a doctoral fellowship to Radcliffe to marry a Presbyterian minister came the closest.

She'd been a music and English major. Now she preferred astronomy.

This afternoon she'd dusted Deane's books and photograph albums, pausing to daydream about Halley's comet—how after reaching the aphelion, its farthest distance from the sun, in 1948, it was on the last stretch of its journey back and would be visible in the sky again in 1986.

Would she be cured of her illness by 1986? She could identify with the comet, freezing and burning at the same time, racing faster and faster out of the darkness toward the sun, only to be shot out into the darkness again, the same journey over and over again—exactly like the rhythm of clinical depression.

She was pulling out of her fifth episode in seven years, tired of its power to take possession, to sleep and wake in her, like a demon. Why the random selection of *her* as a host? She loved her husband, accepted the constant demands of his profession, had three healthy children, and a double master's degree that enabled her to help Nate plan services, liturgies, sermons. But somewhere inside her was the dread that it was

all useless, that this time the world was going to hell to stay
—plus a terrible sense of time urgency. *Why?*

She knew why. She just couldn't acknowledge it con-
sciously, Dr. Hazelett, her psychiatrist, had said. "The heart
has reasons which reason knows not."

"Count no mortal happy." Was it Freud who had said that?
Shakespeare? Dr. Hazelett? Depression muddled her memory
for names, dates, quotations.

Tonight she couldn't concentrate even on the comet. She
felt restless. The room was too warm. She took off her robe
and threw it across the room, not caring what passing parish-
ioner might look through the living-room window and see
her in her flimsy blue nightgown—or what used to be blue,
bleached off-white with a load of diapers long ago. Old Mrs.
Swope across the street watched her with binoculars, Maddie
had learned from her babysitter. For many people, ministers'
wives were objects of infinite interest. Maddie had been sim-
ilarly watched by neighbors in other parishes. With a smirk,
the sitter suggested that Maddie and "the Rev" might put on
a show some night for Mrs. Swope—something to fog her
binoculars. But Maddie refused to buy window shades. Feeling
closed in was even more uncomfortable than being watched.

Now she wished she could take off her nightgown too.
Her grandmother once told her Deane used to practice nudity
around the house, long before he went to Alaska and enjoyed
igloo nudity and ghost stories with Eskimos around a glowing
whale-oil lamp. He had loved the Great Land, the severity of
its beauty, the "warmth of the cold."

The telephone rang. She jumped in her chair as if a gun
had been fired behind her head. She rose and walked slowly
to the hall, dizzy at first, her irritable nerves scrambling to
reorganize themselves like a colony of panicked ants.

"Hello?" she said, stabilized, in her calm, minister's wife
voice.

"Maddie," her father said, his voice also artificially calm, "something has happened."

Her father was rarely indirect. Maddie felt a turning and tightening in her stomach, a reflex against church criticism or bad news.

"Bert is dying," he said.

Usually good at matching her father's controlled response to unforeseen events, Maddie was too shocked to say anything. Then, as if she hadn't understood, she said weakly, "What?"

He explained that her grandmother had had a massive stroke. "Her whole left side is paralyzed," he told her. "And she's bleeding internally."

"No," Maddie said, gripping the phone with a white-knuckled paralysis of her own. And yet the stroke was logical, a voice inside her commented. It could never be Bert's heart that failed.

"She can't last more than a few days," her father said.

"But I can't come home right now," she protested on the absurd grounds of timing. "There are so many special services I have to play for, the Brahms *Requiem* rehearsals, study groups, kids' choir rehearsals . . ."

"It doesn't matter," he reassured her. "She doesn't recognize any of us."

"It isn't possible," she said, too softly for him to hear.

"The doctor says he doesn't know where her strength is coming from. She can't hold out much longer."

Oh, yes she can, Maddie thought with a furious surge of energy that made her lean against the wall for balance. Bert couldn't die until Deane came home—which he never would.

Ginny, Maddie's mother, took the phone briefly and repeated her father's reassurance: it was useless for Maddie to make the long trip home since Bert wouldn't even know she was there. They must all just wait and pray. At least, she added before hanging up, Bert would soon be reunited with her husband, "beloved Howdy," who had died ten years ago.

Maddie hung up the phone and went back to her chair in a state of strange anticipation. What would happen now? She stared straight ahead, as if into a vacuum—which wasn't a vacuum at all, but only a huge space she had placed in herself between Then and Now—between childhood, when Deane had been her idol and Bert her mentor, and her own fast-approaching middle age.

She went over to the bookshelf where Deane's old albums were stored (stolen out of a trunk in her father's attic before she had moved away from Pittsburgh), took up a pile of them, and spread them out in front of the floor fan. The fan blew the disintegrating edges of the pages across the rug like a little flurry of snow, and she felt a flash of tears burn across her eyes —reabsorbed instantly. She could never really cry in depression.

She opened the Shishmaref album first, bending over the bleak, monochromatic landscapes that still fascinated her. There was a black-and-white picture of the windblown Bering Sea backed by a brooding ghostly sky, another of Deane setting out on a walk across the tundra, a third of a collapsed walrus skeleton lying on the beach beside a storm-dismantled dwelling that looked like another pile of bones. At the top of the first page he had written, "Man is astonishingly impressive when faced with any adversary but his fellow man."

Deane had suffered from depression too, Bert had told Maddie many times. He had the blue nature—meaning that special quality of mind that all the family's most driven achievers had: restless, intense, wanting neither and both of every choice of philosophical options, subject to soaring highs and sinking lows. But he had never, even in his worst lows, come to Maddie's sorry state of physical weakness and color blindness

by which everything—earth, sky, the impressiveness of man
—turned gray.

How had he resisted it? How had he kept his balance?
He'd prescribed radical changes of scene and culture for himself, she guessed. And it had worked.

Tonight she had to take his word on the beautiful Arctic
colors—"perdition oranges, reds, indigos," he had written under a black-and-white photograph. Years ago she'd been able
to imagine them vividly. She had even believed herself destined
to set out into that same threatening but irresistible territory
whether he'd been there to search for or not. But she hadn't
done it. She smiled faintly at the idea now, liking to think it
might still be possible.

Instead she directed choir rehearsals, taught Sunday
school classes, led devotions for charity luncheons, attended
Women's Circle meetings. Harmless, if not sublime occupa-
tions, she often reminded herself, out of which some modest
good frequently came. But even when she was well, the demon
lay beneath her like a permafrost, and she went about her
duties color-blind, tone-deaf, foul-breathed, deceiving the parishioners into thinking her heart was engaged in her work.

"Is there anything you enjoy doing when you're depressed?" Dr. Hazelett had asked her a month ago. "Anything
at all?"

"Yes," she had said. "I enjoy writing Nate's sermons for
him when he's pressed for time. I lose myself in it."

"The subject of Jesus saves, if not Jesus himself?"

Yes, she had nodded, anxious to please. But despite his
obvious goodwill for her, she was amazed at his ignorance of
any other perspective on her condition than that of his own
profession. Before seeing him, she had read every book she
could find on her illness. She knew every healing strategy he
tried on her before he tried it. But what did he know of the
sagging weight of Holy Mother Church—that anxious, ragged

bag-mother of the 1980s? While telling her to affirm her role as minister's wife, he subtly mocked the church. Perhaps Maddie's younger sister Katy had given her the best advice before she died: the best way to mental health since Deane and so much else was lost was to lower one's standard of sanity, to counter daily horror with a daily dose of vaudevillian humor, and to take what was left of religion and cherish it like a secret.

But now, crouched on the floor, Maddie had to concede that the pills Dr. Hazelett supplied her with worked. It was the laboratory scientists at Roche, not the words of the prophets that kept her going these days. She mocked the church herself.

She opened the Nome photograph album, and a yellowed slip of paper fell out—a few scribbled notes of Deane's describing the first photograph, a grotesque-looking Eskimo mask with blue wooden hands sticking out of where the ears should be. "The use of art:" he had written, "that we should no longer be bewildered and oppressed."

"Oh?" she thought aloud, looking up at that same mask displayed at the top of her dust-covered bookshelf. The new novel she'd tried to read lately had only added to her feelings of oppression and bewilderment—literature of the glands, not the heart, Faulkner had said in 1950—the same year Deane had disappeared.

Stuck in the album was her most recent postcard from Bert saying maybe Deane would come back with the comet. But now, brought down by the stroke, she wasn't able to wait for the comet, or even for Easter evening when Maddie could drive home and tell her how much she loved her.

Maddie took in a gulp of air, feeling almost feverish in the humid March heat, yet shivering in front of the fan. She thought back to the ice-cold Christmas of 1949—four months after the Soviets had exploded their first atomic bomb—when Deane had come home to tell Bert how much he loved her.

He'd come all the way from Nome that night and brought the whole scale and excitement of Alaska into her grandparents' living room, telling them all about Christmas in Barrow—not a pine tree anywhere to decorate, and later, around the gas fire, what spring was like above the Arctic Circle when the makeshift coffins of the Eskimos rose to the surface of their shallow graves in the permafrost and the corpses' eyes melted in the sun with a look of perfect peace in them. He said he wanted to live in the Bering Straits country, where the few occurring species of amphibians were all the more fascinating for their scarcity, where all life was lived near the limits of tolerance. He had even smelled exciting as he sat beside Maddie in front of the hissing radiants of the gas fire and told stories of vengeance-seeking *tupilaqs*—hell-animals made of stray, mismatched bones that would hunt a man down and kill him—no mercy, no hope of escape.

But life could be lived near the limits of tolerance without ever leaving one's own temperate climate. Now, as she hunched over a faded photograph of "The Golden Beaches of Nome" —gray, cobbled, bare as a moonscape—she wondered how Deane could have found them so beautiful. Where was the gold? "So powder-fine," she read his handwritten note, "so exhausted, it can't be recovered profitably."

She stared at the mask. Could the gold in a family's genetic endowment be exhausted too? Growing thinner and thinner with each generation, its original greatness inevitably regressing toward the mean? Could it happen to a religion? To a nation? Tonight, all the vacuity of popular entertainment, of popular music, of popular religion oppressed her. Or was it only her depressed perspective that made everything in America seem so depleted?

She put the Nome album aside and lay down on her back. The beaches were exhausted. The Golden Age was over. The rising star of Bert's and Grandaddy's hopes had fallen, and it was ridiculous to compare her little rise and fall as a failing minister's wife to Deane's spectacular arc.

After some blank moments, she prodded herself to get up and read. But she couldn't move. Where was her energy? she demanded. Eight years ago she could have scrubbed the steps of the Washington Monument and not felt tired. Where was it?

Submerged, she well knew. Storing. Withholding.

Forcing herself up, she went to the window and opened it as high as it would go. She wished for a wind to blow up the curtains—wild, uncontrollable. Then back in the chair, she smiled at a poem stuck in one of Deane's books, a sonnet she'd written to Nate last summer about her love of winter, titled "Comforted by Blizzards." He had liked it so much, he'd printed it in the church newspaper in the "Poet's Corner." But the overworked church secretary had been in a hurry typing up the stencil, so instead of "Comforted by Blizzards," the title of her premiere poem had read "Comforted by Lizzards." Her kids had had a good laugh over it. But a prominent Elder had protested the "unorthodox content," and Maddie had used the criticism as an excuse not to write any more. Too much was at stake for Nate in this fourth, large parish, with twentieth-century Christians at each other's throats about sexist language in hymns and the rights of homosexuals to mainstreet housing and where the church's mission dollars were really going in Nicaragua.

Her throat felt constricted as she gave way to the thought of Bert dying in the nursing home, and her vision blurred again with tears of emotion. But that was good, some objective part of her mind noted, monitoring the strong feelings. The dullness of depression was definitely giving way. She was thawing.

She heard Nate's car in the driveway and looked at the clock: 12:25.

She worried about him in this college-town church. Since the chaos of the sixties, some members had retreated into a narrow, paranoid fundamentalism. Others flaunted a reckless, humorless radicalism that inspired only utilitarian art, proclaimed politics as the new religion, and afforded no mystery at all. While Nate spun a hundred simultaneous plates trying to walk a reconciling line between them, she made Styrofoam rummage-sale crafts and washed dishes after Medical Mission teas. This wasn't what either of them had thought the ministry would be.

Nate came up the cellar stairs slowly, tired, she could tell, and rounded the corner of the kitchen with his overt-covert minister's face still on—always up, always affirmative for Christ. (The church had taught them both duplicity.) Are you all right? he asked without speaking. Any change? Is everything all right?

"A little better," she said. "You?"

He nodded okay, too weary to tell her about the Presbytery meeting. He kissed her, then puttered at his desk, his fingers blue and puffy. Church nerves, she recognized. After throwing down pens, date book, notes on the desk, he went to the hall to look for messages.

"Ann Smith called," Maddie said. "Her poor mother is starting to shrivel up inside the body cast. Her diabetes is—"

"I know. I stopped at the hospital on the way home. She can't sleep at night, so they let me in. She hasn't lost her spirit, Mad. Still lecturing me on the evils of cardplaying with my son. We had a good time together."

He went to the kitchen and looked over the mail on the counter.

"I got a letter today from Vi McCinney telling me my hemlines are too short," Maddie warned him. "She's advocating Christian clothes now. And she's going to join another church if you don't back her up."

"What are Christian clothes?" he said absently. Then,

"She's a big giver. Practically supplies the interdenominational food pantry."

"You got a letter from the science teacher at the high school who dropped into church last Sunday. He said yours was the first church service he's attended in five years that didn't insult his intelligence."

Nate looked up and smiled. "Really?" He went to the cupboard and poured himself a glass of cream sherry, then pulled off his tie, came over to her chair, and bent down to kiss her again. She reached up to hold him, surprised by a wave of strong desire for his physical nearness. How long had it been since they had spontaneously made love, without the psychological chaperone of the church, phone calls and visitors at all hours, the kids—or the sexually numbing effects of depression? When had they abandoned all roles, all proprieties, even for an hour? Ministers were called "the third sex" for good reason.

"I have a nursing home service in the morning," he said, apologetically extricating himself from her arms. "A Lenten meditation."

His words brought back the thought of Bert's dying. But as he sat down at his desk, his forehead creased, neck stiff, she decided not to burden him with the news about the stroke tonight. Was there something wrong, some crisis or criticism in his congregation that worried him? She recalled that the last pastor of this church had left the ministry altogether. He'd told Nate he used to go down to the train station every Saturday afternoon to watch the trains go out because they were the only thing in the whole town he didn't have to push. He said he'd gotten tired of playing fireman in a succession of small-town churches, always putting out fires set by a few anonymous members who had disliked him from the start, the church "arsonists" who practiced Christianity like some people played Monopoly—for fun and the illusion of power.

Let Nate handle it, Maddie thought selfishly tonight, feel-

ing the precariousness of her recovery from her illness and the
certainty of no recovery for Bert.

As he settled down to work, she pulled her favorite album
of Barrow onto her lap and turned the big, fragile pages. And
page by page, she felt a gradual change in the back of her
head, a loosening down her neck and shoulders. As smoothly
and unpredictably as a weight of snow sliding off a roof, she
felt a giving way somewhere—silent yet abrupt, like the last
inching of a glacier over an edge of rock, just far enough to
crack, break off, and fall—a piece only—through free air into
the ocean below. And then a sense of surfacing, of coming up
alive, and floating, lighter than she'd felt in months.

Could Bert's stroke be causing this? she thought with a
shudder. Or was it happening anyway? She felt a wave of
euphoria, like a soldier hearing the news of an enemy's rumored
but unexpected surrender.

Her eyes fell on an enlarged photograph of Deane standing arm-in-arm with an ancient-looking, happy-faced Eskimo
who, four decades ago, had lost all his children to starvation.
Underneath Deane had written a line of Scripture to express
the Eskimo's philosophy: "Thou hast mourned the not-to-be-
mourned"—not from the Bible, but from the *Bhagavad Gita*.

What was the use of mourning anymore? Deane smiled
out at her. Why mourn the not-to-be-mourned?

Suddenly her stomach felt full of air bubbles. Sometimes
she felt as if she had the bends when she shot up out of
frozenness into passionate feeling. That was the amazing thing
about depression. That without anything being solved, without
making any change at all, it could give way and let her go.

But what was the use of it then? She still had enough
Freudian—or Calvinist—faith left to believe every feeling had
its reason. And now she felt the vaguest insinuation of disappointment. For what had it taken her down again? Like the
orbit of the comet, it took her a million billion miles farther

out into the cold and dark than she needed to go to make a revolution. And precisely at the aphelion was the point of turnaround, trailing fire and ice all the way back to where she started: an enormous distance traveled, but no progress made.

I want to see Bert before she dies, the thought intruded urgently. *Please God*, knowing full well You don't intervene in such matters, though Bert is suffering, *keep her alive until I get there.*

She stared at Nate's back as he worked. She wanted to tell him she was getting better, that she was coming up fast and would be herself, full of energy, in a week or two, maybe less. Yet he couldn't know what a victory it was or wasn't. She recalled something Virginia Woolf had said about her own depressions—that one's lowest ebb was probably the truest vision.

Perlerorneq: an underlined word in a list of Eskimo nouns caught her eye. She had never looked closely at Deane's lists of Eskimo vocabulary before, only the photographs, and could barely make out his penciled translation: "Extreme winter depression; to feel the weight of life; to retreat. *The Eskimos regard this as a sacred state.*"

Tears welled up and overflowed. Melting ice, streaming down her cheeks.

She closed the album and cherished the realization of her returning health, keeping it a secret tonight, with all the legions of her conflicting selves chattering and muttering excitedly, like flattened grass-blades rising up out of a giant's footprint.

2

KEYS

Maddie counted her years before the age of ten as Before; everything else was After. When, against Dr. Hazelett's advice, she lost herself in memories of the past, her eighth year— 1948—came back most vividly: her father's older brother, Uncle Deane, Grandmother Bert and Grandaddy, Great-Aunt Essy, her parents and two-year-old sister Katy frozen in characteristic poses in the old Tudor house in Pittsburgh, like the dioramas of lost civilizations in the Carnegie Museum where Deane worked. The rooms of that house were both bright and dark in her memory. On the spiral-legged refectory table, now sold off, Bert had kept her well-worn volumes of Shakespeare and the American poets. From these she had read aloud to her sons, Deane and Willy, since they were five years old. On the Mason and Hamlin grand piano was the Schnabel edition of Beethoven, the page-corners of favorite sonatas turned down by three generations of musicians. Hurricane lamps glowed in all the corners and alcoves, casting circles of light on the ceiling that hovered over everyones' heads like halos.

When the diorama began to move in her mind, everyone

laughed, resumed arguments, or sat down to play impromptu recitals as they used to, with Bert, the costume-jeweled, black-velveted matriarch always strenuously overacting, always leaning toward Deane when he was home—who would, as Maddie recalled, lean back in a chair or lounge against a doorway with an air of bemused detachment, the family audience.

He'd been working on his doctoral dissertation that year, and, because of his special knowledge of the Arctic, had just been hired by Johns Hopkins University to work on a Survival Project for the Office of Naval Research beginning in 1949—something about geodetic surveys, photographing Soviet islands from the air, and conducting secret experiments in the limits of human endurance above the Arctic Circle. What the secret was, nobody knew. But as Deane prepared for an expedition of his own in March of 1948, he was already looking forward to this bigger one next year. His letters from Nome were full of strategies for keeping the Navy from dragging its feet or bogging down in delays. And at home, nobody was even trying to talk him out of it—not even Bert, who hated expeditions of any kind that took family members out of her sight for more than a few days.

"You might as well migrate up there!" Great-Aunt Essy, Bert's widowed sister, had said when he came home in June, thin-faced and hard-muscled, and told them all about eating raw caribou meat with the Eskimos—the Inupiat, he called them—and sleeping stark-naked in igloos of driftwood, whalebone, and sod. He had been hunting walrus with Eskimos and accepted the valuable tusks as a gift. (Twenty years later, those tusks would be in Maddie's possession, stolen out of a rotting trunk in her father's attic.) On past trips, he had always brought her back beautiful souvenirs: in 1946, an Inuit doll dressed in white fox fur; in 1947, a copper box filled with tiny whales, seals, fish, and polar bears carved out of ivory from a little town called Wales; and now, this year, for her eighth birthday,

a pair of gray and white sealskin mukluks, as soft and elegant
as anything she had ever seen.

"But they're too small!" Bert had cried woefully when Maddie tried to pull them on over her socks—meaning, why didn't
he come home from Alaska more often so he'd know his niece's
shoe size? But Maddie held them up on her hands and didn't
care about the size. They were works of art, flawlessly stitched
with rings of perfectly symmetrical diamonds all around the
ankles. She loved them.

"If you wear them in the snow," Deane said, his eyes warm
and deep (unreachably quiet, she remembered, no matter what
Bert said), "you have to do what the Eskimo mothers do—
chew them for hours and hours until they're soft again. And
then your husband's and sons' boots too."

"Chew them?" Bert said, aghast. "The very idea! I would
never."

But she had, Maddie thought, looking back. She had.

Bert's house had been only a block away from Maddie's,
and when Deane came over to visit, which was often when he
was home, she would bring her souvenirs into the living room
to play and listen to the conversation between him and her
father. Her father would talk first, telling Deane everything
that was going on in the orchestra (he had played tympani in
the Pittsburgh Symphony—the youngest member in its history, Bert boasted—personally invited in by the great Fritz
Reiner when he was seventeen years old). It was getting harder
to work nine hours a day as an engineer and play long concerts
at night, he said. Then Deane would take over and tell about
his latest adventures in the Alaskan wilderness. Maddie would
watch and listen with fascination. Something about him attracted her like a warm-glowing human hearth. Some evenings
she played the snake-and-rabbit game with him. As he went
on about some new species of frog he'd discovered on an
expedition, she'd walk back and forth in front of him ten or

fifteen times trying to distract his attention. Just when she was
sure he wasn't going to play, he'd reach out and grab her, throw
her up in the air like an ornamental pillow, then catch her and
squeeze her so tightly she couldn't breathe.

"You weren't alert, rabbit," he reproached her the evening
after he'd given her the mukluks for her birthday, "and now a
Python reticulatus is going to squeeze you to death, so slowly
your insides will come squirting out between your ribs."

"Don't start, Deane!" her mother called from the kitchen.

Maddie squealed and struggled to get away, as if it were
possible. But his arms were an inescapable cage, and they got
tighter and tighter the more she struggled. He said he'd let
her go only if she promised to hold still and not make a sound
no matter how much tighter the snake squeezed. She promised,
and when she did manage to will herself to be calm, subduing
panic (would the snake ever stop?), he slowly opened the
cage—but still kept hold of one wrist.

"That isn't fair!" she protested.

"You're a fluffy girl," he said as she yanked and pulled with
reckless abandon. "A bundle of cobwebs tied with a ribbon."

"I can get away if I want to," she bluffed.

"No one gets away from me. You're nothing but *mah-
nau-nau*."

She glanced at her father, who knew a lot of Eskimo words
by now. "Eiderdown," he said. "Duck feathers."

"Oh no—I think she's an *ook-pik-e-lo*," Deane said, studying
her closely, then staring off into space as if in deep conjecture.
He always called her an *ookpikelo* at least once during the game.

Her father didn't know that word. "An Eskimo flute?" she
guessed.

Deane's eyes narrowed and glowed so darkly, she wanted
to get up close and look into them with Grandaddy's magnifying glass. "It's an Arctic marshmallow," he said. "Sled dogs
eat them all the time."

Then suddenly he turned her upside down and pretended to sweep the rug with her hair. "You know, Willy, I have a luna moth in my collection that looks a lot like Maddie. But he's bigger, stronger, and prettier."

Her upside-down face reddened as she tried to look up at him, and she appealed to her father for help. But he sat with arms folded, a look of resignation on his face that said no one could control Deane. So she grabbed onto Deane's leg and tried to climb up his side, slipped, and tried again.

"I have a *Thamnophis sirtalis* in a jar that's more intelligent, too," he said. "I brought it all the way from my tent in Icy Cape."

"That's a lie," she croaked, her face purple as she recognized the scientific name for garter snake. "There are no snakes in Alaska. You told me."

In a moment he set her upright again and let her go, wrist and all. "What? You believed that? I've got a rosy boa from Shishmaref right here. Took it out of Bert's refrigerator this morning. He's probably real lively by now." He rummaged in his pockets for the snake, then wriggled around as though it were crawling down his pant's leg. She backed away, half-believing it was true. But then, like a snake striking, the manacle of his thumb and finger was back on her wrist, and she knew she had fallen for one of his acts. She wrestled and pulled, gnawed at his knuckles, bit him as hard as she could, but he just sat down, turned to her father, and started talking about the rarity of two-legged ajolote lizards.

They had played this game many times. And she loved battling this unbeatable adversary who never pretended to weaken for her sake.

But sometimes her squeals got too loud, and her mother would march into the room and stop the game, frowning at Deane, who always acted as though he were unjustly accused and had nothing to do with it. "You're too rough," she

had berated him the night he threatened Maddie with the
rosy boa, making him let her go, refastening the loose barrettes
that dangled in her hair. "You don't understand little girls
at all."

He had winked and grinned at her as her mother dragged
her out to the kitchen. (Even then, there had been a special
collusion between herself and Deane, Maddie thought years
later; surely it hadn't all been in her imagination.) Flushed and
breathless, she had stood at the kitchen sink while her mother
washed her face, tucked her blouse back into her overalls, and
then asked her to help with some bowl-stirring or pot-washing
duty. But as soon as her mother's back was turned, she slipped
out of the kitchen and tried to get his attention again.

But most times after her mother stopped the game, it was
over for the night. That evening, once back in the living room,
she had walked back and forth in front of him fifty times, but
he was so deep in conversation with her father he really didn't
seem to see her. So after a while, she gave up and climbed up
on the couch between the two men, slid under her father's
arm, and listened to Deane talk for another hour about the
sheer, sharp-edged slopes of the Brooks Range and the shining
lakes in the Yukon-Kuskokwim Delta until she fell asleep. She
dreamed about what she'd just heard, of turquoise-blue mountains rearing up like walls straight into the clouds, and of houses
made of snow, shining like scoops of ice cream under a dazzling
azure sky. But then, without warning, it all turned upside down,
and she felt herself falling, slowly at first, then faster and faster,
in a thrill of beauty and terror into the enormous vault of blue.
She looked up at the ceiling of the tundra and saw her face
reflected in a thousand polygonal lakes and ponds, like fragments
of a broken mirror or pieces of a puzzle, changing places and
shapes, all gradually receding out of her sight. Then everything
grew dim as the blue turned indigo, then purple, then black.
She jerked awake, afraid of the black, both relieved and dis-

appointed to find herself safe in her own bed, Deane gone, the house silent and dark.

Those were the days when Deane kept a cluttered little office at the Carnegie Museum of Natural History in Oakland. His ambition had been to collect a hundred new species in one year, he had said, though after his last expedition, he wrote to say that he might have to settle for fifteen at best. When in July he had a new rare species of spider named after him— *Tarantula cameroni*—he had sent Bert red roses.

"Nine-tenths of the museum is stored underground or behind these locked doors," he told Maddie one warm evening in August as she and her father walked with him along the corridors of the first floor of the museum. She had come along at his special request. He wanted to show her something.

As they rounded the waterfall exhibit and passed through the Hall of Dinosaurs on to other hallways lined with more doors on either side, it occurred to her that Deane had keys to all these doors. He knew what was behind every one. Though it was after hours now and the museum was closed, here she was walking around in this wonderful shadowy place, like the inside of an Egyptian pyramid, free as she pleased to look at and touch any of the exhibits. Because Deane was her uncle, she was an insider here. Last week he had taken her on a tour of the Bone Room in the labyrinth of underground passages where visitors weren't usually allowed to go. She had seen woolly-mammoth fossils ride in on special railroad carts, the bones wrapped in protective shells of tissue paper, burlap, and plaster of Paris. He had given her a flashlight and let her explore the long dusty shelves of skulls and skeletons. In the same way, because her father had been invited into the orchestra by conductor Fritz Reiner, she was an insider at the Syria Mosque concert hall, where she could wander among the velvet-lined instrument cases strewn all over the backstage floor while her father rehearsed—or, as he had arranged last year,

sit on the same piano bench with Rudolf Serkin's daughter—
just her age—and play a duet. And it would always be this
way, she thought with a thrill of joyful privilege. Always.

Deane led them up a flight of marble stairs to a huge, glass-
encased exhibit, "a masterpiece of nineteenth-century taxi-
dermy," he said, first shown at the Paris Fair of 1869—a fierce-
looking North African Arab on a one-humped camel fighting
off two attacking lions. "A famous and familiar tableau of frozen
fury," the sign beside the case read. "Walk around it, Maddie,"
Deane told her. "Study it for a while."

The female lion lay dead at the camel's feet—killed, she
guessed, by the Arab's rifle, which had fallen out of his reach
in the sand. But the enraged male lion's jaws were only inches
away from the Arab's elbow. The Arab was poised to strike at
its throat with a long dagger. But the camel's leg was injured,
and he looked as though he were about to fall. The taxidermist,
Deane said, had left the decision of who would win the life-
and-death struggle up to the person looking at it.

"Well?" he said, after a while. "Who wins, Maddie?"

She walked around and around it. The taxidermist had
done a good job. The odds seemed perfectly even. "Is there a
secret clue hidden in it somewhere?" she asked.

He shook his head.

As she walked around it again, Deane and her father began
to argue about it—about the distance of the dagger from the
attacking lion's throat, the angle of the blade, the probable
tiredness of the Arab's arm muscles, the desperation of the
lion's hunger and fury at the loss of his mate. It was her father's
opinion that the Arab would win. But Deane wouldn't commit
himself either way.

"Who do you *want* to win?" Maddie asked him, not much
liking the cruel eyes and clenched teeth of the Arab.

"That's the question, isn't it?" he replied.

She didn't know what he meant.

"I want to know who *does* win," she said, anxious to know his opinion so she could form her own.

He glanced at her father and smiled. "Well then, you and your dad are going to have to get inside the case and start slashing up the upholstery—shorten the hind legs of the lion, move the camel forward, lengthen the blade of the knife—slant the situation as you like. Force the certainty, eh, Will?"

Maddie sensed, as she had at other times, that there was an ongoing argument between Deane and her father that had nothing to do with the the subject at hand. It could make them flare up at each other one minute, shout and argue furiously, and then, the next minute, when no one won the argument, laugh it all off as if it were nothing. (Later, Maddie began to understand that they had been best friends as well as brothers, though of radically different natures. Deane could live with, even celebrate, ambivalence. Her father couldn't stand it.)

They had taken the streetcar home that night after looking at more of Deane's favorite exhibits. Neither her father nor her uncle could afford a car, but she felt rich anyway. "What's your decision?" Deane had whispered in her ear after they had taken their seats, as though hers were a valuable opinion. "Who wins?"

She hesitated. Then, embarrassed, feeling like a failure at an important test, she said, "I don't know. I can't make up my mind."

Deane had given her father a little cat-grin of triumph.

"You know," he said in a confidential tone, "when I was a little older than you—in sixth grade—I went to Africa to capture the rare Schnozzle-nosed Bazoop for the Smithsonian. And after all that trouble, the Institution said they didn't want it because it had gone cross-eyed in the heat."

Maddie laughed.

"That's the way it goes sometimes," he said. "No one will

ever see a Bazoop now. Like your father, they wanted a perfect one, and now they have none."

He paid her carfare when they got off the streetcar and took her hand at the crossing.

He approves of me, Maddie thought happily. He thinks I'm worth something. But as they walked up the hill toward home, his attention shifted to her father, and they began to argue again, this time about rumors of communists at Johns Hopkins University and Russians disguised as fishermen along the Arctic coast. He knew more about it than he was saying, her father accused him. Then at something else her father said, she saw all the light go out of Deane's eyes, and only the darkness and depth were left.

The argument blew over as usual, and Deane decided to come home with her father to play chess. Maddie was glad, since the games often lasted all night and Deane would still be there in the morning when she woke up. She liked to stand by the card table until after midnight, watching both men think and plot, heeding Deane's threats to "crunch" her if she touched any of his chess pieces. Finally, her mother would come and make her go to bed. On the nights when Deane stayed, her mother would sleep beside her all night long. With the light of the living-room lamps filtering up through the stairway bannisters and the muffled conversation of the two men still audible below, her mother warm and close, Maddie would feel as safe and thrillingly happy as a child growing up in a palace. From what she saw of her friends' families in the neighborhood—people who listened to popular music on the radio for hours and played Bingo on their back porches at night—she knew her family was different, so caught up in arguments and high goals.

Downstairs was someone who had been to the top of the world and climbed sharp cliffs ("of friable schist," he had taught her, rock like razor blades) until his hands bled down his arms. He had lived with the Eskimos and written stories about them that were published in foreign languages. He had discovered new bugs that no one knew existed. And he intended to go on exploring, higher and higher, and maybe one day might even take her with him on one of his trips. In the meantime, he brought her back signs of the strange and exotic places he had been—keys to other worlds. Her collection was growing year by year. She couldn't fall asleep anymore when he was in the house.

But tonight the chess game ended early. Maddie heard her father putting away the pieces. Who had won? She crept out of bed, went to the stairs, descended one by one, and listened. They were talking about Deane's upcoming expedition to a river valley near a place called Point Barrow, a preliminary trip for the bigger trip with the Navy next January.

"I have a veteran pilot," he was saying, showing her father a photograph. "He's got a single-engine cabin plane, equipped with new skis and everything. He's flown the Berlin Airlift and knows the territory. You'd like him, Will."

She knew Deane wished her father would share his work as he used to before he got married. They had argued about it before. On the bottom step, she watched through the bannisters as Deane took out a large folded map. "We begin on Tigvariak Island—here," he said, "but we'll spend most of the time in this area here, about a hundred thirty miles southeast of Barrow, along the Northern Slope."

Her father stared at the white area Deane pointed to. "But it's nothing. A big wide expanse of nothing."

Deane traced probable flight paths with his finger. "I'll have plenty of time to work on my own projects. They've promised me my own contract."

"What on earth do they want a frog expert for?"

Deane leaned back, paused, then looked at her father

intently. "You're the best engineer your company has, Will. They'd give you a month. So would the orchestra. Come with me."

Maddie studied the look on her uncle's face, both open and closed, as though he wanted to order her father to come with him without wasting any more time, but of course couldn't or wouldn't. Had he been born with that look? she wondered. Some part of him always disengaged, held back?

"No," her father said after a moment. "I camped out in snow in Germany. I like my life, nine to five, golf on Saturdays—"

"And church on Sundays. For God's sake, you're not even in a foxhole. Essy and your country-Methodist wife are ruining you."

They laughed at this. Essy's born-again religion was a joke between them, Maddie knew, though sometimes less funny to Deane. Essy nagged him about his refusal to go to church anymore when he came home.

Then Deane leaned forward and said quietly, "Willy, I need you."

Maddie noted the changed tone in his voice.

Her father noted it too, looked at the pilot's picture, back at the map, then got up and started to pace.

"You're tempted," Deane said, watching him closely.

Her father hesitated, then shook his head. "No. I'm only tempted to make you still think so. Some people belong up there. I'm not one of them."

"It's incredibly alluring, Will," Deane said quietly. "You haven't seen Denali, or Nunivak Island, or what happens to light when—"

"Spare me the travelogue. I've read your notebooks. I went with you to the Yukon ten years ago, remember? I know all about the long, dreary days you put in, the slow treks from nowhere to nowhere, the cramped little tents and millions of buzzing insects. You can't get anywhere up there without a plane or a boat, and half the pilots go down in their own crates."

"You're exaggerating," Deane said, as though entertained by his brother's impassioned manner. "No way to win an argument with me."

"And those smelly shacks you come back to, full of lamp oil and preservatives. Rows of jars of frogs and lizards floating in their own juice."

"Preservatives can get into your blood," Deane smiled, "like printer's ink, or—"

"*Your* blood, not mine. I didn't like the North Atlantic, and I'd hate the Bering Sea."

Deane looked hard at him, a long, unsmiling look that surprised and then frightened Maddie. "You don't know what you're talking about," he said at last.

Her father picked up the map and tossed it at him. "You listen, Deane. This isn't concocting adventures over corn-silk cigarettes under Bert's back porch. You're taking real risks. You won't even tell Mother or Dad what you're doing up there."

"Scared, little brother?" Deane said. "I'll take care of you."

Her father looked away in exasperation, then saw her peering through the bannisters on the bottom stair. She shrank back; but to her surprise, he motioned for her to come in and join them. Then, as she squinted in the bright light, he put his hands on her shoulders and positioned her like a museum exhibit in front of Deane. "Tell me," he said, "who will take care of *her?*"

Deane folded up the map and stuffed it back into his pocket. Seeming to sense her embarrassment, he didn't look at her.

"Madeleine!" her mother called from upstairs; but she hardly heard. She was watching Deane's attention, which had been so focused and powerful a moment before, sink away from her father and everything in the room.

"*I'd* come with you," Maddie said, feeling his disappointment with a queer intensity.

He looked at her and said absently, "I bet you would." Then all at once, the absent look disappeared. His eyes lit up with resolve, like a lion deciding to attack a complacent passing Arab. "Well," he said, "I'm going to have to show your father who's boss. All right with you?"

She nodded.

Before her father knew what was happening, Deane had pulled him off his chair and onto the floor with a crash. "If I win," he said, pinning him down like an expert wrestler, "you do what I say for the rest of your life, as God intended. Agreed?"

Though taken by surprise, her father loved to wrestle and got into the spirit of it right away. "Agreed," he said, pushing Deane off with a powerful shove.

"Mother's going to be mad," Maddie said, laughing as the two men began to maul and roll each other around the room like two huge boys. They weren't allowed to wrestle in the house, and they knew it.

Though Deane was two inches taller, her father was ten pounds heavier and a good match. Neither one gained the advantage at first. But then in a quick move, Deane got her father into a stranglehold, sat on top of him and gloated, declaring himself the victor. Maddie didn't know whether to cheer or boo. But as he raised his arms over his head, in a fast, sudden maneuver her father rolled him off balance and threw him hard against the wall. Her mother's knick-knack shelf rattled, and two glass birds fell onto the floor. A wing broke off one of them.

Deane leaped back and attacked. Wanting to join in, Maddie jumped on his neck and held on. Awkwardly he shook her off, accidentally jamming her lower lip against her top teeth with his elbow. It stung, and she tasted blood.

"Get away, Maddie," her father ordered. "You'll get hurt."

Who cared? She jumped onto Deane's shoulders to ride him like a horse. But she jumped too far, and in an effort to keep her from rolling over his head, Deane caught his outstretched left leg in the cord of her mother's best floorlamp. Then as he forced her father's arm up behind his back and jerked his own leg to the right, before Maddie could get out of the way the heavy lamp came crashing down on top of her, and the porcelain globe smashed into a thousand pieces. Losing her balance, she fell onto the pieces of glass and cut her hands.

"I didn't do it!" she screamed, hiding her bleeding hands behind her back as her mother charged down the stairs and into the room.

"Will you ever grow up?" her mother shouted at Deane and her father, seeing the damage. "For heaven's sake, Will, it's two o'clock in the morning!"

Deane set the broken lamp upright. The shaft was badly bent. He tried to straighten it against his leg.

"We can't afford a new lamp," she flew at him, her face turning red. "With all your fancy knowledge, you act like a barbarian in my house. You wouldn't try this in Bert's house, would you? Too many fine things."

And then to Maddie's surprise, at the sight of the broken glass bird, her mother started to cry, though she obviously didn't want Deane to see it.

"I'm sorry," Deane said, as Maddie moved in front of him.

"It was an accident, Mom," she said in his defense.

Then Deane saw the blood on the back of her pajamas. He turned her around and examined her palms. "Well," he said simply, and with his thumbs probed for pieces of embedded glass, squeezing the cuts. But her mother pulled her away. She had been a registered nurse before Maddie was born. With her more experienced hands, she extracted four splinters of glass, skillfully but no more gently than Deane.

"Talk to you later," Deane said to her father, who was very busy straightening couch cushions and pillows.

Maddie waved to him as he went out the door, but he didn't see her, so she went to the window and watched him walk down the steps to the street and out into the dark. His head was down, his hands thrust in his pockets. As he passed out of sight beyond the streetlamp, her stomach felt full of huge air bubbles. Her hands stung. She hadn't wanted him to go home. It was her fault. She should never have gotten into the wrestling match.

She looked around and wondered how the atmosphere in the house could change so much when he left. The rooms seemed bigger, the lamps glaring. Why didn't her mother like him?

She pressed her palms together to stop the bleeding, but also to make them hurt more so she wouldn't feel the strange pressure in her stomach. But it didn't help. She could hear her parents arguing in the kitchen and tried to make out what they were saying. Her mother was calling Deane "arrogant," talking about a "forced march" he'd taken her on the night before her wedding, and how he'd tried to talk her out of marrying his brother because she wasn't right for him—"a country hick," she was shouting now, "beneath the Camerons." Her father replied angrily that his brother was incapable of saying such a thing. Her mother shouted she wasn't sure what he was capable of. And then Maddie didn't listen anymore.

She went upstairs and washed her hands at the sink, wrapped washcloths around them for bandages, and got into bed. Could Deane have said such things about her mother long ago? She thought of him at Bert's house now. What was he doing? Was he angry at her? Maybe he hadn't gone home at all but had taken a streetcar down to the museum to work all night, as he often did. She pictured him there now, letting himself in one of the little side doors, making his way through the Hall of Architecture, past the rows of motionless birds and mammal skeletons, through the room of Egyptian mummy cases, not bothering to turn on the big lights since he knew his way by heart. He wasn't afraid of the dark even surrounded by mummies. Sinking down deep in her bed, she went with him in her imagination, following the sound of his confident footsteps down the black corridors, around the corners, in and out of the long echoing halls. But then, against her will, the sound of the footsteps receded. They grew fainter and fainter as she grew sleepier. She couldn't keep up with him. He was in that place alone. And so, she dreamed, was she.

A few days later, Deane gave a lecture at the museum for the annual meeting of the American Society of Ichthyologists and Herpetologists. Forty scientists competed for recognition and prizes, and Deane won the first prize of twenty-five dollars for "Growth and Variation in Plethodon wehrlei." Bert, Grandaddy, Aunt Essy, and her father all clapped loudly as Deane went up on stage to accept his prize. Maddie clapped her bandaged hands, and ran to find him afterwards. Now he could buy some of the equipment he needed for his next expedition.

"How are the cuts?" he asked, bending down to inspect the bandages.

"I don't even feel them," she said. "Congratulations! Are you famous?"

"Nah. How's your mother?"

"She's okay. She's home trying to glue the old globe back together. Katy's sick again."

He thought a moment. "Will you do me a favor?"

She nodded gladly.

"I'm leaving town this afternoon and won't be back for a

while. Would you give this check to your mother and tell her
to buy a new lamp for me?"

Before she could protest, he tucked the check for his prize
money into her coat pocket.

In another minute, other scientists were on either side of
him asking questions. He turned to one of them, then to another, and soon was escorted away, lost in the crowd.

That afternoon he left for Alaska and was gone for four
months.

On Christmas Day, everyone gathered around Grandaddy's great annual extravagance, a ten-foot balsam fir specially
ordered from Nova Scotia. In keeping with family tradition,
Maddie and Essy strung popcorn and cranberries to decorate
it. Deane, who had flown in from Seattle two days before, lifted
Maddie up to perform her Christmas duty, the placing of the
silver star on the top of the tree. As she rode up in his arms,
she thought it had seemed like forever since he'd been home.
But as everyone applauded after the star was placed, and he
turned her upside down to sweep the rug with her hair, Bert's
house took on its rightful holiday color and mood. They were
together again.

After basting the turkey one last time, Bert, festively
dressed in a dark-green velvet dress and red satin, spiked high
heels, took off her apron and declared the gift-giving officially
underway. Maddie raced for her traditional place on the couch
between Katy, who, at age two, never let her out of her sight,
and Grandaddy, who had the highest spirits of anyone at holidays and festivals. They were a festival family—so many rituals
and traditions and reunions to look forward to, seasons to
celebrate, everyone taking such loud pleasure in hanging ornaments or dyeing Easter eggs or carving pumpkins.

Bert took her place on a little stool beside the great stack
of gifts, and Grandaddy, dressed in his best suit and tie, clapped
his hands like a ten-year-old boy. "Here we go!" he said. Hold-

ing her folded glasses up to her eyes (she was too vain to ever actually put them on her face, Essy had said), Bert bent to examine the names on the tags of the gifts closest to her. After long deliberation, she chose a gold-foil box and held it expectantly on her lap. When everyone was silent, she straightened, cleared her throat, and beamed at Maddie and Katy, a signal for everyone else to pause and admire them in their puffsleeved, full-skirted Christmas finery. (Maddie's mother had dressed them in the crinkly crinoline dresses Bert had given them last Christmas.) Compliments were lavished by all, especially by Grandaddy, who leaned back, gasped, and pretended to be newly awestruck by their "dazzling pulchritude." Maddie smiled and said thank you. But Katy thrashed around in her place on the couch, complaining that her dress scratched her back and that she wanted to change into her pajamas. "Beauty must suffer," said Bert, reciting her favorite fashion adage as Maddie reached over to pat Katy's arm. But Katy jerked away. Why was she such a moody creature, Maddie wondered—so sensitive to touch and sound?

"Katy won't last long at this, so please keep the hilarity down," her mother said pointedly to Deane, as Grandaddy, struck with a thought, got up and started to root through the pile of gifts, sending the ones Bert had carefully balanced on top tumbling down all over the place.

"Howdy, sit *down!*" Bert said. "I have already chosen a first presentation—and a second and third."

In vain, Grandaddy tried to press an alternate selection on her, one he couldn't wait to give—a musical stuffed polar bear for Katy, he whispered to Maddie. But Bert held firm. Used to it, he put his package back, turned and grinned sheepishly at them all, and sat down again. How different he was from Bert, Maddie noted, yet how much he loved her.

Bert sat with hands folded and lips pursed, waiting again for everyone's attention.

But Deane was making faces at Katy to get her mind off

her scratchy dress. He made a series of loud hooting monkey noises and gorilla motions.

"Maddie was a more placid baby," her father said as Katy begrudgingly smiled.

"I've seen animals born skittish like that in the wild," Deane said. "Enough nerves for a whole litter. If the mother's over-protective, they can grow up weak and defenseless, and get hurt or—"

"I'm waiting to give a *gift*, Howdy," Bert said firmly to Grandaddy as if he were her sergeant-at-arms. "*Nobody's* listening."

Grandaddy told Deane and Willy to be quiet, that it was Christmas and no time for science.

At last Bert gave the gift to Maddie, but not until after she'd read a long poetic tag expressing her misgivings about it. It was a Cameron tradition to present special gifts with long melodramatic poems either puffing up the gift's value or apologizing for its alleged shortcomings. But often the greatest gifts came with the most elaborate apologies. Bert's poems were always the best—clever, flawless sonnets. Essy, who had none of Bert's writing talent, wrote "ghastly verses for ghastly gifts," as she called them, though her presents were always the most fun, like six-foot-long water rafts in the shape of crocodiles or all-day passes to Kennywood Amusement Park.

But everyone knew how hard Bert shopped and worried over her Christmas purchases, so no one ever dared express any reservations about them but her. As Maddie opened the box and separated the tissue paper reverently, she prepared to exclaim gratefully over the gift no matter what Bert said.

But she hadn't the faintest idea what it was.

"It's a muff!" Bert said, prompting her. "Isn't it *beautiful?* It's genuine mink! Look, Willy. Did you ever see such a beautiful thing? Deane, you're not *looking!*"

Grandaddy helped Maddie put the braided cord over her

head. Obligingly, she stood up to model, trying to show how much she liked it. But she didn't like it. It looked like a big brown beaver lying on her chest.

But everyone said how elegant she looked, so to please Bert, Maddie stroked the fur and thanked her. But when Bert's attention was back on the pile, she glanced at her mother, who was smiling beneath a smile, and put it back in the box. Would her mother make her wear it? she asked with her eyes. Maybe not often, her mother's eyes answered.

By three o'clock in the afternoon, the pile was down to the last few presents.

Bert presented Katy with her last gift, a smaller version of the muff in white fur. Katy, who had no use for any gift but Grandaddy's musical polar bear, and fiercely restless from sitting so long, opened it, studied it a moment, then threw it at Bert as hard as she could, knocking off the little black velvet hat she always wore, indoors and out, to keep her hair in place.

"She thinks it's a ball," Deane laughed.

At the affront to Bert's dignity, Grandaddy laughed so hard he started to wheeze. Then Bert and everyone else laughed too.

Essy read a grand poetic apology for her last gift to Grandaddy, a box of a hundred stamped envelopes that he accepted as if it were a box of gold. As he held it up for everyone to see, Deane explained that when Eskimos gave gifts, they also made elaborate apologies, pretending a gift was an insult to the receiver when, in fact, it was rare and precious, the best that could be offered. It became a challenge to the Eskimo hunter's cleverness: after ranging a hundred miles for the fattest seal or largest walrus of the season, how could he present it to his wife's father as if it were nothing, a piece of rotting scrap? The more abject his posture, the greater his generosity.

In anticipation of Deane's gift to her today, Maddie thought that he himself gave gifts like an Eskimo, quietly offering some little thing that seemed odd, even unidentifiable at first, yet of subtle, secret significance that became more apparent as time went by. But now, as if reading her mind, he leaned over and whispered a real apology: he had nothing to give her this year, he said. He had gotten in from Seattle later than he expected with no time or money left to shop. Could she forgive him?

She tried not to show her disappointment. He had brought her so many beautiful things before. But he was home. That was all that mattered. "It's okay," she said, smiling.

The last and star gift of the day was presented to her father from Bert and Grandaddy: a movie camera with screen, projector, and one roll of film. With a grin, her father protested: they had spent too much money on him already. But as he read the instructions so he could take movies of everyone around the balsam, it was clear the gift was a great success. As the camera began to roll, Grandaddy watched with delight as everyone waved and postured and tried to look natural at the same time. Bert smiled coquettishly, extending her legs in a position flattering to her red satin shoes. Deane tickled Katy to make her laugh, but she howled in irritation instead. Essy and Maddie got up and danced. And then it suddenly occurred to Grandaddy that the film was for outdoors. Since they had no spotlights, the movie would probably turn out all black.

"Ah nuts," her father said as the film ran out. Everyone drooped tiredly. Bert sighed and tucked strands of dyed auburn hair under her black velvet hat. Grandaddy and Katy stood up to stretch.

But then Deane announced that they must all sit down again. There was one more star gift to be given. Everyone looked baffled as he rummaged under cushions, behind drapes, in desk drawers, finally pulling a tiny, folded slip of paper out from under a corner throw rug. He looked around at all of them for a moment, then handed it to Maddie.

He had not forgotten about her, she thought excitedly. Here it was.

She unfolded the paper and saw four Eskimo words, one of which she recognized as *ook-pik-e-lo*. She handed it to her father to translate. But he shook his head, unable to make sense of it.

"Let me try," Grandaddy said, winking at Bert, who looked offended at having been left out of the planning of this gift, whatever it was.

He put Maddie on his lap, and they studied the words together. "Do you see?" he said. " 'Me,' " the first word says. "Then 'you.' I can't make out this last one."

"It's a construct," Deane said. "It means 'beast-igloo.' "

"Beast-igloo?" Bert said, mystified.

"I've got it!" Grandaddy said triumphantly. "It's a poem, Maddie: 'Me / You / *Ookpikelo* / Beast-igloo.' "

"Well, it rhymes," Bert said. "That's more than Deane's poems usually do. I detest free verse, don't you, Howdy? Walt Whitman's to blame for it."

Maddie didn't understand it.

"I'm going to take you to the zoo," Deane said. "Just the two of us, right now."

"What?" Bert said, astounded. "You're not *leaving* us?"

Maddie's eyes shone with surprise—and then joy. Grandaddy slapped his knee. "What did I tell you, Deane?" he laughed. "I knew it would be a hit."

Deane nodded to her question, his eyes warm and deep.

"The zoo's closed on Christmas Day," Essy said, trying to help Bert discourage the idea. "I think you ought to think of something else."

Deane went to the closet to get his coat. "I thought you were a religious woman, Es. Weren't there animals around the manger at that first Christmas?"

"Not gorillas and giraffes," Essy said.

Maddie laughed gleefully, picturing gorillas and baboons jumping around the baby Jesus's cradle.

"Maybe at the Second Coming," Deane said, "Christ will come back as a whole different species of mammal. The first gods man worshiped were animals, you know."

"Don't blaspheme on Christmas!" Essy commanded, glancing at Bert to see if she had heard this last comment.

"Don't worry," Grandaddy said, looking for his car keys. "Deane will get into the zoo. It's a sunny day. Most of the animals will be outside anyway. I'm going to drive them over."

Maddie ran to the closet for her coat, but Deane was already holding it open for her. Her heart beat fast. This was the first time he had ever invited her to go anywhere by herself, as a person separate from her mother and father. She pulled on her bonnet haphazardly, letting the strings hang down, and waited at the door.

Bert knelt in front of her. "This won't do," she said, tying the strings in a dainty bow to the side of her chin and tucking wisps of straggly hair inside the bonnet. "Such a flyaway. Not one curl."

Retrieving the muff from its box, she put it around Maddie's neck. "Put your hands inside," she said. "There—like this. It will keep you nice and warm. See? Now look at you."

At Bert's prompting, Maddie took a step back for a beauty inspection.

"Look at her, Howdy," she said admiringly. "Isn't she *darling* in that?"

Maddie hated beauty inspections. The muff made her feel girlish and ridiculous, not at all like the sealskin mukluks Deane had given her. But for Bert's sake, she turned in a circle.

Then Bert turned to Deane. "I don't like you two deserting the rest of us," she said poutingly. "We should all be together today. I've hardly seen you! Essy's making your favorite oyster dressing, and Ginny has made two *sumptuous* pumpkin pies. We must sing carols around the piano—"

"Shush, Bertie," Grandaddy said, kissing her. "Maddie loves the zoo as much as Deane did at her age. She'll remember this."

Maddie kissed them all good-bye as though she wouldn't be back for a month.

"You'll be back in time to carve the turkey," Bert called after Deane as they walked down the front walk. "It's tradition!"

They drove away, waving from all the windows.

As Grandaddy turned the car onto Penn Avenue, Maddie leaned back, untied her bonnet, and took it off. The cold interior of the car felt surprisingly good after the heat of the celebration in the house. She felt a pleasant sense of lightness and relief in getting away from it this way, knowing that it was there to come back to. As Deane and Grandaddy talked about a new weather front moving in, she watched the leafless trees go by, enjoying their look of stark randomness against the sky. This starkness was Christmas too, and as they drove through Highland Park, she felt almost physically drawn into the bare winter woods. Lately she could understand why, in the middle of family celebrations, Deane would often disappear for a while without telling anyone where he was going. Some part of him needed more space than the rest of them—as though he had to get outside and breathe cold air to keep from smothering. Most of the time he didn't want anyone to go with him. But today he wanted her.

They arrived at the zoo. To commemorate the occasion, Grandaddy took a picture of her and Deane standing in front of the entrance gate, her hand in his. Above the rotating barred gate behind them a big sign said "IN."

(When Maddie studied that picture years later, when she was sinking into or coming out of a bout with depression, she would wonder at her open childish face as she smiled straight into the camera that day, and at Deane's distinctly melancholy face looking down at her. Behind them were bars and gates, high wire fences, stone steps leading up to trees and buildings.

In black-and-white, the picture interested her primarily because
of the look on his face, which she studied again and again as
a possible key to her own present emotional condition: a kind
of *melancholia obscura*, a temperamental sadness in conflict with
philosophical affirmation, and a power of concentration which
could be frightening if it were turned inward. Every moment
for him—as it had become for her—was unavoidably serious,
though not at all humorless. A man like Deane could never
get drunk, she had heard her father say once. He couldn't
afford the time. Everything he did or saw or heard converged
toward an obligatory decision: *yes* or *no* to something—benevolent design in nature, maybe? Or some destination he had
set for himself?

    She could never know what he finally decided, or what
he would have advised her to decide. But she wished she could
go back to that day, and instead of smiling into the camera,
look up into that brief revelatory expression on her uncle's face
as he looked down at her and perhaps discover once and for
all who he really was—if he was as related to her in temperament as she suspected. If he was, in fact, her forebear in this
strange, preoccupying illness, perhaps he would have understood her peculiar sense of being onto something both frightening and irresistible. Ironically it separated her from people,
requiring so much time and energy for analysis. Perhaps he
had already recognized it in her and meant something more
by his Christmas gift than a mere child's tour of caged animals.
If that were true, then her grief at losing him would not be
diminished. But her sense of lonely freakishness would be relieved. She would have a frame of reference.)

    Grandaddy wished them a good time, waved, and drove
away.

    She looked up and down the sidewalk. There wasn't an-
other human being in sight. As Essy had predicted, the high
barred gates were padlocked. A chain wound through the bars.

We'll never get in, she thought uneasily, and Grandaddy won't be back for two hours.

But then Deane rummaged in his pockets the way he did when looking for snakes; only this time he produced a big black key and held it up. "To the Kingdom," he said solemnly. (Where was that key now? she wondered thirty years later, feeling defeated after shuffling her own children through the zoo on a visit to Pittsburgh, knowing they much preferred a rock concert or an afternoon of video games at the shopping mall to polar bears and walruses. Kids were older than their parents in the 1980s, she thought—impervious to the pleasures she had enjoyed at their age, as though the shell they wore to ward off being disturbed when watching television had become permanent. Nothing that wasn't shocking or earsplitting could get through.)

Deane opened the padlock, unwound the chain, bowed, and motioned her in. He followed her and locked the gate behind them. "You're my personal guest, Madeleine," he said. "Today the ark belongs to you."

"Where did you get that key?" she asked.

"I used to work here during the summer. Four years ago I redesigned the reptile house. It's more habitable now for some of my best catches."

"You caught some of these animals?" she asked, newly amazed at all he did.

"A few copperheads, a rattler when I was in Arizona in '46, and also some of the Vespertilionidae and Molossidae for the nocturnal zoo."

He wanted her to recognize the names of species. Yet if she pretended to understand them when she didn't, he'd see right through it.

"The bats," he said, smiling to relieve her anxiety. "They're not my specialty either."

But he knew about them, specialty or not. And she admired

his great knowledge above all things. He had studied everything—nothing was out of range. That was what she wanted for herself.

"I hate bats," she said, to show she knew something about them. "We had them in our attic when we first moved into our house. Mom said they were filthy and wouldn't let me go up there."

"Some species do carry disease. But so do a lot of people. Everything alive is filthy, if you look at it that way."

"Yes," she guessed, thinking about it.

She took his hand, cool and smooth, like soft leather, after the inside of her hot muff. "But they suck your blood," she said.

"Oh?" he said, leading her off the cement path. "Not an ookpikelo's blood."

He lifted her over a fence and showed her a secret passage to the Bird House. To her surprise, the door was unlocked. Inside, two uniformed men were cleaning out cages, and Deane greeted them cheerfully. He led her past clutches of grave, motionless bats, ragged parrots and parakeets, and on to the owls. "Here," he said, stopping in front of a stack of wire cages and lifting her up to see the one on top. "I want you to meet yourself."

She looked into the dim, deeply recessed cage. Barely visible in the corner, on an artificial tree branch, stood a fluffy ghost with huge yellow eyes. "What is it?" she asked, fascinated. The eyes were wide and segmented, on guard, yet perfectly calm.

"A Snowy Owl," he said. "I brought it back from Alaska six months ago. An ookpikelo is an owl chick—a baby—undersized like you."

The owl stared unblinkingly at her. "Do you know," he said, "he sleeps in the blue shadows of the ice all night long and doesn't even shiver?"

It was an Arctic marshmallow, she thought, so soft and

still, with fur on its feet like little mukluks. How could such a fragile thing survive on such a barren nest?

"Looks like fluff," he said, lifting her down, then resting his hand on top of her head. "But don't be fooled. He's tough as can be."

She understood. Straining on tiptoe, she peered up again at the exquisitely poised creature—as silent and white as snow. "Can I hold him?" she asked. "Can you open the cage?"

"No. But you can shake hands with another friend of mine next door. His name is Aristarchus."

He led her out of the Bird House and into the large brick building beside it. Apparently it housed no animals at all, only storage rooms and long corridors with big doors on either side all the way down. It reminded her a little of the museum, only darker and gloomier.

"Can you open all these doors?" she asked curiously.

"If you want me to," he smiled. "Every species of filing cabinet is right here."

"That's okay," she said, smiling back.

At the end of the second floor hallway, a woman sat bent over a big sheet of paper in a circle of yellow light—the zoo secretary, she guessed. Why was she working on Christmas?

"The key to 377, Martha, please," Deane said.

She turned and drew a large key off a rack of many other keys. Out of her desk she took a smaller key. "This too?"

He nodded. "This is my niece, Madeleine," he introduced her. "Madeleine, this is Martha Zearn."

Martha held out her hand. "Are you going to be a zoologist someday?"

"I want to be a nurse like my mother, I guess," Maddie said, unsure.

She nodded. "You can go right up."

"Merry Christmas," Maddie called over her shoulder as they hurried off.

They climbed three flights of stairs with Deane turning on

light switches as they went. "Why does she have to work today?" Maddie asked as he turned down a brick-lined corridor that felt colder than the others.

"She doesn't have to. She's an ornithologist working on a design for a new aviary—big enough for bald eagles to build their giant nests in. Sometimes she works all night until the secretary comes in the morning."

"Oh," Maddie said, impressed. "Who will catch the bald eagles for her?"

"Maybe you?" he suggested with a smile.

Out of breath, she had a hard time keeping up with his long strides; her muff banged rhythmically against her coat with each step. Eagle-catchers didn't wear muffs, she was sure.

"Does Aristarchus have to work on Christmas too?" she asked.

He didn't answer.

At the end of the corridor he opened a sliding door into pitch blackness. Frigid air hit Maddie like a wall. "He isn't a man," Deane said matter-of-factly. "He's a gorilla."

She stepped back. "In *here?*"

"Come on," he said, searching for the light switch.

"Is he loose?" she asked.

He found the switch. Row after row of blinding fluorescent lights flickered on. He pulled her into the room and slid the door shut to keep in the cold air. "Don't be afraid," he said. "This room belongs to the museum."

She looked around in amazement. Bones lay all over the place, on long rows of stained tables, in dripping sinks, sticking out of ceiling-high storage cabinets. In the center of the room was an eight-foot glass case, and Deane motioned her toward it to see what was mounted inside—a massive gorilla skeleton, so tall and broad its dangling arms seemed to overhang every-thing in the room. His enormous skull had eye sockets the size of lightbulbs, and his pinched triangular brow gave him a look of perplexity and mopiness that repulsed Maddie at first, then gradually touched her. He looked like a malformed old man who couldn't figure something out, taking a slow, painful walk. She approached slowly, half afraid to look up at him.

Deane opened the case with the smaller key. He pulled out Aristarchus's slender right arm. "He was a silverback," he said. "Over a thousand pounds."

Cautiously Maddie touched the thumb bone. It felt smooth and light, like a stick of sanded wood. He must have been wonderful and terrible when he was alive. "What happened to him?"

"He lived here for sixteen years, had a mate, two sons, and a daughter. When he died last spring, the museum asked to have his skeleton. I helped to undress him. We're going to transfer him in a few days."

"You mean you took off his skin and everything?"

"Look at the massive rib cage, Maddie. You and Katy could both fit inside there, with room for the Christmas turkey."

Maddie shook Aristarchus's hand. "Nice to meet you," she said, concentrating on the dark hollows of the nose and cheeks and the jutting tooth-filled jaw. He looked as though he could take off her head with one bite if he wanted to. "Aren't you afraid he's mad at you?" she asked.

"Why?"

"For doing this to him—hanging him up like this?"

He smiled. "Not at all. He was named after a man who knew the earth was not the center of the universe seventeen hundred years before Copernicus. We used to give him the key to his own cage and let him walk around and look at the other apes. He had a scientist's curiosity about things, Maddie. For dinner, we'd bring him a huge platter of vegetables, and with all of us standing around watching him, he'd sit right down, the centerpiece in his own salad, and study us studying him. He considered himself one of us."

Deane took off her muff and fit the skinny strap over the head of the skeleton. The muff hung down crookedly between his arms. Carefully he inserted the oversized gorilla fingers halfway into the brown fur. They laughed together at how silly he looked.

"I hate that muff," she said.

"I know," he said. "But you didn't let Bert know."

He looked at her with respect, and she felt both happy and painfully self-conscious.

He took off the muff and locked the glass case. She was pleased to have been so closely watched by him at Bert's house. How often did he watch her that way, without her knowing it?

"Now let's find some live specimens," he said. "The cages outside are a lot roomier than they used to be."

Outside, the winter sun blinded her eyes. He showed her how to make Eskimo sunglasses with her fingers to keep out the glare. First they looked at the great cats, the white and yellow tigers, the leopards, and lions.

"It's sad they have to be in cages on such a pretty day," Maddie said, disturbed by the small circle of the Bengal tiger's restless pacing.

"Noah thought so too. But zoos aren't the cruel show-off collections of rich people and big countries anymore. The way things are going, someday they might be the only safe place for some of these species."

Maddie noticed a bony, haggard-looking lion that prowled endlessly back and forth against the far wall of its cage.

"He's sick," Deane said, noting her absorption. "He's going to die, and he knows it. But he has a strong spirit. He'll fight to the end."

Maddie felt sorry for him, except for the look in his eye when he turned toward her.

They looked at the walruses and seals next, then the

Kodiak bears, and finally the polar bears which, Deane said, once wounded, could track a man for six hundred miles without giving up. He knew everything about all the animals without even looking at the information signs posted in front of them. "These are the big showy ones," he lectured her as a giant male polar bear stood up playfully on his hind legs and begged for food. "As if he had to beg," Deane laughed. "I wish you could see some of the lesser animals of the Arctic—the little burrowing and crawling things. You ought to study the voles, the lemmings, and the ground squirrels. Everything depends on them."

She listened closely, trying to remember everything he said.

Later, she would remember very well that he said all life depended on the small, seemingly negligible creatures. In depression, she would come to feel like a small burrowing thing compared to her own lost self, more and more reduced by the passing of time.

But what she remembered most about that winter day was Deane himself, his face close to hers as they leaned over the railings, his reposed, sky-reflecting eyes, one minute laughing at the gray seals playing on the artificial rocks, telling her how their skins could be stretched and sewn into the most beautiful coats she had ever seen, the next minute looking far beyond the seals, off into the blue horizon, preoccupied, forgetting where he was or why, forgetting even that it was Christmas. Deane was elsewhere, Bert would have said: concentrating on the Problem. The present time and place could never wholly absorb him. Pleasure, it seemed to Maddie, came to him only as little vacations from the habitual concentration, the thinking and re-thinking of theories for coordinating every day's new evidence.

She began to feel uneasy about the empty walkways. The popcorn machine in the monkey house was dark; the concession stands were all closed. At last, after a tour of the spider monkeys and baboons, she asked if they could rest for a few minutes. They sat down on a wooden bench and watched a sparrow fly back and forth in a brisk, chilly wind. The sun was in and out, the temperature falling.

"Tired? Want to quit?" he asked her.

"No." She shivered.

They studied the bird in silence for a while, his slow, labored headway into the wind, then his graceful falling back. She was cold, but felt perfectly contented.

"How about if we finish up with the reptiles and amphibians?" he said. "The building's warm."

This was his specialty. He knew more about them than anyone in the world. "Yes," she said enthusiastically, jumping up.

But she couldn't get as interested in the ugly, knobby frogs as he wanted her to. She commented on the stripes of the lizards and the spots of the salamanders as he narrated case after case. But what really attracted her attention was a twenty-three-foot anaconda, wound around a tree limb like a row of fat rubber tires. She was both horrified and fascinated by the problem of the snake's shape. She had never seen such a big snake before. It was nothing but its own thick neck grown foot after foot after foot for no good reason except to need more food so it could grow some more. It had no arms or legs, no voice, no way of going anyplace, and absolutely nothing to do. Did it have a brain? What was the use of its heavy body? This was life for a different reason than hers and Deane's, and something about it made her feel sick. It was as if a telephone pole or a big hollow pipe should be alive, not right somehow—and yet interesting. What was a creature's life *for* if it didn't do anything but live? The snake was closed. It couldn't tell anyone anything that was on its mind, not even by a look in its glazed eyes. Yet she wondered: if it *could* tell her something, what would it be?

All of a sudden she realized that Deane was studying
her as she studied the snake. Then in a flash he whisked
her up and sat her on his shoulders. "We're late," he said.
"Hold on."

He ran at a half-trot out the door, around the corner and
down the paths. "This is what it's like to ride a camel," she
laughed, bouncing up and down, the cold air canceling out all
thoughts of the snake.

At the zoo entrance, Grandaddy was waiting in the car.
He waved—not a bit angry at them for being late.

"We had a good time," Deane said enthusiastically, opening the door for Maddie, who was more out of breath from
riding than he was from carrying her.

Grandaddy heard all about it. But Deane did most of the
telling since she was too tired even to talk. As they turned
back onto Forbes Avenue, sleet streaked across the windshield.
She leaned against Deane and sank down into her coat, a warm
depth of comfortable satisfaction. "Did you have fun?" he asked
her softly.

"Yes."

"Me too."

As he and Grandaddy talked about the new aviary for
the zoo, she thought of the turkey waiting for them at Bert's.
She could picture perfectly what everyone was doing. Katy
would be playing her xylophone by the fire, or maybe Essy
was rocking her. Her mother was in the kitchen arranging
spiced peaches on a relish tray, wearing an apron with sprigs
of holly printed on it. Bert's apron was black taffeta with big
red poinsettias, and by now she was probably wringing her
hands first at one window, then another, wondering where
Deane was, what was taking so long. Maddie's father would
tell her not to worry, that Deane had been in riskier places
than the Pittsburgh zoo, then sink down deeper into the
couch and read another *National Geographic,* or else prowl out

to the kitchen and steal snitches of white meat. She could see it all in her mind, curiously even better than if she were there. She wondered at the part of her that was half-enjoying this distance from it.

She yawned. Deane invited her to lie down across his lap. "This is what muffs are good for," he whispered in her ear, tucking it under her head.

Grandaddy turned up the car heater. Against the cold twilight outside, the sleet made a soft foggy blur of all the windows. "It's turning to snow," Deane said in her ear as if confiding a secret to her, and she felt floatingly free and exultant, drifting on a wave of peace. How she loved her mother and father and sister. How she loved Essy and Bert and Grandaddy. But how she loved *Deane* forever and ever. She decided in some alert part of her just beneath the surface of her sleepiness that she wanted to be exactly like him. She wanted to study and explore her whole life long as he did, and never, never be like the terrible heavy snake who did nothing but hang in the air and contain itself.

Then she realized that Deane and Grandaddy weren't talking about the zoo anymore. Grandaddy was saying something about a Senate speech he'd heard on the radio, about communists being hired at the Arctic Institute where Deane was going to work next year. Deane said no, that his pilot spoke Russian and knew of only one Soviet in Nome who was mapping the coastline and taking mineral samples. The Senate speech was an exaggeration.

Then Deane talked about a socialist friend of his at Johns Hopkins who had gotten into an argument with him about the Manhattan Project. Grandaddy said something about Franklin Roosevelt. Deane described a professor named McCafferty whom he was at odds with at Johns Hopkins.

After that, Maddie fell asleep.

She remembered little of the Christmas dinner that followed that evening except that there was a lot of laughter and the usual energetic arguing about anything and everything. Bert read some poems by Emerson and Santayana. They all sang around the grand piano, and Deane told Eskimo ghost stories that gave everyone the shivers.

The gas fireplace, turned up as high as it would go, hissed cheerfully all night long.

Tonight, on the third Wednesday in Lent of 1982, sunk in the soft chair, Maddie studied the photograph Grandaddy had taken of her and Deane at the zoo entrance and realized she was over a decade older than Deane had been when he was lost. How long had it been since his keys had opened locked doors for her? While her children slept and Nate was out calling on new members, she thought back to the signs Deane might have been trying to give her at the zoo that day about his future, about her future, or about nothing at all. In the Snowy Owl he had shown her an example of endurance, not just in making a home on the blue ice, but in standing alert and calm backed into the corner of a wire cage. In the pacing cat he had shown her a pride that didn't puff itself up with hope at the expense of objective awareness. And in the polar bear he had shown her a playful-seeming creature who, once wounded, never stopped tracking the wounder, never pardoned the offense—like Bert.

She thought of all the anguish her grandmother had gone through since Deane had disappeared. Somewhere between the pacing cat and the wounded bear, she had held out against going into the nursing home valiantly year after year, in the irrational fear that maybe Deane couldn't find her there if he did come back, but also in dread of leaving her home, like leaving the stage where all the best theater had been played. Maddie couldn't believe the beautiful house was really sold, along with almost everything in it—the piano, the spiral-legged refectory table, Deane's massive old globe. Back in 1976, four years after Grandaddy died, when Bert was still struggling to keep it up alone, neighborhood boys had begun to vandalize the weedy flower garden and front porch, peering through the downstairs windows at all the dusty antique teapots lined up on the windowsills, making faces at her. Not to be intimidated, she had made a grotesque seven-foot scarecrow out of Grandaddy's old clothes and set it on a living-room chair to frighten them off. But it hadn't worked. She couldn't hear a window break or a teapot shatter when she was upstairs, and they had plenty of time to run away and laugh at what she would find in the morning. By that time her legs were so crippled she had to crawl up and down the stairs on all fours, yet preferred that indignity to shutting up a single room. And then, finally, her right leg had broken under her; she was rushed to the hospital and never came back to the house again.

The clock on the mantel struck eleven.

Recalling Dr. Hazelett's advice to try to stop retreating into the past, Maddie put the zoo picture aside and turned on the television for pictures of the present—the eleven o'clock news. In the space of fifteen minutes, it showed a series of violent deaths—civil war in Central America, a drug raid in Miami, a terrorist bombing in Lebanon. The late movie that followed showed a second series of deaths: quick, casual, multiple. Irresistibly, a thought occurred to her. How could her children be taught what just *one* premature death could do? How it could matter?

They could not be told. A year ago she'd traveled to Pittsburgh for a visit, and all three kids' faces had been blank as she had taken them to the Carnegie Museum to see the new tropical rain forest exhibit. The museum was too slow for them, she discovered. Dutifully, they had followed her upstairs to the Arab and lion exhibit—still there, still as inconclusive as when Deane had showed it to her long ago. But they had barely looked at it. There were no special effects. Nothing moved or lit up. In response to her question of "Who wins?" Merrill had glanced at Kate and giggled their contemporary answer: "Who cares?"

How could she tell them what life had been like just a generation ago? What gifts had been given that cost so little but signified so much? A few months ago, at bedtime, Maddie had gotten out the carved ivory animals Deane had given her when she was eight and shown them to Nathan. Requiring no batteries, their power to interest paled in comparison to his remote-controlled, factory-assembled racing car. What could be more futile, or more important, than to try to convince him they still had power?

In February, Merrill had asked Maddie to give her ten dollars to buy her boyfriend an expensive after-shave cologne for Valentine's Day. (To give a homemade card or a pound of fudge was out of the question. The gift had to be something only money could buy.) Both Maddie and Nate had said *no*, that the boyfriend didn't even shave yet. Frustrated, Merrill had sulked for days, especially after he gave her a fourteen-carat gold bracelet—"and a candy heart," she added glumly, worried about its effect on her wispy, thin figure. Glad he had conformed to the candy tradition, at least, Maddie asked to sample the heart. But when Merrill lugged it home from school, it struck Maddie as the ideal Valentine for the madam of a brothel—five pounds done up in broad-pleated crimson satin and lace topped off with a bouquet of red plastic roses secured with a cardboard medallion prominently displaying the price: $16.95.

"I don't want it," Merrill sighed, stashing the heart under her bed as if it were a nuisance. Just as well, Maddie thought, after trying one of the chocolates. They were awful, packaged to impress, not to satisfy. And a week later, Merrill's boyfriend had a new love.

Sublime: the word inexplicably surfaced in her consciousness tonight like an escaped bubble. She stared at the television
screen without seeing it. "Exalted." "Lofty." What was sublime
in their lives?

Or was it only the aftermath of depression speaking, the
distortions of illness throwing her back and back into the past
to verify what was no longer true? When the passing of minutes
or the movement from one chair to another involved more
effort than she thought possible, she had to acknowledge that
her subconscious mind had a will of its own, slamming on
brakes when something enraged but helplessly inarticulate inside her raced out of control, insisting that velocity was no
substitute for direction and that comfort was not equivalent to
well-being. One could make a dying man comfortable.

But how could she stop it? How could she explain it to
her growing children? Perhaps there was so little endurance in
them because there was nothing for them to endure but their
mother, who, when she wasn't well, ranted about the useless-
ness of inheriting a set of keys to doors that had passed out
of existence before they were born.

Some nights she wanted to tell Dr. Hazelett that she felt
like the Arab in the museum—a loser to paralysis, stared at
by neighbors, by parishioners, by psychiatrists all around the
showcase. Or like Aristarchus, hung up by his bones, remembering what it was like to have had powerful muscles attached
to them. Children of the "Me Generation," Nathan, Kate, and
Merrill were learning that the self and its safety mattered most.
But Deane had taught her there was something more than safety
to be achieved, something to be reverenced even more than
the sanctity of the individual life. Ironically, in pursuing what
he believed to be worth the risk of his life, he became all the
more precious as an individual, and died precisely at that
height.

Maddie got up from her chair and tiptoed into her children's rooms to kiss them good-night, praying (as Bert had undoubtedly prayed over her sons) against everything she had just thought—that God would keep them safe, simply safe. Watching them sleep, she also wanted to tell them not to worry about her, that an essential part of her wasn't sick at all, only waiting for Deane—or something else that was lost—to come back.

3

THE MASK
WITH HOLES
IN ITS HANDS

Maddie remembered her ninth year, 1949, as thirty-eight days
long. That was how many days Deane was home from the
Arctic and everyone was happy and together. When he arrived
at the Pennsylvania and Lake Erie train station in June after
over five months away, she drove to the station with her father
to pick him up. He was glad to see her and held out his arms
to swing her around, his handsome face full of slants and
hollows, his eyes as sparkling as ever.

But when she went over to her grandmother's house the
next morning for a welcome-home breakfast, he and Bert were
already in an argument. Torn between relief at having him
home again and anger at his staying away so long, Bert had
accused him of embracing destitution as a way of life and of
recklessly cutting himself off from the family when he set out
alone east of Barrow along the Arctic coast. "You didn't even
hear of Mama's funeral until May!" she cried, the thought of
it bringing tears to her eyes.

As she ate breakfast, Maddie thought back to all the people who had come to her great-grandmother's funeral in April.

Some had said that she was the strongest, most unselfish woman they had ever known—and the very best cook. Many of them had asked how Deane was, and what he was doing, but Bert hadn't been able to tell them because she had no idea.

"The mail sleds can't get through in the spring," he explained as he helped Maddie clear the table when breakfast was over. "The Kogmolliks are afraid of being trapped by the soft ice. Their families would starve if they—"

"You don't remember," Bert persisted, scarcely hearing, "how Mama walked the floor with you when you had those terrible ear infections and nearly went deaf, and how she got you through double pneumonia!"

Deane was nodding, but Maddie saw the same look in his eyes she had seen at the zoo half a year ago. He was only half-listening, concentrating on something else.

"And how she used to spoil you down at the campground in West Virginia," Bert went on, not seeing what Maddie saw. "Cooking all day long while you and Willy played Tom Sawyer and Huck Finn, leaping off rooftops and setting fields on fire! At the service, everyone said how proud I must be of you, and what could I *say* but that I hadn't heard a word from you in *two months?*"

Deane poked through her ice-jammed freezer in an effort to dislodge an impacted pint of ice cream. "I thought I'd seen the tundra," he said.

"And look at you! You can't weigh more than a hundred fifty pounds. Giving all your money away to those people, eating raw fish livers and owl soup."

He was much thinner, Maddie noted, straight and narrow as a poplar tree. Even in his manner, he reminded her of a tree trunk, covered with invisible plates of protective bark.

"I'm sorry," he said simply, then turned and left the kitchen.

But Bert followed him through the dining room into the

living room and out onto the front porch. In fact, Maddie watched her follow him around all day, wiping tears away with her apron, asking him over and over how he could be so resigned to his own dear grandmother's death. She hardly stopped long enough to let him answer, as if to spare herself knowing for sure that he wasn't going to answer no matter how many times she asked.

That evening, Deane announced to everyone at dinner that he was going back to Nome in five weeks to work through the rest of the summer and fall. Immediately sorry for what she'd said in the morning, fearful of driving him away, Bert said that of course she knew he must fulfill his obligations to Johns Hopkins, the better to come home early next year and get a permanent job in town with the museum. But later that night, Maddie heard her tell Essy she was afraid there was more than the lure of science drawing him to Alaska. Someone was influencing him up there, she said. He wasn't acting like himself.

The following Friday night, everyone but Maddie's mother and Katy gathered to watch Grandaddy's new television set. Bert set up five old easy chairs covered with bath towels and throw rugs to convert Grandaddy's map room, where he liked to retreat to read maps and plan imaginary trips, to a home theater. As Grandaddy tuned in a snowy, flipping channel, Bert served ice cream and trolley cakes, and Maddie took a place on the floor between Deane's and Essy's chairs. Grandaddy couldn't get a good picture, so her father got up to help him. To pass the time, Essy dug into her purse for the bulletin to last Sunday's church service. "The new minister was installed last week," she said, handing it to Deane, poking at the name at the top of the first page.

Deane looked at it briefly, then balanced it at a distance on the arm of his chair.

"Oh yes!" Bert said exultantly. "The Reverend James

Thaden Rutke. How good to have dignity and literacy back
in the pulpit! You must hear him preach once, Deane. He's
nothing like his predecessor."

"He's a liberal," Essy said warningly.

"Won't you come just once?" Bert pressed him. "Maddie
sings in the Youth Choir now."

"No, Mother," he said with a quick, disappearing grin. The
bulletin fell on the floor, and he didn't move to pick it up.

Why? Maddie wondered. Why wouldn't he come to
church to please Bert? She liked the new minister too. He was
completely different from the last one who'd always worn slick
shiny gray suits to match his slick shiny gray hair. In a way,
the shadowy light in Reverend Rutke's eyes reminded her of
the light in Deane's. He had the same quiet, compressed-inside-
himself look about him, serious, but not stuffy or grim. And
he gave the impression that, deep down, sometimes he thought
the church was a big funny joke.

Bert pulled an afghan up over her stiff arthritic knees.
"There's nothing lonelier than one who casts himself out," she
said. "I'm not orthodox myself, Deane, as you well know. But
I go. I search."

He leaned back and regarded her with a level gaze, as if
to say, *So do I, Mother*. But at that look, Bert averted her eyes,
and Essy sighed loudly, "All that religious sensibility you had
as a child, turned to such industrious fatalism!"

"I am no fatalist," he said with a wave of his hand, as
though dismissing a foolish guess.

Not entirely understanding the conversation, Maddie
drew closer to Deane's chair and put her arm around the calf
of his leg. It was so good to have him home. She had turned
nine years old while he was away, but he hadn't forgotten to
send her a present—a beautiful ink drawing of a white Arctic
fox done by an Eskimo woman. She took it out of her pocket
and held it up to him now. "See?"

He nodded in acknowledgment. "You like the drawing?"

"I can see every hair. I didn't know Eskimos could draw."

"At your age, Madeleine," Essy said, "Deane used to draw the organ pipes and choir members and take notes on the sermons. He went to church every Sunday."

"You did?" Maddie looked up, surprised.

"That was in Reverend McMurdock's day," he admitted, "until a small group of members hounded him out of his pulpit for inviting a black man and his wife to join the church they janitored. Then came the Reverend Ernest "Jolly" Stark, a theological mushroom growing in the cosmic dark. Everybody loved him."

"Not I, you will recall," Bert said, looking aside at Essy.

"I drew a picture of Stark one Sunday," Deane said to Maddie, "with fat frog eyes and bat wings. Not as good as that fox, but a pretty good caricature. Dropped the labeled portrait in the collection place, signed."

"You didn't!" Bert said, horrified. "Oh Deane, you didn't!"

"So that's why the man was so standoffish," Grandaddy laughed. "I thought it was just me he couldn't stand."

"His soul had the wideness of a crack in the sidewalk," Deane said with no laughter in his voice.

"Then Deane started bringing books to church," Essy addressed Maddie again, "with 'hymnal' taped across the covers. First it was astronomy, then penguins, then alpine botany. While the minister was talking about eternal life, he was reading about exploding stars and galaxies and pygmy pine trees on the edge of the timberline that grow for one hundred years and attain the majestic height of two feet."

"Perhaps that was Stark's problem," Deane said thoughtfully, stroking Maddie's hand where it rested on his knee. "He might have been a California Redwood if it hadn't been for a long stretch of bad weather, eh, Es?"

"Ah," Bert smiled meaningfully. "And the altitude."

Maddie detected a glint of pride and longing in Bert's sidelong glance at him, and a momentary appreciation of her in his. Despite all their arguments, they seemed a lot alike sometimes, like members of some secret society the rest of the family didn't know about. She guessed that both her father and Deane had attained their heights partly because of the good weather she had provided for them in that big old house.

Essy took Deane's hand to gain back his attention. "You must study the Bible, Deane, not as mere fiction and poetry as Bertha does, but as the inspired and inerrant word of God. You think you know what's in it, but you don't. The Eskimos are good people. But as I read somewhere, *Eskimo* means 'eater of raw meat.' They're heathen. They share each other's wives. They don't have the Gospel."

Deane laughed and shifted his position. "Don't be fooled by the bread and wine, Es. Christians are carnivores. The body and blood of the Lamb, and then the raw hides of the Brunos and Galileos. Jesus would pound the nail in his own left hand if he knew what the church is doing to—"

"Oh!" Essy said, throwing back her head in dismay. "Do you hear this, Bertha? Where have you learned to talk like this, Deane?"

"I taught myself," he said quietly.

Maddie began to feel nervous. It seemed that as much as everyone loved to have Deane home, there was always a lot of arguing until they got used to him again. As her father said, Deane would never pass up a chance to defend a truth, even if it killed him—or someone else.

"Let's drop the Eskimos for now," her father said, pretending to be bored with the conversation.

"They prefer to be called 'Inuit,' not Eskimo," Deane said to Essy firmly, "meaning 'the People.' " Then more gently, "But perhaps you're right. Genesis is correct about the fallen nature of *Homo sapiens*. We are considerably lower than the angels. I've

seen for myself over the past months that the Soviets aren't
looking for quartz crystals in Alaska. When they finally test
their atomic bomb, which I have reason to believe is imminent,
this postwar euphoria of ours will be over. Moral men might
have to start thinking about migrating off this planet. We'll
have to adapt to environments that make pre-Cambrian times
look like the Garden of Eden."

"You believe in evolution," Essy said with a hurt, troubled
look.

"I'm Secretary of the Society for the Study of Evolution
here in town. You know that."

"Yes," she said. "But a lot of people think that, like communism, evolution is a conspiracy."

Deane covered Maddie's ears. "Don't listen to this," he
said.

"Evolution isn't a conspiracy, Essy," Bert said firmly, tugging at the afghan. "Whose would it be?"

Essy sat up, poised and alert, ready to witness for creationism.

In an effort to discourage that, and after a look from Willy,
Deane said, "Maybe it's God's conspiracy, Essy. Let's leave it
at that."

But Bert, piqued at Essy's anti-intellectualism, picked up
the church bulletin from the floor and held her glasses up to
her eyes. "Well, I believe what is printed at the top of this
page," she pronounced after a solemn pause. " 'Better to beg
for crumbs on the doorstep of God's house than to live well-
fed in a house without hope.' If we must leave it, let it be at
that."

They were all silent for a moment. Maddie liked what
Bert had said. If it came to such a choice, she guessed she
would choose the crumbs, even if everyone else in the world
were eating steak and living in houses with swimming pools.
Those bits of crumbs would be the real reason to eat at all.

(*Sublime* was the word she wanted but did not yet know.) She thought back to the big anaconda in the zoo, fat and heavy in a house without hope. Deane must feed on the crumbs in secret, since he was the thinnest of them all.

"No!" Essy contradicted Bert. "That's *not* the Gospel. That's not salvation in Christ. We can have the feast—the whole feast, Deane. You've forgotten your invitation to the table."

As they continued to argue, Maddie watched Deane as he looked away from both of them, stared at the arm of the chair, then down at a pattern in the carpet until, caught up in their own points of view, they gradually forgot all about him. Once out of the conversation, he took up a section of newspaper and began to read. He had a photographic memory, and she loved to watch his eyes fly across the lines. But he wasn't really reading now, she could tell—just pretending. And all at once the eyes of both Essy and Bert were back on him, realizing he'd gotten away. Sensing it from behind his paper, he said, "Don't you worry about me, Es. Someday man will break through the entanglements of his genetic strings to real responsibility. I have faith."

"No," Essy replied firmly. "That's your heresy. Man is helpless. There's no cumulative progress. Evolution is a communist myth."

What was she talking about? Maddie wondered. Hadn't Essy seen the trilobites in the museum, and all the fossils of what Deane called the "Cambrian explosion"?

Deane slouched. The newspaper collapsed. He looked at Willy, whose back was turned. Then very quietly, he said, "My dear Aunt Esther, anyone who believes that is a damned fool."

Essy heard. Maddie heard. Her father shot him a furious look, as if he thought he had lost his mind. Maddie had never heard him swear before.

Essy broke into tears. She looked at Bert, then back at her nephew as though he had physically struck her.

"I don't understand," Bert cried, as shocked as anyone by Deane's uncharacteristic profanity. "After all the love we've lavished on you, after all the sacrifices so *happily* made. . . ." She stopped and searched Deane's face in bewilderment, for once at a loss for words.

"I guess I should just go home," Essy whimpered into a ragged bunch of Kleenexes she had dredged from her purse.

"Apologize," Grandaddy ordered Deane calmly. "Nobody's going anywhere."

Deane said nothing.

Then he looked down and saw Maddie's face turned up at him. He stared at her thoughtfully a moment, pulled her up on his lap, took her hand and curved it into a fist. "Punch me," he said, pointing to his nose. "Punch me right here. I deserve it."

"Go ahead," Grandaddy said with a smile. "Do it, Maddie. Sock him."

"Oh *no*," Essy sobbed angrily. "He'd prefer that to humbling himself. That's not an apology. I'm afraid for him, Howard! God punishes pride most severely of all."

"Punch him anyway," Maddie's father said, yanking the heavy television to the left and right, getting no improvement in the reception.

At a loss for what to do, Maddie stared at the snow-filled screen. Barely perceptible human figures looked like doubleghosts of themselves, groping blindly through a blizzard, their speech unintelligible. She looked at Essy, then back at her uncle, who, she sensed, really wanted her to hit him—to flatten his nose for all the unwitting little ways he had hurt and provoked everybody in less than a week.

She dropped her fist. She couldn't punch him. He shouldn't have said what he did to Essy. But on the other hand, he had seemed so closed up inside himself ever since he got home, like someone locked in a box, and this was the first time

he had actually said what he really thought. Should he be
socked for that? And besides, even if Essy was right about the
big feast, she preferred not to come to it if Deane wasn't going
to be there. "Just tell her you're sorry," she said softly and gave
him a kiss on the nose.

"Ah," Bert said, pleased by her action.

Obediently, he reached over to take Essy's hand. "A fool
for Christ, I meant," he said in a conciliatory tone that Essy
strove to resist. "I apologize," he added, and raised her hand
to kiss it. "I'm the damned one, not you. We both know that."

Essy pulled away at first, but then after the kiss, helplessly
gave in. She loved him as much as Bert did, Maddie could see.
The two of them competed for him, it seemed sometimes,
courting him when he was home to try to make him come
over to their side, as if he were some kind of ultimate trophy,
the spoils of a philosophical war.

"We must *not* be unkind," Bert pronounced passionately,
raising a crooked finger in the air. "We can't be careless of one
another's hearts, or—"

The television picture suddenly righted itself, and Essy
squelched Bert's pronouncement with a call for instant silence.
"Oh—look!" she said. "There's Milton Berle in an evening
gown! Turn it up, Willy. I want to hear this."

In a moment, Deane was forgiven, and everybody was
laughing at Milton Berle.

For half an hour, Maddie lay in Deane's lap, seeming to
watch television with the others. She knew he really wasn't
watching it either. He was thinking about something, smoothing her hair over and over as though mentally trying out paths
in a maze. She thought of her mother at home with Katy, who
was sick again, the third upset stomach in ten days. What was
wrong with her? She'd eat, throw up, then eat again, and lately
she'd been rocking back and forth on the couch or in her crib
for hours at a time. The bolts in her crib were working loose.
"Nerves," the doctor said. "High-strung. It runs in families."

"You know what I think?" Essy leaned over to Deane during a commercial break in the show. (The expression on his mouth altered slightly, Maddie saw.) "You are specially touched by God. I've always thought that, from the first day I saw you in your crib. But you are at great peril, Deane. The Devil sets traps for gifted people. You can walk into them with your eyes wide open."

To Maddie's surprise, he neither agreed nor disagreed with what she said. (Later, Maddie would think Essy had been right about the traps. At least partly because of their gifted minds, Katy and Deane had both fallen into traps. But if the Devil sprang them, wasn't it God who set them? He gave gifts with strings attached. Was that why Deane didn't go to church?)

Essy wanted to say something more to Deane, but a look, a special focusing behind his eyes, stopped her. He patted her hand noncommitally.

When the program ended, everyone went downstairs for coffee. After the warmth of the cozy chairs upstairs, the living room felt cold and drafty. It was June, but only forty degrees outside, and Bert lit the gas fire. As the radiants flared, Deane sat down in front of the fireplace with Maddie beside him, and, without anyone else knowing, they played a game they had played many times before; he squeezed a rhythmic pattern into her hand and she squeezed it back until, after a while, the pattern became too long and complicated for her to follow. Then, to her disappointment, he stretched out full length on the hearth and fell asleep.

Sorry he was too tired to tell stories, she lay down beside him with her arm across his chest. His muscles felt lean and hard under his shirt. Yet over the past few days, he had looked heavily pulled down in himself somehow when he was walking around, as though he were carrying extra weight. She had a sense of how deep down he was even now; his skin not so much like tree bark at all, but like an insect's wingcase or a cocoon under his clothes. He reminded her of the happy-sad nesting dolls that Essy had given her two Christmases ago, brightly colored hollow dolls that fit snugly inside each other, each one smaller than the last, with alternating happy and sad faces, until the last one was so tiny its features were indistinguishable. You couldn't tell if it was happy or sad.

For the first time in her life, Maddie felt anxious for Deane for no logical reason. She stared into the blue wells at the base of the softly hissing gas flames, then at her uncle, his arm drawn over his eyes, his palm turned up. The world was full of invisible forces, she thought uneasily. Not all of them could be sensed or controlled. And then suddenly, without knowing why, she felt sorry for him, lying there sound asleep.

In July, he flew back to Alaska. When Bert asked how long he'd be gone this time, he said he didn't know for sure—he'd let them know.

In August, Maddie heard that he had published two chapters from his forthcoming dissertation and was winning great praise from other scientists in his field. Essy sent him a "care package" of canned tuna, dried fruit, and Bible verses; Maddie tucked in an ink drawing she'd made of Reverend Rutke (since she liked him, she drew him as a benevolent-looking string bean with droopy eyes), and Grandaddy tied up fifty dollars in a pair of red woolen socks, knowing Deane would keep the socks and either send the money back or give it away. Essy warned in a postscript that Bert had been depressed since he left because she thought he was "spiritually distancing himself" from the family. Though they knew he was constantly on the move, she added, could he possibly write more often?

He wrote in September to announce in big bold type that he was officially Dr. Rodgers Deane Cameron. But he was afraid he might not get home for Thanksgiving, and possibly not even for Christmas. When Bert read the letter to Maddie and her mother, she wept for joy at the culmination of so much effort, but also in bewilderment at this casual announcement that for the first time in thirty years, he might not be able to celebrate Christmas, nor even the completion of his degree, with his family.

After a week, she wrote back vowing she and Grandaddy would not decorate a Nova Scotia balsam unless both their precious sons were there to see it. "My knees are *failing*," she added in the last paragraph. "Some days they are so bowed, I hardly recognize them as mine!" (It undoubtedly went back, she told Maddie, to those terrible days of the Depression when poor Grandaddy lost his job; in desperation, she had taken in huge quantities of laundry—stood on her feet for twelve or fourteen hours a day ironing men's cotton shirts. Forty shirts in one night, she recalled with heavy sighs, while Grandaddy sold shoe polish from door to door. But they had kept the house, she said proudly. They had kept Deane and Willy supplied with books, clothes, a typewriter, and a microscope.)

But a week before Christmas, Bert changed her mind about the tree; she would decorate as usual, "as an act of faith," Maddie heard her tell her mother. She knew Deane, and Deane knew his priorities. Somehow he would find a way to get home— at least for a few weeks.

But on the evening of December 20, as they were all gathered around Bert's hearth for popcorn, he called long-distance to say a new deadline with the Navy had been set; given the weather, there was no way he could fly out of Nome and get back on time. He said he was sorry and wished them all a Merry Christmas. Bert and Grandaddy returned his greetings over the phone, then Willy and Ginny and Essy. Bert put Maddie on the phone to say the last good-bye. But just at the point of hanging up, Bert took the phone back again, broke down, and wept that he was disappointing Maddie and everyone. Couldn't he have planned things better? Weren't there any Christians left in the U.S. Navy?

She sat by the phone the whole rest of the evening. No one could comfort her. Not knowing what to say or do, Maddie went upstairs and looked into Deane's room. Bert had put fresh holly and bittersweet in the empty specimen jars and dusted his Eskimo art collection until the spooky masks and ivory carvings shone. She had polished the oversized globe with furniture wax, washed and mended the Aztec sun-yellow drapes, and scrubbed his rug on her swollen knees. Maddie could understand how she felt. This was his great moment of triumph. He was a Doctor. But he was a million miles away. On the verge of crying herself, she sat down on his bed and tried to feel Deane there in the room with her. She sensed him in the house, as always, but not close by. If she went into Bert's room, Deane's spirit beckoned from her father's old room. If she went into her father's room, he receded into Grandaddy's map room. Or downstairs into the kitchen, or out into the backyard—always somewhere else, as if drawing her on and on with more games.

On Christmas Eve, a dark, snowy afternoon, Bert sank into a chair in Maddie mother's kitchen, clutching a white cashmere coat around her shoulders. (Ever since the Depression, Grandaddy had lavished every extra cent on her, Essy said, especially at Christmas.) "I won't stay," she vowed to Maddie's mother, her powdered eyebrows arched with anxiety. Her favorite black velvet hat with the spiderweb veil was perched at a sharp angle on her head, and she spread a pair of pleated black velvet gloves over her lap. "I've had pneumonia four times in eight years—and pleurisy!" she said, smoothing the gloves over and over. "And twenty-seven ovarian cysts removed. He doesn't know *that*."

Maddie sat down on the floor to look at her grandmother's shoes. Her mother said Bert must have a hundred pairs, ten in every color, all with high spiked heels and elegant pointy toes. Today she wore cobalt-blue satin ones with jeweled ornaments—fairy godmother shoes, Maddie thought, sending off sparks of light in every direction.

"Do you think I should tell him how sick I am?" Bert asked her mother intently.

"Would it make any difference?" her mother said, offering her a steaming cup of tea from a Blue Danube pot. She knew the things that pleased Bert even when she was "on her high horse."

"My knees *lock* in the morning," Bert said. "I can't put any weight on them at *all*."

Three-year-old Katy clomped across the floor with a crust of half-eaten jelly toast hanging out of her mouth. She stamped her heavy-soled corrective shoes (she had flat, pigeon-toed feet), enjoying the noise they made, and supercharged with energy, banged on the table beside Bert with sticky fists.

Bert patted her head. "Does her face still break out in streaks every time she eats?"

"She's allergic to almost everything," Maddie said.

Katy moved around Bert's chair in a little dance, smiling winningly. She was the most unpredictable creature in the world. Now, drawn to the texture of Bert's coat, she suddenly reached out and grabbed the pocket as if to examine it closely, and—to Bert's horror—left a long streak of grape stain across the fabric.

"Oh no, Kathryn!" Bert wailed, pulling away. "Don't touch the pretty coat! Oh Ginny, look at what she's done!"

Maddie pulled Katy away to a far corner as her mother went to the sink to get a damp cloth. As offended as Bert, Katy howled.

"Howdy bought me this coat for our thirtieth anniversary," Bert said. "Oh, what if it's ruined? He'll be heartsick!"

"It's coming out," Ginny said, working gently at the stain with the cloth.

"It will have to be dry-*cleaned*," Bert said. "And even then—"

"We'll pay for it," Ginny said. "But look—it's gone."

Bert sighed deeply, seeing that the stain had indeed disappeared, leaving no trace. But instead of looking pleased, she waved her gloves in a gesture of futility, falling back into a troubled musing more distracted than before. It was almost as though she'd half-enjoyed the problem of the jelly stain since it took her mind off Deane. "Do you know," she said at last, "I think he might be interested in a girl up there. I know he was receiving mail from her last summer. Of course I'd never look into his things, but I did notice a return address. The name was Marian Komuk." She lowered her voice to a whisper, as if Maddie shouldn't hear. "I'm glad to see him take an interest in a woman, you understand. But she must be an Eskimo."

Ginny sat down beside her at the table. Bert leaned forward and pressed two fingers deep into her arm. "Essy's blind faith in Providence is not mine, you understand," she said confidentially. "Religion can't fill the whole void of the heart. Only other hearts can. Deane has never—" She broke off her sentence as Ginny's attention was distracted by Katy's bellowing. She sat back resignedly and began to massage her swollen arthritic knuckles. "Will you look at my hands, Madeleine?" she said. "I'll never play the piano again."

She held them up, and Maddie touched the bulging joint of her right index finger. It felt hard as stone.

"Isn't that awful?" she said. "That's *my* hand!"

Not so awful, Maddie thought. (Years later, she remembered her grandmother's hands with particular love and affection. They had looked like eagle claws with painted tips that winter day, blue-veined and stiff, immaculately scrubbed with fresh-smelling soap. Her right hand was set off with an enormous diamond ring, a thirty-fifth anniversary gift from Grandaddy—and Maddie loved her hand exactly as it was.

Bert's hands had suited her, deformed, yet surprisingly strong and graceful in their curled-up expressiveness, gentle at the heart, helpless even, yet belying an iron will, like the stony bone underneath her pink, old-woman skin.)

"I used to write poetry, mind you," she addressed Maddie alone now, since her mother was preoccupied with tying Katy's corrective shoes. "I haven't published anything since the jingles I wrote to help pay for Deane's first year at Pitt. They were contests, you see, and I won. Over two thousand dollars in all—imagine! It's strange that, now that I have the time to write for pleasure, I don't have the will. But the market for poetry has changed so! It's all Whitman's fault—passing off words as cheaply and numerously as grass-blades! Deane used to claim he actually *liked* Whitman!"

Her face clouded. She turned back to Maddie's mother. "I ask you, what kind of son would give a passionate mother's love a merely *dutiful* return?" she pleaded, dabbing her eyes with her gloves, leaving smudges of powder and rouge on the black velvet.

"Deane can be selfish at times," Ginny said sympathetically.

Bert stiffened. Maddie handed her a Kleenex for her tears, but she crushed it in her fist. "Selfish? Oh no, *never* selfish! He won't take a thing from *anyone*!" She pointed her crooked finger at Ginny accusingly, and Maddie thought her grandmother could be frightening if she wanted to. "Willy *knows* how we've tried to send him money. He sends it right back—with interest! He won't take so much as a postage stamp." Then she sagged in her chair as though deflated. "Ask him for anything, and he'll *give* it to you. He gave away the *gorgeous* coat I gave him last Christmas, a heavy, fur-lined parka with the warmest hood, in smoky blue . . ."

Her voice trailed off. She fell into a kind of pensive hum, like a cat purring—but not in contentment. Maddie had heard that sound many times over the years, as if Bert were trying to figure out how to outmaneuver an adored adversary she couldn't afford to defeat.

Maddie sat at her feet again and wished she could try on her shoes. Even if Bert's hands were crooked, her feet still looked young and pretty. Maybe that was why she wore such splendid shoes—so she could look down and see some part of her that hadn't changed or turned old. Bert didn't like being old, Maddie knew, which was why she dyed her hair and wore so many cosmetics. She didn't want to lose anything, not her youth, her knowledge, her physical strength or beauty, or either of her sons. She let nothing go easily, begrudging every waste and loss, even when it couldn't be helped.

"Shouldn't you get off those high heels if your legs hurt so much?" her mother said to Bert, seeing Maddie's absorption in them. Maddie felt the question go through her grandmother's pride like a pearl-headed hatpin.

Bert looked at Ginny, stricken for just a moment, then recovered and ran her fingers through Maddie's hair. "When will you get this child a permanent wave? Her bangs shouldn't hang down in her eyes like this."

Ginny said nothing.

"If I gave it as a gift?" she pressed. "In addition to the piano lessons, of course. And ballet."

Katy was up on her feet again, balanced on pigeon-toes and rocking back and forth. "For Katy, dance will be a necessity!" Bert laughed, drawing her cashmere coat around her protectively. "Poor, poor Katy! Look at those little feet."

Katy frowned and kept her distance.

Then in a surprising gesture of emotion, Bert pulled Maddie close and held her tightly against her side, stroking her arm softly and rhythmically. "It is such suffering," she said as if confiding a special sorrow to her. "Not knowing where he is, or what kind of danger he's in. *You* understand . . . ?"

Yes, she wanted to say. She had felt it when Deane had lain asleep at the fireplace.

"You're good with words," her mother said to Bert after a silence. "Why don't you write and tell *him* how you feel?"

Bert studied her daughter-in-law's face as a baroness might study a kitchen maid's for fresh, unthought-of solutions to things. She straightened her posture, pulled on her gloves with short, hard tugs, and Maddie saw she still had remarkable strength in her inflamed fingers. "Perhaps," she said. "But I couldn't beg him for anything. If he's so fond of geographical distance—"

She stopped in mid-sentence. "But no," she reconsidered. "That's *not* the tack to take. I can't expect him to be like other people's sons. The Deanes were never like other people." (It was then that Maddie realized that "Deane" was Bert's maiden name.) "It amazes me how completely he's taken on the family character."

"He's a character all right," Ginny said, laughing.

"We were always a *distinguished* family," Bert explained to Maddie, ignoring Ginny's joke. "Intense and apart. Private. Absorbed. Always absorbed in one idea or another."

"Obsessed, I would say," Ginny commented. "Sometimes Deane puts his love of knowledge before everything else, even before his own family."

Was that wrong? Maddie wondered. Was it so wrong?

Katy tripped on the corner of a chair and sat down hard on the floor. She thrashed her legs and cried loudly.

"It's those shoes," said her mother, picking her up and rocking her. "It's those big dumb shoes."

Bert rose from her chair, and while Ginny lulled Katy back to an agreeable state, stood in an isolated stare by the stove, as deep down in herself as Deane had been by the fire. They were both thinkers and schemers, Maddie thought, always working on solutions to something; but Bert worked with a kind of hampering powerlessness (and a compensating cunning, Maddie would see later) that Deane didn't have.

When Katy stopped crying, her mother put her down

beside the cupboard of pots and pans. "Daddy's tympani," she said, setting a big aluminum Dutch oven and a three-quart saucepan before her. She placed two wooden spoons in her hands. "Watch this," she said to Bert.

Katy's mood changed instantly. She looked up at her mother, back down at the pans, then began to beat slowly and precisely in a strong, steady rhythm, then faster, in a more excited syncopated one.

Bert's head began to nod. And in a few moments, Maddie saw her grandmother's eyes grow wide with astonishment as her grave anxiousness gave way to pleasure and delight. "Why, she's good!" she exclaimed. "She's very good! When did she start doing this? She's going to be a percussionist like Willy! Maddie, listen to Katy!"

Katy didn't care if anyone listened or not. She was, in the tradition of a Deane, absorbed. And Bert was thrilled, looking at Katy as if seeing her for the first time. "Do you know, Ginny," she said excitedly, "that *I* was beset with allergies when I was a child? Almost everyone in our family manifested a talent early. Sometimes the talent could be so strong, it would make *rags* of the one who possessed it. But oh, the music!"

"Talents and allergies," Maddie heard her mother say softly as she turned back to the sink.

Bert went home, energized by Katy's drum-playing and her resolution to write to Deane. Two hours later, she returned with the letter in her hand. "I've done it," she said, waving off Ginny's preparations for supper. "Maddie, darling, listen for your father in the hallway if he comes home from work. This is not for his ears. You both must tell me *honestly* if you think this is right."

She poised herself to read, holding her folded glasses up to her eyes and shaking out five typewritten pages. " 'December 24, 1949,' " she began. " 'My dearest Deane: How I would have *loved* to welcome you home, *warm* and *safe*, this Christmas Eve.

How few Christmases we are given in a lifetime! Here, it is softly snowing, a winter *wonderland*. I fear that where you are, surrounded with those dimly-lit cabins and saloons backed up to a frozen ocean, it is a winter *wasteland*. Are you still in Nome? How we miss you! I pray that you are not imposing undue hardships on yourself, physically or spiritually, and that you are not trying to *protect* us from anything we should know about your sit—"

"Daddy's home," Maddie said, hearing the front door open and close.

"Oh *no*," Bert said, frustrated, "I'll skip to the last page," and paused to recover her concentration. (Whenever Bert read, she always waited for the mood of the piece to possess her, Maddie knew; nothing could hurry her. As she prepared, there would be an amazing transformation in her, from anxious to calm, depressed to lighthearted, whatever the words suggested. She had perfect emotional control then, and only then, it seemed, becoming one with the author's will, her voice beautifully affecting and true.) " 'Have you considered my servant Job?' " she read now. (Maddie saw her mother smile; Essy had said Bert loved to throw Job into everything.) " 'A man who had done nothing wrong in his life? Yet in an instant, everything was taken from him. *Too late!* Too late for changing priorities or retrieving lost opportunities for kindness! Lost sheep and cows—or shall I say frogs and snakes?—can be restored, my *dearest* son, but not a father, a mother, a brother. We are so proud of you! But you are being driven to higher and higher latitudes, not in search, but in escape from something, it seems to us—from what? You used to say the Eskimos were a mystery. . . .' " She stopped, took a tissue from her purse, and wiped her nose roughly back and forth. " 'You used to wonder how cold—how dark it could get before life ceased altogether. I have never questioned the direction your questions have taken you. But now *you* are the one who is a mystery.

You are growing cold, I fear. I actually wake up at night in *dread* that—"

Maddie became so absorbed in the letter, she didn't see her father standing in the doorway listening. Now he strode into the kitchen and grabbed the letter out of Bert's hands. "You're not sending that," he said, turning his back and scanning the pages briefly.

"Give it back to me!" she demanded, struggling to rise out of her chair.

"You aren't going to bother him with this nonsense, Mother."

"Bother?" she said, appalled. "I can if I want to!"

She reached for the letter, but he tore it up, folded it, and tore it again.

"Daddy—?" Maddie said, shocked at his action.

"You don't know the situation," he said to Bert.

"It was Ginny's idea!" she cried helplessly, pulling Maddie tightly to her side again. "She suggested it! I was telling him that I have this terrible sense that something is wrong, that he's in trouble up there."

He threw the pieces of the letter into the wastebasket. "He's fine," he said. "Why won't you ever trust *my* judgment?"

She got to her feet as though she wanted to strike him for insolence. But as her glasses fell from her lap onto the floor and she almost stepped on them, Maddie saw she meant no such thing.

"Oh thank you, thank you, darling," she whimpered, leaning on her heavily as she handed her the glasses.

"Don't you think he would be here if he could?" her father said more gently.

"I don't know!" she cried. "How do *you* know? What does he tell you that he doesn't tell his own mother?"

He shrugged. She looked at him tearfully and ordered, "Please take me home."

He put on the coat he had just taken off and led her on his arm to the front door. "I never raised my sons to be so harsh!" she called over her shoulder to Ginny. Maddie noticed that her severely bowed legs looked like perfectly rounded parentheses.

When her father returned from Bert's, he was in surprisingly good spirits. Maddie had noticed that Bert's mood swings never bothered him for long. If the Deanes were "absorbed," he told Maddie and her mother in the kitchen now, they could also be absorbing, draining the emotions of everyone around them. One had to know when to walk away, as Deane had learned long ago. He said he had apologized to Bert for tearing up her letter, had reassured her of Deane's safety, and after a while, she had accepted it. She could never stay angry at him for long. He predicted she would be her old self again for the tree-decorating party that night.

As her mother worked on supper, Maddie joined her father in the living room to run the electric train under the Christmas tree. They shared an enthusiasm for the American Flyer steam engine that her mother did not. Year by year, his layouts covered more and more of the living-room floor. ("Excess is not enough," was the Cameron motto, her mother had said last Christmas in exasperation.) This year, the layout had trestles, homemade cardboard grades, tunnels through mountains, and an automated crossing, better than any of the Christmas train displays she had seen in the department stores. A few nights ago, he had built a wooden box to mount all his controls on, which he didn't want Maddie to touch. But she didn't mind. She enjoyed lying flat on her stomach, watching the train come out of the tunnel toward her, imagining it trudging through snowed-in mountain passes or crawling along rocky ledges. Sometimes she loaded plastic cows into boxcars or pieces of hard candy into hoppers, although she noticed tonight that all the candy on the coffee table was gone. Katy must have stolen it again. So she took the Baby Jesus out of the creche and gave him a ride to Egypt in the hopper instead.

"It's snowing again," her father said enthusiastically, pointing to the window. "Eight inches by morning, they say."

Snow was another of their shared enthusiasms, learned from Deane. Tonight, just as always, they would all trudge through it over to Bert's house, and eat and sing, and decorate the tree. Only for the first time ever, Deane wouldn't be there.

"Another perfect Christmas," her father said, throwing switches, turning green lights red.

"Yep." She knew he was reading her mind—not wanting Deane's being away to spoil things for her. Like Bert, he worked hard to force the ideal of every holiday, as if anything less would be a failure.

"Do you think Santa's left the Pole yet?" he asked, looking at his watch, playing the game they always played—that every myth and legend was literally true, or could be made true by unquestioning faith. "Just heading out over the Yukon, I'd say."

There was a funny noise in the fireplace. It sounded like a shower of pebbles falling out of the chimney. She looked up, puzzled. Apparently her father hadn't heard it; he was busy reversing switches.

She went to the hearth and looked behind the cardtable her mother had set up against it to cover up the old discolored bricks. There, scattered on the floor, were thirty or forty pieces of hard candy wrapped in bright green-and-red foil. She picked them up in amazement. "Look, Dad," she said, "look what fell out of the chimney."

He looked surprised.

"But how could it?" she said. "It's all bricked up!"

"Maybe it's a sign," he said casually. "Santa Claus is going to come down that chimney, bricked up or not."

She couldn't resist looking up the chimney to confirm that

it was still solid bricks. Where had the candy come from? Deane said that now and then there was real magic in the world, and whoever didn't believe it deserved not to. Her father had been sitting right beside her at the transformer and somehow made all that candy fall out of a bricked-up fireplace. Or else, as he wanted her to think and she wanted to believe, this was real Christmas magic.

Happily, she loaded a boxcar with the candy, and felt pulled like a piece of string between joy and sadness, faith and doubt. She felt it more and more often the older she got, especially when Deane was away. At times the string was relaxed and had a comfortable slack. But at other times it pulled so tightly, she felt as though she would snap in two and go tumbling into craziness. Even if the string did break, she wouldn't be able to tell for sure which end was joy and which end sadness. Sometimes she didn't know one feeling from the other.

Sensing her distraction, her father turned off the transformer and went to the window. He looked at his watch, then back out at the snow again. Was he waiting for something? she wondered.

Her mother called them to the kitchen for homemade potato soup and cornbread. In the kitchen, all the windows were steamed over, and Katy was banging lustily on the table with her Rudolf-the-Red-nosed-Reindeer cup.

Joy, Maddie decided. Joy.

Then, in a tradition of her own, full of longing, she looked out the window and up through the snow-covered hemlocks for the Christmas star. Unlike Deane, sometimes she couldn't disbelieve in anything.

That night, Essy got out her violin and played carols to Grandaddy's improvised accompaniment. (He had never had a music lesson in his life, but he could play by ear—a mystery to Maddie.) She sat on the piano bench beside him and picked out the melodies an octave higher, trying to keep up with his modulations to higher and higher keys. "I can't even carry a tune," her mother laughed, listening to the music from the couch. Outside the window behind her, gusts of wind blew powdery snow in showers and spirals. It sparkled in the reflected lamplight.

Bert moved restlessly from table to hearth, rearranging balsam branches on the mantel, turning up the gas in the fireplace, humming an independent carol.

"It's already eighty degrees in here, Mother," Willy protested. "Turn it down!"

"I want the children to be *warm*," she said, looking hurt, turning it up anyway.

"Do you know Bert used to compose?" Grandaddy said to Maddie. "Come sit, Bertie. Play the 'Romance' you wrote at Carnegie Tech."

"Oh I couldn't, Howdy. Don't ask me."

Maddie thought she wanted to be coaxed, took her hand, and pulled her to the Mason and Hamlin.

"You polished the lid for an hour yesterday," Grandaddy said. "Shouldn't you play it?"

"She won a Composition Award for it," Maddie's father told her mother. "Beat out the whole music school."

Bert smiled coquettishly, drawing nearer. But she hesitated at the bench, as though thinking over a momentous matter.

"Oh, play it, Bertha!" Essy said impatiently. "You used to play it all the time. Nearly drove Mama crazy."

"That was a hundred years ago," Bert said sharply.

She looked at Grandaddy, then cast sad, blinking eyes down at the keys. "I don't have the heart to play this year. Everyone isn't here."

Essy sighed loudly. Maddie saw her father look at his watch with the same preoccupied look he had worn before supper.

Grandaddy refused to humor Bert. He pulled her down on the bench and said "Play."

Giving in at last, she turned on the rose-globed hurricane lamp at her left to set the mood. She loved that lamp, Maddie knew. But she didn't really need extra light since she could memorize the notes of a piece after playing it through only once, just as Deane had a photographic memory for words. Now she addressed the piano with complete seriousness. The room grew quiet. Maddie silently stepped to the treble end of the piano and watched her place her crooked fingers on the keys without even looking down. She stared out through the raised lid of the instrument as if trying to find her memory of the music in the far wall. "I can't," she said after a long pause, dropping her hands. "I can't remember."

"Please," Maddie said, seeing real anxiety in her grand-mother's eyes.

She looked at Maddie, considered, and renewed her con-centration. After a false start, she began to play hesitatingly, then deliberately, ten or fifteen bars of the loveliest music Maddie had ever heard. As the music came back to her, Bert bent her whole body into it, yet her head seemed detached and free from the performance, able to listen critically, as though someone else were playing. And she liked what she heard. The melody descended and ascended liltingly like a conversation, at one point slowing and turning on itself as if having second thoughts about its original gay mood, then recovering and repeating its first statement. "Unabashedly ro-mantic," Essy said from her chair.

But then Bert came to a difficult transitional measure and couldn't get past it. She winced at wrong notes and grabbed awkwardly at worse ones.

"Keep going," Grandaddy said. "Play anything to get through that section."

To Maddie's delight, she began to sing to fill in the missed phrases and soon relaxed into the music again, swaying and laughing with the spirit of her own composition. What a grand time Bert was having, Maddie saw, her grandmother's watery eyes shining with the pleasure of coming out on display and performing before her favorite audience, the family.

Then all at once she stopped, shook her head, and massaged her left hand. "I can't go on," she said bitterly. "I want to and can't."

"But look at Katy," Ginny said encouragingly. "She loves your piece, Bert."

Katy was dancing to Bert's music even after it had stopped, flushed with excitement, bowing and hopping with a quirky kind of grace in her clumsy shoes.

"Play anything, Bert," Grandaddy commanded. "Did you ever see a child with such a musical sense?"

"Willy had it!" Bert boasted, and began again, weak in the bass, not as strong as before, but looking over her shoulder with pleasure at Katy's happy twirls and hops.

There was a loud knock at the front door. Maddie saw her father look at his watch. "Eleven-fifteen," he murmured. "Want to get that?" he said to his mother.

"No," Bert said. "Willy, can't you see I'm playing?"

"Who would call at this hour on Christmas Eve?" Essy complained, taking up her violin to join in again.

"It's got to be for you, Mom," Willy said, sinking down into the couch. "Probably one of the neighbors."

Bert stopped playing and looked at him as though he were incomprehensibly stubborn—nothing new. She got up from the bench, straightened her dress, and walked stiffly to the door. "What difference would . . ." she reproached him, opening the door.

Outside in the blowing snow stood Deane.

"Merry Christmas, Mother," he smiled, holding out a bouquet of bedraggled pine. "This is pretty rare flora where I come from. It's for you."

"Oh!" she staggered backward, then forward into his arms, receiving him wildly, joyfully. ("Like the mother of the Prodigal Son," Essy whispered to Ginny with tear-filled eyes.) Bert turned him around, then flashed a look at Willy, aware that there had been a conspiracy between the brothers. "Oh Howdy, look who's here!" she exclaimed to Grandaddy, as though he couldn't see for himself. "And nobody *told* me!"

She allowed Deane to hug his father, then took him back for herself. "I *knew* you couldn't stay away!" she said, crying, holding his face. "Didn't I tell you, Es?"

She laughed and cried, kissed Deane again and directed everyone else to kiss him. Then she kissed Willy passionately. "You knew it all along, didn't you? Oh, but why didn't you give me a hint? Why *didn't* you? I've been so *miserable!*"

"He didn't call until dawn yesterday—at five-twenty," Willy said. "Said he'd gotten a flight out with some cowboy pilot desperate for money who promised to get him back on time. Probably cost him a fortune."

Grandaddy took Deane's suitcase while he stamped around shaking melting snow off his overcoat. Maddie couldn't believe it. It was as though he had brought the Arctic back with him into the living room. The whole atmosphere of the house had freshened, everything lighting up with color and energy. It was as though before, even with the music and fun, they had not all been completely awake.

"Guess what, everybody?" Deane said as Bert presented him with a cup of steaming coffee in her best blue Spode china cup. "Congress has passed one million dollars for a granite seawall in Nome. Another bad storm would have wiped us off the map—including Marks Air Force Base, Willy. It's cause for celebration."

He raised his coffee cup, and everyone applauded for Congress.

Bert pressed on him a plate of homemade cookies big

enough for ten men. Maddie laughed as he ate greedily, stuffing his mouth to please her. But then, for a moment, she felt herself sink back from them, as if into a separate space. She realized she had been playing a game with herself this past week—had been made to play it by everyone but Bert. The game was to accept Deane's absence cheerfully and to go on with Christmas as though everything were fine. But it hadn't been fine. Yet somehow she had almost been fooled. Now with Deane standing in the living room again, his exceptional presence turning up the brightness and volume of everything, she wondered how she could ever have been persuaded to accept his not coming home. Only Bert had held out against it.

When he had finished his cookies—about a dozen and a half, Maddie figured—he dug down into a shabby traveling satchel and pulled out a paper bag. "I know it's not official gift-giving time, Mother," he said. "But Santa said to deliver this to Maddie Cameron personally tonight. It took two weeks by dogsled from the North Pole." He handed it to her. "Sorry it's not wrapped."

Maddie pulled an exquisite blue-and-red-beaded sealskin pouch out of the bag—present enough. But inside was another gift, a heavy book called *Eskimo Tales*, with ten full-page ink illustrations drawn by native Eskimo artists. "It's a treasure," he said, as she smiled to thank him. "Not many Eskimos confide their tales to the white man."

The book was wonderful. Its pages were snow-white, glossy, and cold to the touch. "Look!" she said to her mother, holding it up. "It even feels like Alaska!"

"Merry Christmas," he said with the full strength of that warm light in his eyes she had not seen since July. Oh, thank you, she thought, returning the look happily: *Welcome home.*

She sat on the floor and turned the pages, fascinated by the strange mythical creatures in the drawings. Some of them were funny, others terrifying. She was only vaguely aware that, as she studied them, Deane, Grandaddy, and her father were talking about Russia, its first successful testing of an A-bomb, and rumors of an "underground" in Nome, whatever that was.

"Planes from Siberia can be over us in six minutes," Deane said in response to a question from her father she hadn't heard. "Somebody slipped a copy of *Pravda* under my door last week."

"And you think the scare is exaggerated!" Essy said, horrified.

Deane held out his coffee cup to Bert for a refill. Maddie took the opportunity to slip the Eskimo book on his lap and point to a drawing of a fat little Eskimo man being chased across the tundra by an enormously long serpent with sharp fangs and a hundred legs. "What *is* that?" she asked.

"That man has offended a nature spirit," Deane explained, pleased by her curiosity. "He was selfish and gluttonous. While his wife and children were starving, he ate the puppies of his own sled dogs. And then he was caught stealing from other hunters' blowholes."

"He ate puppies?" she asked incredulously.

Essy asked to see the book. "There's a lot of violence in these stories," she said after looking over the pictures. "I thought the Eskimos were supposed to be a gentle people."

"These stories are their religion, Es," Deane said—"their Jonah and the Whale, the Serpent in the Garden. Beneath their mildness there's plenty of violence and, at the same time, an almost unlimited reserve of spiritual endurance. I envy it."

"What's this one?" Maddie asked over Essy's shoulder, pointing to a drawing of children playing in the air.

"That's supposed to be the aurora borealis—the northern lights. The *angakok* or priest believes that the souls of stillborn children dance and play a kind of football game with their umbilical cords."

"Oh my!" Bert said, reaching for the book, as Maddie followed it and took a stand over her shoulder. Putting her glasses to her eyes, she pored over the drawings with intense concentration, pausing at a drawing of an old woman sitting in the middle of an enormous white plain, all alone. Far off in the distance, a dog sled was speeding away.

"The Inuit understand perfectly the conditions and circumstances of their own lives," Deane explained. "That old grandmother is very weak. She can't work any longer, and she believes it's her time to die. So she leaves the *igloovigak*, her son takes her out on the ice, says good-bye, and rides away."

"And she lets him?" Bert asked, looking up at him.

"She orders him," Deane said.

Maddie stared at the tiny form on the snow, left there like a crumpled bug on a huge white tablecloth. It wasn't right, she thought. Understandable, but not right.

"Eskimos are afraid of all kinds of things," Deane said quietly. "Death isn't one of them."

"Is Maddie old enough for this book?" her mother said, taking her turn to look at the pictures.

He stretched out in his old place in front of the fire, motioning for Maddie to come sit down beside him. "Sure," he said.

"I am," Maddie said, glad to know he didn't think she was a child anymore. She had grown deeper in herself this past year, and stronger, she felt, in her love and respect for the things he loved.

She took the book back from her mother, grateful to Bert for having taught her how to read before she went to kindergarten. She could read most of the words in the book easily. "I love this present," she whispered to Deane.

"You've grown," he said admiringly.

At Christmas dinner the next afternoon, Essy said a long Christmas grace, Deane carved the turkey, and Bert carried a made-to-order plate to each one around the table. Willy took movies from every angle with his one-year-old camera, exasperating Bert with his fussing with the light meter and spotlights. "You'll thank me for this later," he said as she kept waving him out of her way but smiling charmingly every time the camera focused on her.

"What's this?" Deane said, pulling a soggy paper bag from the turkey's chest cavity and holding it up on his knife.

"Bertha!" Essy groaned. "You didn't clean the turkey! No wonder Ginny couldn't find the giblets for the gravy!"

Bert's cheeks burned as Maddie's mother exchanged looks with Essy. "I scrubbed the outside," she stammered. "I must have forgotten . . ."

Deane laughed and said Eskimos ate uncleaned things inside other uncleaned things all the time. "You should see what they do with seal embryos," he grinned at Essy.

"Never mind!" she said, her mouth full, holding up her hand. "I don't want to hear it."

But Deane told it anyway and ate the whole bag of giblets himself—"a new high standard" for dinners, he said, as he always said. (It *was* the best of all dinners, Maddie would think later. Bert served Deane three plates because he looked so gaunt beside the rest of them.)

When the meal was over, Maddie blew out the candles and helped Essy clear the table. She looked for Katy, who had fallen asleep under the piano bench, and covered her with a blanket. Then, more drawn to the conversation in the living room than in the kitchen, she picked a puzzle from Bert's game cupboard and spread out the pieces on the floor beside Deane.

"I collected an *Anas acuta*—a young Pintail—at Kiana on Kobuk River," Deane was telling her father and grandfather over a frayed map spread out on the coffee table. "Its stomach was packed full of mosquito larvae—a surprise. I'd thought the Pintail's diet was nine-tenths vegetable. This might lead to a partial solution to the bug hordes in the summer."

As Deane talked, Maddie watched her father yawn and settle down into an easy chair with his legs spread out on an ottoman. In contrast, Deane sat like an Indian chief on the floor, back straight, his stocking feet folded under him. Grandaddy drew his legs up to his chest in a corner of the couch and hugged a velvet pillow like a little boy hearing a bedtime story.

"Would you believe," Deane continued, "that the Alaskan Railroad imported frogs to eat the mosquitoes? Might have worked if the frogs had weighed two hundred pounds each."

Everyone laughed. "Tell Maddie about your concert debut," Grandaddy urged.

As Deane folded the map, it occurred to Maddie that all the men in the family relaxed with their shoes off after dinner, while all the women worked in the kitchen with their shoes on. She kicked off her patent leathers.

"Well," Deane said, warming to the telling, "I found an old Kurtzman upright in a tin shack in Teller. No one knew how it had gotten there, and no one could play it. So one day I sat down and murdered a few bars of the 'Mapleleaf Rag.' You should have seen the Eskimos come running from everywhere. They gathered around me with broad blissful looks on their faces, as if I were a god."

"And you loved it," Willy smiled, eyes closed. "You ate it up."

"There was one very intelligent little girl named Nauja. I taught her how to play Brahms's 'Lullaby' and 'Onward, Christian Soldiers,' and now she's an aristocrat among her people. Keeps bringing me little gifts all the time—fresh salmon, seal liver, auk that has been soaked underground in blubber for five months—"

"Aaughh!" Maddie made a face and pretended to choke —jealous of Nauja.

"I ate it raw," Deane said, peering down at her. "*Peechook!*

All gone. In the Arctic you have to keep an open mind to keep a full stomach."

He picked up the lid of her puzzle box and studied the picture—two Trumpeter swans gliding across a calm blue lake. "You know," he said to all of them, "I wouldn't mind living in Teller. There's one town commissioner, one radio operator, and an ancient postmistress by the name of Mrs. Tweet. Enough government for anybody."

Oh no, Maddie thought with alarm. This was what Bert feared the most: that he'd move up to Alaska to stay. But she doubted he could mean it. He couldn't leave them all for good. He had come all this way just to be with them for the holidays.

"What's the commissioner do?" her father asked, obviously unconcerned by his words.

"Issues marriage licenses, mostly, stops fights, talks to Eskimos who commit offenses against the public interest." He rummaged in his traveling satchel under the couch, took out a .45 revolver, and handed it to him. "I bought this on his recommendation."

"What for?" Willy said with surprise, holding up the gun admiringly in his hand. "Rowdy Eskimos?" He aimed it directly through the holly wreath in Bert's picture window.

"Wolves and rabid foxes. They'll follow a sled for days. And there are other dangers."

Willy passed the gun to Grandaddy. "I've heard they're reducing the military force in Nome," he said. "A lot of people are frightened."

"A lot of people get hysterical," Deane said.

There was a silence in the room.

"Why would you want to live in such a tiny isolated village?" Grandaddy asked after inspecting the gun.

Maddie looked up from her puzzle, especially interested in this question.

Deane laughed. "The land is free. The world's bigger. You

just pick a vacant place on the sandspit, and it's yours. The natives speak English well enough to pack the Dream Movie Theater in Nome. I bet Teller could support a newspaper. I could be the editor—'The Midnight Sun' or something."

"You're crazy," Willy said, sinking deeper in his chair.

"May I see the gun?" Maddie asked as Grandaddy handed it back to Deane.

Her father shook his head, but Deane gave it to her anyway. "Oh!" she said, finding it much heavier than she expected. The metal was silvery and silky smooth. Holding it with both hands, she put her finger on the trigger and pointed the gun toward the fireplace. It felt full of unimaginable power. "I bet it's loud," she said with a nervous laugh.

"I didn't know there was a movie theater in Nome," her father said, taking the gun from her.

Deane smiled. "The Dream Theater is a rickety, barn-like old building. Mostly the Eskimos delight in Dorothy Lamour Technicolor dramas of the South Seas. The first time I went in, I sat down, leaned back, and fell into the lap of the man behind me. The chair had its back broken out. I apologized, moved up a row and leaned back cautiously, found my chair had a back, relaxed, and the whole row fell over. The bolts had pulled out of the floor. All around me Eskimos were happily munching popcorn and staring at the screen. My commonplace mishaps weren't worth a glance."

Deane put the gun away and took out his ancient box camera, unloaded a used roll of film, and loaded it with another. "You'd love the puffins, Maddie," he said, "little white-breasted, orange-beaked guys. I backed up on a slippery rock in a cliff face trying to get a picture of one for you. The surf soaked my camera, but they just kept flying in circles over my head, laughing at me."

She imagined him hanging on the side of a cliff like someone in the movies, trying to get the picture for her.

"It's a wonder you get anything with that old relic," Grandaddy said. "How about a new one as a Christmas present?"

"Thanks," Deane said, but shook his head. "You'd have to see this place, Dad. As soon as you put any weight on the cliff-face, it crumbles into little knife edges that cut your fingers and clothes. It was thirteen below zero, but I was bathed in sweat by the time I got to the top. Coming down was worse. I could easily have dropped the camera onto the rocks below. At least it wouldn't have been any loss."

Maddie abandoned her puzzle for a moment and tried to picture his adventure in her mind. She imagined Alaska as a vast, beautiful, but cruel place where nights could be three months long and storms could come lashing out of nowhere at fifty degrees below zero. Outside Deane's tent, such a storm could moan and blow for days, he had said, leading a person into thoughts that ruled him out-of-business for a normal, practical life. The temptation to rest in peace could be overwhelming then. And yet, she thought, how pleasant it was in this house tonight, with everyone hearing about the threats and dangers of the Arctic by the warm fire, waiting for dessert. Deane loved this place too. How did he go back and forth between this world and that one so easily?

He took an interest in the puzzle now, drawing her attention back to it. She had almost finished the swans, but was having a hard time filling in the blue sky and lake behind them. "Several pieces are missing," she said. But after a quick scan of the puzzle, he located one of them and reached across her to pick it up. "What's that?" she asked, noticing a pale, thick, white line across his hand.

"A scar," he said.

She studied it. "Did something bite you?"

"Yes and no," he said, studying the puzzle.

"A fox?"

"No."

"A wolf?"

"No."

Interested, her father bent down to look at it. "The wound was ragged and deep, whatever it was," he said.

"Guess again," Deane said to Maddie, making a game of it.

She reexamined the scar, turning his hand over and back. The line felt smooth and yet tough to the touch. "The beak of a Great Blue Heron?" she said. He shook his head. "The claw of a polar bear?"

She gave up.

"A rusty can opener," he said, deflating the mystery with a grin. "I was in a hurry to get out of camp one morning and stabbed myself." He stretched out the flesh between his thumb and forefinger. "The point was embedded here. When I pulled it out, a piece of muscle came with it."

"Good Lord," Grandaddy said, noting a stiffness in Deane's hand for the first time. "You could have had lockjaw. How far were you from a hospital?"

"Far. But the Eskimos have a good remedy for infection. They do amazing things with urine and saliva."

Maddie saw her father roll his eyes and look up at the ceiling.

"But I decided to trust to whiskey, the cold, and chance," Deane said.

"Did it hurt?" Maddie asked.

"It hurt to find out I couldn't use my thumb for a while. Do you realize how important an opposable thumb is?" He took her right hand and bent her thumb under. "Now try to finish your puzzle without it."

She tried. It was hopelessly awkward, like Bert must feel with her arthritis some days.

Bert, Essy, and her mother came into the room, flushed with the steam from the kitchen, wiping their hands on their aprons.

"What's going on?" Bert asked, seeing Maddie's struggling motions and everybody watching her.

"I'm putting a puzzle together without thumbs," she said matter-of-factly.

"Good practice for real life," Deane said, smiling.

Bert looked perplexed. Grandaddy fluffed up the couch cushions and held out his hand. "Come here and listen to Deane, Bertie. You too, Es."

Maddie's mother sat on the arm of her father's chair. He pulled her down into the cramped space beside him and kissed her loudly, then grinned at Deane.

"Now tell everything again," Bert commanded him. "What have I missed? What's going on with the Navy? Your letters have been *so* few and far between."

Deane moved back from the puzzle to let Maddie finish it herself. "We're stalled again," he said in a subdued tone. "And they altered my contract without telling me. Aside from that, there's not much to tell."

"What do you mean—altered?" Bert said. "You said the terms were clear before you left."

"They were. Position of Assistant Director of my part of the survival project at five thousand dollars a year, my own contract, plus a two-thousand-dollar grant for my work on frogs at the Institute."

"You mean you didn't get the job McCafferty hired you for?" Grandaddy said.

"When I got there in July, I was no more Assistant Director than Willy is. A man named Sidorkin put me through as a rider on McCafferty's contract with a nine-hundred-dollar cut in salary. McCafferty put Sidorkin in charge of hiring all the scientists on the project. I think he deliberately deceived me about my status just to get me up there after funds were cut. Didn't even give me the right to say no."

"How *dare* he!" Bert said. "Didn't he know your reputation?"

"I fired off a letter to McCafferty telling him what Sidorkin had done. He wrote back and said he'd look into it. I've been waiting for him to straighten it out ever since, but I don't think anything's going to happen. Meanwhile, the Navy sits and sits on the next stage of the project and doesn't move."

"So what have you been doing all this time?" Willy asked. "Getting into local politics?"

"You can use your thumbs now," Deane told Maddie, who was grimacing painfully, trying to pick up a tiny piece. "Actually yes. I've gotten into a few discussions with some of the Diomedes, natives of a little island in the Bering Strait less than a mile from Russia. Also trying to find out if a salamander that occurs just across the Bering Strait in the Anadyr Peninsula of Siberia can also be found in North America. And I want to establish the utmost northern and western limits of the frogs that range into Alaska."

"Amazing," Maddie's mother said, as though he might as well be working on Mars.

"The freedom's been fine—though it's over now. All of a sudden, the government wants to talk to me again."

Ginny sighed. "I don't understand it. What do you do on a typical day up there? What do you do when you get up in the morning?"

Deane shrugged.

"I'll tell you what he does," Willy said. "In good weather and bad, he gets up at four A.M., gets out a hundred little vials of alcohol, assembles his shotgun, makes a crude butterfly net, nails together a plant press, hangs himself all over with fifty bags and knapsacks, fills his pockets with shells, and sets forth to explore."

Deane laughed. "Sure," he said. "Roses and monarchs all over the place."

"Isn't it lonely?" Ginny asked. "How do you stand it month after month?"

He hesitated, searching for words. "Loneliness becomes irrelevant after the first few weeks. Sometimes it can actually clear and intensify the senses. When I first saw the steel-gray waters of the Tuksuk and the Kigluaiks soaring in the air, I was alone, but I was so elated it didn't even occur to me. All I wanted to do was yell for joy at the top of my lungs."

"I can't imagine it," Ginny said, as though chilled by the idea.

"Remember that quote from Robinson Jeffers you sent me?" Deane turned to Bert. "That man is only a passing evil in a world of heartbreaking beauty—'beauty that will remain when there is no heart to break for it'? That's what I've felt up there. Ecstatic heartbreak. It works like a drug."

"I've read Jeffers," Essy said after a silence. "Now there's a great soul in peril."

"Did you yell?" Maddie asked, thinking about the Kigluaiks.

"No," he smiled. "I just gasped like a man in a very cold shower."

No one said anything for a while. Deane stared into the fire with that strangely intent absence of his that had become familiar to her since the day at the zoo. He is different from the rest of us, she thought, watching him closely. He's different from everybody. And something about his difference attracted her, though she couldn't put it into words. (When she was older, she would think of it in terms of balanced forces; he was the most highly conscious, sensing person she had ever known, yet also the most controlled and emotionally disengaged. One could never be as conscious of him as he was of you. He radiated energy, yet exercised a restraint that was utterly dependable.)

"Don't you ever want to get married?" her mother asked him now.

"Is Maddie interested in marriage?" he joked. But the joke didn't distract Maddie's or her mother's curiosity. Everyone in the room was listening for the answer.

He looked down at his hands, tracing the lines in his

palms. "The Inuit have a name for a man who likes loneliness,"
he said. "In our language, it's usually something suspect like
'recluse' or 'eccentric.' In their language, the word 'lonely' is
equivalent to our word for 'poet,' or 'priest.' God knows I'm
neither one—"

"God knows," Essy interrupted with a little laugh.

"Sh!" Bert said. "Go on."

"I've come to understand another Eskimo word," Deane
continued. "*Qarrtsiluni*—that kind of isolated concentration that
literally means 'waiting for something to break.' The *angakok*
goes off into the wastes, into the ice and snow, and waits for
fire—for something in himself to ignite and burst open or
bubble up from the bottom and explode into the air."

He paused. For the first time Maddie saw pure uncovered
feeling, as well as something like awe, in Deane's eyes. It astounded her.

"Some of their poetry is quite beautiful," he said, his voice
low and confiding. "It offers a kind of recovered humanist
fundamentalism to the white man."

"We do *not* need any more humanism," Essy said.

No one said anything for a few moments. Maddie wondered if there was a bubble in her that might rise up to the
surface someday.

"Would anyone like more coffee?" her mother said at last,
guessing Deane wasn't going to answer her question directly.

Grandaddy, Essy, and Willy said they would like coffee.
Bert said nothing, but sat quietly, staring into space.

As Deane went back to Maddie's puzzle, everyone
slumped in their chairs and stared into the glowing radiants.
After a while, Essy turned on the radio for the Christmas service
from the First Presbyterian Church downtown. A choir was
singing a Bach chorale—"How Shall I Fitly Greet Thee?" Bert,
who knew it by heart, began to sing along distractedly in her
quavering soprano. "You know," she said to Deane, after the

THE MASK WITH HOLES IN ITS HANDS

second verse, "it's a love song, pure and simple, isn't it? Passionate love for an absent God who has come back."

Deane looked up and nodded. And Maddie saw a look pass between them that convinced her Essy would never win the competition for him. In some indeterminate way, Deane was Bert's, at least when he was home from Alaska.

"Ready for dessert?" her mother called from the kitchen when the Evening Prayer on the radio was over.

"Yes," Willy said, rousing himself from a half-doze.

"The Presbyterians have done a lot for the Eskimos, haven't they?" Essy asked Deane as she browsed through Bert's bookcases. She took down her old King James Bible, full of ragged place markers.

"We've given them the match," Deane said. "The benefits of that are incalculable. And metal tools. The younger women's hands don't look like wood anymore."

"I mean spiritually," Essy said. "Our Sunday School supports the Alaskan mission in Wainwright. And such good things we've heard—about their openness and love of learning, no lying or stealing; and yet also about strangling infants and abandoning old people on ice floes, and sharing women like a pair of favorite boots or a good sled. Now, at least, they're hearing the Gospel."

"A mixed blessing," Deane said. "Do you know the missionaries in Wainwright who translated the Lord's Prayer couldn't find a word equivalent to temptation in Eskimo? There's no such concept—or wasn't, before we got there. Now more and more of the natives are preferring chocolate bars and tobacco to *muktuk*. Some of them will do anything to get them."

"Is it true," Essy asked, undeterred, "that Eskimo mothers lick their newborn babies clean? That children take unborn seals out of the bodies of their harpooned mothers and sled-ride on them?"

Exasperated, Deane looked at Willy and didn't answer.

"And I've heard that their sexual practices are—"

"Christmas dinner isn't over yet, folks," Grandaddy interrupted heartily as Ginny entered with a tray. "Here's the Christmas pie!"

"You have to understand the environment," Deane said measuredly as Maddie passed out napkins and forks. "A woman who kills her infant in hard times is respected by her people. She has saved it from a slow, agonizing death by starvation."

I can understand having to do it, Maddie thought. But then, once the baby was killed, how could the mother go on living remembering what she had done?

"Try to imagine," he went on, "a place where even in the best of times, birds build their nests in the skulls of your ancestors, where ice-floes float all around you like the pieces of Maddie's puzzle—your whole world coming apart. And in bad times, the unrelieved darkness of the winter months can induce a state of madly enlivened wakefulness. The movements of the caribou herd—your food supply—change unpredictably. Imagine, Maddie, a supermarket that migrated and your having to walk miles and miles looking for it everytime you wanted to shop. Or having to eat the linings of your own boots for lunch. What is inhumanly difficult by our standards can grow so much worse in the Arctic that survival becomes impossible. Then life is like 'swimming through rock,' the old women say. It becomes 'heavier than death.' The weak must die to spare the strong. And yet, as a people, the Inuit have great faith in the worthwhileness of life. The greatest I've seen anywhere."

Essy sat in thoughtful silence. "Are they translating the Old Testament for them? Genesis and Exodus?"

Deane hesitated. "There are crosses on many of the Eskimo graves." Maddie saw him look at her father again, who was staring a warning at him to be careful what he said. He balanced his piece of pie on his knee and continued. "But in my honest opinion, Es, in the darkest of times, their own myths and legends serve them better."

"Oh," Essy said, opening the Bible to Genesis. "You don't mean that."

"No he doesn't," Willy said. "Eat your pie, Deane."

"Listen to this," Essy said, turning to a passage and reading: " 'In the beginning, God created the heavens and the earth. The earth was without form and void, and darkness was upon the face of the deep. . . .' " She looked up to measure the effect of the words. "You're a brilliant scholar, Deane," she said. "You must know that Adam and Eve were our real parents. Not simians. Not knuckle-walking apes."

Maddie thought of Aristarchus at the zoo. Perhaps Essy could do worse than have him as her great-grandfather.

Deane hunched his shoulders over as though his muscles ached.

"I don't agree," he said simply and turned his eyes on Maddie, who was searching under chairs and rugs for a missing puzzle piece like a puppy looking for a lost bone.

"But everything is explained here," Essy said, turning over the pages of the Bible. "Oh Isaiah is wonderful! And Jeremiah!"

"Essy," Deane said patiently, taking one bite of his pie, then pushing it aside, "sometime in your life you should see the advance of a Bering sea fog. It comes in silently, against the wind. The sky turns dark. You look back at steamers in the roadstead off a coastal town and see them gradually blotted out as the fog comes between you and them. The temperature drops. The sea begins to work, and on come the blankets of gray—without haste, without delay, *against* the wind. Now I want to know how that happens. Where shall I find the answer? In Jeremiah? Revelation?"

"We're not meant to know some things," Essy said.

"Why not?" he said. "For how long?"

"I agree with Essy," Ginny said quietly. "The tree of knowledge in the Garden of Eden was forbidden to us for our own good."

Maddie watched her father gulp pie at a furious pace. "I better eat this quick," he said, "before this conversation wrecks my appetite. Why not have another piece, Deane?"

"I thought the point of the Genesis myth," Deane said, ignoring him, "was that God willed man's *submission* to his lordship over creation, not his arbitrary ignorance of it."

"No," Ginny said hesitantly, as though not entirely grasping the distinction. "I don't think that's right. The apples were evil."

Essy searched the Bible for more passages to read. Deane reached out and gave his brother—who was sitting now with arms folded—a quick, jolting kick. "What do you think?" he challenged him. "Can apples be inherently evil? I've known some pretty sour grapes in my time."

"Oh no," Willy said, putting up his hands, "I'm not getting into this."

"Why not?" Essy said. "Tell him what you think."

"He reminds me of Switzerland," Deane said. "A whole nation of conflicting opinions with one neutral voice."

"He thinks you're his ally, Willy," Essy said. "I'll have you know, Deane, Willy's been going to church."

Maddie wondered at the weary look her father gave Essy. Then, caught between Essy's prodding and Deane's insults, he sat up and stretched. "You know I don't take it all literally, Essy. But I can't go as far as you do either, Deane. Halfway, maybe. I don't think Genesis is just another myth in a grab bag."

"Not good enough," Essy sighed, disappointed.

"Not good enough," Deane agreed.

Maddie put the last piece in her puzzle and looked up at Deane for his approval.

"What do you call the babies, Maddie?" he said, seeming glad of the change of focus.

"Cygnets," she said, recalling that bit of information from her trip to the zoo. "The babies start to fly after a hundred days."

"Good," he said, and sprawled in front of the fire with his hands across his chest like a mummy in a sarcophagus. As the congregation on the radio sang "It Came Upon the Midnight Clear," Maddie left the puzzle and sat on top of him. "Want to play funeral parlor?" she whispered, not sure if he was in the mood.

No answer. He would play.

She tickled his ribs, lightly at first, then harder, trying to make him "come alive." But as part of the game he lay there with perfect willpower, eyes closed, not moving a muscle, as though he really were dead. He'd always been extremely ticklish as a boy, Bert had told her, and still was. "How do you *do* that?" Maddie asked the corpse, tickling between all his ribs. But he was dead and said nothing. So she took off his shoes and tickled his feet. No response. Then she studied his face, wondering how he could control even his eyeballs and keep them from fluttering under the lids. She felt his chest to make sure his heart was still beating. It was—slow and steady. She put her ear down to listen. And as she listened, the dead man's arm's rose up and closed over her in a long affectionate hug. She put her head down on his chest and, while the minister on the radio preached the sermon, watched the gas fire for a long time.

When the sermon was over, the conversation in the room turned to her father's recent promotion to Assistant Director of Manufacturing of his company for designing a special new oxygen mask for the Navy. At Bert's prodding, he explained to Deane that there had been a submarine disaster off Norway last October; every man on board had drowned because the old oxygen masks, stored next to cold bulkheads, had failed to work at low temperatures. So the Navy had sent out an urgent call for a new design, and in one weekend he had designed a mask that worked perfectly at any temperature. It would make millions of dollars for his company, his boss had said. The design was flawless.

At the end of the story, everyone applauded for Willy—except Deane, who was sound asleep.

Maddie yawned, half-asleep herself.

"It's almost midnight, Will," her mother said, gathering up cups and saucers. "We ought to get Maddie and Katy to bed."

"Oh, why not let Maddie sleep here?" Bert suggested. "She can go right upstairs and climb in her father's old bed. Tomorrow morning I'll make a nice breakfast, and we can make plans for a trip to the museum or the zoo."

Maddie said she wanted to stay. She thought maybe she and Deane could go to the zoo by themselves again, or maybe he could show her the herpetology lab he'd told her about at the museum.

Her father gathered Katy up in a blanket against her angry protests. "You ride with us, Essy," he said. "You haven't even seen the inside of my new car." (For Christmas, Bert and Grandaddy had given Maddie's parents the down payment on a car, and it had thrilled her mother. But Maddie worried when her mother said she wanted to spend next Christmas at her grandparents' farm in Tionesta. Maddie loved to visit the farm in the fall when she and Katy played in the barn and bounced along dirt roads in Cook Forest in the back of her grandfather's pickup truck. But what would Christmas be like without Bert, Deane, Grandaddy, and Essy?)

Deane dragged himself up to a sitting position on the floor.

"You're worn out, and so am I," Essy said, bending down to kiss his cheek. "Go back to sleep. I'm praying for you."

An icy draft made the drapes billow out as Grandaddy opened the door. Maddie shivered and backed into Deane. "Be careful on the steps!" Grandaddy called after her mother and Essy.

"Merry Christmas!" Bert waved, smiling broadly from the window.

There were no throw rugs on Bert's bathroom floor. The turquoise and white octagonal tiles felt like cold marble under Maddie's bare feet. Bert helped her scrub her hands and face, then tucked her into the high mahogany bed her father used to sleep in when he was a little boy. Worried she might forget where she was in the middle of the night, Grandaddy pushed the bed up against the wall. "There, Gink," he said (to Bert's irritation, he sometimes called Maddie "Ginky" when she wasn't dressed up because she reminded him of a street orphan from the Bowery in New York). "Sleep against the far wall and you won't fall out."

"Thanks," she said gratefully, reaching for a hug.

He kissed her, then squeezed her cheeks between both hands in a head hug and studied her face. He loved to do this to both her and Katy, though they didn't like it very much. "You're going to be a great lady someday," he said.

"I am?" she smiled through her scrunched lips.

He looked at her sideways through squinty eyes, as though he knew a wonderful secret about her which he'd never tell. "Do you suppose Deane would come up and kiss me good-night too?" she asked when she couldn't stand the squeeze anymore.

"Sure," he said with a wink that assured her he understood her love affair with Deane perfectly. "Sleep tight, Gink."

After he left, she settled down into the bed and looked around. She felt as though she were sleeping in one of the display rooms at the museum where a king or president had slept. Bert's house was decorated so differently from her mother's. Her mother had lots of bright ceramics and plants and knickknacks everywhere, all shiny and new. But here everything was old, scores of antique pitchers and glass hurricane lamps, Blue Danube and Blue Willow china displayed on high, ancient wardrobes, draperies of rose, and mauve satin pillows. She loved the rich look of it. But there was an undusted ghostliness about it at night that made her nervous. She was suspicious of the dark closets and archways that loomed between the rooms; in the dim light they seemed too high and narrow. And the house was dead quiet, as though listening for something that was long gone but still remembered in the walls, the old boyish sounds of Willy and Deane perhaps, shouting, running, catching escaped snakes, wrestling as they used to years ago.

She leaned back on a starched rose pillow sham to wait for Deane, resting her eyes on the turquoise hurricane lamp that stood on a wicker table in the corner of the room. The lamp leaned at a funny angle on a too-tall, crooked stem. (So many of Bert's antiques were cracked or chipped, inherited from her grandmother and great-grandmother, who were, she reminded Maddie frequently, first and second cousins to Mark Twain.) The table itself was off balance, too short in one leg. She studied the dancing human figures painted in a circle around the globe of the tilted lamp, blue ribbons floating out from their wrists, long hair flying up into a robin's-egg blue sky. How fragile and otherworldly they looked, dancing like grown-up children around and around in a perpetual summer, like no real people would ever do.

"Well," Deane said, appearing silently at the door. "You don't look sleepy anymore. Your eyes are as wide as an *ook-pikelo's*. Want me to turn out the light?"

"No." She motioned for him to sit beside her and pulled the Eskimo book out from under her pillow. "Read to me," she said, leafing through the pages. "I want the one about the snake." She put the book in his hands and pointed to an Eskimo word in italics. "What's this mean—*tupilaq*?"

"You read well," he said. "Can you figure it out from the story?"

"I tried. I can't."

He settled down beside her and put his arm around her. "Do you believe in evil spirits, Maddie?"

"I don't know."

"Good," he said. "But decide for a minute that you do. Imagine an evil spirit is angry at me for something I did."

"Like what?"

"Oh, say this particular spirit used to be inside a friend of mine, and I killed him after a big argument and left his body lying outside uncovered on the ice. His spirit would change, lying there. He'd become evil with anger, and to get even with me, he would rise out of his body and put a *tupilaq* together —a hell-animal—out of all the stray bones of dead animals he could find scattered on the tundra: a whale bone here, a wolf rib there, maybe a caribou skull . . ."

"Like this snake with the legs?" she asked. (She had decided she didn't like snakes, but she couldn't tell that to a Doctor of Herpetology.)

"Yes," he said. "The spirit would say some magic over the assembled bones and suddenly the *tupilaq* would come alive. He'd jump up and shake and become the body of the wronged man's anger, then run away and hunt me down. And sooner or later he'd find me. Nothing could save me."

"Not even God?"

"No."

She thought a moment. "Are they ever real? In Alaska, I mean?"

Deane turned the pages of the book back to the beginning. "Who knows?" He smiled. "But let's read another story." He directed her attention to a drawing of a sly-looking fox and a beautiful white rabbit standing face to face in an empty field of snow. "This one's about creation. You remember what Essy read tonight—from Genesis?"

She nodded.

He began to read. " 'In the beginning there was nothing but water and darkness—"

"It sounds the same as Essy's," she interrupted.

"Yes. 'But then after a million ages of waiting, showers of stone and storms of rock began to rain down from the sky. And land was created.' " He paused. "What does that make you think of?"

"Volcanoes?" she guessed after a moment.

"Exactly. Imagine how old the Eskimo's memory is, Maddie." He continued: " 'In these times, animals and humans lived among each other in the dark, making love as they pleased, assuming each other's shapes without order or reason . . .' "

She laughed. "You mean a person could marry a cat or a horse or a whale?"

"Or a grizzly bear if she wanted to."

She liked the idea.

" 'But into this blessed darkness words were born,' " he went on. " 'And since words were new and never had been used before, they were as powerful as magic formulas. And strange things began to happen in the world because words were pronounced.' "

Like *abracadabra*, she thought—making candy fall out of chimneys.

" 'And it was at this time that the sly fox met the snow hare. "Dark, dark, dark," said the fox. He wanted it to stay dark, you see, so that he could easily steal from the meat caches of the human beings among the cliffs. "Light, light, light," said the snow hare. He wanted it light so that he could see to find his own bits of food in the grass. And at that very moment, it became as the snow hare wished. It became light. And since then, light and darkness have alternated upon the earth.' "

Deane closed the book. "Well? What do you think?"

"So the snow hare won," she said thoughtfully.

"Yes. But only half of the time."

She nodded.

He kissed her on the forehead. "Good night, Maddie," he said, moving to the corner to turn off the turquoise lamp.

"No! Leave it on, please."

"Why?"

She hesitated. "I don't know."

Deane looked around the shadowy room and back at her. Then suddenly he threw open the doors to the big black wardrobe at the foot of the bed and got inside. He banged around and shouted a lot of Eskimo words, knocking on the sides and back, came back out, then opened the bedroom closet with a wild yell, shook Bert's piled-up shoe boxes, pounded the walls, and jumped around waving his arms up and down. "*Peechook!*" he said. "Gone in an instant. No *tupilaqs* or evil spirits in this room."

She laughed. He had read her thoughts, her fears.

"Wait!" she ordered, as he turned to go.

He folded his arms. "Now what?"

"In the museum—remember that big glass case you showed me last summer with the man fighting the lions?"

"Yes. What made you think of that?"

"I think about it a lot. The fox and the hare reminded me. With nobody winning, I guess."

"I'm still waiting for you to tell me who wins," he said.

"No, no, no. That's what Dad said you'd say if I asked you. He says you know who wins—what the taxidermist himself thought. But you won't tell anyone."

He sat back down on the bed. "He said that?"

"Yes."

"He thinks I have all kinds of special knowledge that I really don't."

"Yes you do," she said. "More than anyone in the family."

He said nothing.

"And I want to get it someday. I want to be exactly like you."

"Maybe," he said, looking at her so hard she dropped her

eyes, "you won't have to get it so much as you'll have to acknowledge it."

She didn't understand what he meant. "I don't care," she said. "I want it anyway."

He looked at her with a mixture of expressions now, and after a moment said, "Well then, you will. And as for the Arab and the lions, I think a decision can't be made by your father or me until Maddie Cameron looks at it with her own two eyes."

She shook her head, confused and unsatisfied.

He got up and saluted her like a soldier. "What the taxidermist really thought," he said, "was that everyone must decide for themselves." He bowed and left before she could think of another excuse to keep him.

She lay awake for a long time afterward, thinking about what he'd said. The light from the blue lamp blurred into a smoky circle, darkening everything around it. She felt herself slowly pulled into it. And then the circle of light itself faded and shrank as she slipped through it into sleep, sliding as if on a sled into a well of empty air, hovering over a string of islands of Arctic white and Christmas silver, floating in a blue-black sea. She was huge and strong in the dream, and rode the islands like skates.

She woke once in the middle of the night to go to the bathroom. The room was black; someone had come in after she'd fallen asleep and turned off the lamp. She felt her way to the bedroom door and along the hallway, trying to remember how far the bathroom was. She found it. The house was so still she could hear her bare feet on the ceramic tiles.

By the time she got back to bed, the sheets were cold, even the place where she'd been sleeping. She balanced on the edge of the bed with her arms tucked around her knees and put off getting back under the white muslin Bert had tucked in so tightly. The clock said three-fifteen. This was how the old woman on the ice must have felt, she imagined. It was cold where she sat, but every place around her was colder. She wondered how Deane could stand sleeping in a tent night after night on the tundra, or in cabins when three inches of frost coated the inside of the walls. She wished Katy had stayed overnight with her. Katy was always warm at night, almost hot, as though she had her own burning furnace inside her.

Then out in the hallway she noticed a hairline of light under Deane's door. How had she missed it before? He must still be working. Comforted by that, she decided to brave the sheets and try to go back to sleep.

But the line of light kept appearing under her eyelids in red, blue, yellow. The more she blinked it away, the more wide-awake she felt.

She got out of bed, walked to Deane's door, and listened. There wasn't a sound. She knocked softly.

"Come in," he said, as though expecting her.

She opened the door slowly, feeling like an intruder in a forbidden time and place. Deane sat under a fluorescent desk lamp, his back to her, stark naked. The lamp cast sharp black shadows on the walls and ceiling. He was holding something in his hands, a funny-looking painted mask with hands coming out from where the ears should be. Not seeming to care that she saw him without his clothes, he laid a blanket over his lap, turned to her, and held up the mask. "Do you like it?"

"You don't have any pajamas on," she said. "Aren't you freezing?"

She remembered that a long time ago Bert had told her Deane loved to sit around naked in his room when he was a little boy. She couldn't get him to dress at all on Saturdays. He had eaten, read, and slept naked, and had been delighted to discover that Eskimos often sat around in their igloos naked too.

"Not at all," he said, holding out the mask for her to examine.

"Why do the hands have holes in them?" she asked, a little frightened by the misshapen object.

"Because the hunter who made it knows that man isn't the master of nature, though he likes to think so. Some of the game he hunts will always slip through his fingers, right through these pierced palms, and get away. Do you see? In his wisdom, the artist is saying that man can never completely rule the world, no matter how clever or strong he is. And that's just as well."

"It is?"

"The game that gets away goes on living and multiplying, providing more game for his descendants."

He held the mask up to his face. The long neck of a bird projected out of the chin with a mangled fish in its mouth. She was disturbed by the little human face at the very center of the mask. Deane's eyes looked threatening as they shone through the two narrow slits set over long rows of grinning teeth. "You look like a jack-o'-lantern," she said nervously. "That would be a good mask for Halloween."

"My favorite holiday," he said, smiling as he took off the mask and held it out to her. "Would you like to have it?"

"What do you mean?" she said, unbelieving.

"I want you to have it. And one other thing too."

He knotted the blanket around his waist like an Indian chief and reached up to the shelf above his bed. Just then Maddie noticed the disorder of the room. Every drawer was turned inside out; books and papers were strewn on the floor and piled up on the bed. Cardboard boxes were half-filled with notebooks and magazines. What was he doing?

"Look at this piece," he said enthusiastically. "I thought of it when I was reading to you tonight."

He held out a curved black piece of driftwood, satiny

smooth and shaped like a boomerang with little branches growing out of it. "This traveled two thousand miles or more to get
to the Eskimo who picked it up on the coast of the Bering
Sea. It's very old."

She liked the feel of it in her hand, like something magic.
It had been polished to a bright shine by the water and wind.

"It's a great treasure, Maddie. I want you to keep it for
me."

She was overjoyed to keep it, but perplexed. "For how
long? Why do you want to give it away?"

He pointed to four faint lines scored into the wood. "You
see here? The Eskimos I lived with in Alaska don't tell the story
of the fox and the hare. They believe the world was created
by a great Raven. The Raven was Lord over all, and still is.
But he's in hiding now. Sometimes he's in the clouds, in the
rocks, in the sea, or blending in with the flight of the Great
Blue Heron. . . ."

"You mean invisible—like the real God?"

"No one ever sees him directly," he nodded. "But every
now and then the Raven leaves a footprint. Lucky is the one
who finds one of those footprints, for he's standing in a place
where the Creator of the Universe has passed by."

She looked at the marks of the driftwood with awe. "This
is his footprint?"

"The Eskimo who found it gave it to me as a token of our
friendship. Her name is Marian Komuk, and if she says it's the
Raven, it is. Most of the good luck of finding it stays with her,
but a little of it was passed on to me, the new owner—and
now to you."

Yes, she thought, examining it; the splayed lines looked
as though they were left by the claw of a great bird. "Have
you ever found a footprint of your own?"

"No," he said. "But I'm always looking."

She lined the driftwood up beside the mask on the desk.

They were wonderful objects. "Are you sure you want to give them away? Don't you want them anymore?"

"Will you take good care of them?"

"I promise."

"Someday you'll have to go to Alaska and look for your own Raven footprint. You'd like it there, Maddie."

"But if he's the Creator, he could be walking around here too sometimes, couldn't he?"

He smiled. And then suddenly she got the feeling that he wanted to be alone and back at his work. She noticed that his eyes were red with tiredness as he scanned the debris on his desk. "Aren't you going to sleep?" she asked, taking up her gifts in her arms.

"Soon," he said, poking into a birchbark basket of feathers and bones.

"Thank you very much for these presents, Uncle Deane."

"You're welcome, Maddie."

And then she felt utterly removed, instantaneously distanced from him as he bent over some other object in his art collection. She turned to go, then looked back from the doorway, his bare muscular shoulders reminding her of a statue in the Hall of Sculpture at the museum, displayed by itself in a position of frozen, hunched-over thought under a spotlight— receding now as she backed away. She wanted to tell him how much she loved him. But when he was concentrating like that, it would be like trying to tell the marble statue how beautiful it was. It didn't need it.

She went back to bed and lay awake for a long time.

At breakfast next morning, Bert complained to Grandaddy that before anyone else was up, Deane had carried ten boxes of books and equipment over to Willy's house to store in his attic. "You should see his room," she said, dabbing her eyes with her apron. "He worked all night tearing everything apart! The collections in the closet, under the bed, in his bureau, his ulus and skeletons, everything taken out and stacked in the middle of the floor. He's sealing it all up in cardboard boxes!"

"You've been after him to clean out his room for years," Grandaddy said. "Maybe he just wants to get it all organized now that his degree is finished."

"But why is he taking it over to Willy's?" she lamented. "His contract with Johns Hopkins and the Navy will be up in six months, and then he can look for a permanent job here in town. I didn't mean for him to move everything out of the house!"

Maddie was as mystified as Bert, but glad that all Deane's things would be in her attic now. In between lamentations, Bert presented her with an artistically arranged breakfast on a Blue Tower Spode plate. "It's the day after Christmas, Howdy!" she said. "I wanted to make plans, and he won't even stop to eat. I thought we could all go to the new International Art Gallery today or maybe to Buhl Planetarium to see the Christmas Star exhibit. And next Friday night, the symphony is playing Mahler's 'Resurrection' Symphony with—"

The telephone rang. Grandaddy got up to answer it.

"Wouldn't it be fun to plan a big celebration for Deane, Maddie?" she continued. "We could wear our new clothes, ride downtown on the streetcar to the Nixon Theater, and then go across to Klein's restaurant. Deane hasn't been out to dinner with us in *three years*."

"I have to go over to Will's," Grandaddy said, returning to the table.

"What? You too?" Bert wailed. "Nobody cares about my breakfast!"

"I do," Maddie said, eating hungrily, the way she'd seen Deane do last night to please her.

"Ginny wants me to bring Maddie with me. She's not feeling well and needs help with Katy."

Disappointed, but then rethinking her plans in a moment, Bert cleared the table hurriedly. "All right, I'll go with you. Maddie can try on her new dresses and model. Wait until Ginny sees her in the pink dimity!"

But as Grandaddy searched for his car keys, he said that Deane had piled up boxes in the back seat of the car and half of the front seat. She couldn't ride with them. There was hardly room for Maddie.

Bert scraped the dishes carelessly, splashing water all over the sink. "Well, I guess you'll have to go without me then, Maddie. My legs are too sore to walk today. Run upstairs and get your shoes."

Maddie did. She made her bed neatly with hospital corners as her mother had taught her, then stopped to look once more into Deane's room. It looked terrible. The shelves were completely bare. The big globe was still there, and a few torn wall maps. But all the artwork and books were gone. The sealskin balls, the sitting mats, the skin scrapers, even his prized harpoon and walrus tusks were packed away. Normally dim, cluttered, and alluring as a cavern, it looked boxy and bright, like a vacated business office.

Grandaddy called to her to hurry.

"You come back for lunch," Bert insisted. "I'll fry some big sandwich steaks and make a fresh Waldorf salad. Deane loves that. You tell him lunch is for twelve-thirty. We'll make our plans then."

Maddie followed Grandaddy to the garage, skipping along the garden walk, aware that Bert was watching from the dining-room window, her hands clenched with anxiety. Maddie looked back and could see Bert's lips moving—talking to herself, still going over the problem of Deane's strange behavior. Maddie wished she could stay behind and help her clean up the breakfast dishes. Bert had warmed a beautiful big cinnamon roll for all of them, and no one had even taken a bite of it.

* * *

At home, Maddie ran to find Katy, who was sitting under the dining-room table banging her toy xylophone. Her sister smiled up at her, happy in her music, glad to see her.

"Hold the door, Maddie!" her father yelled as he and Deane carried in the first boxes from the car.

"You're not going to put them there, are you?" her mother said irritably as they dropped the first load in the hallway.

"What have you got in here, Deane?" her father asked, panting. "Dead bodies?"

"Mostly books," Deane said. "A few dead bodies too." He picked up the box he'd just dropped and carried it up another flight.

"Keep Katy out of the way," Maddie's mother ordered her as she massaged the small of her back and sat down to fold clothes.

After ten minutes, Deane went out to the car to get the last two boxes. As the door closed behind him, Maddie saw her father take her grandfather aside in the hallway. "What's going on?" he asked in a hushed tone.

"What do you mean?" Grandaddy said.

"Deane came up here this morning at six A.M., took a long distance call at precisely six-fifteen, then gave me this." He took an eight-by-ten photograph out of a brown envelope hidden behind a chair and handed it to him. Maddie moved closer. The photograph showed Deane standing in front of a big map of Alaska, pointing with a double-barbed harpoon to a blurry place on a stretch of jagged coastline.

"Who took the picture?" Grandaddy asked, puzzled.

"Who knows? Know what he told me? Not to show this to the newspapers or anyone else unless he doesn't come back."

Maddie's full attention was caught by these last words— like a weight of submerged fear yanked to the surface.

"What do you mean, 'unless he doesn't come back'?" Grandaddy said.

"I asked him, and he shrugged it off with one of his looks. The phone call had something to do with the Navy project. All of a sudden it's go again. It's probably more dangerous than he's telling anyone."

Willy heard Deane on the porch and slipped the photograph back into the envelope, out of sight.

"C'mon, Will," Deane said, coming in. "Let's get the rest of these boxes up to the attic, out of Ginny's way."

"Don't you ever get tired?" Maddie asked, running ahead of him as he took the steps two at a time to the attic landing.

"I don't know," he said, passing her by.

"Wouldn't you ever just like to stay home with everybody for a couple of years?"

He stopped on the landing to get a better grip on his boxes and didn't answer her. From the look in his eyes, she wished she hadn't asked him that question.

He and her father worked for the next half hour in the back room of the attic, arranging the boxes as Deane wanted them along the wall of a long cupboard, numbering them according to their contents. "I might send for a couple of these in a month," she heard him say from her seat at the top of the stairs. "I'll send you the money and the address in Seattle. Gabe Waite will pick them up from there."

"Forget the money," her father said.

"Nah, I'm rich. Essy's sending me a care package every week now—dried figs, aspirin tins, inspirational verses, and five-dollar bills. The Lord doth provide."

"Bert doesn't even know she does it."

Maddie heard the long line of doors to the room-length cupboard slam shut one by one. The sound echoed through the whole house.

"Is Ginny all right?" Deane asked, after a silence.

Her father laughed. "She asked the same thing about you last night."

There was another silence, then a few words Maddie didn't understand, and finally one word she did: *pregnant*.

"You're a glutton for punishment," Deane said with a laugh. "You're never going anywhere with me again, are you, little brother?"

Maddie ran to join them. Seeing her face, her father caught her up in his arms and swung her around five times.

"Another baby's coming?" she cried. "Why didn't you tell me?"

"We were going to wait for New Year's," he said, "and make a big announcement, big ears."

"I hope it's another girl," Deane said, watching Maddie stagger around dizzily with a big grin on her face after her father put her down.

"What's going on?" Grandaddy called from the bottom of the stairs. "It sounds like a caribou stampede up there!"

Maddie raced down to tell him the news. Deane and her father stayed behind for a few more minutes. But when they came downstairs, she thought the faces of both men looked strangely solemn and subdued. The feeling of fear rose up in her again, a vague heavy weight caught on a hook. Unable to hold it, she let it drop down into the dark again, out of her sight and sense.

Maddie watched Bert fry hamburgers for lunch. Restored in mood, she had changed into a red taffeta apron with sprigs of mistletoe printed all over it, and tended the patties of meat with overconscientious care. "Don't they smell good?" she said. "Deane never could resist 'steakburgers,' as we used to call them during the Great Depression."

Deane came into the kitchen and kissed her on the back of the neck. She smiled up at him radiantly.

"Maddie has some news for you," he said.

"I have news too!" she said. "While you were gone, I called the Nixon and made reservations for next Saturday night, the front row balcony. And we're going to dinner at Klein's for fried jumbo shrimp right by the window overlooking all the lights—all for *you* and your *degree*, and it's on Grandaddy and me. It's about time we celebrated this grand accomplishment."

Maddie clapped her hands and did a little dance around the stove. Bert had something in the oven that smelled good. She must have put the cinnamon roll back in.

Deane hesitated. "That sounds fine," he said quietly. "But you'll have to cancel my reservation, Mother. I can't go."

"Oh no? Well, I suppose I could change the date."

Maddie saw Bert's smile falter as she caught a look of warning in Deane's eyes. "Of course *any* day would be all right," she said, turning her back, patting the meat down hard. "I know we have to accommodate your schedule. We always have."

"Mother," he said, "I have to go back to Alaska this afternoon."

Bert's body went stiff.

"What?" Maddie said, stopping her dance. "But you just came!"

Bert turned around, her spatula dripping grease, poised as if to strike him with it. "What—are—you—talking about?"

Deane eyed the high gas flame licking at the puffed-up bow at the back of her apron.

"Surely you can spend a single week out of this year with your family," she said angrily. "I won't permit you to go. You are underfed and overextended. I won't permit it."

He pulled her toward him, away from the stove. Thinking he meant to embrace her and give in to her plea, she realized he hadn't meant that at all and pulled away. "Don't you *want* to stay?" she cried. "To just—sit and look at things here?"

"Mother, I have schedules to consider—and personalities.

There is a connection in Seattle tomorrow I have to make. If I miss it, I won't be in Anchorage in time for my flight to Nome for . . ." He hesitated.

She turned away. The meat patties were frying too fast, spitting grease on the stove. Tears rolled down her heavily powdered cheeks. "Of course I am not among your 'personalities,' " she said.

"You're going to burn yourself," he answered, reaching past her to turn down the flame.

"Will you concentrate on *me?*" she shouted. "Here I am preparing your after-Christmas lunch with such love and care—all your favorite things—and you are packing to leave! Now I see it. You've been getting ready to leave all night, haven't you? To leave for another year!" Without a potholder, she yanked the iron skillet off the burner and burned the palm of her hand. She shrieked, and Maddie backed away. Deane reached out to examine the burn, but she held it back. "You get all our hopes up," she cried. "I don't even have a *gift* for you because I thought you weren't coming! Your father was going to drive you down to Walley's Photography and buy you a new camera, and I wanted to surprise you with a new leather traveling bag and—"

"I don't need them, Mother," he said.

"Just once I'd like to give you something other than money that just keeps coming back to us."

"I don't need anything."

She stared at him. "Oh, you are so strong!" she cried, new streams of tears running down her face. "You don't need anything or anyone. You've forgotten what it is to need, as if the whole world existed only to be studied under your magnifying glass."

"Go upstairs and call Grandaddy for lunch, Maddie," Deane said calmly.

Looking from him to Bert, Maddie obeyed and left the

kitchen. But she stopped in the living room to listen as the argument resumed. She could hear Bert jabbing again at the half-burnt meat stuck in the pan. "When I think of all I went through to make this house a liveable place, to get you a typewriter and a microscope, a hearing aid after your mastoiditis, a desk —and piano lessons!"

"I use the microscope every day."

" 'Use'! Exactly!"

"What do you mean by that?" he said.

"You don't remember how sick I was, frantic to get you a bicycle so you could go back and forth to the museum without having to pay carfare. I stayed up all night writing commercials for soap manufacturers and washing other people's clothes— me! a laundry woman—with a fever week after week of a hundred and two! And what did you do after you got your bicycle? Ride to the train station without a word of explanation in the middle of the night to hitch a ride on a boxcar and take up residence in the Philadelphia Zoo!"

"I was fourteen," Deane said. "I thought I could get—"

"You had no right to think! Do you *remember?* We waited *three days* without a word from the police, not knowing if you were kidnapped or—or—and then you called as if everything were just fine: 'Come and get me, Mother, please. They won't let me stay.' And Howdy and I drove hundreds of miles, and me carrying a quart milk bottle out of the refrigerator to hold the blood from uterine hemorrhaging the whole way. And there you were, hosing out filthy Kodiak bear cages in the zoo, with the bears in there *with* you. You might have been killed!"

"How long ago was it, Mother? I wanted to save Dad money. I—"

"Oh yes! But you never thought to save us from heartbreak!"

Maddie heard her scrape the bottom of the heavy skillet,

dump the meat patties onto a platter, and throw the smoking pan into the sink. The splash of the dishwater was followed by the hiss of a cloud of steam. "Over and over, you leave us without a single regret," she sobbed. "And for what? For mosquito larvae frozen in a duck's stomach! For six months' camping-out on an iceberg where people don't know Robinson Jeffers from a dead walrus!"

Maddie peeked around the corner. Deane said nothing, but backed away to the far side of the kitchen as if to give Bert's anger room to disperse. She slumped at the sink, whimpering softly to herself.

At last he said: "Do you remember a sonnet you used to read to me when I was growing up? It was called 'Euclid alone has looked on Beauty bare.'"

She nodded stiffly. "I read you many sonnets."

"About how lucky the man is who hears—what was it? —'though once only and then but far away . . .'"

"'Her massive sandal set on stone,'" she finished.

"Yes. I grew up on that poem, Mother, thanks to you. And in the Arctic, I've seen it. Beauty *bare*. For now, I don't need or want anything else but to see it again and again."

"You mean just landscapes—Arctic landscapes instead of people?"

"No. Not landscapes only."

Maddie peered farther around the door. Bert's face was burning bright red. She looked at him with narrowed eyes. "Oh," she said, "if I had known it would separate you from us, I would have torn up the sonnet and burned it!" Perspiration broke out like blisters on her forehead. Maddie had never seen her so upset, as though she wanted to punish Deane like a little boy, to break his will, a will that had grown stronger than her own. But instead, she thrust her arthritic hands into the wet pockets of her apron like weapons in cotton holsters, their weakness humiliating to her. "Why did you bother to come home?" she demanded. "You're moving up there to stay, aren't you? You told your father you want to live in Teller."

Maddie started as she felt Grandaddy's hand on her head. He walked past her into the kitchen. "What's going on here?" he said. "I could hear you two all the way upstairs."

Bert burst out crying and collapsed into his arms.

"I have to go back this afternoon, Dad," Deane said.

Grandaddy nodded calmly and rocked Bert back and forth.

All at once she looked up and read the look of acceptance on his face. "You knew this? You knew he was leaving today?"

"I knew it had to be soon. What did you expect, Bertie?"

"Wim Steiger called this morning," Deane explained. "He said he could fly me from Anchorage to Nome. Gabe will be there to pick me up to fly to Barrow. Otherwise I'd have to wait another two weeks."

"And what would be so terrible about that?" Bert cried. "Answer me!"

"I can't change it," Deane said, looking away.

"Oh no?" she pointed a crooked finger at him. "I don't believe you. The next stage of your project with the Navy doesn't really begin until January twenty-first, and you know it. You could stay, if you wanted to. You *could*. Even Marian Komuk knows that much!"

"You read my mail?" Deane said, staring at her.

"And I'd do it again," she spat back. "I *will* know what's happening to my own son, and what communistic professors are corrupting his politics!"

"Bert, what are you talking about?" Grandaddy said.

Without another word, Deane walked out of the kitchen.

"Bertie," Grandaddy said firmly, "you don't understand. The Navy moved the date up again."

"Never mind!" Deane called from the living room—at last a shout, the first and only one Maddie ever remembered hearing from him. "I'm going right now, Dad," he added in a more controlled tone.

Maddie watched from the dining-room archway as he searched for his traveling satchel under the chairs. "Don't leave now," she said barely audibly.

He didn't hear her.

Grandaddy came in, took two twenty-dollar bills out of his wallet and held them out to him. "Take this. I'll send more later to help pay for the cost of the flight home."

"No," Deane said, waving the money away. "Give it to Will. He needs it."

"Please. In lieu of a Christmas present from us. You know your mother. She's just disappointed. She'll get over it."

Deane forced a brief smile.

"Losing Mama in April demoralized her. You know how dependent she was on her for stability."

"Yes," Deane said objectively, betraying, Maddie thought later, a trace of contempt for that and any dependence.

He looked around for missing objects—his fountain pen, a Wien Airlines flight schedule. Bert came into the living room, head down, with a brown paper bag. "Here," she said formally, handing it to him. "I packed a lunch for you on the plane."

He didn't answer or take it.

"What about your laundry? And all the rest of the things in your room? That beautiful globe is worth—"

He took a deep breath. "They serve lunch and dinner on the plane, Mother. As for my room, you can sell or give away anything that's left. There isn't much."

"Sell?" she said, astonished. "Sell?"

He packed his last few things in silence. She held out the sack again as he zipped the satchel shut. "Listen to me," she said. "I want you to *take* this. You used to love hamburgers cold with bread and ketchup. I've wrapped everything up for you."

"Mother," he said with forced patience, "I don't want it. I have no intention of eating out of a paper bag when everyone else is eating the hot meal provided by the airline."

"The meals are part of the fare, Bert," Grandaddy said, trying to cover for Deane's tone. He slipped the two twenty-dollar bills halfway into the barrel of the .45 pistol in the satchel when Deane's back was turned.

Bert looked from Deane to Grandaddy, then back to Deane. "I see," she said scornfully, marching past both of them as well as she could on her bowed legs. "You're in conspiracy against me." (Thirty years later, Maddie would vividly remember her clutching the sack, steering her eyes straight in front of her like one who knew she was outside all power to change anything in the lives of her husband and son, then climbing the stairs to make a grand, pathetically awkward exit.)

"I'll call you a taxi," Grandaddy said to Deane. "I'd drive you, but . . ."

"Stay with her," he said.

Maddie felt sick to her stomach as Deane looked around the room, then took his coat and hat out of the closet. The bouquet of pine he had presented to Bert at the door on Christmas Eve fell out from the top shelf, looking more be-draggled than ever. Bert had forgotten about it. He tossed it aside.

How could things change so much in one day, she wanted to ask him? What could make him stay a little longer?

She ran upstairs to get the Eskimo book she'd left by her bed. As Deane stood at the glass storm door waiting for the taxi, she held it up to him. "Would you write your name and my name in it?" she asked.

He looked down, taking a moment to comprehend what she had said. Then he sat down with the book and wrote.

In a few moments, Bert reappeared on the stairs, laboring under the weight of Deane's suitcase. "Why do you carry fifty pounds of books everywhere you go?" she demanded of him. "How much did you expect to read in just thirty-six hours?" She flung the suitcase at him. "I finished packing for you. A fresh-ironed shirt on top. Good-bye. Happy New Year."

Maddie heard the horn of the taxi. "Good-bye," she said, as Deane hugged her quickly, then Grandaddy. He turned to Bert. She looked at him and turned away.

Deane picked up his suitcase and left without saying another word.

He did not look back out of the taxi window, but Grandaddy waved to him anyway, watching out the storm door long after the taxi had disappeared in the snow. Bert went back to the kitchen, crying aloud now, banging pots and pans.

Maddie's throat ached. Everything had gone wrong. All wrong.

Grandaddy turned to her, saw her reddened eyes, and said not to worry, that Deane and Bert had fought since he was a little boy—it was all right. They would make up.

She nodded. But it wasn't all right. She ran upstairs to the map room to be by herself. After a while, she opened the book Deane had signed to see what he had written. "To Maddie," she read. "Enough for a new sled, if not for a team of puppies. All my love, Deane."

Forty dollars fell out in her lap.

Many years later, Essy told Maddie what else Bert had done in her outburst of anger that day after Christmas in 1949.

When Deane unpacked his suitcase in Anchorage, exhausted from his trip, frustrated at bad weather that had postponed his connection to Nome for forty-eight hours, he found on top of his freshly-ironed shirt the two ketchup-smeared hamburgers Bert had intended for his post-Christmas lunch— unwrapped. Foul-smelling grease had soaked through his clothes and books. On top of the hamburgers, wrapped in

waxed paper, was a sonnet—not the one Deane had referred
to in the kitchen, but one by George Santayana entitled "On
the Death of a Metaphysician." He sat on a cot and read it:

> Unhappy dreamer, who outwinged in flight
> The pleasant region of the things I love,
> And soared beyond the sunshine, and above
> The golden cornfields and the dear and bright
> Warmth of the hearth,—blasphemer of delight,
> Was your proud bosom not at peace with Jove,
> That you sought, thankless for his guarded grove,
> The empty horror of abysmal night?
>
> Ah, the thin air is cold above the moon!
> I stood and saw you fall, befooled in death,
> As, in your numbèd spirit's fatal swoon,
> You cried you were a god, or were to be;
> I heard with feeble moan your boastful breath
> Bubble from depths of the Icarian sea.

Bert had underlined "numbèd spirit" and "boastful" and the
last two lines. She had scrawled "Think of Icarus!" across the
bottom of the paper.

Worried that his mother's mind was overburdened by all
her physical illnesses and too few outlets for her creative ener-
gies, Deane had probably smiled at her efforts to wield power
over him, Essy told Maddie. Maddie could picture him calmly
folding up the poem, throwing the hamburgers away, and dipping out water to wash his clothes. His hotel room would have
been drafty, perhaps with its one small window opaque with
frost. He might have made a clothesline out of a spool of sinew
thread. By morning, his laundry would have dried stiff and
hard. But in the other world now, he would hardly have noticed.

* * *

Deane didn't write home for four weeks. Then, finally, in response to a letter from Essy reporting that Bert had been in a distracted condition since Christmas, he wrote to tell her about the hamburger incident, asking her to promise not to tell even his father. No one but Essy ever need know about it. He also instructed her to tell Bert not to worry about what was over and done with. It was forgiven and forgotten. But, as Maddie learned later, Essy was so angry over what Bert had done, she put off giving her the message until it was too late.

Grandaddy wrote regularly, asking Deane to keep them informed about his approximate location and to stay away from can openers. He praised him for his new short story about the Canadian mounties that was published in *Adventure* magazine in February. Bert signed her name to the letters, but wrote none of her own. Weekly, Essy lectured her on the sin of pride.

In March, Deane wrote to Willy requesting that he send him two of his stored boxes of equipment. Willy sent them off, returning Deane's postage money to him. Then on April 20, a letter from Deane alluded briefly to an expedition west into the wilderness; the main survival experiments were at last underway. He was having more to do with them than he'd expected, he said, and was looking forward to the results "with interest." Two members of the scientific team had quit; one other man had gotten mysteriously sick and had to be flown out. But he himself was doing fine, he assured them, though they should not expect to hear from him for a long time. Essy thought the letter was uncharacteristically short and formal in tone. "It doesn't sound like Deane," she confided to Grandaddy.

Three weeks later, on a warm spring morning in May, Bert went out to sweep her front porch, and a young man delivered a telegram marked "Urgent: To the Parents of R. Deane Cameron." It informed her that her son and a hired bush pilot by the name of Gabriel Waite had taken off from Tigvariak Island near the Alaska coast in the Arctic Ocean;

that they were last heard from an hour later when they radioed Point Barrow, their destination, to say they were in the air; that they had not arrived at Point Barrow; and that the Naval Tenth Rescue Squadron was in the process of organizing a search for the men's bodies and/or wreckage of the plane. Cameron and the pilot were either stranded on the Arctic ice, or presumed dead.

An hour later, returning from mailing a letter to Deane at the post office, Grandaddy found Bert collapsed on the front porch steps. He took the telegram from her hand, read it, and called Willy and Essy to come immediately. But, as her father told Maddie later, Bert was conscious and sitting up calmly by the time they arrived. "It's all part of the experiment," she said. "The two men meant to lose themselves. The Navy knows exactly where they are and are monitoring their survival skills. The airport just wasn't informed."

Ironically, Maddie thought, going over the albums of photographs of Deane's expeditions many years later, Bert had been right. It all *had* been part of an experiment in survival. But it had been set up by some other power than the U.S. government. And they, not Deane, were the objects of it.

Her eyes glittering with animation, Bert had assured them all that even if Deane had gone down in his plane, he knew how to live in the wilderness. He could build an igloo and was an expert hunter. And Maddie had believed her completely. She looked at the gifts Deane had given her at Christmas with every confidence.

But late at night, the mask with holes in its hands stared down at her from the shelf in her bedroom with something less than reassurance. Some things got away, it said; they could slip through your hands, and there was nothing you could do about it.

All through the late evenings of May and June, the pierced blue palms wagged in the air, outstretched, as though the mask could flap them like wings if it wanted to, and fly down at her under its own power.

She decided to put the mask away up in the attic with the rest of Deane's things, for him to take back when he got home.

4

ARCTIC SUMMER

Maddie's grandfather was informed by telegram that the airline that had employed Gabriel Waite, her uncle's bush pilot in Alaska, had joined the Navy rescue squadron in the search for the missing plane. The area in which the men were lost was a vast open expanse on which the debris of a wreck or the trail of two men walking might easily be seen from the air. ("Like blood on a handkerchief," Maddie remembered Deane's describing any irregularity on the tundra.) Deane had carried rations and supplies for thirty days.

Bert withdrew to her bedroom, but couldn't sleep. Strangely energized by the sedatives prescribed by her doctor, she sat in bed for six days and nights holding the telephone. "He's traveled as far north as Coppermine many times," she lectured everyone excitedly, incessantly. "He *knows* the country. How could he be lost on a little routine trip over open tundra in broad daylight, in good weather, *without even a distress signal sent out?* It's all part of the experiment."

The seventh night, sick and feverish, she fell asleep. Grandaddy dozed fitfully beside her. Then at four o'clock in the

morning she awoke as serenely as someone rising out of hyp-
nosis, full of energy, as though her bed had been rocking on
a floating cloud. She breathed out long exhalations of "Oh,"
then suddenly cried "Howdy!" and sat bolt upright, knocking
the phone off the bed.

She clambered over the covers on all fours, unaware of
any pain in her crooked legs, and stood at the foot of her bed
breathing heavily. Disoriented at being startled from his doze,
Grandaddy was at first appalled at the sight of her haggard,
parched-lipped smile and wild eyes. Tears bathed her face. "He
was here," she panted, half-crying, half-laughing. "Deane was
here."

She pointed to the throw rug at her feet, brushing its
fringe with her bare blue toes. "He stood there—right on that
spot. Howdy, it's still cold!"

Grandaddy stared. Tears ran down her chin, under her
throat.

"He was wearing the red flannel shirt I gave him two Christmases ago. His hair was blowing. He looked right at me and
smiled. Oh, he never smiled so sweetly!"

She swayed and gasped "O my God!"—then, clinging to
the foot of the bed, shook with ecstatic shivers.

The corners of Grandaddy's eyes were scalded with days
of withheld tears. "It was a dream," he told her. "You fell asleep,
Bertie."

"No," she said. "I *wasn't* asleep. I was wide awake. He came
to tell us he's all right. It wasn't a dream. Howdy, I could smell
the Arctic air. It made the curtains blow!" She poked at them
to show exactly where.

He came to her and held her close, massaging her shoulders and neck, feeling the hot-cold clamminess of the skin
beneath her nightgown. She smiled up at him exultantly, looking for a sign that he shared her joy.

Then her whole body drooped as though power had gone

out of it. Her head fell to the side, and she pressed her fists against his chest.

"The Valium," he said, seeing the empty prescription bottle by her bed. "How many did you take?"

"He *came*," she said in a croaking whisper. "I saw him."

She crawled weakly back over her bed, but wouldn't lie down or allow him to pull the covers up over her trembling legs. He put the phone back into her lap. She wound the cord tightly around her wrist to secure it and rested her hand on the receiver.

"Don't," Grandaddy said. "You'll cut off the circulation. Look at your hand, Bert."

She doubled over. He sat down beside her and waited for retching, but despite a few violent shudders, there was none. Soothingly he caressed her matted hair and saw white roots next to the gray scalp. For the first time in twenty-five years she had forgotten to dye her hair. He hadn't realized her hair was so white.

Sensing the observation, she straightened up. "Hand me my hat," she ordered. "And my hairpins."

He handed them to her. She pressed the old velvet hat over the crown of her head and stabbed at it with the hairpins until it was immovably in place. "It improves me," she said with a failed attempt at a smile, painfully aborted by lips too cracked and dry to stretch. Over the past week she had licked and chewed them compulsively until they had bled when she talked in fits of ammation. As she looked at herself in her antique hand mirror, he offered to rub them with ointment. Horrified, she rejected him and the mirror. "I'll call Essy and tell her what happened," she said. "*She'll* believe me. That he *could* come to me."

"No," he said. "Look at the time, Bert. Let her sleep."

She looked at him perplexedly, then lay back, too exhausted to argue.

"Let me turn the light off," he said. For seven days, she had kept all the lamps in every room burning around the clock.

"*No*," she replied. Then, after a pause, "I have to think what to do about Willy."

"What about Willy?"

"He's withdrawing. Don't tell me you haven't *seen* it? He can't stand it. He's turning away from us."

Grandaddy was also concerned about Willy's quiet reaction to his brother's disappearance, never an unseemly outbreak, never a lapse of self-control. "I pray Deane comes to see him, too, tonight," she wept, hugging the phone.

Grandaddy glanced back at the rug at the foot of the bed. Perhaps Deane's spirit *had* come to tell her he was all right, he told Maddie and her father later. But that was no guarantee he was still alive. He reached for the light in a rare defiance of her expressed preference. "I'm turning it off," he said. "I can't stand it."

They lay in the dark, eyes open, not speaking, for five more hours.

Bert started out of her half-conscious stare as though she had been waiting for the knock on the door all night long. "Get it!" she ordered Grandaddy while the knock was still going on, and he hurried downstairs without robe or slippers to see who it was—what messenger, what message.

The living room was flooded with light. Morning sun streamed through the storm door window. Outside, Ginny held out a tray and Maddie a bunch of tulips and spiraea. They smiled and waved through the glass.

"Who *is* it?" Bert screamed from the top of the stairs.

"Ginny!" Grandaddy shouted up, opening the door.

Although eight months pregnant, Ginny still moved gracefully and efficiently. "How is she?" she asked, glancing up the stairs. "I thought it might do her good to see Maddie."

Maddie listened as Grandaddy told her mother everything that had happened the night before, about Bert's strange behavior, her worries about Willy, and her vision of Deane standing at the foot of the bed. It sent chills down Maddie's spine —and a shiver of envy.

"Howdy! I can't *hear* you!" Bert cried from halfway down the stairs. Maddie saw a flash of her naked thighs, loose, bluish-gray, under her robe. "I haven't the strength to get down these steps," she wailed, trying to come farther down anyway.

Grandaddy rushed up to meet her. When Bert heard it was Ginny and Maddie, she fell limp and weeping into his arms. He carried her back up to her room.

"Slow down," Ginny ordered him, as he ran back down the stairs. "You'll have a heart attack. Then where will she be?"

Maddie folded back the dishtowel that covered the tray and laid the pink tulips across the top of the plate. She thought the whites of Grandaddy's eyes looked the same color as Bert's thighs.

"What a beautiful tray," he said with emotion. "Blue linen and Bert's favorite china . . ."

"It's for both of you," said Ginny.

He would not let her carry it up the stairs.

"Willy thinks you should go back to work," she said. "To get out of here for a little while."

Grandaddy sighed. "She won't let me out of her sight. She wants me alert, silent, and motionless as a Buckingham guard."

Upstairs, Bert lay stretched crossways on the bed, staring at the ceiling. "Good morning," Ginny said in an easy voice, noting the mess of the room.

Bert's looks frightened Maddie. Her face was chalky-white, yet with two patches on her cheeks that burned bright red. Her brow was moist, as though her body were running a great race while she was lying perfectly still.

She looked up at Maddie and tried to focus her eyes,

groaned, pulled herself up to a sitting position, then fumbled awkwardly among the litter on her night table. "Where are my glasses, Howdy? What did you *do* with them?"

"Ginny's brought breakfast," he said, showing her the tray.

"Oh no," she said, averting her eyes in revulsion.

"Now listen to me," Ginny said, finding her glasses. "You have to keep up your strength for what is going to happen. What if the Navy called and said he was in the hospital and you must come right away? Remember the Philadelphia Zoo?"

Bert looked at her suspiciously. "Yes," she said bitterly. "I didn't have the strength *then* either. But I went."

"I'm going to give you a bath and air out this room. Tonight, you're coming to my house for supper."

"Oh no," Bert protested, amazed. "I can't possibly leave the telephone. Howdy, explain to Ginny—"

"You have another son," Ginny interrupted firmly.

Ignoring Bert's weak gestures of resistance, Ginny fluffed up the pillows, smoothed the tangled sheets, and set the breakfast tray on her lap. She lifted a glass of orange juice to Bert's cracked lips and waited for her to take a sip. "Good," she said, as Bert grimaced at the stinging citric acid. "Now a piece of toast."

Grandaddy sat on the bed and ate a bowl of oatmeal. His hand was shaking, Maddie saw, as he raised his spoon. She peeled a banana, gave him half, and sat beside him.

"Go on, Howard," her mother said. "Take a shower. I'll take care of Bert. She added with a smile: "I don't have many talents, but I'm good at this."

His eyes filled with tears, as though deeply touched by her words. He got up to leave, but Bert shot him a look of panic. "Don't go, Howdy. Please, don't!"

"Go," Ginny ordered. "After you're cleaned up, come back and get Maddie. You two can walk to the drugstore for a newspaper. It's a beautiful day."

He hesitated, then turned and left. Bert buried her face in her hands. "Oh, how can I ever face this?" she moaned in a tone that made Maddie back away. "How can I live? *How can I live?*"

"You have to live," Ginny said. "And so does he."

Maddie didn't want to come near Bert when she was like this. It was as though she were full of some terrible power. But at her mother's commands, she helped her grandmother get out of bed while she stripped off two sets of damp, yellowish sheets and pillowcases and opened the windows. "Give me your nightgown and robe," she ordered Bert. "Maddie, you run a tub of hot water."

When Maddie came back, Bert was staring at her mother vacantly. "What season is this?" she asked with a knitted brow.

"It's spring. I know nobody in this family likes spring very much, but I like it, and that's what it is. Warm and breezy. You should go to the window and smell the lilacs."

Bert didn't believe her. She shook her head and started talking about the snow in the bedroom last night, how she'd actually felt the pinpoints of cold on her bare skin where the flakes had fallen and melted.

Clutching the backs of chairs and dresser tops for balance, she made her way to the vanity, sat down, and began to open and close drawers distractedly. She found what she was looking for, a sheet of paper smudged with lipstick and rouge. "What I want to know is, why did the Navy *wait?*" she demanded of Ginny, thrusting the ragged sheet in her face. "Look at this report."

"I've seen it, Bert. You showed it to me days ago."

Maddie looked over Bert's shoulder. The margins of the paper were covered with overlapping lines of illegible notes. Key phrases were underlined once, twice, or three times in red, green, and blue ink. Bert poked at it hard with a crooked finger. "Why did they wait *forty-eight* hours before they even started

searching? The flight should have taken no more than an hour
and a half!"

"Because no distress signal was sent out," Ginny said quietly, stripping Grandaddy's bed. "Maddie, put these sheets in
the pile to take home."

"They didn't give the story to the newspapers until two
days ago!" Bert continued in an anguished tone. "*Why?* 'We are
investigating suspicious areas and incidents,' the Navy says.
What is a suspicious *area?* What incidents have there been?"

"What would you like to wear?" Ginny asked, adding
towels from the bathroom to her pile of laundry. Knowing
Bert's normally obsessive cleanliness, Maddie knew that the
filthy towels were a sign of how badly upset she was. She
watched her grandmother open and close all the drawers again,
turn over broken pots of rouge and face powder, then throw
them all aside in frantic agitation. "What are you looking for?"
her mother asked, approaching her with a clean robe.

Bert looked up wonderingly. " 'As gossips whisper of a
trinket's worth / Spied by the death-bed's flickering candle-
gloom . . .' What is that poem? Who wrote that?"

"I don't know."

From under stacks of turquoise nightgowns in the bottom
drawer, Bert pulled a slim volume of poetry by George Santayana. "I can't see! I swear to you I can't focus on words to
read them. Find me the poem entitled 'As in the Crevices of
Caesar's Tomb. . . .' No, that's not it. 'As in the Midst of Battle
There is Room.' *That's* it!"

Ginny found it in the Table of Contents and turned to
the page. "It's torn out," she said, "along with another poem
on the same page—'On the Death of a Metaphysican.' "

Bert sighed as if under a new weight, a new staggering
blow—overplayed, Maddie would think later, but convincing
enough now. Bert wanted her and her mother to believe that
the poem had been inadvertently lost, not torn out and de-

stroyed by herself days before. Perhaps Bert believed it herself by then.

"Give me your robe," Ginny said, putting the book aside. "And take off that silly hat."

Bert did not come to Maddie's for supper, but Grandaddy did. Aunt Essy was deeply affected by his retelling of the story of Bert's dream of Deane appearing at the foot of the bed. She wiped away tears all evening long and said God must have sent Deane to relieve Bert's soul of guilt and anguish. (Perhaps, Maddie thought, when she was older, Deane had come to do what Essy had failed to do: to deliver the message of his forgiveness to Bert.)

"What guilt?" Grandaddy said, still unaware of what Bert had put in Deane's suitcase at Christmas.

"She wants forgiveness for letting him leave like that," Essy said evasively.

"Oh, they've fought like that for years," Maddie's father said angrily, waving her off. "He's forgiven her a million times."

"Perhaps too many times," Essy said, defiant at his harsh tone, as though wanting to tell him he didn't know everything.

"Deane can take care of himself," Willy said. "If he's alive, he'll stay alive, and one of these days he'll walk in the door like nothing's happened and everything will go back to the way it was."

Maddie was relieved to hear him say this. He'd said almost nothing about Deane for the past week.

"*Yes,*" Grandaddy said. "Tell your mother that. Why not go over and tell her that right now? She's worried about you as much as him."

"About me?" Willy laughed. "She's the one who can't eat or sleep."

"She thinks you don't have any hope for the air search—

that you've resigned yourself to the worst," said Essy, wiping away more tears.

Maddie studied her father as he looked at Essy. His jaw was set in hard lines, his eyes cool and composed. And yet he seemed half out of breath when he talked to her mother lately, or as if he had more air than he knew what to do with. "That's ridiculous," he said now. "I'm trying to be realistic—Deane's first and her last resort. It's possible, Es, that the plane could have disintegrated in the air and he didn't have a chance." After a pause, he added more quietly, "But I don't believe it. Anyhow, she doesn't want to see me anyway. She wants to see *him*. I hope and pray she will. It might take the Navy a month to find him, but when they do, he'll probably greet them with a 'You're interrupting my work' and a meat cache big enough to feed the whole squadron."

Grandaddy and Essy laughed.

That night in bed, Maddie prayed that God would find Deane soon. She also prayed that, in the meantime, He would make him appear at the foot of her bed too. Why shouldn't He? She lay awake for an hour, daring to think up the words of an invitation that might conjure Deane out of the darkness, half-hoping, half-afraid he would come. But after a while, a part of her didn't want him to come. Who could be in two places at the same time unless he were a ghost? She thought back to the story he had told her about the Eskimo's dread of being killed and left unburied out on the ice for animals to drag around and tear apart. What if Deane's body lay out on the ice somewhere right now? What would happen to his spirit? Would it turn evil with anger and want revenge on someone? No, she answered; Deane's spirit could never turn evil—no matter what. Yet she turned over in her bed restlessly, facing the light in the hallway away from the dark side of the room. In such darkness, she didn't trust the laws of nature to hold perfectly.

If Deane were dead, she went on thinking—not believing
for a minute he was—he might be angry that he couldn't go
on with his work. And who would he blame? If there were no
one to blame, where would the anger go? What form would
it take? Could it be willed to his closest relatives, like the mask
with the holes in its hands or the piece of driftwood he had
given her at Christmas?

The next morning, before the sun was up, Maddie was
awakened by Aunt Essy bending over her, shaking her shoulder.
"Wake up, Maddie! I have wonderful news!"

Maddie could see through sleep-blurred eyes that Essy
was crying for joy. So Deane had been found, she assumed;
God had answered her prayer right away. She had just been
dreaming of him, and now it was all over. He was safe. She
wanted to jump out of bed and run over to Bert's house to see
how happy she was.

But that wasn't Essy's news.

"You have a new baby sister!" Essy said. "And your mother
has named her Esther, after me!"

Maddie was torn between joy and disappointment.

And then Essy turned away, overwhelmed with weeping.
"The Lord giveth, and the Lord taketh away," she said, smothering her raw red nose in a handkerchief.

After two months, the Navy called a halt to the search.
Conflicting reports baffled, then infuriated Grandaddy, who
brought each one over to Willy as soon as it arrived. Every
night they went over maps and papers as Maddie looked over
their shoulders, growing more and more interested in the mystery. They wrote letters and made long-distance phone calls,
trying to determine the exact facts of Deane's disappearance.
But not a trace could be found of the missing plane or its
passengers, which included, Maddie learned, a small pet Arctic
fox of Deane's. She remembered the story of the fox and the

hare he had told her, how the fox had wished for "Dark, dark, dark," and the hare, who wanted light, won the argument only half of the time. She guessed the story meant that one had to take one's chances. Yet she couldn't believe a life like Deane's was balanced on the same chances as everyone else's. She was convinced he had special powers and controls; he could live in the light *or* the dark without danger.

Her father sent the eight-by-ten photograph Deane had left behind to two local newspapers. Both papers printed it and ran articles entitled "Facts Conflict" and "Mysterious Disappearance of Local Scientist." Willy hoped a reader somewhere might make some sense of the vague outline on the map Deane pointed to with the harpoon, but no one responded. The outline on the map was too faint and didn't match any section of Alaskan coastline that anyone could identify.

"Perhaps the harpoon itself is the clue," Grandaddy suggested. "Maybe it's typical of a certain hunting village or island?"

Her father checked. One of Deane's old friends at the museum wrote letters to anthropologists around the country and sent them copies of the photograph. No one knew.

Then on a cool afternoon in July, Bert told Maddie over the telephone that she was coming out. She intended to make a short visit to see her mother and father that evening and wanted everyone to be there. She had an announcement to make.

She called back five minutes later and told Maddie's mother she preferred that Essy not be invited.

When she arrived with Grandaddy, she was dressed all in black and carried a large black tote bag. Even her high-heeled shoes were black suede, Maddie noted with surprise. (She would wear no other color for three years.) "I've come here for one reason," she began in the controlled tone of a prosecuting attorney making an opening statement; and Maddie thought she looked surprisingly strong, not so much wasted by her months of mourning as reduced to essentials. "You know our hearts are wrung out by this ghastly thing," she continued. "Howdy can't concentrate at work and is in danger of losing his job. We will never know another day of happiness until we have an explanation for what happened to Deane."

She took a folder of letters and papers out of the tote bag. "We cannot tolerate one more piece of contradictory or evasive evidence without *acting* on his behalf."

"What are you talking about, Mother?" Willy said. "We've been over all of this."

"No. Listen to what just came in," she said, holding her folded glasses up to her eyes. "This is a report from a Canadian newspaper: 'The men were last heard of working in an area south*west* of Point Barrow—' "

"No," Willy interrupted. "In his last letter, Deane said he was working a hundred thirty miles south*east* of Point Barrow. Tigvariak is east."

"I know!" Bert said. "Another discrepancy. *Siberia* is west. Which is true?"

She took a letter from a stack wrapped in a tight rubber band, her eyes glittering above cheeks that had been rubbed hard with rouge the color of dried blood. Her black velvet hat kept freshly-dyed hair in place. But the dye had been put on wrong and was full of orange streaks. Yet for all her strange appearance, there was no doubt that she was in control and presiding over the meeting. Maddie thought that in this sudden emergence from seclusion she was strangely magnificent, like a ship with broken masts and torn sails keeping a steady course toward a determined destination.

"You remember Cole Cortright, the man who was working with Deane on the mosquito problem?" she asked Willy, opening the letter. "Listen to what he says: 'I think I saw Dr. Cameron, or someone posing as Dr. Cameron, ten days ago, in a doctor's office in Anchorage. But as I was hurrying out of the office and he did not seem to recognize me, I thought nothing of it and left. It was only yesterday that I heard of your son's disappearance. I am deeply sorry to disturb you with these strange facts, but I thought you would want to know. Deane was one of the finest men I've ever had the privilege to know.' "

Bert put the letter down, and Willy picked it up to read for himself. Maddie watched his eyes speed over the lines.

"And then," Bert said, holding up a third letter, "from Dr. David Eston, dated June tenth—a bill for ten dollars for a doctor's appointment for R. D. Cameron that was kept. I've written a letter this morning requesting a statement on the nature of the ailment and the treatment. Willy, the appointment was *kept*."

"This doesn't prove anything," he said. "It could be a person with the same name—a mix-up."

Or, Maddie thought confusedly, it could mean that Deane was still alive, but, for some reason, didn't want any of them to know it.

Bert cleared her throat, rearranging the papers on her lap like one who had them all memorized anyway. "Do you remember a man named Sam Roselund that Deane used to talk about at the museum—an ichthyologist?"

"Vaguely," said Willy.

"Two days ago Howdy received a letter from him in Baltimore. He says he heard a radio broadcast from Washington, D.C., on June twenty-first that stated that communists have been found actively involved in Johns Hopkins University and a *ring* of them in the Arctic Institute of North America, both of which were agencies Deane worked for. You *know* how outspoken Deane was about politics. He hated communism even more than fascism."

She waited for Willy to respond. He didn't.

"Not only that," she persisted, her voice more urgent, "this illustrious Professor McCafferty who was directing

Johns Hopkins' part of the survival project is a close personal friend of Mr. Sidorkin—who is the very communist referred to in the Washington broadcast! And McCafferty flatly refuses to answer any of our questions. We have called three times for information, and he will not come to the phone. Three times!"

Willy looked at his father. "It's true," Grandaddy said quietly. "I know they're looking for communists under every rock in Alaska these days, and Deane scoffed at it. But this Sidorkin is the very one who cheated Deane out of his contract, and he was dismissed from Johns Hopkins for communist activities one week before Deane's disappearance. Then, upon disclosure of his record, he was refused Arctic Institute funds by Congress. So Deane's complaints about him might have triggered the whole investigation, and Sidorkin probably blamed Deane for the dismissal. For everything. Do you see, Willy?"

Maddie saw her father turn away, as if he didn't want them to see what he saw. "If he was in trouble, why wouldn't he have told me about it?" he said, as though more angry at Deane for the moment than at Sidorkin. "He always told me everything."

"I *knew* it," Bert said, striking the papers with her hand. "He wasn't himself at all this Christmas. Didn't I *tell* you? He stayed up all night packing his life away—perhaps writing letters of outrage to people he *trusted* up there! Remember years ago, Willy, that article he wrote for the Pitt newspaper about the 'unmitigated national calamity' of Roosevelt's reelection? He called himself an 'unreconstructed rebel.' I can quote you the first line: 'I am disgusted with the gentlemen of the press, easily recognized by the dorsal flavous stripe and hypocritical smile, who heartily panned Mr. Roosevelt before the recent election, but who lick up to him now. . . .' "

Maddie watched uneasily as her father got up from his

chair as if to clear his head of conflicting thoughts. "I had a sense something new was up," he said at last. "He could never keep his mouth shut about politics or religion."

"You and Howdy saw the photograph," Bert said triumphantly. "You should have *made* him stay home. Didn't I try to stop him? But nobody would listen to me."

Maddie saw something like desperate triumph shine in her grandmother's eyes for a moment—like vindication. But it flickered out immediately.

Grandaddy shook his head. "I think he might have stumbled onto some information he wasn't supposed to know, Willy. Maybe he knew it at Christmas but thought he could handle it."

"That day in the attic," Willy said, his eyes on the floor, "when we carried up the boxes, he told me before we came downstairs that if anything happened to him during the survival experiments, I should give all his boxes to the museum."

"Ah!" Bert said, leaning back against the couch. "All his magnificent work!"

"And he said . . ." Willy hesitated, shaking his head as if at a new recollection.

"What?" Bert prompted. "What did he say?"

Maddie saw her father turn from Bert's searching gaze to Grandaddy's. "He told me he was afraid to go back to Alaska this time for fear he'd never see home again."

Bert stared at him in astonishment. "What?" she cried. "Why didn't you tell us this before? If Deane was afraid, he had more than reason to be. You could have saved him!"

"Hush, Bertie," Grandaddy said, taking her hand.

"He told me in confidence, Mother," Willy said. "Like a lot of other things he told me over the years. As usual, I obeyed him." He sank back into his chair, and Maddie thought he looked as pale and intense as Bert now. "I thought he was afraid of the hazards of the expedition," he said weakly.

"Afraid of the expedition!" Bert mocked, thrashing in her bag for another letter. "You knew him better than that! Read *this* from Alton Marx, a retired pilot in Hamilton, Ontario. He says he understood Deane was on a 'United States Navy scientific mission that was *highly* secret.'"

As he took the letter and skimmed it, Maddie felt sorry for her father. Couldn't Bert see how he felt?

"Read *closely*, Willy," Bert insisted. "He mentions in passing that in addition to his other duties, Deane was helping the U.S. government locate *uranium deposits* in Alaska."

There was a silence. Maddie looked around at everyone's faces. What was uranium?

"He never told me anything about that," her father said in a flat tone.

"Which doesn't mean he wasn't doing it," Bert retorted, implying that he had no more been in Deane's close confidence than she had. "And wouldn't a foreign power like the Soviet Union—right next door—be interested in obtaining that information *any way it could?* We wrote to a Dr. Ira Brent at the Arctic Institute two weeks ago, telling him our misgivings about this." She handed Willy still another letter. "Here is his reply. He says our 'innuendos' are *completely unfounded*, and that our son's death will never be solved by our 'oblique approach.'"

"In other words," Willy concluded after a long pause, "stay out of it."

"Not a single word of condolence! It's not even *human*. He says the project wasn't secret at all, that 'Dr. Cameron and Professor McCafferty were collaborating on a routine Arctic research project.' *Routine!*"

Maddie stared at the accumulated letters in her father's hand, and after a moment, he asked the question she wanted to ask. "So what are you saying, Mother? That Deane was murdered by the communists? That his plane was sabotaged?"

"No! Don't you see? It's clear there was no wreckage because there was no crash. His plane was diverted to Siberia, barely a few hundred miles away, and he was taken prisoner. *Deane is alive.* I can feel it, Willy. Either they perceived him as a threat to security, or more likely, as a source of information. He's as alive as you are."

She lowered her glasses with an air of triumph and finality.

Maddie's mother, who had been nursing Esther in a chair beside Willy, quietly rose and put the baby in her bassinet, followed by Maddie, who stared down at her peacefully sleeping sister, hardly seeing her. No one said anything for a while.

Finally her father said, "I don't believe it"—though from his face, Maddie wasn't sure whether he did or not. "His plane could have simply crashed, Mother."

Bert, exhausted from the exertion of presenting the letters, leaned back, turned her head to the side, and closed her eyes. Her lips moved slightly as though she were still arguing with them. Grandaddy held her hand tightly. And Maddie felt a heaviness inside herself that made it hard to breathe. Absently she reached into the bassinet and touched the delicate blue-veined eyelids of her sister.

After a long silence, her mother approached Bert and said, "You haven't held your new granddaughter yet, Bert. Would you like to now?"

Bert sat up and looked at her blankly. "Oh no. I can't. I have a packet of Deane's personal things here that just arrived from Nome, and I want Willy—"

"Slow down, Mother," Willy said wearily, throwing down the letters he'd already read, resisting the addition of anything more just now.

Proclaiming an intermission, Ginny went to the kitchen.

At a loss without her audience, Bert permitted herself to stand, approach the bassinet, and look down at her new infant grandchild. "Oh how sweet, how sweet," she relented with tearful tenderness. "Look at her ears, Howdy," she said. "She has Willy's ears!"

As they waited for coffee, Maddie stood silent guard at Esther's side, and Grandaddy told her how her father's ears had been so big when he was born, Bert had tried to train them back with masking tape. It hadn't worked, he said.

"It might have," Bert defended herself with a faint, pouting smile.

"Fortunately, Willy grew into his ears," Grandaddy added, "and everything turned out fine."

Maddie smiled at the story. But she was thinking now about what Bert had said about Deane being captured, and nothing Grandaddy said could distract her from it. Could Deane be a prisoner in Russia? Was he in chains in some filthy place with rats? Would they torture him to make him tell them where the uranium was? No. Like her father, she couldn't believe it. It wasn't real.

When her mother returned with the coffee, Bert left Esther's side and resumed her place on the couch. She untied a small packet of Deane's private journals and most recent notebooks. "Come, *everyone!*" she called, though everyone was already there. "There's more!"

Slowly, ceremoniously, she took a battered spiral notebook from the top of the packet and set it on her lap. She waited for silence from Katy, who had wandered in from the kitchen and sat happily by Grandaddy's chair, rocking back and forth against the arm. "I think Maddie should take Katy out for a little while," Bert said.

Grandaddy nodded to Maddie.

She understood. She took Katy back to the kitchen and sat her down at the table with several balls of colored clay. She made a blue snake and a red polar bear for her, and when Katy was contentedly humming and absorbed in the work, stole back into the dining room so she could listen to the rest of the conversation. "Look at this," Bert was saying. "Unaccountably, Deane's wallet and revolver were left behind on Tigvariak Island, and in his wallet Howdy found this—a copy

of Matthew Arnold's 'Dover Beach,' a poem *I* introduced him
to his first year of high school. How many poems he remembered! Apparently, he's carried it with him ever since. Look at
the circled lines: 'Ah, love, let us be true to one another' . . .
and on through the rest of it—the world having 'neither joy,
nor love, nor light, / Nor certitude, nor peace, nor help for
pain . . .' Oh, I never meant for him to believe that!"

"Then why did you show it to him?" Ginny asked quietly.

"Because it's beautiful!" Bert said, gathering her brow de-
fensively. "Many things are beautiful that ought not to be
believed!"

"I wouldn't show it to Essy," Willy said grimly. "She hates
that poem."

"And then there was this," she continued, sighing as she
opened the spiral notebook on her lap. "He was writing his
own poetry, and keeping a journal separate from his scientific
notes. 'Reindeer tracks and skulls everywhere,' he says here,
and talks about the 'sub-conscious tension, that almost-aware-
ness of struggle' he feels 'wresting his existence directly from
nature by personal effort.' "

Good, Maddie thought, not understanding all the words,
but getting a sense of their spirit. Deane loved the wilderness.
He might even be enjoying being stranded in the Arctic somewhere. If he could bravely hold on up there, they should be
able to hold on down here and not lose hope.

"Go on to the poem," Grandaddy urged her.

"I will!" she said, not to be hurried. "These notes are *significant*, Howdy. He embraced the challenges of survival in a
hostile environment. Oh, he *could* endure. And here are beautiful notes on birds, on swans, and the Great Blue Heron. How
he used to love the Great Blue—'like a pterodactyl that had
evolved into grace,' he wrote."

Reluctantly, at Grandaddy's urging, she skipped over several pages. "Here," she paused, "he talks about exploring an

Eskimo cemetery above Port Clarence: 'Because of the permafrost, the tundra is almost impossible to dig in. So most of the
crude wooden coffins are sitting on the surface, some in shallow
excavations, others with tundra mosses all grown up around
them. The box lids are either rotted off, or, I suspect, pried
off. Many of the corpses' skulls are missing—or in the case of
infants, the entire tiny skeleton—stolen, not by wolves, but
by American anthropologists.' "

"They have no right to do that," Ginny said angrily. "Who
are the barbarians? The Eskimos or the scientists?"

"Go on," Grandaddy said.

Bert skipped a few more pages, then continued to read:
" 'The oldest marked grave I could find was that of one Tomy
Kayangoruk of Wales who died the year I was born, 1919. His
skeleton lay in a macabre state, covered with green mold. I
was sufficiently morbid to take color photographs, for he affected me deeply.' "

"Deane used to love cemeteries," Willy said. "Do you
remember the Halloween parties he used to have, Dad?"

"What parties?" Maddie couldn't resist asking from the
archway between the dining and living rooms.

"Is Katy all right?" her mother asked.

Maddie nodded.

"He would write notes to all the girls at school," her father
said, "inviting them to come to the cemetery at midnight for
a party, and then sign their boyfriends' names to them. He
could forge anybody's handwriting. And when they came, he'd
hire me and Bud French to dress up as ghosts and make sound
effects among the tombstones. He wasn't satisfied to scare
them. He wanted to *terrify* them, and then study their reactions
and see if—"

"Willy!" Bert said, impatient with the digression. "*Please.*
May I continue? At the end of this paragraph is a quote from
a book he'd just bought called *Arctic Mood*. Listen to it: 'In that

moment, remembering the rimed beauty of the plumage of dead birds, I saw myself interred, lying there sheened in silver frost—eyelashes and every strand of hair a shining lovely thing—beautiful at last—and dead—the velvet sky and white stars radiant, my shroud forever.' "

As she read these last words, her voice faltered. "Can you imagine," she croaked, "finding these lines among your child's last words?" She began to gulp and cough between phrases: "The image of a fallen bird—after soaring so high—fallen— his wings weighted down with . . ." Then she gasped and gave in to convulsive choking. Maddie ran for a glass of water. "Sometimes I can't swallow," she whispered. "I actually strangle!"

Maddie returned with the water, glad for an excuse to get back into the living room. She wanted to look at the notebook.

"The point is, Will," Grandaddy said as her coughing spell subsided, "there may be clues in these notebooks about his state of mind, or names, places, references that might mean something. If you would go over them while we're gone—"

"Gone?" Willy said. "Gone where?"

Bert straightened herself, taking charge of the conversation again. "We've come to a decision," she said, folding her glasses as if for the last time in a lifetime of study, resolved now to act. "Howdy and I are going to Alaska. We're going to Barrow to search for Deane ourselves. We should have done it six weeks ago."

"You can't," Willy said.

"Of course we can," Grandaddy said. "There are too many questions. We have to turn over all the stones. We would do the same for you, Willy."

Maddie could see their resolve, and so could her father. "What makes you think you can find him up there?" he said, looking alarmed now. "Do you know how big it is? What risks there are? Deane wouldn't allow it."

"If the Soviets have taken our son, we have nothing to risk," Bert said.

"Or, if the plane crashed and he's lost on the tundra, we have to know that for sure," Grandaddy said. "We'll use our savings. What else is it for?"

Listening at Bert's side, Maddie wanted to say that, in spite of the dangers, she approved of their decision and wished she could go with them. Surely their love for Deane would guide them to him. But then, over the next few minutes, as her father brought up all the reasons why they shouldn't go, she thought of the mask made by the Eskimo hunter she'd put up in the attic two months ago. Alaskan hunters—searchers —knew that sometimes a thing could slip through their grasp. In life, some things got away. There were holes even in Bert's and Grandaddy's hands. They would have to search carefully, keeping tight fists.

"Read page sixty," Grandaddy told her father. "The poem. Read it aloud."

He found the page in the notebook. It was "To Tomy of Wales," scratched in Deane's hand. He read it:

> His chin had fallen into a grin
> The mushy remains of trousers and mukluks
> Bedecked what was left of his legs:
> Alyeska—the great land.
>
> Strips of a brightly colored cloth
> Woven with paper and one gold thread
> Were tied to the cross at his forehead.
> I wished him peace—and silence—
> On the windswept hill above the sea.
>
> Is it any farther I will go?
> Is it any farther?

Gladly I turn to the land of the living,
Gladly I regain the warmth of companionship.
But oh the peace in the dead man's eyes!

Sometimes, I groan in anticipation
Of the beautiful cold.

Bert blotted her eyes, chin, and forehead with a Kleenex.
"You recall, Deane and I would argue for hours about Whitman,
wouldn't we, Howdy? About the use of rhythm and rhyme . . . ?"

But Maddie wasn't listening. She was feeling Deane's
poem, the sadness and sense of it, its lovely vague familiarity
to her, even the last two lines. "Is it any farther I will go?" She
responded to its mood of pulling and longing in two directions.
How hard it must be for Deane to love people and warmth
and good times, but also to feel apart from them, to even want
to be away from them in some dark, private way—to look out
a window, reflecting the light from the fireplace inside, and be
drawn out by an owl at the top of the skeleton trees, right out
into the cold. Didn't anyone else in the family understand it?

"Look," Grandaddy showed her father. "Look at the dedication at the top of the page."

" 'To Marian, with love,' " Willy said. " 'Again, to Marian.' "

"You see?" Bert said resolutely. "We're going to find this
Marian Komuk. She might know more about Deane's state of
mind than McCafferty or Johns Hopkins or anyone else. We
want your blessing and your prayers before we set out. That's
all."

Bert's presentation was finished. She fell back, dropped
her glasses into her lap, and lapsed into a musing hum, a million
miles away.

"You aren't well enough for this trip," Ginny said after a
while.

"I am not well enough *not* to go," she said in a low voice.

"I'm going over every inch of tundra myself. Every inch, I tell you."

"Do you have any idea how big it is?" Willy asked for the second time.

"Howdy's hired a bush pilot. He's going to meet us in Juneau in a week. We'll go from there for as long as it takes. I'll write you a postcard every day. You won't have to wonder for a minute about our location."

Her voice had grown thin and quavery. She looked anxiously around the room for her scattered documents. Maddie helped her gather them, except for Deane's notebook, which her father wanted to keep. As Bert organized the letters by date, Maddie put her hand on her grandmother's arm and felt a thousand little bumps, as though she were freezing. She wanted, without sounding childish, to reassure her grandmother that she also believed Deane was alive and could be brought home safely. Of course he wasn't dead. He was more alive than anyone she knew.

But sensing Maddie's sympathy before she said a word, Bert squeezed her arm tightly, reassuringly. Maddie helped her get up, and together they went to look at Esther again. The baby was awake and looked up at Bert with placid, steady eyes. "Essy must be so proud of having you named after her," Bert softly cooed to her. "Nobody would ever want to give a child *my* hideous name."

"You should hold her," Maddie said. "She's as warm as anything."

Bert did not protest this time, and Ginny put Esther into her arms. With infinite care, as if holding the treasure of the family, Bert smoothed the kimono and blanket out until they fell in graceful folds around the tiny body. Then she began to rock Esther back and forth with the slow motion of a swinging bell, singing tunelessly in her high, wide vibrato. The baby gazed up in perfect contentment. "Oh," Bert sighed. "So new, so new . . ." Then the expression on her face changed. "Do you know," she said, as if in confidence to Maddie's mother, "that I found fifty or sixty letters from *Essy* among Deane's things? I hope and pray that she will not compete with you for this child's affections as she has competed with me for Deane's."

"Oh Bertie," Grandaddy said, "she meant him only good with those packages and letters. You know that."

"But why didn't she *tell* me she was doing it?" Bert asked. "What did she mean by *excluding* me?"

Maddie saw beads of perspiration form on her brow and upper lip, and her mother took Esther back from her. Bert sat down, fanned herself with a sheaf of letters from her bag, and asked Maddie for a glass of ice water. She scarcely acknowledged the presence of Katy, who had marched in to show everyone the fine little animals she had made out of clay. Maddie had to make a big fuss over them to compensate for everyone else's indifference. "I want to go home," Bert said after Maddie brought the ice water. "*Now*, Howdy."

Maddie noticed that the color of her face was the same as Esther's transparent eyelids.

Her father did not look up from the notebook, which, by now, absorbed his whole attention. Maddie wondered if Deane's being lost would drive Bert and Essy apart, as it seemed to be driving Bert and her father apart. She guessed that everything would be off-center until he came home again. He had been the focus and balance of so much in their lives. And she wondered if having a strong, exceptional person in a family could sometimes be a little dangerous.

Later that evening, as her mother put Katy and Esther to bed, Maddie watched her father move restlessly around the living room. He looked into the mirror as if to confer with himself about something, took Deane's notebook off the mantel, opened it, and put it back. Then, as if remembering something long forgotten, he strode to the kitchen and called to Maddie to follow him. He set up the movie projector on her mother's ironing board, loaded it, and used the refrigerator as a movie screen. "I have a new movie," he said. "I want you to watch it with me."

Maddie loved to preview movies with her father. She still remembered when he'd gotten the camera for Christmas a year and a half ago, and how the first year he'd taken so many rolls of film—holidays, vacations, family birthdays—that everyone had gotten sick of it. But now she was perplexed. He hadn't taken any movies for over six months, and she had seen all the old ones many times.

"I guess it's about time we looked at this," he said, urging her enthusiasm. "Do you remember it?"

He turned off the light. The movie began.

"It's last Christmas!" she said, clapping her hands. "I forgot all about it!"

"I've been saving it," he said.

Saving it? For what? she wondered. And then she thought she knew for what—for when Deane came home again and they could all watch and laugh at it together. What would Bert say if she saw it now?

Maddie watched closely, fascinated by the rolling back of time, seeing the family do things they would never do again. The camera had preserved perfectly what could not really be preserved. The movie was like a three-minute moving diorama in the museum, stored for reference for future generations.

There was happy Bert serving plates of mounded turkey and dressing with dramatic slowness and fanfare. She waltzed from chair to chair, as if to say: Look!—all of you with your plates overflowing—look at the beautiful Spode china, the polished crystal goblets, the shining candles, the precious people. Feel the warmth, the light, the joy of the season! Do you see? she seemed to say to Deane, who sat at the table as real and strong as ever. Who can spare even one of these celebrations in a lifetime? Someday they will be gone forever.

Maddie loved the movie. She had forgotten the glow of color in Bert's face, the flush of unexpected joy that had come over her that night when Deane arrived at the door with the bouquet of pine. The whole film was color—the lights on the Christmas tree behind the table, her mother pregnant, radiantly pretty, with red lips and shiny brown hair; herself still nine years old and dressed in turquoise blue taffeta; and Katy, a rose-cheeked toddler sitting on a pile of cushions at her mother's side. It was a strange, almost slow-motion piece of film, the reds, greens, and deep blues more vivid than she remembered them. And there was no question about who the star of the movie was. In the center of everything was Deane—the "agnostic black sheep of the Nativity scene," as Essy had jokingly called him that day—the family treasure, the first Doctor of Philosophy, young and strong and full of life. Her father had zoomed the camera in on him just as he snatched a piece of celery from Essy's plate to make Maddie laugh; and he had winked at her—at her alone—at the joke. Then he began devouring his turkey and the bag of uncleaned giblets with exaggerated greed, and Bert bent over to kiss him on the forehead. He smiled up at her, the light of perfectly free intelligence in his eyes, along with the shadow of something else that Maddie couldn't name, a secret he kept within himself, a well of resource that was his alone. If, as Bert had said tonight, Deane wasn't himself that day and had acted strangely burdened or troubled, Maddie didn't see it here.

The movie ended abruptly, a shower of white dots blanking out faces, then nothing. Maddie stood up and shouted "Yea!" for the movie-taker as she always did, and as the last half-foot of film went round and round on the take-up reel, she made shadow animals against the blank white screen. But it went on too long. She looked up to remind her father to turn it off. But he was gone.

Not knowing how to turn off the projector herself, she went to look for him. She found him standing in the living room in total darkness, all the lamps turned off, but his profile clearly visible against the streetlight shining through the picture window. His hands were deep in his pockets, his body stiffly erect. She could hear him inhale deeply as he looked up at the ceiling, hold his breath, then exhale as he looked down at the floor. Then he shuddered violently as if taking a chill.

"Daddy, the movie's over," she said.

He turned and waved her away. There was a glistening in his eyes, a strange wild flash.

And all at once she realized that her father was crying. The realization disoriented her like a burst of fluorescent light in darkness. She felt uncertain of things, caught off-balance just at the moment she had been reassured of the great and certain vitality of Deane in the movie. Not sure what to do, she ran to the bottom of the stairs—should she tell her mother? Katy appeared at the top, fussy and out of sorts with her mother's demands on her. She looked down with a frown.

"Come," she said, holding out her arms in an appeal for comfort. "*You* put me to bed. Mama's mean tonight."

Maddie ran up the stairs and put her arms around her sister's straight, soldierly little body and thought that maybe they both needed comfort their mother couldn't give. Lately Ginny had grown more impatient with Katy's moodiness, and Katy was turning more and more to Maddie for sympathy. Now, as she felt the little girl's gray eyes turn up and look at her with a fierce solemnity, feeling Maddie's fears and taking them on herself, Maddie realized that despite the difference in their ages, they might be very close someday—maybe even as close as Deane and her father had been.

That night Katy decided she wasn't going to sleep in her crib anymore. Instead she slept with Maddie in her double bed, snuggling close to her all night long. In the morning, surprised to wake up to each other, they rolled and wrestled in bed, laughing loudly at each other's silly jokes, jumping up and down on the mattress until at last they both rolled out of bed onto the floor, red in the face and panting with wonderful exhaustion.

Grandaddy and Bert left for Alaska and were gone for eight weeks.

"The waves of the Bering Sea break on the back doorsteps of the houses on Front Street," Bert wrote from Nome on August 1. "This is one of the most inhospitable summers on record. The time for flowering is perilously short. There is wind, intermittent snow, and constant discouragement. We have found the Komuk family to be good people, as grieved for Deane as if he were their own son, but claiming to know nothing of his personal affairs. Marian is not what we expected, very shy and withdrawn, not able to communicate easily with us. Her mother says she was so devastated to hear of Deane's disappearance that she did not eat for fourteen days. The old man meant to comfort us with bits of Eskimo wisdom: 'What chance has a man in Nome?' he says—'In winter he leaves tracks in the snow, and in summer it's daylight all night.' By which he means that the Arctic favors the pursuer! But Deane has left no tracks. We are searching everywhere. Howdy has appealed to the Navy to resume the search, but they refuse. The Institute swears Gabriel Waite had no living relatives, but Marian says Deane once mentioned he had a mother living in Mexico City. We are finding more humanity in our son's Eskimo friends than in his employers."

A week later, Maddie listened as her father read aloud to Essy and her mother a barely legible letter from Grandaddy, apparently scratched in great haste. " 'Bert was rushed to the hospital this afternoon after collapsing in a medical missionary's living room in Wainwright. An Eskimo hunter had come into town the day before with an amputated right hand in his possession—he had found it on the tundra. Local people told him about us and our search for Deane and directed him to Reverend Latterley's home where we were staying. Can you imagine our thoughts?' "

Maddie pictured what Deane's right hand had looked like—the fingers long, no ring, with the white scar from the can opener. She would know that hand anywhere. But then on second thought, maybe she wouldn't know it *anywhere*. She could not imagine it actually detached from his arm, lying by itself in the snow like a dropped glove—a piece of a body instead of part of *him*. It should not be possible to sever any part of him.

Her father continued reading: " 'The Eskimo said it was the hand of a white man, the wrist mangled perhaps from being cut off with a dull knife or piece of bone over a period of several hours, the fingers white as snow. The Reverend, who is also a doctor, examined it closely and said it had no doubt been amputated by its owner as a desperate remedy for frostbite. Several years ago a hunter had brought in a human foot in the same condition. But the hand was found too far south of the coast to be Deane's, he assured Bert. Yet she insisted on seeing it for herself. As the doctor turned back the white linen cloth that covered it, Bert took a look at the hand to see if there was a scar, saw none, and then fainted dead away. She is weakening in morale. But we keep flying.' "

Maddie thought of the amputated hand day and night for the next week, dreaming about it buried under layers of snow, then slowly coming alive and starting to tunnel up. (She thought of the funeral parlor game, how Deane could seem so still and dead and yet be so alive.) Sometimes in her dream, the hand would dig itself out, and wondering where Deane's arm was, float up into the air and flutter its long, loose fingers like strips of paper in the wind, trying to fly. Failing that, it would sink down to the ground again, stretch out each of the digits to ten inches long, like five wriggling white snakes, and crawl over the ice like a reptile, the opposable thumb leading the way.

Maddie would wake up soaking wet. She told herself Deane would never be foolish enough to let himself get frostbite—if he had a choice.

After that, she began indulging in fantasies of rescue. She liked to picture Deane heroically wrestling with his situation on some ice-pillared mountainside, slowly, loyally dragging his injured pilot inch by inch back to civilization. Sometimes she would imagine *she* was the one he was rescuing. He would know by instinct what the right direction was and how to keep her safe and warm until they found their way to a village or camp. Some days she thought of nothing else but this drama, and would act it out in her backyard. Other days, when even the fenced-in yard wasn't privacy enough, she'd crawl under the caves of the late flowering spiraea or Van Fleet rosebushes and imagine the white blossoms showering down exactly like snow. For hours she'd pretend she was lost on the tundra somewhere east of Barrow, camped under an overturned oomiak, with nothing to eat but the grass soles of her frozen mukluks. She would half enjoy it at first, until the cold and dark became so lonely, she couldn't bear it even in her imagination.

On other mornings, later in August, after helping her mother feed Esther breakfast, she would go outside and make tin-bucket stew for her doll out of dirt and birdbath water, adding dead leaves, sycamore balls, and live ants as a substitute for fresh caribou or seal meat. The ants would struggle to crawl out of the stew, but she'd stir them back in, pretending their drownings were part of her desperate life-and-death situation. (The Arctic was a severe, unsympathizing place, Deane had said many times. Life could be like "swimming through rock.") Occasionally she would feel the emergency from the ants' point of view, start to perspire under her overalls, and want to dump the whole stew out; but most of the time she enjoyed having the power—as Deane did, she was sure—to decide whether to keep on fighting the raging storm or to give in and die. But she never died in her imagination—not even when she resolved to. For as soon as she pretended to give up the struggle, to close her eyes and lie back in the bushes in a frozen death-sleep, out of a wild hurricane of snow he would appear, his beard black and stubbly, a gun on his hip, just as she'd seen him in Bert's photograph albums of his trip to the Yukon five years ago. He would laugh at her fear, start a fire, and make caribou soup, then take her under his huge fur coat and keep her warm all night long, cradling her as she cradled her doll, telling her stories about his adventures after the plane crash.

But then, by early September, when the edges of the sycamore leaves began to curl and die, the fantasy became harder to act out. Bert's postcards came less frequently. Grandaddy wrote that they had crossed the northernmost Arctic tundra back and forth five times and hadn't found a scrap of debris. Nothing. And for the first time, Maddie considered what would happen if Deane could not be found. How long could he hold out? Another month? Two months? She felt hopeful during the day. But at night, tossing and turning in bed, she would begin to wonder what it felt like to really freeze to death.

Unable to sleep one chilly September night that smelled like fall through her open bedroom window, she got up, felt her way down the dark stairs so as not to wake her parents, then went to the shelf of books her mother had studied in nurse's training before she got married. She looked up "Frostbite and Hypothermia—treatment" in the index of the *General Health Manual* and quickly skimmed the paragraphs. "Hypothermia victims are never dead until they are warm and dead," she read, "and *must never be abandoned.*" Did hypothermia mean *frozen?* The combination "warm and dead" sounded horrible to her, even worse than cold and dead somehow.

And yet, the words were a reassurance that a frozen person could recover. "The victim's flesh may be gray or gray-white and feel like wood to the touch. The touch test is decisive." She paused, insatiably curious, afraid to read further, but unable to resist: "When sinking into hypothermia, the body shuts down all peripheral circulation to conserve heat in the vital organs. When pain turns to numbness or a pleasant sensation of false warmth, you know that the body is withdrawing circulation from the affected area, usually the extremities, sacrificing them to minimize heat loss."

What would Deane feel, she tried to think, when his circulation was slowly being withdrawn, his blood reduced, as the "extremities" of his body—and maybe of his mind too—were being sacrificed to maintain temperature and circulation at the heart? How much could be sacrificed? For how long? She thought of her father's grief as a kind of freezing too, and also the constant quarreling going on between Bert and Essy.

She scanned the last paragraph of the chapter: "It is possible to walk out of the wilderness on frozen feet. But the pain of rewarming can be agonizing; swelling and blistering may virtually disable the victim for a time." It struck her as strange that the restoration of the blood, so needed and missed, could cause a person to feel agony instead of relief. Why should it? Perhaps it was because the body made so many changes to compensate for what was missing that, after a while, it couldn't change back; what had been good and normal before flowed back into the closed-up, shrunken blood vessels like an attack, a healing that couldn't be withstood if it came too late.

What if Deane came back tomorrow? Would everything simply go back to the way it was before?

She went back to bed and thought of Deane frozen and half-buried on the Alaska plain. Days and nights passed in the thought. At night especially, she thought of the Arctic winter coming on, and pictured his broken arms and legs fixed in the same grotesque positions under the blue moonlight week after week, surrounded by smashed specimen jars and bent animal cages—and maybe the frozen pet fox lying close by his outstretched white hand.

But it was late summer in the Arctic, she reminded herself. Maybe Deane was already a skeleton. In August the temperature might have risen high enough to melt the snow and expose his body to the sun, just long enough for hungry wolves and foxes to attack and scatter his bones. And then maybe some of his bones would be gathered up by an evil Eskimo spirit and combined with dirty walrus and fox bones to make a hell-animal on some terrible mission. Oh, if such things could happen, she thought—then abruptly stopped thinking with an involuntary cry that made Katy stir in her sleep beside her.

No, she decided. In their python games in the living room, Deane had taught her to be calm, how to hold still no matter how hard the huge snake squeezed. Sometimes one had to hold one's mind still too, she reasoned, and not follow the temptation to panic—or even to think at all. And so, for the first of many times in her life, she shut her thoughts off from her own conscious knowledge, closed her eyes, and went to sleep.

Bert's postcards stopped coming.

Grandaddy wrote to say they had hoped to meet with the family of the lost bush pilot, but had been told again there was no next of kin. They had visited the doctor who had supposedly treated Deane on June 10. He was on vacation, but his secretary explained the confusion stemmed from a mistake in billing—that a Mr. C. E. Cameron had received typhoid shots on June 10, but the bill had been sent to R. D. Cameron by mistake. Grandaddy then called on C. E. Cameron in Fairbanks, who said he had indeed had typhoid shots on that date, but had paid his bill before leaving the doctor's office. He bore no physical resemblance to Deane. Who had Cole Cortright seen then? As it turned out, the doctor wasn't on vacation at all, Grandaddy ended the letter, but had been indicted by a grand jury on a morals charge and couldn't be reached. Bert's spirits were sinking further.

Finally, in his last letter dated October 1, Grandaddy reported that Mr. Sidorkin, the communist who had hired Deane and been subsequently dismissed, was no longer in the country. A month after Deane's disappearance, he had accepted a position with Steinman Laboratories in Israel. Surprisingly, Professor McCafferty had also resigned his position at Johns Hopkins "for health reasons." Grandaddy was trying to find out his new address so he and Bert could visit him. Lastly, he told of a talk he and Bert had with two old retired seal hunters, Karl Akaleisik and Joe Toomik, who had been among Deane's closest friends. They wept openly when Bert told them who she was and praised Deane as a "best man" who was "good for many peoples." They also spoke of Deane's pilot, for whom they had fainter praise. Waite was a good pilot, but not a "best man." They remembered hearing him mention a sister living in California, and something about a farm he'd bought in Arkansas where he planned to settle down with his fiancée "after a few more jobs." Either the Institute had lied about "no next of kin," Grandaddy concluded, or Waite had lied to the Institute, even perhaps about his name.

As her father read this letter aloud to Essy and her mother, Maddie saw a poised impenetrableness in his eyes that perplexed her. No one could draw much of a response from him these days. He was more quiet and unrevealing day by day, more like Deane in some ways, and yet lacking Deane's old humor and warmth. He mailed Bert three copies of an article from *The Pittsburgh Press*, written by a Yukon trading-post keeper who reported that Russian engineers disguised as salmon fishermen "had been mapping the coast of Alaska for the last ten years and had infiltrated every town and village in the area." He got into political arguments with people where he worked, and stopped speaking to one department manager who mocked the "red menace" and accused him of losing his perspective. In a letter to Grandaddy, her father enclosed a newspaper report about the disappearance of three men from a camp near the Northwest Territories two years earlier: "The remnants of a meal were on the table, but the three had vanished. An investigation was instigated, and the report that followed suggested—but could not confirm—that the three men, all scientists, had been taken by the Russians."

Her father was feeling Deane's disappearance very deeply, Maddie could see. Yet for everyone else's sake, he showed neither grief nor hope, hardly any feeling at all. It was as though, for him, strong feelings were now either too dangerous or too useless to express.

On September 16, Grandaddy called long-distance to report that the weather was closing in, and Bert was in a state of nervous collapse. They were coming home.

"This is for you, Maddie," Grandaddy said the Friday night after their return. "We found it in a box under Deane's bed. I thought you might like to have it."

It was a poem typed on yellowish paper, decorated with concentric circles of happy-looking frogs drawn in soft pencil. Why was Grandaddy going through Deane's old things? she wondered, noting a few more papers and magazines in his lap. It seemed like he and Bert had just gotten home, and now they were talking about a trip to California to meet the pilot's sister whose address Bert had located through a man in Fairbanks.

"Read it aloud," Grandaddy asked her, and she did:

> *What a wonderful bird the frog are—*
> *When he stand he sit almost;*
> *When he hop he fly almost.*
> *He ain't got no sense hardly;*
> *He ain't got no tail hardly either.*
> *When he sit, he sit on what he ain't got almost.*

"Isn't it wonderful?" he said, pleased with her straight-faced reading of it. "Isn't it perfect *frogness?* Deane loved nonsense poems."

"When did he do the drawings?" she asked, admiring the silvery shading he had done with his fingers. The frogs looked perfectly three-dimensional. She rubbed her own fingers into the smudges he had made.

"In the sixth grade. I remember he got an *F* on the assignment, and was outraged. His teacher asked his class to submit essays about what they wanted to be when they grew up. Already fascinated with frogs, Deane submitted this poem, with artistic embellishments, listing the author as 'That famous Egyptologist, Dr. A. Nonymous.' She wasn't amused."

He was an artist, Maddie thought. He could do anything. He couldn't be dead.

"Anything left that's worth going over?" her father said absently as he bent over the few things Grandaddy had brought over to show him. " 'Don't Always Get Your Man' by R. D. Cameron. Where on earth did you dig this up?"

"He published that in *Adventure* when he was nineteen. I re-read it last night. See the underlined part?"

Her father read: " 'Southeast, there, is no man's land, and no native would be likely to head that way except under pressure. You know the Eskimos hate the unknown, even more than the rest of us, and believe that where no man is known to live, no man *can* live.' So?"

Grandaddy shrugged. "I don't know. The irony struck me. He's talking about the place where the Navy was conducting the experiments."

Could Deane have foreseen what was going to happen to him someday, Maddie wondered? Instead of hating the unknown, he had loved it and been drawn to it.

Grandaddy handed her a heavy gold medal on a chain. "Would you like to have this? I think he meant to give it to you anyway." Then he handed her an old newspaper article showing Deane at age twelve, grinning, shaking hands with a man who was presenting him with the gold medal on a ribbon. "He won this as the state spelling champion."

Her father took the medal from her and looked at it. "Ha!" he said, his face lighting up momentarily. "He won this the same year he bribed me to read a book. I hated reading, Maddie. So he told me if I'd read a book all the way through, he'd buy me a BB gun. And he did."

Maddie laughed. Evidently Deane had been the way he was from the beginning—always playing games with people to teach them things. "How many rounds did he go in the spelling bee?" she asked.

"I don't know," Grandaddy said, "but it was the first time a boy ever won the marathon. The last girl went down on 'polynomial.' Bert never let any of us forget it."

How proud Bert must have been, Maddie thought—her son, famous at age twelve. And that wasn't the whole story, Grandaddy said. "Deane had a lot of trouble with his hearing in those days, and he'd forgotten his hearing aid. Something happened during the marathon, and he had to go through the final rounds almost stone-deaf, gambling on every word pronounced, taking a chance on not understanding it to avoid seeming to stall or make excuses. But when the man pronouncing the words turned his head, it brought a showdown. 'I can't hear you,' Deane said. 'But how have you been getting these words?' the man asked him. 'I read your lips,' Deane explained. The next day the newspaper ran an article about him with the headline: 'No Handicaps for Real Champions.' Bert bought up thirty-five newspapers and sent them to everyone she knew."

"Is the medal real gold?" Maddie asked, admiring Deane's reluctance to make excuses.

Grandaddy nodded. "He was always resourceful. He could always find a way out of a predicament."

Where was he now then? she wondered. How was he doing it?

Grandaddy handed her a small slip of paper. "Here's another poem for you, stuck to an article on Emperor penguins he won a prize for five years ago."

She read the poem to herself:

> *I she went oh, am she gone?*
> *Have her left I all alone?*
> *Will her never come to we?*
> *Will I never come to she?*
> *It cannot was!*

It was funny—sort of crazy-funny, she thought. She didn't like it as well as the other poem, but read it again.

"The Eskimos had such loyalty to him, Will," Grandaddy said. "He taught a bunch of kids in Teller to play the piano. In Nome, he showed a poor, half-crippled old man how to build a sluice from the fuselage of a wrecked plane so he could concentrate up to twenty dollars a day of flour-fine gold dust that lies all over the place and make a decent living. And Burt Mozeek, the town marshal, told me he had almost convinced Deane to postpone his work with the Institute a couple of years and apply for the position of deputy. Deane and five other deputies would have administered the entire Second Judicial Division, stretching from the Arctic Coast beyond Barrow to the mouth of the Yukon—the wildest and least known parts of Alaska."

"He should have done it," her father said emphatically. "He would have loved it."

"He'd never go back on a contract. Not to save his neck."

They sat in silence for a while, turning over the pages. "Our pilot had flown Deane on an expedition to the Mukarcharni Mountains last year," Grandaddy resumed. "They came within a hundred miles of Siberia, and Deane showed him some excellent aerial photographs he had taken of Russian islands off the Alaska coast. These islands were only about four hundred miles from the area Deane and Waite were flying in. If there had been engine trouble, or if the plane had been tampered with and flown off course, our pilot said they might very well have been intercepted and interned by the Russians, who, he was sure, would be in no hurry to notify anyone in the United States."

Barely listening, Maddie read the second poem again, substituting he for she, him for her. The poem was sad, terribly sad. Not really funny at all.

"So now what?" her father said.

Grandaddy said Bert had just sent off a long letter summarizing everything they had learned to the Assistant Chief for Administration of the Office of Naval Research in Washington, D.C. He hoped to find an ally in Waite's surviving sister, who still didn't officially exist. They were still waiting for Professor McCafferty's address.

Her father shuffled the papers together as if to put some order to them. "I wish you'd let me give you the money to fly to the Coast."

"No. We're going to drive through the desert Southwest.

No ice and snow, no planes. Just hot sun and cactuses. I thought the long drive would do Bert good. The desert can be so beautiful—healing, in a way."

"Dad," Maddie heard her father say softly, after a pause, "what if Deane is in the Soviet Union? What if they have him? He'd be no use to them. They'd never break him."

Maddie looked up at her grandfather, whose face and hair were both gray. He had lost a lot of weight in Alaska, she noticed for the first time. His scalp seemed stretched too tight to fit his skull, and blue veins wormed just below the surface through a recent outbreak of dark freckles. His upper arms had lost their muscles and sagged in bags under the sleeves of his starched shirt. Maddie felt a rush of sadness and respect for him as he tried so hard to keep Bert and everyone encouraged, never losing his sense of humor or appreciation of beauty, and never, unlike her father, trying to hide his feelings. Deane had learned a lot from him.

"What will she do if . . ." her father began again and stopped.

Grandaddy sighed and said quietly, "Willy, sometimes I think she hasn't even started to react."

As they fell silent again, Maddie imagined Deane chained up in a Russian prison—a dungeon, she pictured it, with lots of other prisoners. After the first couple of days, he'd probably start telling them stories, or drawing pictures of frogs on the dirty walls to make them laugh and not lose heart. But sooner or later, the Russians would question him. Would they hurt him for not telling them where the uranium was in Alaska? Surely they would see for themselves what he was really interested in, that he was no threat to anyone, and let him go. As Bert hoped, one day soon he would come to the door just as he did last Christmas. Everyone would laugh, gather around, and welcome him home; and he would tell them that all their worries and fears had been for nothing.

It cannot was, she thought of the nonsense poem. It cannot was.

Grandaddy caught the look on her face and held out his arms. "Come here, Gink," he said, giving her a hug and scrunching her cheeks between his hands. "What are you thinking about?"

"Nothing."

"She's going to be a great lady, eh, Willy?" he said, studying her face.

Her father, deep in thought, didn't answer. And for the hundredth time, Maddie wondered what on earth Grandaddy was talking about. As he and her father got out a worn map of North America and opened it on the coffee table, she went to the bathroom and looked in the mirror. Plain face. Brown flyaway hair. Plain brown eyes with nothing in them but little black pupils. No warm light as in Deane's eyes. No sparkly darkness or changing shadows. Deane was the great one in the family, and the only one.

Grandaddy held out his hand as she came back into the living room. "Such a face, Gink! How about going on a trip with me?"

"Oh Dad, don't bore Maddie with that," her father said as she climbed up beside her grandfather. He knew she didn't completely share Grandaddy's enthusiasm for maps and imaginary trip-planning, although she had often pretended to like it to please him.

"Ah, she enjoys it, don't you, Gink?" he said, undeterred, spreading the large map across their laps. "Where do you want to go? The Grand Tetons? The White Mountains? Mexico? Bert and I are planning a trip to Mexico after we go to California. See? All the way over here to the coast, and then way down here."

She put off choosing. It was a long drawn-out process of selecting and trying out different route numbers to a predetermined destination by which he sought to teach her American geography. And yet she couldn't altogether resist his excitement about the mountains and deserts. Bert had said his mother died when he was fourteen years old, and he had been so devastated with grief, he ran away, hopping boxcars and working at odd jobs back and forth across the country for seven years. That's how he'd come to know so much about every town and river she pointed to.

"Where are we now?" he prodded, anxious to play the game.

She pointed to Pittsburgh.

"Good. Now follow this highway west to my favorite place of all." And he proceeded to help her choose a scenic route to the Black Hills of South Dakota. "I used to break horses for the U.S. Cavalry in this little town—here."

She stretched, yawned, tried to be attentive. "Where's Alaska?" she asked, looking for it.

"Ah," Grandaddy said, glancing at Willy. "Don't you know, Maddie?"

Embarrassed, she shook her head. They had never gone to Alaska when they played the map game.

"Well, here is where you are," he said. "And this—way up here—is Alaska."

She was appalled at the distance—and the size of it. "Where was Deane last seen?" she asked.

"Do you have an atlas?"

She ran and got her father's, opened it to the place—already marked by a scrap of paper—that displayed a full two-page map of Alaska. The marker wasn't necessary, she noted; the book opened to the place automatically.

Grandaddy pointed to the topmost tip of land. "Somewhere around here, or to the southeast," he said. "Or perhaps out over this water."

She stared. "But there aren't any towns or villages around there."

"No."

"How many miles is it from here?"

"Well," he paused, "you tell me. In Alaska alone, you could probably fit twelve or thirteen Pennsylvanias. You know how long it takes to drive to Tionesta where your other grandparents live."

She studied the map key, but could not add up the sum of its length laid end to end all the way up to the top of the map. "How did you and Bert know where to look?" she asked, comparing Alaska's immense size to the states she knew. "How do you know he's not here—or down here—or over there?"

"We don't know for sure. But we do know a little more about where he isn't. Deane used to say that in science a negative fact is just as important as a positive one."

What? Maddie thought, hardly hearing. What was he talking about?

Grandaddy showed her Tigvariak Island, barely a speck in the vast Arctic Ocean, where Deane's plane had taken off —and then the course he had followed west toward Barrow, with Siberia a little farther beyond. "Do you see this area here?" he said, pointing to the big empty spot where Deane had been working on the secret experiments with the Navy.

She nodded. But she wasn't listening anymore. What had they all been thinking? No one could find anyone in that enormous space. She had been taking encouragement from the sentence in her mother's medical book, that a man could walk out of the wilderness on frozen feet. But realization of the distance shot waves of hot-cold dread up her spine now, into her head, and out through her eyes and forehead into the air. She had not understood before. No one had explained it to her.

"What Deane meant by that," Grandaddy was going on about the negative fact, "is that it's just as important to know what is *not* true as it is to know what *is*. Do you see?"

Yes, she nodded. She saw. What was not true was that

Deane could ever walk out of all that great blank space alive.
There was no place to walk to.

She stared again at the map, at the unrelieved emptiness
north of the Brooks Range. And as simply and finally as Grandaddy turned over the page of the atlas to show her Yukon
Territory where Deane had worked three years before, everything in the world dimmed, taking on a dark blue Arctic light
that drew her back into it at the same moment she became
aware of the appallingly huge, true scale of things. She felt a
bottomless and terrifying well of emotion open up in her. What
hope was there for Deane? Wherever her life, their lives, had
been going when he was alive, now, without him, they would
have to go someplace else.

Grandaddy was saying something about the pioneers,
pointing out the old wagon trails that had become superhighways spanning the plains and prairie states. She half-listened,
thinking of Deane's death as the narrowing of all these roads,
back to footpaths and ruts from the superhighways he had
opened for her. Oh, she thought in a mounting fever of rage,
he had been the sure route to a place he knew she wanted to
go. But she couldn't get there without him. She wasn't even
sure what or where it was.

Now Grandaddy was saying how, barely begun in their
journeys west, some of the pioneers had been stopped by floods
or other disasters. They often lost their teams of horses or
oxen. Then, no matter what their original destination had been,
they had to set down roots in the place where their progress
had been stopped. Without the pulling power of those teams,
they couldn't go any farther. By a quirk of chance, home became that random plot where their losses left them, and they
had to content themselves with its barren, Midwestern fea-
turelessness for the rest of their lives.

"Where shall we go next?" Grandaddy said, turning back
to the big map.

"I don't know," Maddie thought, feeling tired and sick, wanting to get away from Grandaddy and the map, up to her room to sleep.

In bed that night, Maddie dreamed she saw Deane running, half-flying out of a bright blue horizon into a sea of Easter lilies, pursued by a hell-animal that Professor McCafferty had made. And then Deane was overtaken and *peechooked*, shattered into a million pieces that fell like snow on the waving, sundazzled lilies. Like snow he melted into them, and there was not a trace of him left anywhere as far as she could see. She remembered him telling her once that the Eskimos said *peechook* to express good-natured resignation at the suddenness and finality of the utter ending of certain things—pain, pleasure, good weather, luck. Now she must do that, he said to her out of the flowers in his familiar confident voice: she must resign herself to the reality of losing things with good nature. But the sound of his voice, so alive and intimate through her sleep, did not make her feel resigned. She woke feeling strong, with restored certainty that he was alive somewhere, somehow. She reached for the gold medal under her pillow and held it, cool and substantial in her palm. The medals, the poems and drawings, the mask and the raven print were all symbols of him, just as words were symbols of real things in the world. What did a word mean if the thing it symbolized stopped existing? But here the things were, as much the shadows of his reality as they had ever been.

The next morning, after breakfast, Maddie was surprised to see Bert appear at the back door, her hair hanging down in straggly wisps, a letter crushed in her hand. She wore old black velvet bedroom slippers instead of high heels, and an artificial leopard fur bathrobe full of holes. "Oh, how few people in the world speak with genuine humanity!" she exclaimed to Maddie's mother, falling into her usual chair.

Bert opened the letter with trembling hands. "God *knows* when we can*not* go on without help," she sighed. "This is from one of Deane's true friends—at last a voice I can trust! Oh I hope no one saw me coming through the alley. I kept my head down."

She read all four pages to Maddie and her mother, many of the sentences already memorized. The last few lines she read with her eyes fixed on Ginny: " 'Deane always seemed to be so completely able to look after himself in any emergency. I understand from the press in Canada that the U.S. Navy has put a news blanket on all Alaskan incidents of any kind. Perhaps there have been other recent disappearances. I know it is probably the wrong thing to say, not to give up hope for Deane, Mrs. Cameron. But I do say it. I cannot help but think that he is still alive and well. I, at least, am going to hope for his return.' "

She lowered her glasses victoriously. But something in the look of Ginny's eyes disappointed her. She pulled Maddie toward her, encircling her waist with a strong arm. "We two do not resign ourselves, do we? We do not lose hope."

Maddie shook her head.

After she had gone, Maddie went to her room to look up "resignation" in the dictionary. She remembered hearing Deane use that word when he'd argued with her father about the Arab and lion exhibit in the museum last summer. Deane had said that sometimes one had to resign oneself to not knowing what to decide about the outcome of an action or a problem. But when an action was frozen in uncertainty, how could one decide whether to hope or not? What if someone *loved* the Arab? Bert might be left wondering forever what happened to Deane, trying to put a puzzle together with pieces that would remain missing as long as anybody remembered there was a puzzle to solve. How could she resign herself to a reality if she didn't know what the reality was, or if it could be changed?

As far as Deane's fate was concerned, neither of the alternatives was acceptable. Either Deane was frozen to death in the middle of nowhere, or he was a prisoner in another country from which he couldn't escape. So why did Bert rejoice at getting these letters? Just this morning her father had shown her a book of photographs Grandaddy had taken of the Arctic tundra from the air—lifeless, snow-covered flatlands, going on and on interminably into a pale blue horizon, with streaks of purple and white, pink and white. White, white, white.

But then, thoughts of Deane's strength and knowledge came back to her. She couldn't discount what Deane's friend had written, which was also true. She couldn't forget how prepared and resourceful he always was, how capable of taking care of himself in any emergency, as this man had said.

She got out her doll, wrapped it in blankets, and went out to play once more under the spiraea bushes. She pretended as always that she and her baby were lost in an Arctic storm. She unwrapped the blankets, laid her doll down on top of them, then wrapped her up again as tightly as possible. The baby's cobalt blue eyes looked up at her glassily. She held her tight against her body, away from the icy wind.

This time she imagined it was night, a three-month-long Arctic night, and she was lost in a cold so severe that the only way she could save her baby's life was to lie down on top of her, shielding her with the warmth of her own body at the risk of her life. To make it real, she stretched out on the dirt with her doll underneath her. She could feel its hard rubber arms and hands poking into her ribs.

After holding this position for five minutes, imagining the long night ahead, she felt a sharp pain in her stomach, a wave of real anxiety, and then without warning, an overwhelming feeling of nausea. Her back ached from the awkward posture she was holding to avoid being scratched by the twigs of the bare spiraea bush. To avoid throwing up, she sat up and looked around, crawled out, and dragged the unwrapped doll behind her. She examined its dumb pink face. The cheeks were scuffed from many years of play. The blue eyes were segmented like the staring eyes of the Snowy Owl at the zoo, but unlike the owl's, they were dull and unresponsive. No matter how much she loved and protected this thing, it would never be anything but a doll, a dead drain on her, a senselessly demanding taker of her energy and emotion. Why should she waste so much feeling on it? Angrily, she held it by its legs and shook it as if to punish it for not being alive. Then, without actually deciding to do it, she stood up, hauled back like a baseball player swinging a bat and banged its head against the sycamore tree. Amazed at her action, she repeated it three more times, harder each time. She felt anger flare up in her like fire released from a house when the roof blows off. She wanted to kill the doll for not being alive—to hear its head crack. She hit it again and again, harder than before, starting to pant with the effort.

She stopped and looked at it. The face was cut and gashed, but the head was still intact. Wildly, she swung again, three, four more slams against the tree, and began to feel hot and dizzy with the exertion. Everything is dead, she thought with each slam. Everything that should be alive is dead.

She inspected the face for a second time, both pleased and horrified to see that the forehead had acquired two big cracks and the eyes had rolled up into the head. No more blue eyes. Only empty sockets revealing the mechanism by which the eyes had opened and closed when Maddie had sung it to sleep or wakened it from a nap. The doll was nothing but a breakable mechanism. Maybe that's all anybody was, she thought in a wave of pity for Deane and herself and every living thing in the world.

Her eyes stung with tears. She felt worn out, overwhelmingly tired. She glanced toward the kitchen window to make sure her mother hadn't been watching her, then in a wave of remorse, clutched the doll to her breast. She stuck her finger inside one of the eye sockets to try to roll down the iris, but it rolled back up again and wouldn't stay in place. How fast things could be ruined, she noted objectively, amazed at this simple truth. Years and years of love could be cancelled out in just a few minutes.

She wrapped the doll to hide its face and took it inside up to her room. Her mother must never know she had done this. She crawled into bed with her clothes on. Pulling up the covers, she held the broken doll close to her, and, in just a few minutes, drifted down a long, slanted tunnel into dreamless sleep. If she dreamed of Deane after that day, she did not remember it.

That night, Bert came back to read them all a second letter she'd written to Captain Davis Rigler at the Office of Naval Research requesting a hearing as soon as possible. She read the conclusion as though it were a solemn historical document: " 'We have not had one day of happiness since Deane disappeared. Where such a big *question mark* still exists, a *period* does not properly belong. We seek to enlist your help as the *best* and the *most* we can do for our dear son. We hold ourselves available at any time for *Action* and *Questioning* that will help in any way.' " Bert told everyone she hoped to receive an answer to her request within a week. It came, four weeks later, in the form of a request for confirmation of two dates regarding Deane's contracts and a question about the spelling of Mc-Cafferty's middle name.

For weeks after that, Maddie felt half-asleep all day, but wide-awake at night. She would toss back and forth in bed, caught up in maddening circles of thought that repeated themselves senselessly like monotonous tunes. One of the circles was that Bert had lost her child, and so had she. But at least Bert hadn't killed Deane herself; she hadn't beaten him to death.

Who could grieve when guilt was all mixed up with a loss? What was happening to her? Why was everything in the family and inside her changing just because one person had gotten lost? She felt too hot some nights, other nights too cold. She wanted Deane to appear to her, as a ghost or anything, it didn't matter now, and stop the way things were going, to put everything right again. As someone drowning wanted the air, she wanted him to come home. He would know how all the feelings fit, how nothing was as bad as it seemed—except this, she thought, weeping unconsolably: *needing so much what she could not have.* Sometimes she couldn't understand why Deane had such a hold on the family, or why she wasn't strong enough to follow in his direction without him pulling her along showing the way. Everything was changing, slowing down—demystifying, she would think later—as the hope of his being found alive dimmed.

Yet as her grandmother sat in her mother's kitchen day after day going over the flimsiest scraps and reinforcements of hope, Maddie couldn't help but admire her fierce, obsessed faith that things could still turn out justly. She impressed Maddie with a courage that searched out all the worst evidence yet still remained full of determination to believe that, as Essy said, all things worked together for good. By nature, Maddie thought she shared Bert's determination. She wasn't sure she could share her belief.

Maddie was especially happy when Bert said that, if nothing else, the trip to Alaska had inspired her will to write again. Almost a year to the day after Deane was lost, she sat down by the kitchen stove and announced she'd written a sonnet called "Still Life" and wanted Maddie and her mother to hear it.

Maddie sat at her feet, excited for her. Bert cleared her throat, held her glasses up to her eyes, and composed herself for reading—intense, quiet, proceeding to cast the poem like a spell over the kitchen, over the whole mundane, practical world of their present life. She read:

I have seen the Arctic summer lying nude
Against the tundra's strange, impassive breast,
She cannot melt this chilling rectitude,
A vanquished vestal, she, still unpossessed;
Her days and nights are passionate with sun,
A lovely, shameless pleading to beget,
But the ice-hearted land will not be won,
Importunate Summer is a virgin yet.
Here are no roses and no forests born
To help the seasons' cycle come and go,
Never a single tree to bend forlorn
Under the coming jeopardy of snow.
This is the hardened, unregenerate earth
Where summer dies in trying to give birth.

Her pink-powdered eyebrows converged with feeling as she waited for their response. "It's very nice," Maddie's mother said, not really liking the poem very much, Maddie could tell. There was even the faintest look of embarrassment on her mother's face, perhaps at the use of the word "virgin" in Maddie's presence.

She saw a vague, collapsed look in Bert's eyes. But then, catching the look in Maddie's eyes, Bert turned to her.

5

HALLOWEEN

In March of Maddie's fourteenth year, her mother watched out of the kitchen window as Maddie wove a crown of thorns out of the Van Fleet rosebushes she used to play under. "If you're determined to do that," her mother said as Maddie carried the finished crown into the house, "why don't you wear gloves?"

Maddie tried to explain to her the strange mystical pleasure she felt scratching up her hands during Lent until they were crisscrossed with red lines. Considering what Christ had done, wasn't it appropriate? She'd written a poem about it called "Weaving" to show Bert, and Bert had understood, though warning her not to take it too far. But as the first day of Holy Week approached, Maddie felt that even pleasures had to be painful, symbolic, self-mortifying. What better way to prepare for the crucifixion? Last Easter, she told Katy she had become a Christian mystic. She was beginning to believe everything at the same time she believed nothing.

In February, more mystical than ever, she signed up for communicants' classes at the Presbyterian church, and lately, a few of the church members had remarked to her parents how absorbed she seemed in the minister's controversial sermons. Although Aunt Essy still objected to Reverend Rutke's liberal politics, and also to his habit of quoting English poets and Russian novelists more often than St. Paul, Maddie was falling in love with him. His plain black robe accentuated his height, and the stoop of his shoulders added a slightly burdened look to his stride that attracted her. He was a mystic, too, she bet Katy. Four years ago he had brought back the ancient tradition of the Good Friday Tenebrae service—the Extinguishing of the Lights—that so filled her with wonder the first time she saw it that she couldn't believe this was the same religion Essy practiced or that she'd learned about in Sunday school. A lot of people stayed away from the service after the first year— "too dark," they said, "too sad." But it couldn't be sad enough as far as Maddie was concerned.

As Palm Sunday approached, the day she would officially join the church, she began stopping by the sanctuary after school to sit in the back balcony and think. In the late afternoon sun, the floor shimmered with pools of richly colored light that slanted down from the stained-glass windows—no one else in all that immense, exquisitely structured space but herself and maybe the organist practicing high up in the choir loft. Sometimes, as she watched the back of his head sway back and forth with the music and pictured his feet flying over the pedals in their wonderfully specialized dance, she envied his work—the artistic competence and private enclosure of it.

Reverend Rutke told the communicants' class that the church had been built during the Great Depression. The congregation's faith had been so strong that many of the members had mortgaged their homes to pay for a sanctuary modeled after York Minster in England. The windows had been leaded by a master glass artist from France who worked on the great cathedrals and spared no effort of detail. He'd been passionate about blue, blue so royally concentrated, Maddie could almost hear it hum when the sanctuary was silent. Above the back balcony, the triple crucifixion window could trick her eyes into squinting as if it gave off ultraviolet light. If the stone and oak were the skeleton and muscle of the church, the windows were its rich blue blood.

She was particularly drawn to one window illustrating the Parable of the Lost Sheep: a young, strong Christ holding the wayward sheep on his shoulders, safe and secure, and behind him, in glass, the ninety-nine other sheep who had never strayed from the fold. "Count them," the minister told her class, noting Maddie's special absorption. "They're all there." She was the only one who bothered to count them, mainly because the window posed a problem for her. She knew from her family's experience with Deane five years ago that it was a terrifying thing to be lost. But what a privileged place the lost sheep had achieved once he was recovered. Who would want to be among the undifferentiated ninety-nine who huddled together in a uniform line, fading off into the lead frame?

Her favorite place in the church was the Gothic arch over the door leading into the sanctuary. Last week Reverend Rutke had explained how, back in the thirties, the congregation had adopted a logo for their church to symbolize Christ's sacrifice for the lost and outcast of the world. After much discussion, they had settled on a symbol of Christ that went back to the Middle Ages: a mother pelican, her wings outstretched like a protective cloak around her three baby pelicans gathered to her breast, their beaks poking into her feathers. There she was, the minister told the half-attentive class as they straggled into the sanctuary. They'd all passed under the pelican a hundred times without noticing her. "Why didn't the congregation choose a dove?" asked one of the communicants—doves are "much prettier than pelicans." Maddie listened closely as Rutke told the legend of how, in temperate latitudes, when winters were unseasonably severe and baby birds in danger of starving

to death, a mother pelican would bare her breast and let them
feed on her own flesh. By this act of will against her own body,
she was able, in a cold and hostile landscape, to save their
lives. In fact, he concluded, under such conditions there was
no other way.

"How I envy the pelican's privilege!" Bert had said with
glistening eyes when Maddie told her about the sculpture a
few days later. Then, after a heavy sigh: "But opportunity must
be available for such miracles!"

Maddie had studied her sympathetically. So much guilt
(which she understood better later, when Essy finally told her
what Bert had put in Deane's suitcase at Christmas), as well as
advancing arthritis, had so crippled her that she looked gro-
tesquely handicapped, even half-crazy, to people who didn't
know her. A few weeks before, Maddie had invited a friend
from school to meet her, and poor Bert had hobbled to the
door on her bowed legs dressed in her black velvet rags, her
unevenly dyed hair streaked with bright orange. (She refused
to go to a beauty parlor anymore where the language was too
"common" and conversation "exhausting.") Her friend's eyes
had widened in disbelief. "*This* is your grandmother?" she asked.
Bert looked like a witch who would have been thrown in prison
back in Salem, Massachusetts.

"Will you come to see me join the church on Palm
Sunday?" Maddie asked Bert, dropping the distressing subject
of the pelican.

Pondering her answer, Bert peered into a row of undusted
flow-blue teapots in search of Darvons and Seconals she'd hidden
there. She'd been hoarding tranquilizers and painkillers for
three years, Essy told Maddie recently, afraid her doctor would
cut her off and leave her "immobilized" by pain. In fact, Essy
added, Bert was seeing several doctors at once who were all
prescribing medicine. She took enough painkillers to sedate a
horse.

"I would like to come," Bert said noncommittally. "I used to love to go, you know. But people ask the same questions over and over and then forget what you say."

To please her, Maddie sat down at the piano and played a new piece—a three-part invention by Bach.

"I don't care for Bach anymore," Bert confessed when she finished. "I used to. But I can't concentrate. I can't follow it."

So Maddie played a Chopin prelude. Gradually soothed by this, Bert began to hum along in her tuneless, wide vibrato, waving a listless, black-slippered foot to the rhythm. "You should hear Katy play this," Maddie said brightly. "She can play half my music already."

Going on nine, Katy was a musical prodigy. Bert nodded, though Maddie knew she worried about her sister's irritable temper and persistent stomachaches and nosebleeds. Katy had both a frankness and a secretiveness about her that disconcerted Bert. Her little eyes could take you in and cast you out in one glance.

"I have a surprise for you," Maddie said, swinging off the bench.

"For *me?*" Bert brightened, putting her hand to her breast.

"I've written a sonnet. About autumn—Halloween."

"Oh!" Bert exclaimed. "*You have?* Maddie, how wonderful!" She began to root and search for her glasses in the piled-up stacks of books and papers on the table beside her. "Isn't this *awful?*" she laughed as one unstable column swayed and toppled notebooks all over the floor. Letting them lie, she retrieved her glasses, unfolded them, and leaned back expectantly, falling into the soft little purring sound of concentration she often made. "Let's set the mood," she said. "Light the fire."

It was April, almost balmy outside, but Maddie lit the gas radiants anyway. She took out her sonnet, unfolded it nervously, and handed it to Bert, who bent over it eagerly, making little dipping and nodding motions with her head as she read

it. To pass the time, Maddie looked into the teapots lined up
on the windowsills. She counted nineteen pills in three different
colors.

"It's so well done," Bert said at last with conviction and a
smile. "Come sit beside me." She patted the couch.

Maddie sat down, clutching a dark-red velvet pillow.

Bert read the poem again, this time aloud and with beautiful expression, exactly as Maddie would have wanted it read.
But instead of enjoying it, all Maddie heard was everything
that was wrong with it. It was too gloomy, too melodramatic,
some of it as sing-songy as the poems in her mother's issues
of *Good Housekeeping*.

Bert got up awkwardly on her stiff legs and went to the
game cupboard to get a music case stuffed with sheets of typing
paper. "Isn't it wonderful that we should *share* this now?" she
said, hobbled back, and sat down heavily, her right knee hardly
bending at all. She squeezed Maddie's hand affectionately.
"Now I have something I want to show *you*. Howdy wants me
to send it out somewhere, but I'm afraid. Oh, Maddie, it's been
such a long time since I *tried*."

She took a creased, dog-eared, and obviously much worked-
over page from the disorganized mess. "Some people think
sonnets are old-fashioned," she said, "but I disagree. The poet
can muster forces—conspire with the limitations. Do you see?"

She held her glasses up to her eyes, paused, and waited
for the moment to begin. "It's called 'To a Very Little Girl—
When She Was Seven.' Actually I began it some time ago, but
because . . ." She paused again, gave up the explanation, and
read:

> *You will be vulnerable. Your little hand*
> *Has pleading in its touch. Your eyes are fed*
> *By the invisibles; you wear the brand*

Of those to whom intangibles are bread.
Your feet are set to music, they shall dance
To lovely overtones that few can hear;
Your days are prisms, beamed by Beauty's glance,
(You have not learned she wears a sword, my dear).
For you, no griefs ephemeral,—wounds must flow
From greater depths for one in Beauty's thrall,
But, like a vanquished planet, you shall know
The bosom of Elysium ere you fall.
I pray that you need never count the cost
Of a remembered heaven that is lost.

Bert leaned back and sighed deeply. "It's to you, Maddie. My dear Maddie."

Maddie didn't know what to say. She felt honored and amazed. There were tears in Bert's eyes.

"Do you understand it?" Bert asked, searching her face.

"Yes—I think." She certainly understood the last two lines. They were about Deane and the cost of losing him. Bert was still counting it. So was everybody. But what did the sword mean? She wasn't sure of that at all. Did Bert mean it as a criticism of her?

"You take a copy of it home," Bert said with a faint trace of disappointment in her eyes. "When you've had some time with it, we'll talk about it together."

Maddie felt embarrassed by her tongue-tied response—and her ignorance. She had no idea what the bosom of Elysium was. "I should know what it all means," she apologized.

"Ah, well, 'sometimes it's the things we know that we have to learn,' as Deane used to say." Bert cast her eyes down in an effort to control upwelling tears, a gesture Maddie had seen a hundred times over the past few years.

To save Bert the trouble of getting up again, Maddie returned the case of papers to the game cupboard and scanned the top row of books and notebooks. "Were some of these Deane's?" she asked.

"All I have that isn't in your attic."

The Brothers Karamazov. How Green Was My Valley. Wind, Sand, and Stars. Paradise Lost. The Little Prince. More typical of a Ph.D. in literature than in herpetology, she thought. He'd read everything. She chose a notebook at random and read a few paragraphs on the first page in Deane's writing, scattered notes on what the evolution of *Homo sapiens* owed to the Ice Age. There were quotations in all the margins, but she couldn't make many of them out. "Could I borrow this?" she asked, wanting to pore over it in private.

Bert hesitated. "No, Maddie," she said at last. "I never let any of those things out of the house. If Deane came back, I'd want him to find them just as they are."

Surprised at not being trusted to take it, Maddie put the notebook back. She sighed and suddenly felt weak and weighted down, a feeling she'd had many times over the past few years but had learned to ignore until it went away. But it was strong this time, as it used to be three or four years ago. Bert had such a strong claim on Deane's memory, just as Essy and her father and Grandaddy had. But she, barely ten years old when he disappeared, had never been anything to him but a child. If he ever did come back, he probably wouldn't even recognize her.

"May I read a few more poems to you—not by me?" Bert asked, half-shyly, not wanting to force her.

"Okay," Maddie said, sinking down into the soft, over-warm pillows again. She leaned back, her face away from Bert, and listened to Frost's "Desert Places," Emerson's "Days," and the first of Elizabeth Browning's *Sonnets From the Portuguese*, all read in Bert's soft, lyrical inflection. She relaxed a

little, and the feeling of heaviness passed away. Her grandmother's voice could always reach her heart somehow.
Maddie was especially moved by the last lines of the Browning poem:

> ... how a mystic Shape did move
> Behind me, and drew me backward by the hair;
> And a voice said in mastery while I strove,—
> "Guess now who holds thee?"—"Death!" I said. But
>   there,
> The silver answer rang,—"Not Death, but Love."

She thought again of her own poem, its rhythmic mo-
notony and high melodrama. Now Grandaddy came into the
room looking for a section of newspaper, and Bert told him
all about it and read it aloud again.

When she finished, he raised his hands up high and applauded for Maddie. "How do you two *do* that?" he asked, as
if it were totally beyond him.

But when Bert left the room to search for a misplaced
volume of poetry by Edna St. Vincent Millay, Grandaddy read
it again silently, then asked Maddie if she remembered the
name of the Tragic Muse of Greek mythology. (He had taught
her the names of all the Muses last year.)

"Melpomene?" she said.

"Good. She's my favorite. But you know, sometimes even
the tragic poets ought to let Melpomene slip on a banana peel
every now and then. You must never lose your sense of the
ridiculous, Maddie. Listen for the sneezes at the opera. Be
grateful for the—"

"Howdy, what are you telling her?" Bert said, hobbling
back with the book in her hand.

He smiled at her and winked at Maddie. "Only that, in

spite of all the conflicts she feels, she should thank God she's
as northeast of the clock as you are. That it's a gift."

Maddie laughed, understanding at once. And Bert nodded
in agreement.

But Maddie knew Bert most loved the dark poems that
went all the way to the precipice of hopelessness, turning away
only at the last possible moment with an affirmation. Ever since
Deane disappeared, it seemed that Grandaddy's goal with Maddie was to teach her how to have second thoughts: how to
stop and think again when the world looked too bleak or the
human condition too sad. But Bert had third thoughts, too,
which Maddie detected in a look behind her smiles, or in her
sagging posture after a poem was read when she thought no
one was looking at her.

Bert had never quite recovered from the trips to California
and Mexico four years ago when she and Grandaddy had gone
to search for Deane's pilot's missing relatives. Both trips had
been failures, thousands of miles for nothing. In Corona Del
Mar, Gabriel Waite's sister had nervously admitted them to a
filthy flat and, huddled under a torn shawl, claimed to know
nothing. In Mexico City, Waite's mother had refused to see
them at all. Though Grandaddy had brought Bert a whole new
wardrobe in California in an effort to raise her spirits, once
she got home she wore the same old rusty dresses and hats,
and also kept her shades drawn and doors locked to ward off
calls from the neighbors. Lately, she and Grandaddy had been
quarreling about it. Essy said sometimes he was at wit's end
with her and would lose his temper and hole up upstairs in
the map room for days. There, under an ever-growing pile of
maps and *National Geographics*, he plotted alternative routes to
the Black Hills. But then Bert would begin to sigh and cry
around the house, and after a while, he'd give in, take her in
his arms, and for the next week so overwhelm her with flatteries
and endearments that Essy said they both made her sick.

Essy was losing patience with Bert's endless grieving over

Deane, which she still displayed before everyone but Maddie and Katy. Essy let no one forget one afternoon in November two years ago when she'd dropped in on Bert for an unexpected visit, and to her horror, had found her on the living-room floor crouched on all fours, "carrying on like a wild animal." Her hair had been disheveled, her bathrobe torn open, and her face bathed in sweat. Appalled at being discovered in that condition, Bert had claimed she was praying and that Essy had no right to barge in on her unannounced. Essy had replied that God was not won over by raised fists and screamed curses; if Bert couldn't pray "Thy will be done," she shouldn't pray at all.

But Maddie had more sympathy. She could picture Bert swaying on the floor, torn between pain and hope, misery and love. In matters of hope and love, Bert had almost too much stamina. But, unlike Essy, Maddie admired it. She could understand the grief that erupted again and again through her uneasy composure. If she were Deane's mother, she would probably do the same thing. He had been more than just a son. His death had amounted to the bankruptcy of the family's greatest investment—the hyphen between two times—the day-world of the hare and the night-world of the fox. And she knew Deane would approve of her daily visits with Bert now, as she knew Grandaddy approved—sharing her music and poems to help Bert keep her balance on the hyphen since she couldn't move off it.

"Did you write many poems when Dad and Deane were growing up?" Maddie asked Bert now as Grandaddy took his newspaper out on the porch. She knew Bert loved to talk about the days of the Great Depression.

She smiled faintly. "There wasn't time, Maddie. Oh, but the most voluptuous vases could be made out of clay in those days! I wrote only for ad contests and jingles for Campbell's soup to help pay the mortgage. But I saved the house, you know."

Maddie wasn't sure what she meant by the vases.

"I was good at what was needed most," she added, "salvaging value out of things that had no value. Nothing was lost. Not the smallest thing."

The look on her face showed second and third thoughts: she had saved everything but the most valuable thing.

"I've told you before," she continued, "that Grandaddy sold shoe polish. We always managed to find enough loose ends and pieces. And somehow, they all fit together, like taking two or three pieces out of each of those puzzles in the cupboard and finding they fit together into something impossibly lovely . . ."

Her voice trailed off, and Maddie could hear her thinking on the other side of her words—that now, nothing fit together as it should, and never would. Deane, who had been the best of them, the opposable thumb of the family's hand, was lost. Melpomene walked confidently, not a banana peel in sight.

Yet how hard Bert was trying to keep going, Maddie thought admiringly as she said good-bye and walked down the back steps along the garden walk, resolved to help her anew, to excel in school and become a new, if smaller, opposable thumb.

But as she turned to wave good-bye to Bert standing at the back door, she could tell by the way Bert lowered her head and turned inside that she was already thinking of something, someone, else.

Bert didn't come to the Palm Sunday service.

"Will you be Christ's disciple all your life long?" Reverend Rutke asked the communicants' class as they lined up at the chancel.

"Yes," they all said in a mumble.

"Yes," she said softly, and then repeated, "Yes."

She caught a glimpse of Essy's beaming smile behind her and smiled back. But she was disappointed Bert hadn't come.

It was her grandmother's idea of the church she was joining, not her aunt's. Bert had begged off the occasion by saying she was too embarrassed to walk down the aisle with her legs so crooked. But Essy said she knew the real reason—that Bert felt the gazes of her fellow-worshipers like scourges on her back rather than looks of love, and was sure they all gossiped about her. "Bertha is losing her faith," was Essy's final judgment. But Maddie knew better. She had learned more about God from Bert than anyone else, except maybe Reverend Rutke. When Bert had read to her from Isaiah—"I create the light, and I create darkness; I make peace, and create evil; I am the Lord, there is no other"—she and Maddie had debated it excitedly for days. What did it mean? they wondered. Given God's dual nature, was there no use for a Devil? Maddie had begun to understand what Reverend Rutke meant when in one of his sermons, he quoted Dietrich Bonhoeffer, the great theologian who was hanged by the Nazis: "The God who is with us is the God who forsakes us." It struck a note of divine common sense in her—though not a terribly comforting one.

Maddie wasn't surprised that Bert didn't come to the Tenebrae service on Good Friday either. Essy coaxed her, saying she might take comfort from witnessing the drama of God's offering up his own Son on the cross. But Bert firmly said no. She couldn't possibly.

Maddie went to church early Good Friday evening so she could be alone to watch the last rays of light fade from the windows. The blazing reds, blues, and purples deepened slowly at first, growing richer and more concentrated every minute, then turned in a matter of moments to a stark opaque black. As always for this service, the chancel was stripped of its ornaments, and everything was draped in black. Reverend Rutke had replaced the gold Celtic cross with a seven-foot wooden one he had made out of a dying sycamore behind the church. At her last communicants' class meeting, Maddie had given him the crown of thorns she'd woven to hang at the center of the cross—and there it was now, looking sinister and real, with black rags draped behind it. Reverend Rutke, also in black, stood at the lectern checking the microphone. This minister was on terms with the dual God of Isaiah, she was sure. Maybe that's what made Essy so suspicious of him. For him, as for Bert, Good Friday was unspeakably beautiful and true; but Easter Sunday was a worse ordeal because it was only beautiful, not exactly, simply true. Or at least not true in a way most people could celebrate.

The people began to arrive—not many. The choirs rehearsed in the loft. At the piano, Maddie followed the junior choir director, sensitive to the quick changes he made in tempo and interpretation. It delighted her to anticipate his feeling about the music even before he felt it. Two acolytes lit the candles. She knew them—two seventh-grade boys who cared no more about the symbolism of candles than about the vitamins in the green beans they'd been forced to eat for supper. Yet she liked seeing them sober-faced and in their robes like this, looking more salvageable than they really were.

She saw her parents and Essy and Katy come in the side door. Katy spotted her, stuck her fingers in her ears, and made a face. She didn't want any part of coming to church tonight; one morning a week was more than enough for her. But Maddie had made her mother promise to bring her anyway. She wanted Katy to experience the Tenebrae service; she was sure she was now old enough to appreciate its spell.

She motioned Katy to come sit with her in the junior choir stall. Reluctantly, eyeing the looming cross and stripped chancel dubiously, she came.

"No fooling around," Maddie said. "No barnyard imitations."

Katy smiled noncommittally. Last Christmas Eve, she had audibly mooed as the Wise Men took their places beside the

cardboard cattle in the pageant—anything to nudge her mystic
sister out of her staring religious trance. Easter Sunday had
been even worse. In the middle of the prayer, Katy had excused
herself to go to the ladies' room. In a few minutes, Maddie
heard her doing true-to-life harp seal imitations, which she
usually reserved for the bathtub, from one of the toilet stalls.
Maddie got the joke right away: Easter seals. But Katy didn't
know when to quit. She kept it up all through the prayer.
Though her mother was furious, Maddie couldn't stop laughing
for the whole rest of the service. Even Reverend Rutke had
laughed.

"This is serious," Maddie said now, wanting to impress
Katy with the exceptional power of the Tenebrae.

Begrudgingly, Katy gave in to her earnestness. In fact, her
eyes grew wide as the service began with a silent choir proces-
sional, the only one of the year: no organ prelude, no introit,
no voices at all, just the hollow, chilling sound of seventy feet
walking on stone in unison. Reverend Rutke gave a prayer about
darkness and desertion. "One of you shall betray me," he said,
and the congregation responded by saying, "Is it I, Lord? Is it
I?" There was a hymn, then a brief sermon on a poem called
"Christmas Mourning," which, thanks to Bert, Maddie knew
already. Rejoice at Calvary, the poet said. Mourn at Bethlehem.
Yes, she assented. Yes.

After the Offering was taken and the Doxology sung, all
the big electric lanterns in the church were extinguished, and
the whole sanctuary was plunged into darkness except for two
seven-tiered candelabra on either side of the cross and a dim
amber light behind the crown of thorns. Reverend Rutke, barely
visible in his black robe, ascended the pulpit and began to read
the passages of scripture that contained the Seven Last Words
of Christ spoken from the cross—*Father, forgive them, for they
know not what they do. My God, My God, why hast thou forsaken
me?*—and so on, each followed by a choral response from the

choir in the darkened loft. With each of the responses, two
candles were extinguished by the acolytes, who in the shadows,
Maddie noted with satisfaction, were now faceless, anonymous,
and perfectly synchronized. The putting out of the candles
two by two symbolized the falling away of the disciples, Reverend Rutke said to the silent congregation—"and of ourselves."

With each word and response, the vaulted ceiling receded
higher and higher into the blackness. "This is the descent into
Hell," Maddie whispered to Katy, who was very quiet now,
not making a move. "Imagine what Jesus felt. He was deserted
by everyone. Even by God for a little while."

"Not by his mother," Katy said, recalling this bare thread
of knowledge from Sunday school.

Maddie sighed, scarcely breathing. Then as if taking a
cue from Katy, the soprano stood up from the choir and sang
a solo response about Jesus's last words to his mother when
He gave her away to the disciple John's keeping: *"Woman, behold
thy son . . ."* The song was called "At the Cry of the First Bird,"
an exquisite lullaby sung by Mary to her dying son as she
recalled what His cheek had felt like as an infant—as soft as
a swan's. Listening with an almost anticipatory greed, Maddie
felt the floor give way under her everyday way of looking at
things. This was what she had come for.

She felt Katy's hand rest on her arm—soft, moist. "What
is this?" she whispered to Maddie as the Word *I thirst* led into
a solemn Bach chorale, like deepest twilight sinking into night.
Katy was feeling it, Maddie sensed. She had known she would.
More and more she and Katy felt things identically.

"Answer me!" Katy demanded. "What are they singing
now? I can't understand the words."

"They're printed in the bulletin," Maddie said, resisting
talking. "Read them for yourself."

"How can I read in the dark?"

The choir was singing the second verse of the chorale:

"What language shall I borrow . . . ?" and Maddie sat in an island of emotion, hypersensitive to sound and sight. Everything good was dying. Everything true was losing its way, falling into the dark.

How could the woman in the pew behind her be coughing, shuffling her bulletin, unwrapping a stupid piece of candy?

"O Lamb of God that taketh away the sins of the world," Reverend Rutke read from a million miles away, "have mercy upon us."

"How does the organist play without any light?" Katy whispered.

Maddie said nothing. Then, at Katy's prodding, she said, "This is the last moment of crucifixion. It's every sad, hopeless thing in the world. Everybody's admitting it. Even Jesus."

Very softly the choir began to sing the "Lacrymosa" from Mozart's *Requiem*. The exquisite rise and fall of it, like human sighing, subdued even Katy, who listened with still, unblinking eyes.

The last two candles went out. The smoke from the wicks spiraled up into the darkness out of range of the weak light behind the crown of thorns. "*Kyrie eleison*," the choir chanted without accompaniment, like the ghostly prayer of a people that had died ten thousand years ago: "Lord have mercy upon us. Christ have mercy upon us. Lord have mercy upon us."

Tears blurred Maddie's eyes. For some things there was no mercy. That's what the service was about.

"I don't feel good," Katy said, shifting position, staring at her shoes.

"Sh," Maddie commanded.

Now the choir sang to the general broken heart, a Negro spiritual, "Were You There When They Crucified My Lord?" The line of it rose and fell, rose and fell, and Maddie stared at the cross.

"Is he finally dead?" Katy said.

She nodded.

"Why? From just hanging there?"

Maddie said nothing, could say nothing.

"Poor Jesus," Katy said.

Yes, Maddie agreed.

The service ended. Reverend Rutke gave the Benediction and asked the people to leave the church in silence just as Christians used to leave the Tenebrae a thousand years ago. Maddie was glad there were no greetings, none of the usual friendly exchanges of Christian small talk. She scanned the faces of the people who filed past her to see how moved they had been by the service. Many of them, to her surprise, just looked blank. A few were crying. One woman couldn't wait to get outside to tell another woman the price per pound of Easter hams at the A & P.

Her head and heart ached. While Katy went to the bathroom, she hung around the chancel—touched the wooden cross, pressed a thorn into her finger. What must it feel like to have a whole crown of them pressed down on your head?

Outside, walking home with Katy behind their parents, she thought how completely at home she had felt in the service. She smiled with satisfaction at Katy's face, deep in thought, concentrated into what her father called her "storm cloud" look. In that moment, Maddie realized how intensely dear Katy had become to her over the past year. There was a bond of like natures between them. They were different from each other, yet more different from everybody else than from each other. The gap between their ages hardly mattered at all. She wanted to reach out and hug her, but she knew Katy would push her off with an embarrassed "Quit it!" No one could get a willing hug out of her.

As they rounded the first corner, Katy said irritably, "I have to go to the bathroom again. I'm sick, Maddie."

"Throwing up or diarrhea?"

"And my nose is bleeding!" she cried, looking down at her spotted blouse, and started to run.

Maddie explained the situation to her mother, took her keys, and ran ahead to hold the front door open for Katy. This was the third time this month she'd gotten suddenly sick for no reason.

Red in the face, her nose dripping, Katy ran past her into the bathroom, slammed and locked the door. Maddie stood outside and listened. Katy was crying and throwing up at the same time.

"You okay?" Maddie called through the door.

"No!"

"Can I come in?"

"No!"

Maddie waited. "How's your nose?"

No answer.

Maddie felt sorry for her, and responsible. Maybe she shouldn't have made her come to the service after all, knowing how Katy could get emotionally affected by things. Just going on nine years old, she wasn't as old as she acted.

Five minutes later Maddie heard the toilet flush, followed by silence, then two sudden loud thumps against the bathroom door that made her jump. "What are you doing?" she yelled through the door. "What's going on?"

"My feet," she yelled back. "I hate my feet! I'm never going to sit with those stupid choir kids again in my whole life. Everybody looked at my barges."

"What are you talking about?" Maddie said. "Open the door."

There were two more thuds, louder than before. For the second time, Katy had hurled her corrective oxfords for her flat, pigeon-toed feet against the door. She'd been wearing "barges" since she first learned to walk, but they didn't seem to do any good.

"Everyone was sitting there with pretty church shoes on," Katy yelled, pulling the door open with a yank. "My shoes are ugly! My feet are ugly. Something is crazy with me, and it's getting worse and worse." She stopped, lowered her head and her voice. "I *heard* it in the church."

Maddie laughed, pulled her out, and patted her head. "Oh, everyone knows you're—"

"Our whole family is crazy!" she said, wrenching away. "Do you know anybody like us?" She picked up her shoes and threw them against the wall, picked them up, and threw them again. Then she slammed the palms of her hands against the wall, so hard the tips of her fingers started to turn blue.

"Stop it!" Maddie ordered, pulling her down and sitting on top of her. Katy's body felt overheated to her, as if she had a fever. "It was just a church service. You're acting like a baby." But Katy pulled away and started pounding the floor. Maddie was afraid her nose would bleed again.

Suddenly her mother appeared. She saw what Katy was doing, moved close over her head, and clapped her hands loudly behind her ears. The sound surprised her out of her tantrum long enough to break its momentum. Panting, Katy looked up at her mother resentfully, collapsed, and lay on her back.

"It's her barges," Maddie explained, at a loss to understand her sister, how she'd hoard her feelings for weeks at a time, then suddenly splash them out all over the place.

Her mother picked up the scuffed shoes. She had just shined them that afternoon. They'd cost sixty-five dollars.

Katy whimpered, a watchful ball in the corner now.

"Couldn't she have a pair of patent leathers to wear to church?" Maddie asked on her behalf.

"The orthopedist said she should wear these all the time," her mother said. "I can't afford another pair."

"But who cares about just a few hours a week?" Maddie pleaded.

Katy stared at her with bright feverish eyes. Maddie had *better* plead her case, those eyes were saying, or she'd never set foot inside the church again.

Her mother sighed and said she would think about it.

Next Sunday—Easter—Katy wore shiny black patent-leather shoes to church. Maddie had enlisted Bert as an ally to convince her mother the shoes could be handed down to Esther in a few years. Bert even offered to pay for them if they were too expensive, since "all little girls liked to look pretty sometimes"—though she wasn't absolutely sure about Katy.

Now Maddie watched her sister stick her feet out from the pew and bounce them up and down to the organist's opening bars of "Jesus Christ Is Risen Today." Katy smiled vainly, responding to the pulse of the triumphant hymn as though it had been written just for her and this occasion. Maddie smiled back. Everything had turned out all right, she guessed. Last night, after getting the shoes, Katy had said she really liked the Tenebrae service—that it was scary, but wonderful, like Halloween.

But now, as Maddie breathed the warm, lily-scented air of the crowded sanctuary—fewer than a fourth this many people had been there Good Friday—and counted the gold-wrapped flowerpots arranged in the shape of a cross on the chancel ("like the overpriced flowers in the funeral home," she had overheard Bert comment to Essy when she declined to come to even this service), she admitted that she didn't feel nearly as triumphant as she was supposed to feel as a new member of the church. In fact, crammed into this creaking pew, she felt like one of the ninety-nine sheep lined up in the stained-glass window. It wasn't that she merely sympathized with the Tenebrae service with its ceremony of darkness. She actually preferred it. There was something sickeningly sweet about these Easter proclamations, a forced euphoria, everyone trying too hard. Even Reverend Rutke seemed at a loss for exactly what to say. People in fancy clothes and flowered hats were participating in the celebration of a victory they hadn't witnessed. They hadn't come to the Tenebrae; they hadn't sat in Gethsemane for one hour. So they had no understanding of it, she judged irritably, and scarcely any right to it. They probably put chocolate marshmallow crosses in their kids' Easter baskets.

By the time she finished singing the last alleluia, Maddie was blinking back tears. Today she could understand why Bert didn't come to church anymore. "The God of the Lamb is the God of the Tiger," she had told Maddie many times; Christ was both risen and not risen. It was the tension of these contrary beliefs that distinguished Bert's strangely evolved theology, which now, whether by nature or by choice, Maddie began to think was probably right. Unlike Essy, who affirmed Jesus's resurrection as the fact upon which all faith depended, Bert believed it and didn't believe it at the same time. Since Deane's death, she hardly even had a preference. She had lectured Maddie on paradox, how opposites must both be true to be true at all. There was hope; there was no hope. Deane would come back; he would never come back. Faith; doubt. Yes; no.

Yet unlike Deane, who had left the church, Bert was still powerfully attracted to it. Like many members, she was moved by its extravagant claims of hope in a tragic world; but like almost no one else, she still believed in the Puritan-Calvinist idea of an inscrutable, terrifying divinity whose blessing was hardly any easier to bear than his curse, except perhaps at the very last outcome. She was cut off from the majority of the worshipers in this, Maddie knew; the rest believed in something simpler and gentler and would probably have thrown her out as a cracked holdover from Jonathan Edwards's day—a heretic—if they knew.

But they are God's heresies, Maddie thought today with conviction. They are God's.

As Reverend Rutke raised his hands for the Benediction,

her eyes fell on the picture of the resurrected Jesus on the front cover of the bulletin in her hands—benign, robed in white, his hands outstretched—with holes in them.

As the months went by, things were going on inside Maddie she couldn't even tell Bert. They were too embarrassing, she thought, too silly—and yet absurdly irresistible. She was becoming obsessed with Halloween. Maybe it was its pagan independence from church she liked, despite its association with supernatural power. Whatever the reason, she began to flirt with gothic romances of vampires and demon lovers, and to read every good ghost story she could find. Disgusted with the immature boys in her freshman high school English class, she fell in love with Milton's Satan in *Paradise Lost*, the once glorious angel with a proud, brooding intelligence second only to God's who embraced evil as an unavoidable second choice. Her Uncle Deane had loved both John Milton and Halloween. Bert had told her how he and her father used to save up all their money every October and buy up a truckload of pumpkins and cornshocks to decorate the whole backyard like a haunted cornfield; on Halloween night they'd sit among the lights of the jack-o'-lanterns until midnight, telling ghost stories, summoning the spirits of fallen angels, feeling the mood.

The older she got, the more she felt it too, long before Halloween arrived. She told Katy in July that she was beginning to hate spring and summer. By mid-August, she was already longing for fall with a kind of lust, waiting for the hot muggy days to come to an end so she could wake up and feel alive again. By early September, when the nights had turned cool and crisp, she felt so increased in physical energy, she broke into crazy fits of it and ran up and down the stairs thirty or forty times a day to drain it off. Her mother looked at her sometimes as though she'd lost her mind. Maddie tried to explain how, at Easter, the smell of spring had made her feel

half-sick—season of mud and swarms of new bugs, and little
green shoots sticking up out of the ground like the fingernails
of monsters poking up out of last year's graves.

How could Maddie explain how she felt in October when
she walked through the woods in Frick Park behind her house?
As she kicked at the autumn leaves—brilliant reds, purples,
golds—she felt entirely and wonderfully in her right mind.
"How is it there should be / So much of life in truly valiant
dying?" Bert had written in a poem about autumn recently. Last
Sunday, Maddie had even heard the seductive spirit of it in
the chants and anthems at church: dissonant chords of out-
castness, lamentations of sorrow, the sighs and whispers rising
up out of mist-harboring cornfields, or muffled cries from the
chimneys of abandoned houses in Massachusetts, where secret
sins festered in the closets and cupboards, and distraught ghosts
of the un-elect who had thought good works could save them
glided down the hallways. This year she had picked up the
scent in the air as early as August 20. "Here it is!" she had
yelled to Katy as they ran through the woods looking for
pockets of the fall smell. "And over here!"

Now, at age fourteen, with Halloween less than a month
away, she felt a peculiar sense of foreboding that something
great and terrible was about to happen to her. ("You're a
hundred miles northeast," Grandaddy had laughed when he
caught her daydreaming in the middle of the map game again
last week, "just like your grandmother.") Many of the people
in her neighborhood and on television were talking about a
national sense of impending atomic war. Some of her friends'
parents were even building bomb shelters. The principal at
school had decided to conduct monthly air-raid drills. But this
had nothing to do with her strange feeling. She wasn't bothered
by fear of any political evil. After all her reading in the occult,
a more subtle and seductive kind of evil preoccupied her. "The
Devil is a gentleman," Bert had quoted to her from *King Lear* a

few months ago. He could drop in on people without so much as a walking stick in his hand, let alone an atomic bomb, and wreak utter havoc.

More and more she liked to be alone to think about it, without even Katy. She began to paint, trying to express in color what she couldn't—or didn't want to—express in words. She wasn't good at the oils Bert had bought her, but got gradually better with practice. Then, for a surprise, her mother said she could have one of the closed-up rooms in the attic for a "studio" if she wanted it, away from Katy and Esther. She could spread out her oils and canvases without messing up her bedroom downstairs and have all the privacy she wanted.

Maddie was overjoyed. She set up an easel in the studio and began to paint furiously—stormy seascapes with lots of threatening clouds at first, because they were easy to draw and required a lot of black—then on to dead and dying trees, winter elms and locusts with bare, snaky branches twisting up into pale moonlight. Each tree was a maze of offshoots, like a human nervous system. In one of them, she painted a pair of tiny shining eyes peering out of the knothole in the center. She told Katy, who kept coming up to the studio despite her rule against it, that it was a self-portrait.

"What do you mean 'self-portrait'?" asked Katy, who was not a fan of her artwork but always eager to offer comments. "How can you be a tree?"

"No," Maddie said impatiently. "I'm the little animal *in* the tree and—"

"Having babies in there?" Katy laughed, having just discovered the way babies were made and finding it hilarious.

"No," Maddie said. "I'm hiding."

"Why are you hiding?"

She took a long breath. "Because I have to. Because I'm different." She hesitated. "And so are you."

She took some pleasure in Katy's narrowed brow and pretense of puzzlement.

"I don't hide," Katy said at last. "No matter what, I wouldn't do that. You're a chicken in that tree. That's what you ought to call it—'Chicken Eyes.' "

"Oh?" Maddie said. "I'm a chicken, and you're not?"

She nodded.

"Then how come you won't play any pieces on the piano for anyone but yourself? How many times do you think you can get away with throwing up before recitals so you don't have to perform before an audience like everyone else?"

Katy frowned as though the question were irrelevant. "I can't help throwing up."

Giving up on explaining the painting, Maddie picked up a flashlight and led Katy to the algae-clogged aquarium she had just carried up from her bedroom. It sat in the darkest corner of the studio, a slimy green cemetery of Atlantis ruins and sunken ships with a few live guppies. "Walk slowly," she said. "An inch at a time."

"Why?" Katy said suspiciously, approaching slowly.

"Look in there," Maddie ordered.

There, spiraling up an inch out of the sand like miniature swaying cobras, were nine or ten semitransparent red worms.

"Yuck!" Katy jumped back. "What *are* those?"

"I don't know. They just appeared a week ago after I bought the seaweed. There must have been eggs in it or something. Watch."

She nudged Katy closer, then surprised the worms with a sudden beam from her flashlight. In an instant, all the worms withdrew into the sand and disappeared, perfectly hidden. "Isn't it amazing? They won't dance in the light. They dance only in the dark. I named the longest one Katy."

Katy stared, not entirely pleased with the comparison. "If Mother sees that, she'll make you dump it out in the backyard."

But as the worms cautiously reemerged in the shadow and Maddie returned to her painting, Katy studied them for a long time.

That same day, at the supper table, Maddie's mother announced that she was pregnant again. Happy to see Maddie's and Katy's joyful reaction—even Esther clapped her hands excitedly—her father expressed one worry: where would the new baby sleep? They were running out of room.

Maddie suggested—magnanimously—that she could take over all three rooms of the attic as her apartment. She could sleep and study and completely live up there. Esther could move in with Katy, and the new baby could have a room of her own. It was perfect.

Her mother said there wasn't any heat in the attic, and only one room had electricity. What about the wintertime? But Maddie said she didn't care. It would be romantic, she argued, like a poet's garret. She could burn candles, take hot-water bottles to bed with her at night, and pretend she was Emily Brontë.

Katy rolled her eyes in disgust. She didn't want to sleep with Esther, who not only snored but didn't like to stay awake to talk for hours as Maddie did. But the next Saturday, for a bribe of $5, Katy helped Maddie carry all her stuff up to the attic. They bought candles and remnants of black cloth at Woolworth's to decorate the apartment "in early Tenebrae," Maddie said, trying for a cross between a medieval Gothic castle and a New England haunted house. On orange-crate shelves she arranged her books and all the gifts Deane had given her. At a sporting goods' store she bought a papier-mâché raven to hang from the ceiling in honor of Edgar Allan Poe. Her mother gave her two warm comforters for her bed of piled-up mattresses, an oval mirror, and a potted philodendron. By the second week in October, it was all finished.

Seven times that month, Maddie's mother thanked her for

giving up her bedroom so unselfishly. Seven times Maddie graciously said "you're welcome." But Maddie had an ulterior motive for moving up to the attic which she hadn't told anyone. If something extraordinary was going to happen to her this season, she decided she had to make it happen. Now was the time to look into the forbidden cupboards in the back room. And so, late at night when everyone else was asleep, one by one Maddie began to cut open the seals of all of Deane's boxes and explore the contents.

At first it was frightening, like being the first person on an expedition to open the treasure chamber of an Egyptian pyramid with a curse on it. Part of her believed, like her father, that Deane's things shouldn't be disturbed for a thousand years. But once she opened the first box, it got easier. She found collections of small bird and bat skeletons, preserved lizards and snakes, notebooks, scrapbooks, beautiful boxes of copper and ivory, odd little objects of Eskimo art, the treasured walrus tusks, and many albums of black-and-white photographs. By candlelight, she pored over them night after night, looking for clues to the mystery nobody had been able to solve. She hoped by sheer luck she might be able to find some overlooked fact or detail that everyone else had missed—some letter or picture that would enable her to put two and two together and not get three or five or zero.

She stashed several of the photograph albums under her mattresses so she could look at them more closely before falling asleep each night. Sometimes when the wind blew hard outside and the falling sweet gum leaves stuck up against the window like splay-fingered little hands, she imagined Deane's ghost hovering over her shoulder looking at the photographs with her. There he was in the 1948 album, she noted with fascination, slouching like a brush-haired bum in baggy leather jacket and pants, his hand on the propeller of a fragile-looking plane: "On beach at Wales, facing Siberia," he'd written underneath. In another picture, he was down on his knees doing something with an ax to a dead bull walrus, taking out the tusks probably: "On Arctic beach between Wales and Shish-maref." In another he was striding between flimsy tents spread out over a vast expanse on the shore of a frigid ocean: "ATG rescue huts." What a harsh, alien world it seemed to her. Yet a part of her felt drawn to its austere beauty as perhaps he had felt drawn. The world she and Katy lived in was a miniature by comparison.

But the nightly work of discovering and sorting Deane's treasures had an unforeseen effect. She began to remember something that for over five years she had managed to forget: that Deane wasn't a legend. He wasn't a family romance. He was real. He had been theirs once. He'd been her uncle, Bert's son, her father's brother, Katy's uncle, Grandaddy's son, Essy's nephew. Now, by an accident of fate, he was reduced to so much bonepicked matter in a place that could never be searched thoroughly enough to find him. The wind moved. The snow moved. Places changed places. Her uncle and friend and teacher, her flesh and blood, Bert's beloved exceptional son, was scattered like so many sticks and stones across a frozen planetary vacant lot.

Poor Deane, she thought, sitting on her bed long past midnight, trying to imagine his remains further reduced. He might be as fine as gold dust by now. If she ever went to look for him herself—which she resolved to do someday—she would have to sift for him, to try to discern the recognizable grains of him in the whole shifting circumference of the Arctic Circle. But then, in a wave of drowsy weakness, she recalled a poem Bert had read to her once, about how the circumference of the poet's search for God expanded outward and outward, forever adding new unsearched area to the circle within. One could never search it all. The poem was by Emily Dickinson.

To please Grandaddy, in September Bert had sent a sample of her poems to a new professor of American literature at the

University of Pittsburgh for critical evaluation. Now, a week
before Halloween, Grandaddy interrupted Maddie's painting
in the attic with a phone call. Bert had gotten her poems back,
he told her, but the written response was not good. Bert was
beside herself with disappointment. Could Maddie come over
right away and cheer her up?

When Maddie arrived, Grandaddy met her at the front
door to explain that Professor Leeds had said Bert's poems,
though lovely "here and there," were, on the whole, "stilted,
archaic, and unpublishable." Reading between the lines, Bert
concluded that he meant politely but firmly to commend her
to her kitchen; housewives who hadn't published poetry before
the age of sixty were not likely to do so thereafter. There were,
he implied, no dormant geniuses. Bert was crushed, Grandaddy
whispered to Maddie, as weak in her own defense as a lace
curtain set up against a speeding freight train.

"Professor Leeds admires Whitman!" Bert burst in upon
them from the kitchen, savagely dabbing at a saucepan with a
ragged dishtowel. "Maddie, he holds Whitman up to me as an
example! As if extravagance were richness!"

She threw the pan on the couch and rooted among the
stacks of papers on the end table in search of her poems. At
last she found Professor Leeds's evaluation and handed it to
Maddie—rather brutally short, Maddie noted.

"Beauty must be *resident* in the *form* of an artwork," she
cried, wringing her hands, as if afraid Maddie wouldn't believe
her. "One must *extract* the art from the experience. Whitman
has no use for tradition—he is *outside* the temple! He levels
rather than reveals."

"Yes," Maddie said to encourage her. "I don't like Whitman."

"Whitman speaks and speaks and avers and avers," she
lectured hoarsely, *"but he is without comment!"*

"I like Whitman here and there," Grandaddy dared to say

cheerfully, sitting down on the couch beside the pan and curling his stocking feet under him. "I love the one about
compost—what's it called, Maddie?"

Maddie knew his strategy. If he agreed with everything
Bert said, she'd accuse him of humoring her and rage all the
more.

"Howdy, how can you *say* that?" she responded. "He is a
graceless onion among the exotic blossoms of the real poets!"

"He repeats endlessly," Maddie said, giving her the majority rule, as Grandaddy wished.

"Of course!" Bert pounced on the observation. "Maddie
understands how far a reader has to go in Whitman's art to
bring home so little! Neither rhyme nor reason." Perspiration
beaded her forehead as she searched for words, then at a new
wave of outrage, threw up her hands in dismay. "A professor
of American literature, indeed! I'll have you know I've read
some of Professor Leeds's *own* poetry—published at *his* expense,
mind you. Free verse, he calls it! Free *of* verse."

She sat down on the couch in a great collapse. Deep cuts
of grief lined her mouth as she stared at the floor—feeling
Leeds's criticisms all over again, Maddie knew—incapable of
dismissing them now or ever. Shaking her head, Bert said a
little more quietly, "The rhythm in art, Maddie, as in a great
passage from Shakespeare or the Bible, beats like heartbeats.
What is that passage from Micah, Howdy? Or is it Isaiah? 'It
grieves like the old ram's bell in the lonely wastes—truly an
objective arrow falling to the side of thee, to no hurt.' Now
that is poetry."

Bert was deeply hurt by the professor, Maddie could see.
She thought of the sonnet about wearing a sword Bert had
written to her when she was a little girl. Bert wore no sword.
She had no defense against Leeds's words. "What is that quote
from?" Bert asked with confused, brimming eyes. "The use of
art is that we should no longer be bewildered and oppressed.

I taught that to my children *years* ago. And now all the modern poets wallow in bewilderment! In crass illiterature! 'I am large, I contain multitudes,' Whitman said. That was the confession of the demoniac among the stones—'My name is Legion!' The split personality of our time, the frenetic, disordered soul! Christ sent the multitudes over the cliff with the swine, Maddie. *Over the cliff."*

"I don't think that's what Whitman meant when . . ." Grandaddy began, but seeing Bert's face, let the point go.

He had wanted this evaluation to encourage her, Maddie knew. The act of writing had worked on her own disordered soul like therapy.

At last, Bert calmed down a little. Maddie urged her to send her poems to another professor, someone older and more experienced.

"How?" Bert wept. "I am utterly demoralized, Maddie. Professor Leeds has weakened my *will."* She rested her head in her hands.

Feeling her pain helplessly, not knowing what else to say, suddenly all Maddie wanted was to get back to her own quiet attic and be alone with Deane's things. She told Bert her poems were beautiful no matter what anyone said. Then with an apologetic look at Grandaddy, she made an excuse to leave, and kissed her good-bye.

On the way home, she began to understand why Deane had gone into science instead of art, even though he had at least half the nature of an artist. A scientist looked out at the world; an artist looked in. The scientist was a witness to what he saw; but the artist was responsible for what was or wasn't seen. Deane could study a moth with a broken wing under a microscope and perhaps be criticized for failing to describe it accurately. But Bert could be criticized not only for a poor description, but also for being that broken thing itself under the glass. In real life, she walked on bowed, arthritic legs. But as a poet, she must walk in an unfailing straight line at an even, unremitting pace, like a cripple on a high wire performing miraculous feats for an audience of safely seated, able-bodied spectators. And yet, if she were able-bodied herself, she would have no act. She would be like all the other healthy spectators in the undifferentiated mass below—seeing, but not seen. An unthinkable alternative for Bert.

Most of Deane's notes were hopelessly technical, Maddie had to admit that night as she opened the last of his boxes. The scrapbooks, though captivating at first, had become familiar enough to her to put away again. She knew by now she wasn't going to come upon any overlooked clue to the mystery of his disappearance. She loved all the bird skeletons and frog specimens, but except for a few volumes of poetry, his books, most of them already dated, were all for specialists in herpetology. As she opened the last box, she could predict by its weight that it was probably just more books. It was.

But on the top was a surprise, a long silver dagger with an eagle and swastika on it, wrapped in a silk handkerchief. Here, among Deane's books, the unexpected sight of it sent chills up and down her spine. What was a weapon like this doing on top of Hobart Smith's *Handbook of Lizards of the United States and Canada?* Her history teacher in school had recently taught a unit on World War II and Nazi Germany, so she knew exactly what it signified, so sleek and cool in her hand, a castoff prop in a terrible drama that had closed forever, yet still able to inspire terror. She turned it over and over. Sinister as the symbolism of the swastika was, the dagger was beautiful as an object, like something a Prince of Darkness would carry. Why did Deane have it?

She put it under her pillow. But as she lay in bed, unable to sleep, thoughts translated into feelings and back into thoughts again. The dagger was affecting her like an evil work of art, suggesting a further work—something she might make or do in response to it.

By two o'clock in the morning, she had an idea. Since Katy mocked her paintings, why not try her hand at a piece of sculpture? Why not sculpt a man—life-size or bigger—of a Prince of Darkness to carry the Nazi dagger and stand in the corner of her attic bedroom for Halloween?

The next day, a Saturday, Maddie felt bursting with energy as she plundered kitchen drawers and cellar shelves for materials.

"What are you doing?" Katy asked suspiciously as Maddie hurried past her with armloads of rags, string, coat hangers, masking tape, and old curtain rods.

"Nothing. Just stay out of the studio."

Wanting privacy and knowing Katy wouldn't give it to her, she asked her mother to keep Katy busy in the backyard raking leaves or pulling up dead geraniums. Her mother promised. "What are you up to?" she asked.

"Nothing," Maddie said firmly.

She began the sculpture. She decided the Prince would wear her father's black yard-boots and her mother's old nurse's cape with the red lining, and be supported by a skeleton made of curtain rods. In less than half an hour, she had finished a rickety skeleton that looked as though it could support the weight of a six-foot stuffed man.

For the body, she filled the arms and legs of one of her father's old black tuxedos from his symphony days with rags and blankets, trying to sculpt a lean, muscular look in the legs. But it didn't go well. Once attached to the skeleton, it looked lumpy and fat, and wouldn't stand upright. She took it apart and restuffed it. But it turned out even worse. It leaned spinelessly to the left and the right, looking more pathetic than frightening. She tried sticking curtain rods down through the legs, then propped it up against the wall, nailing the tuxedo collar to the plaster. But it looked no better, just hung there like a scarecrow on a hook. Then the nail let go. Disgusted, she turned her attention to attaching the dagger and glove to the limp right arm.

Suddenly Katy burst into the studio to see what was going on. "I heard the pounding through the broken attic window," she said, grinning. "I sneaked right past Mom."

Furious, Maddie jumped in front of the sculpture and told her to get out, that she wasn't wanted. Katy pushed her out of the way.

But instead of mocking the project as Maddie expected, Katy admired it right away. "It's Jack the Ripper," she said delightedly, recalling a movie she'd seen about him on television. She walked slowly around it. "I like him, Mad! He changes the whole room."

"Thanks," Maddie said, sitting on the floor. "I've worked all morning, but he won't stand up. I'm giving up."

Katy propped up the dagger arm where it had flopped down unnaturally. "Quitter," she said. "If you don't want him, I'll take over."

She began to fool with the curtain rod down the back of the left leg and almost toppled him completely.

"Stop that!" Maddie ordered protectively and felt a new interest in her work. "You'll wreck him. I can fix him. But I need help."

Putting pride aside for a higher cause, Katy agreed. "What do you want me to do?"

At Maddie's bidding, she ran up and down steps until she was red in the face, brought wire and string, a rusty old hat stand, then a rubber Halloween mask, black cloth for a hood, black leather gloves, and more string.

In an hour and a half, Katy cheered as Maddie got the Prince to stand up as she wanted him to at last—almost seven feet tall, his head inclined downward at a menacing angle.

Katy stepped back. "The idea of the hat stand was great,

wasn't it?" she said, complimenting herself. "He's solid." "Now everything's good but the face. The mask looks stupid."

She was right. So with her oil paints, Maddie revised the mask so it wouldn't look so much like a Halloween ghoul from Woolworth's anymore, but more like a real man. She darkened the eyes and made the cheeks sunken until the face looked sick, malevolent, tormented by thought. She turned up the collar of the nurse's cape to add a hint of her favorite Halloween character, Count Dracula, the nobleman who was also a savage, brilliant but merciless, evil with anger at something in himself he could never change. For a final elegant touch, she stole a gold chain from her mother's jewelry box and put Deane's old spelling championship medal on it.

"Wow," Katy said, as they both stared at him quietly. "He's good, Mad. He's really good. The medal does it."

Yes, Maddie agreed with a pleasurable shudder, both repelled and attracted. He was better than Katy knew.

Then, against Maddie's orders, Katy ran downstairs to get her mother.

"No!" Maddie screamed after her. But her mother was already on the way up, Katy's hands covering her eyes. "Don't come up, Mom," Maddie pleaded warningly. "You won't like it."

Ignoring her sister, Katy positioned her mother in front of the Prince. "Now look!" she commanded, uncovering her eyes with a thrill of assistant artistic achievement.

"Maddie!" her mother gasped.

"It's Jack the Ripper," Katy said proudly. "We made it together."

"No, it *isn't* Jack the Ripper," Maddie said.

"Madeline," her mother said sternly, after a considerable pause, "when I let you have these rooms, I didn't intend for you to turn them into a house of horrors!"

"Look," Katy said, her enthusiasm undimmed, showing her the Nazi dagger. "Isn't this neat?"

"But why?" her mother said, looking genuinely upset. "What did you *do* this for?"

"For Halloween," Maddie said. She was at a loss to explain it any further.

"But Halloween is five days away. Are you planning to sleep with this thing looking down on you every night until then?"

Maddie hadn't thought about that. But she supposed it could be done.

"I want you to take it apart right now. Isn't that my best gold chain?"

While her mother expressed dismay at having her jewelry borrowed without permission, Katy ran to get her father.

Maddie sighed in despair. Katy couldn't keep anything a secret. She didn't even understand why it *should* be kept a secret. Her father would probably make her take it down immediately.

But to her surprise, he inspected the Prince with calm, objective detachment. He even complimented her engineering, given the raw materials, then pinched her and Katy's noses with casual approval, as though it were nothing, an innocent amusement. "That's the kind of project Deane and I would have done at your age," he smiled, not looking at their mother. Then he noticed the dagger that Maddie had tried to tuck under the cape before he came into the room. "Where on earth did *that* come from?" he said, lifting it up, touching the blade. "I brought that back from Germany in 1945. I thought I gave it . . ."

He looked at Maddie. She looked over at Katy with helpless anger. It wouldn't do any good to lie. She would make Katy pay for this later. "I opened Deane's boxes," she said, pointing toward the room with the cupboards. "I wanted to see what was in them."

Now it was Katy's turn to gasp. "You did? You mean that's where you got the knife, Mad? You really did? You told me it was from Dad's drawer!"

Her father went into the back room, looked into the cupboards briefly, came back, and said nothing.

"I put everything back just the way I found it except for the dagger," she assured him, not mentioning the albums under her bed. She was confused by his calm reaction.

He said simply, after a silence, "There's some wonderful stuff in them, isn't there, Maddie? They all ought to go to the museum."

These last words she had heard many times before, every time he came up to the attic, which wasn't often anymore. But the boxes never went to the museum. It was as though he couldn't bring himself to act on a decision about them, not so much out of sadness now as a habitual forgetting or denial of their existence once they were out of sight. It occurred to Maddie that it was the same with his old suitcase full of percussion instruments and drumsticks on the attic landing. He had quit the orchestra a year after Deane disappeared, put the suitcase on the landing and not opened it since. There was a thick layer of dust on it.

Not even much interested in the dagger, scarcely looking at it after first recognizing it, he told her and Katy not to play with it—that it was still sharp—and to come down for supper soon. He left them with their mother, who was angrier than ever.

After supper, despite her mother's orders, Maddie refused to take the Prince down. He had taken too much work, and her father didn't mind him. So her mother called Bert, sure she would take her side. To Maddie's alarm, although Bert was still depressed about Professor Leeds's evaluation of her poems and complaining about a flare-up of pain in her legs, she walked three blocks through the back alleys to Maddie's house in her worst rags, determined to climb the attic steps to see the "scarecrow," as her mother now called it.

"You should wait," Maddie said, trying to stall Bert as she stopped on the attic landing to pant. "It's not finished yet."

"Yes it is," Katy said. "Come on."

Driven by curiosity, Bert couldn't be put off. She entered the studio, held up her glasses, then leaned back on one bowed leg, as if balancing on a perch, to study the creature. She looked from the scarecrow to Maddie, back to the scarecrow, then once again to Maddie, as though Maddie had transcended all boundaries of logical expectation and committed an utterly inexplicable act. "What is this *for*, Madeleine?" she asked sternly at last.

"For Halloween," Maddie said casually, as if all the kids did it.

Bert saw the dagger, raised the arm cautiously to look at it, and frowned. "But *who*—is it?"

Maddie shrugged. "I don't know."

"She thinks it's Hitler or Dracula or somebody," Katy said. "But it's Jack the Ripper."

"No, it isn't!" Maddie said angrily, feeling her face turn red with embarrassment. This was the last thing she would have wanted Bert to see. "It's a Prince of Darkness. His name is—Legion."

Bert looked at her through narrowed eyes. "Oh." She moved closer to inspect the rubber-lidded eyes of the Prince. "My granddaughter!" she said, halfway between an exclamation and sigh. But was there the slightest trace of a smile around her mouth?

Maddie relaxed a little. She was glad to see Bert smile for any reason after the incident with her poems. And certainly Bert would appreciate the name Legion better than anyone else. She knew evil when she saw it—the courtly, glass-eyed gentleman who was as attractive as he was ruinous. But Maddie felt a shiver of wonder. Was she a little evil herself? Was this another self-portrait like the creature in the tree, only this one of a different side of her character, a side that flirted with violence and perversion as a solution to the conflicts inside her? But then, as Bert exchanged glances with her mother, Maddie wondered if, rather than recognizing and respecting Legion, Bert was really only secretly amused by him. Was she trying to hold back laughter?

Katy stood under Legion's outstretched right hand and thrust the dagger out swiftly by swinging the arm. "I saw a movie about a wax museum on television," she said excitedly, "and Jack the Ripper had an automatic arm that swished out when people went by—zap! like that. Let's make ours do that, Mad. I could hide under the cape and when—"

"No!" Maddie snapped, embarrassed again. "What's the matter with you?" It wasn't a mechanical fun-house monster she had meant to create, she wanted to explain to Bert. Didn't Katy understand that? The Prince was an aristocrat, a great fallen power in despair of all truth and justice who would rather reign in hell than serve in heaven. He should just stand there in perfect motionless silence.

Bert looked hard at Maddie. Then she turned to her mother. "Deane and Willy used to do things like this," she said. "It runs in the family."

Katy smiled at Maddie at the disclosure.

"Once Deane built a demon named Thom in the linen closet," Bert said, shifting her weight from the perch of one bowed leg to the other. "Rather I should say it was half a demon—an upper torso made out of papier-mâché and suspended on a wire. When I opened the door, the vacuum of air made the thing swing out at me. I shrieked, Ginny! The thing was so real, with curled horns and long fangs. Willy said Deane refused to put legs on it for fear it would take on a life of its own and slay its creator. Deane would never admit that, of course."

So Deane *had* been afraid of something once, Maddie noted.

The smile was still tugging at Bert's lips. After a few more stern looks, she left the attic to confer with Maddie's mother in the kitchen.

In half an hour, the verdict was to let Maddie keep her creation up until Halloween.

That night Maddie slept with the Prince standing at the foot of her bed, mostly to prove to Katy that he had no real power to scare her beyond the power she granted him, which, now that Bert had seen him, he hardly had. She couldn't decide if he looked truly menacing or just plain shabby. Her mother had taken back the gold chain, and without the accessory of Deane's spelling medal, the whole thing looked rag-taggle and unfinished. It was amazing how one little detail could make the whole creation work. Without it, it didn't work at all.

Or how one person could make a whole family work, she thought vaguely in her bed, aware of Deane's boxes, repacked and silent in the cupboards.

The next day, on an angry impulse, she tore the Prince apart as fast as she could.

"Are you crazy?" Katy said, trying to stop her.

Maddie said she had decided the sculpture wasn't any good. Maybe she'd build another one next Halloween, she told Katy.

"At least keep the mask," Katy said in a rare concession to the value of Maddie's artwork. "The mask is really scary, Mad. Let me have it."

"No. I'll keep it for next year."

Maddie propped the mask in the corner of her bedroom on the lampshade of an old floorlamp Deane had broken years ago. She pretended to Katy that she had forgotten all about it. And for that day, she had.

But getting ready for bed that night, she was intensely conscious of it. After her candles were blown out, she discovered the mask had a more suggestive power without the body; it actually worked better if the body were left to the imagination. Staring at it for a long time, she could see the outline of the nose and eye sockets quite clearly. Yes, she had done a great job on the eyes, she complimented herself—better than any pictures of real Nazis or demons she had seen in books. In the dark she couldn't tell it was only a painted mask; it looked like a real face emerging out of the juncture of the walls. Her imagination filled in details of the mouth, ears, hair, and neck until a real personality stood out in vivid relief, staring intently back at her.

Who was he really? she wondered, provoked by the combination of threat and suffering in the eyes. How did he get that way? If he were alive, what would he want or do?

Her thoughts wandered to her girlfriends in school. They didn't care at all about the Nazis or Milton's Satan, or anything except clothes and Elvis-the-Pelvis Presley. But Elvis Presley was nothing, she felt now, repulsed by the image of his dull sleepy eyes and greasy hair. Everyone thought he was so sexy. So had she for about three weeks. But then he had struck her as the most ridiculous rock-and-roll idol yet, with no real authority over himself or anything. That's what she thought was most attractive, she realized now with some bafflement: knowledge and authority. She could love a bald troll under a bridge if he knew something more than everybody else. And though she knew she was alone among her girlfriends in that definition, she felt absolutely satisfied with it.

The attic was cold tonight. Outside, massive sycamore branches creaked back and forth in the wind, and thin scudding clouds made a ghostly lace across the full moon. She sank down into the sheets of her bed, and the mushy mattresses folded over her like soft fat arms. Whoever you are, she addressed the mask of the Prince, I wish you would come. It's you I'm interested in—in love with, she might as well say. Part of the feeling was an undeniable physical attraction to him. While she and Katy had been building him, she had indulged in fantasies of being sexually overwhelmed by someone so superior, who had achieved a strength so supernatural and a knowledge so vast, that—that what? What would happen? She

pursued the conclusion in her mind, but it eluded her. Perhaps
what she wanted, she guessed at last, was to be taken over by
someone so extraordinary, she could give up her whole troubled mind to him without guilt. If he were truly worthy and
knew everything about life and death, she could forfeit responsibility for her own personality by being absorbed into
his. She thought of the masterly "mystic Shape" in Elizabeth
Browning's poem, drawing the poet backward by her hair,
saying "Guess now who holds thee?" He was Death *and* Love
somehow. He would know what to do with her.

She laughed at herself in the dark, a little laugh of futility.
How could there ever be a real man like that? He could exist
only in her fantasy—or, she half-formed the thought, in her
memory.

She couldn't let the fantasy go. Come, she invited the
mask, daring it to take on form, a body of its own. Come out
and stand over my bed and tell me everything about life and
death, good and evil, and why I am different from almost
everybody else in the whole world.

For over an hour she held her body taut and alert, waiting.
But despite the open invitation, nothing happened. Gradually
her muscles gave way to resignation and tiredness. She woke
up in the morning irritable and aching all over.

That day, her history teacher resumed class discussion of
World War II and Nazi Germany by urging everyone to watch
a documentary on television that evening called "The Final
Solution." It had to do with the concentration camps, he said.
Preferably they should watch it with a parent who could answer
questions. The movie clips of Auschwitz were quite horrifying,
he added, and shouldn't be watched by any students prone to
stomach upsets or nightmares.

When the time came for the program that evening, Maddie's father wasn't home from work yet, and her mother was
ironing in the cellar. But Maddie didn't mind. With the dagger

in her possession, she felt superior to the other students in her knowledge of Hitler's evil, and quite capable of confronting it head-on. Katy had a low-grade fever and was already in bed with Esther, out of the way. So she watched the program alone.

Later that night, after the program was over, she lay rigid in bed, revolted by the mask that stared out at her. She wanted to get up and put it and the Nazi dagger out of the room, out of the house forever. But she couldn't move. Once in bed, too upset to take even the smallest action, she stared at the mask passively, breathing shallowly, thinking in tight little circles for over an hour.

As from a great distance, at last she heard her father come home from work, his car pull into the driveway, his footsteps on the porch, the opening of the front door, and then the slam that made all the windows on the front side of the house shake. To her horror, with the rattling of the window beside her bed, the mask moved in the dark—slipped silently off the tilted lampstand and hung by one rubber ear in a slant half-grimace. A vacant slitted eye stared out at her.

She couldn't breathe, she was so senselessly frightened. She stared back at it motionlessly, feeling that *her* paralysis would somehow prevent it from moving again. Of course she knew the mask had fallen by the force of gravity—and was amazed at her reaction. But the Final Solution had made her irrational with fear, and perversely vulnerable. She knew *nothing* about evil, she had learned tonight. How could she ever get those pictures of Auschwitz out of her mind? How could people ever recover from such things? *Or do them?*

Terror now took a new form for her, the form of a Jewish skeleton rising up out of the ashes of an oven, then putting on the mask she herself had made and walking out of the corner of her room toward her. It had nothing to do with Jack the Ripper or ghosts or vampires in a cemetery at Halloween. *This* was the thing that knew everything there was to know about life and death: it knew that evil wasn't elegant or seductive at all, but filthy and infinitely ignorant. The skeleton was omniscient, and yet could not sanely endure what it knew. Once as alive and healthy as she, now it was mutilated in body and mind, as sick as a living thing could get without dying; yet it had died a million times and came back to life again and again to bear witness, unable to accept or change its fate.

In dread, Maddie turned away from the corner of the room, squeezing her eyes tightly shut. With an exertion of will that was an attempted abandonment of any responsibility to see, wanting only to keep it at bay by cutting off her thoughts altogether, she huddled into the wall.

But the thoughts kept coming. She knew there was no defense against them. (She had seen such a realization in Bert's face many times, not knowing what it was.) There was no defense against a ghost that had virtually no power of its own and nothing whatever to lose. *Her* vulnerability was that she had so much to lose. She was a treasure-store of wealth in the presence of this deranged beggar stripped of flesh who had once had imagination, memory, desire—sanity. There could be no cross to hold up to stop it, no words to comfort it, no sexual fantasies to romanticize it or distract her from what it really was—a hell-animal. For so she identified it, recalling the Eskimo myth Deane had taught her years ago. A *tupilaq*: a composite of all the bones in all the piles in all the camps—powerless, but with massive strength, and on an unstoppable mission. And she knew, identifying it a second time, its other name was Legion—and its heart was grief, its brain rage, and its consciousness horror. And it was here in her room to hold *her* responsible, as easily as anyone else, for the everlasting nightmare of its condition.

She tossed back and forth in her bed, assaulted by thoughts and images of the television program. There could be no escape from them except sleep. But she couldn't sleep.

Much later, she did fall asleep. But it was no escape. She

dreamed of the other mask, the one Deane had given her five
years ago with the hands with holes in them. She dreamed it
rose up out of one of the boxes in the attic cupboard and beat
its blue wooden hands violently on the cupboard door. Then
it burst out and flew around the room like a bird lost in a
snowstorm. The mask squawked and circled over her bed as
the room filled up with snow falling from the ceiling. Then it
began to writhe and swell. The human face in the center of
the mask elongated into a body and the hands grew arms, and
somehow it became Christ on the cross. The holes in the hands
flowed with blood onto the attic floor, but the floor was covered
with an icy crust as hard as marble, and the drops of blood
froze and clinked on it like shards of stained glass, unable to
penetrate. Then all at once, the walls of Maddie's bedroom
gave way, and she was in bed in the church in the middle of
a Tenebrae service. There were candles everywhere, but no
acolytes. Two by two, the flames were going out by themselves.
There was chanting—the *Kyrie eleison*, but no choir. No one in
the whole sanctuary but her and the Christ-mask on the cross.

The last two candles went out. But Christ was not dead.
He was still barely alive, raised up over the chancel, looking
down at her.

In spite of her fear, Maddie stepped out of bed and came
toward the cross to see him better. She stopped. Almost dead,
everything but dead, he came down from the cross toward her,
a Jewish skeleton who, as he walked, shed his skin like a
snake—another layer gone—leaving hardly any flesh on his
bones at all. His eyes glittered ice-blue at first, then as he came
closer, kindled to bright orange, like the flaring up of the gas
radiants in Bert's fireplace, blazing with anger for a moment,
then dying out to black ashes. Wisps of smoke rose out of the
sockets, as from the last two candles in the sanctuary.

Brokenness, was all she could think. Not death, but brokenness. And depletion. The Bread of Life eaten down to the
crumbs.

He spoke. But the sound of his voice came out of the holes in his outstretched palms, not his mouth. *Some things get away,* the holes said. *Some things slip through my hands.*

The words struck her as a revelation. It was not in God's power to save everything, it meant. Some things slipped even through His grasp. And there was nothing He could do about it.

It horrified her. This wasn't what she believed. She wanted to believe that, at the end of all things, God would somehow relent and save everyone, everything.

No, the holes said, contradicting her. He wouldn't.

They said something else. For an instant she understood it perfectly and felt an inexpressible comfort and wave of relief, like the relief logic would be to a person who has lived a whole lifetime of superstition. But then, in the next instant, as the figure withdrew back into the dark, she forgot it. The sound and the sense of Him were simultaneously withdrawn. There was no cross, no church, nothing at all.

Maddie awoke, not frightened, but in a terrible state of tension trying to remember what His last words to her had been. What had she heard that had given her so much peace for the last few moments? Had they been in English? Were they in Latin or some other language her conscious mind didn't know? Or had they just been nonsense syllables her brain made up?

She knew one thing: that the speaker of those words was not deranged by his condition. He was balanced. Even at some kind of peace. And she also knew she would never see Him in any state of consciousness or unconsciousness again. She got a sense that He had appeared to her at the end of something, a farewell—as if to say, *Now you are on your own;* strange, since she thought she'd been on her own ever since Deane died. If there was a second revelation He wanted her to have, it was that He'd been with her all along, but for some reason was now withdrawing to an unutterable distance.

But that was enormously wonderful. Her excitement mounted rather than subsided as the sun came up. Whether near or far, at least He *was*.

She was just thinking of telling Katy about the dream when Katy yelled up to her from her bedroom downstairs. "Maddie, come *down* here!" she ordered impatiently, as though she'd been calling for hours.

Maddie went down. "What's the matter?" she asked, surprised at Katy's pale skin, the queer look on her face. She didn't look well at all.

"I feel weird," she said.

"What do you mean?"

"I don't know. I guess I got tired running up and down the stairs getting all that junk to make Jack." She shook her head. "I couldn't believe you tore him up."

"Should I get Mom?"

"No."

Maddie felt her sister's forehead. She had a fever, though not high.

"My head aches," she said. "It ached all night."

Esther, a heavy sleeper, groaned in the bed beside her.

"Climb in," Katy said, pushing Esther roughly over to the edge. "I got a bad nosebleed last night too. I'm getting sick of them. It was real dark red."

"Well, what other color would it be?" Maddie said lightly, climbing in beside her. The sheets around Katy were damp and hot. There were dark brown spots all over her pillow. What was wrong with her?

They lay beside each other in silence for a while, and Maddie couldn't help thinking about her dream again. Should she tell Katy?

Katy moved closer. "I miss you sometimes," she said softly. "Esther hogs the bed. I wish you and I still slept together."

A tone in Katy's voice made Maddie uneasy. Katy was never this nice unless she wanted something or felt really bad.

"I dreamed it was snowing in the attic," Maddie said to distract her. "The mask of the Prince slid off the lampshade when Dad slammed the door, and it scared me to death."

"It did?" Katy brightened, delighted to hear that her sister had been scared. "What did you do?"

She told Katy everything about the flying mask and seeing Jesus in the sanctuary, and how he'd said something extraordinarily wonderful to her but she couldn't remember what it was no matter how hard she tried.

"You're bonkers," Katy said, shifting restlessly in the bed after listening intently, her favorite dismissal of everything lately. "Like everybody else in this family. Jesus probably told you you're bonkers."

"No," Maddie laughed. "Just blue. You know, after seeing the Prince, Bert told Mom that I definitely have the blue nature, almost as much as Deane did. And she says you might have it even worse."

"Ha!" Katy snorted, sitting up and rolling up the sleeves of her nightgown. "I'm blue all over. Look."

Maddie stared at her arms. They were covered with bruises, like little bunches of navy blue flowers. "Where did you get those?" she asked.

"I don't know. From carrying the hat stand up to the attic, maybe. I banged into a lot of things."

She lay back with a sigh.

"Deane wasn't bonkers," Maddie said after a silence. "And even if he was, he knew what to do about it."

"What do you mean?"

"He got away. Not just from here, I mean, but from himself. He never stopped moving out and out and out."

"Do you think Esther's going to be crazy too?" Katy asked. "She's starting out so cheery."

"I don't know."

"She never gets sick. She never has bad dreams. I hate her."

Maddie laughed. "She can't carry a tune in a paper bag

either. You could win the Pittsburgh Concert Society Competition if you had the guts to try out."

They were silent again, Maddie thinking about her dream.

Feeling too warm, she kicked off the sheets. But Katy, her teeth chattering, protested loudly and pulled them back up again. Maddie noticed more bruises on her legs. "Bert and Grandaddy say we should thank God we're northeast," Maddie said, putting her arm around Katy to warm her up. "That it's both a good and terrible place, like holy ground."

"What's 'northeast'?"

"It means you have to pay for your blue genes by being different—by seeing things differently from other people. Deane was different from everybody else when he was growing up. Bert says he was really awkward around other kids and spent a lot of time alone. Do you know he never went to a school dance in his whole life?"

"Maybe he should have paid for blue genes that fit him a little tighter," Katy said, laughing. But the laughter turned into a cough.

"Bert says you have to accept it, and then be grateful for the bonus you get. Are you getting the flu?"

"What bonus?" Katy asked through a froggy throat.

"A musical talent like yours. Or a strong sense of words like Emily Dickinson or of colors like Vincent van Gogh. Think how many really great artists were cracked. Born much more eccentric and crazy than you, they were given the ability to make connections and see things beneath the surface to make up for it—or maybe because of it. Michelangelo got painting, Einstein got science, Mozart got music—"

"Mozart *didn't* get nosebleeds."

"Your piano teacher was mad when you sent that tape to your lesson instead of coming yourself. You'd better not try that again."

Katy sighed and said she wished they could stay in bed all day and keep talking to make up for all the nights they had missed. In answer to her persistent questions, Maddie told her more about what Bert had said about Katy's blue nature—"intense and full of conflict and power." Also about how sometimes the gene for blueness could skip a generation in a family or mix with someone else's practical or aggressive genes and create all kinds of funny combinations. Together they wondered what could happen when a person with some blue in him like their father married someone without any blue at all like their mother. Would it make the children feel pulled in opposite directions? Or would it make for an ideal combination? Could someone be a happy, pragmatic artist, or a prize-winning research scientist who believed in, as their mother said, "moderation in all things"?

But after a while Katy's interest in the conversation faded. She seemed too tired to talk. So Maddie lay beside her and followed her own thoughts. In Deane, she supposed, the blueness had found a perfect balance with motivation: a cool, clear passion for the outward-bound adventure and neutrality of science, even at the cost of leaving people behind who loved him. He learned to endure loneliness, sleeplessness, and Arctic desolation for the sake of pursuing something he believed was worth living for: intimacy with the sublime—taking off from the island of doubt into the wilderness toward the infinitely distant God. He had completely come to terms with himself on this, not trying to deny what he knew to be true about himself or the world. His mind hadn't devoured itself with third thoughts—or maybe it had. But he went out and found a landscape big enough to swallow it all up and to distract him from the poem he carried in his wallet.

But the poem was there, she recalled, resolved to look up "Dover Beach" this afternoon and read it to Katy—like his identification card. No matter what, he was still a Cameron-Deane.

"Do you think he really loved that Eskimo lady?" Katy piped up now, evidently also thinking of Deane.

"Marian Komuk? I don't know."

"I hope so," Katy said, sighing. "I hope so."

They heard their mother get up from her bed and run to the bathroom with morning sickness. This fourth pregnancy was harder on her than the other ones for some reason. What would the baby be like?

"Maybe it's a boy," Katy said. "That's why it's making her so sick."

They laughed and listened until their mother stopped vomiting and ran water in the sink.

Then suddenly Katy made a hissing sound and sat straight up. "Oh no," she said, then yelled at Maddie, "Get a towel! Something's happening!"

Maddie rolled over. Katy's gown and pillow were covered with blood. Her hands were clamped tightly over her nose, but blood was streaming out through her fingers. She looked whiter than the sheet pulled up around her.

Frightened, Maddie ran to get her mother. Katy started to scream.

Half an hour later, Katy was lifted into an ambulance. She looked back at Maddie with the white rolling eyes of a fox that in spite of all its cunning finds itself caught in a trap.

"You'll be okay," Maddie yelled to her and waved.

"Stay with Esther," her mother called as she climbed into the ambulance after her. "I'll call you from the hospital. Your father's meeting me there. Call Bert and Essy."

Maddie watched the ambulance pull away. She was hardly aware of Esther's frightened crying beside her. Ten minutes ago, she had heard her mother say something to the doctor over the phone: *acute lymphocyt*—something. Maddie took Esther inside and looked it up in the medical dictionary.

Once she understood, she began to shake uncontrollably. She went to the phone and picked it up to call Bert. But she couldn't do it. How could she tell Bert Katy had leukemia? Or Essy?

Who then?

She thought of the dream: Now you are on your own—without Katy. Maybe that's what it meant. God couldn't save her. He wouldn't.

Hardly knowing what she was doing, she picked up the phone and dialed the number of the office at the church. "Is Reverend Rutke there?" she asked the secretary.

He was at the door in fifteen minutes.

PART II

"Ayii, ayii,
There is one thing
and only one thing,
To rise
And greet the new day,
To turn your face
From the dark of night,
To gaze at the white dawn.
Arise. Arise.
Ayii, ayii."

THE WHITE DAWN
by James Houston, 1971

6

THE ELECTRIC
LAST SUPPER

Maddie looked into the bedroom mirror. For the ninth Sunday in a row, she was perfect. Her dress was halfway between Puritan drab and missionary sweet, navy blue, below the knee, with a ring of antique lace around the collar. Her heels were low, the black leather scuffed, but shined with a light rub of Vaseline. (At age twenty-four, she was not materialistic, the parishioners would think, but meticulous.) She chose a pin, a small oval of roses, artificial gold. The master stroke was the watch, a no-nonsense Timex with a masculine brown band that indicated she meant Christian business. Sanctify me, Lord, she thought as she studied herself in the mirror and approved the effect of unstudied modesty. Make me an instrument of Thy —something. Not peace. This morning she felt anything but instrumental of peace.

She hated these calculations, even as week by week they were growing more subtle. How to dress for a role she was preparing to live, not merely play? To be a Presbyterian minister's wife, she needed guileless sincerity, transparency of spirit, not this cunning analysis. So far, she had learned how to achieve perfect inconspicuousness. That was the safest look if she wanted to maintain her privacy, Nate had told her; for she would be watched, her values judged and her character studied by each of the congregations they visited. Last Sunday he said that some members might even try to infer his theology from how she looked. Was he a Bible-believing conservative? A naive, idealistic liberal? Or, worst of all, a radical, God-is-dead agnostic? (Considering what had happened to the Reverend Rutke at her home church last year, she could believe it. His late marriage to an outspoken Jewish woman who touted a new book called *The Feminine Mystique* at Circle meetings made him the scandal of the Presbytery. Some of his loyalest people hadn't been happy until he left the church. Now they had a benign old man who lost his place in his sermons.)

But they also had Nate Hart, the young student assistant from The Pittsburgh Theological Seminary.

Nate was a strong and eager beginner in the church, and she wanted to serve as a recommendation for him. But at five-thirty A.M., she was already on the verge of her usual Sabbath nausea. With stiff fingers she buttoned a bulky sweater over her dress and scanned the lineup of great doubter/believers on her desk: Deane's old copies of Milton, Dostoyevski, and Melville; Bert's favorite collections of poetry; and her own stash of post-Auschwitz twentieth-century theologians. They had prepared her well to be a pastor's wife, trivializing simple atheism as effectively as simple fundamentalism, showing the troubled, modern church to be nothing more than the slushy tip of the iceberg of real Christianity. Even Deane had suspected that, or so she'd learned from reading between the lines of the notebooks her grandmother had finally relinquished to her one by one. There was forgotten substance underneath. But what would it take to uncover the depths hidden beneath the false floors of the churches now?

She passed the bedrooms of her parents and sisters—still

sleeping. Downstairs, she paused at the front door window. Outside it was dark, but grayly glowing with ten inches of new snow. Her father's car looked like a frozen tortoise under the drifts. Against the streetlight, she could see snow still coming down. "The God who is with us is the God who forsakes us," she quoted the old line from Bonhoeffer. Imprisoned in a cold Nazi cell, he had come to appreciate all the ironies of his fate, and had darkened but not lost his faith. Fogging the window with her breath, she made the sign of the cross in it. Then, irritably, she rubbed it out.

In the kitchen, shivering over the stove, she fried eggs and bacon for Nate. Why was he always starving before preaching and she always sick to her stomach? It was part of his nervous immunity, she guessed, one of the curiosities that had first attracted her to him. When she first met him six months ago, she had assumed that he would be like all the other student assistants that had worked part-time at the church to satisfy degree requirements for graduation from seminary—over-confident, pious, certain that the solution to the contemporary church's problems was to ditch all the pipe organs and accompany the hymns on guitars, or maybe ditch the hymns, too, and sing popular camp and folksongs about love and harmony. "Everything Is Beautiful" was their favorite song and gospel. (Like hell it is, she had angrily dissented to Nate in one of their earliest discussions, telling him about the end of Reverend Rutke and the Tenebrae services. It was a long way from Mozart's "Lacrymosa" to "Micah, Row the Boat Ashore." Instead of Father, Son, and Holy Ghost, now there was Peter, Paul, and Mary, and everyone who didn't sing along was lumped together under the excommunicate "establishment.")

But Nate was different. He was theologically liberal, as militant as any of them, but more soft-spoken and yielding to people's differences. He sought her out early at the church. When they sat in the pews after services and debated Paul

Tillich or Karl Barth, her eyes often focused on his slender, delicate wrists and restless fingertips, so sensitive to the texture of the oak of the pew. His fingers moved lightly, like sensors, over everything he touched. Just as she was trying to explain her theories about the tragic nature of reality, how sooner or later God dropped the Rock of Ages on everyone's head, those fingertips had touched her arm and muddled her whole point. "I need a visionary who can scrub floors," he said one Sunday, smiling into her eyes as if to estimate the depths hidden from him.

She had resisted the invitation at first. How could she explain to him that, more and more, she felt like a freak mixture of intelligence and lunacy, faith and heresy, and that she didn't want to date anyone at all—let alone marry, as her mother was hoping for soon. Nate had seemed so relentlessly cheerful the first Sunday he preached. Katy would have hated him.

He apologized for making that bad first impression. His cheerfulness was a means of "professional disarmament," he said; she shouldn't take it, God forbid, seriously. He then described himself as an unorthodox, experimental Presbyterian who had gone to seminary to see if he really was a Christian. There had been no moment of sudden revelation, no mountaintop born-again conversion.

As they sat in the empty church Sunday after Sunday, Maddie told him all about Deane and Kate, and how she had come to believe what Christ himself came to believe—that tragedy was the only means to redemption and that God was inscrutable and often strategically unavailable.

"In other words, you agree with Nietzsche," he interrupted her one hot Sunday in July.

"I do?" she had said.

" 'I tell you, one must still have chaos in one, to give birth to a dancing star.' "

She was pleased by the quote, having never heard it before.

Then with unexpected decision, he kissed her—gentle, long. And she thought this was the only way anyone could do such a thing. No warning, no asking permission. "You were created to be happy," he said, twisting and turning the cameo ring Bert and Grandaddy had given her for graduation, Phi Beta Kappa, *summa cum laude*. And paradoxically, in his restraint, she felt his considerable sexual energy waking her up like an academic Sleeping Semi-Beauty. He made no demands on her. But she felt a license, a readiness.

Despite having just won a fellowship for doctoral studies at Radcliffe, which had thrilled Bert, she, or some part of her, was sick of study and wanted "to fall out into the real world," as she told Grandaddy when she first introduced Nate. She was ready to take a risk.

Was she really getting married? she asked herself this morning, as if there were a third person in her to consult. Was it possible to change direction this easily? She couldn't help but admire the extra effort Nate was making for their future. In September, he had joined the Preaching Association, a group of volunteer student pastors who traveled hundreds of miles every Sunday to fill the vacant pulpits of rural churches that couldn't afford full-time ministers. They weren't paid for it, only money for gas. In return for bringing the Gospel to these remote little congregations, they got experience in preaching and familiarity with problems in the Presbytery. Girlfriends who went along got exposure to life in a small town or rural pastorate. Nate said that he might be called to a church not much larger than some of these.

She measured out coffee and massaged two knots of pain in the back of her head. For some reason this morning, her usual sense of spiritual adventure wasn't with her. Her throat was sore from the cold she'd caught in the unheated sanctuary of Grant's Hill last Sunday. But it wasn't that, or getting up early that bothered her. Since she was now finishing up a double master's degree in music and American literature at the

University of Pittsburgh, she had come to look forward to
these Sunday outings as diversions from the predictable round
of organ recitals and research papers. She had wanted experience outside her own limited world. And at first, the bizarre-
ness of some of Nate's assignments had provided it. In the
remotest rural areas of Pennsylvania and Ohio, America was
not as far removed from its Puritan past as she had expected.
The first Sunday, they'd been assigned to the two-hundred-
year-old church of Nortontown, Pennsylvania. Nate climbed
the old spiraling staircase to the elevated pulpit and looked
just like Father Mapple in *Moby Dick*. Maddie took his picture.
In isolated Seaton, West Virginia, she found a treasure pushed
into the sanctuary corner: a portable pipe organ with sterling
silver pipes and silver filigree, still playable, a work of art from
the late eighteenth century that put modern squalling electric
organs to shame. Original pewter sconces and candelabra still
lit the services—no electricity. It was Arthur Dimmesdale's
church, she thought romantically. Still there.

But most of the churches fell far short of that, out of touch
with their own histories. Two Sundays ago, after driving a
hundred and forty miles into the barren Appalachian landscape
of southeastern Ohio, they had arrived at the one-room church
of West Guntly, a bare garage-like structure that stood on a
slant, treeless elevation of earth and sheltered a congregation
of three old ladies, all wearing babushkas and black farmer's
boots. It was the weather, they apologized to Nate. Usually,
when "real" ministers came, they had fifteen to twenty in attendance.

She needed these experiences for her perspective, Maddie
reasoned as she waited for the coffee to perk. But today she
felt dull and tired. She looked out the kitchen window at the
shadowy eastern hemlocks in the backyard. Her sisters, Esther
and Lynne, thought she was crazy to take these trips every
Sunday. Why did she want to marry a minister? (Maddie could

only imagine what Katy would say if she were still alive.) And now her digestive tract felt crampy and full of air. She thought she would prefer standing out there with those trees all morning long than go through with another preaching assignment in Ohio.

At six o'clock the coffee was ready and Nate was at the door. Looking lean and handsome, a quite unfallen Dimmesdale in his black suit and white clerical collar, he gave her a greeting kiss full of energy. He was like Katy used to be, she thought, as he pulled her into a long hug: physically warm all the time. Enthusiastically he sat down to breakfast and told her about their assignment for today. It was the hundred-and-ninety-five-year-old Presbyterian church of Pottsfield, Ohio, a hundred and twenty miles away. Dead as religion was in America, she thought, why was it so much deader in Ohio?

"You'll like this one, Mad," he said. "Before the Civil War, it was the biggest, most influential congregation east of the Mississippi."

Splendid. What could a hundred and ten years of steadily declining membership do to a church? They must be down to negative members by now.

"Slavery divided it right down the middle," he said. "Aren't you eating?"

"Can't."

"Nerves?"

"Sometimes Sunday divides *me* right down the middle."

He smiled sympathetically. "I bet it would be easier if you were doing the preaching. You wouldn't have to sit there and listen for my embarrassing syntactical errors and strings of literary quotes taken out of context."

"I don't do that."

"You're a better scholar than I am," he said earnestly, his dark, long-lashed eyes pulling her in, mood and all. "But consider," he said, grabbing her hand as she reached for the ketchup bottle to put it away, "I've given you warning. The adventure is just beginning." He put her hand, bottle and all, to his lips and kissed it.

I knew all the warnings long ago, she wanted to tell him, but instead said cheerfully: "I'd make a good preacher. But I'd be a terrible pastor. That's your strength. I'd preach, pray, and run out the back door to avoid having to actually talk to the people."

He let her go and went back to his eggs. She wanted to say more—that this morning she was afraid something was hopelessly wrong with her whole attitude, that it was becoming harder to function as a reflection of him each Sunday, to smile and smile and communicate nothing specific about herself, and try so hard to care about people she did not know. She was a private, eccentric person—she accepted that by now. And yet, like Bert, she still believed with all her heart in the value of a community of flawed, vulnerable people—sinners for want of a better word—who came together each week in search of a larger perspective, with the image of the cross to bind them together. She still heard the power of that cross in the music, in the great Passions and Requiems.

Breakfast over, Nate wanted to be on his way. Glad to leave the fumy kitchen behind, Maddie put on her most practical coat, black gloves, and white scarf, and compared herself to Nate's black topcoat and hat. They were both impeccably funereal. Jonathan Edwards couldn't have faulted a thing.

Nate shoveled a pathway for her from the front door to the car. Once outside, the cold December air made her feel better. With customary skill, Nate backed his car out of the driveway onto the snow-covered street. Thanking God for four-wheel drive, she settled into the trip. On Interstate 70, he offered to practice his sermon on her, which he had memorized.

"Oh, lucky for me," she said. "Is the heater still broken?"

"Sorry. I spent my car money on books. But I threw a couple of blankets in the back seat."

She piled the blankets on her lap. "Do you think when we're married, we'll have things like other people have—like food?"

"Maybe not at first," he said, pulling her across the seat close to him. Then gesturing with one hand and steering with the other, he elaborated on the text of the day, one of his favorites: "Judge not that ye be not judged."

"But it's Advent," she said. "The kids will be making clothespin shepherds and cotton sheep in Sunday school. The parents will be looking for prophecies of the baby-in-the-manger."

"It relates," he said, and proceeded into the first page of his sermon, which touched briefly on the problem of evil as it related to the Christmas hope, the inevitability of human weakness, and hence the absurdity of self-righteous judgments. He provided a good scholarly exegesis of the passage, then suggested that conservative churches need not feel alienated from modern Biblical criticism or social change. The virgin birth did not have to be taken literally; but Jesus's birth in poverty surrounded by animals, his strength made perfect in weakness—these were the miracles that had to be believed. "What do you think?" he said at last.

"It's good," she said honestly. "But do you think it might be too much for a conservative country church like Pottsfield?"

"How do we know it's conservative?"

"All these congregations are, Nate. Remember last week? Some of them got pretty upset when you said Adam and Eve were mythical figures."

"Sooner or later, somebody's got to take the risk, Mad."

"It *is* a risk," she said, recalling the arguments about creationism Deane and Essy used to have in Bert's living room.

He said nothing.

She thought about what had happened to his friend from seminary, Warren Jackson, when he questioned the literalness of the Virgin Birth in a sermon in Mechanicsville. The Elders of the church had written a letter of outrage to the seminary demanding his dismissal from the Association and expulsion from seminary.

"Your language is a trifle lofty in places," she said. "After what happened to Warren, and our experience in Grant's Tomb last week . . ."

"Hill," he laughed. "Grant's Hill. What happened to Warren, Maddie, was a perfect example of what's happening between the seminary and the churches. The gap is getting wider and wider. Warren was only repeating what he had heard in class many times. The seminary reprimanded him for tactlessness—that's all."

She wished Nate could meet her mother's parents on their farm in Tionesta. They had a simple Methodist faith and kept their open Bible on a doily on top of the piano in the parlor. For them, everything was either true or not true. There were no levels or dimensions or interpretations of truth.

"This is the advantage of circuit-riding," he reassured her, putting his right hand and her left in his warm pocket. "We sow the seeds, and leave."

"But someday we'll have to stay," she said.

"That's true. But I can't turn into a Billy Graham to please them, Maddie."

"I know," she laughed. And in her heart, thanked God.

Two and a half hours later, they arrived at the church. From the distance of the highway, it looked reassuring. The Pottsfield Presbyterian Church stood on a hill like a beacon of Christian endurance, gleaming white in the snow. Adjoining it was a cemetery that looked big enough to contain ten generations of its members. As they turned up the road that wound behind it, Maddie couldn't see another building anywhere in sight. Only snow-covered hills surrounded the church, a silent circle of empty fields and white horizon that made her wonder if all the members of Pottsfield were in the cemetery, waiting for a definitive sermon on the resurrection.

They drove around to the parking lot. To their relief, six cars and a truck were parked there. There was a living congregation here—perhaps even children in Sunday school classes right now. Her relief wasn't complete, however. She cast a longing look at the outhouse off to the left, situated at the edge of the woods near the oldest gravestones. It was in an oddly crumpled condition, as though someone had picked it up, then dropped it in a heap. "That can't be it," she said, knowing from past experience that it might very well be.

"Grant's Hill didn't even have that," Nate reminded her.

Blessed with an inhumanly superior bladder, he smiled as she trudged through the snow and wrestled open the rotten door against a snow drift. There was paper inside, at least.

Five minutes later, she rejoined him at the door, and they went inside the vestibule. The door slammed behind them. Maddie heard a hoarse whisper from somewhere inside the sanctuary.

"Vida! He's here. Turn on the Last Supper."

After that, silence. It seemed that taking off her cloth gloves made too much noise. There were people in this building—but where? She peered around the plaster archway and observed a stout, elderly woman—Vida, she presumed—move with steps ceremoniously slow toward the chancel, past a battered communion table and folding chair, past the faded pink, white, and gray American flag to the pale green far wall —a fine network of hairline cracks, like structural varicose veins. Hanging crookedly from a nail was a ten-by-twelve inch reproduction of Leonardo da Vinci's "Last Supper" from which dangled a heavy extension cord.

"I have a sickening foreboding," Maddie whispered to Nate.

"Shh," he said, all attention and solemnity, assuming his pastoral right-at-home look.

Slowly, ritually, Vida connected the cord to another extension cord lying on the floor and pushed a little button situated under Judas's feet. The thing lit up. It blinked once or twice as Jesus took on the colorful radiance of a cartoon character. This, she surmised, signified the beginning of the service.

Nate left her to organize himself at the lectern. She looked around for an out-of-the-way place to sit close to the rude chopping block that served as a pulpit. (Why am I so irritable today? she wondered nervously.) She was met halfway down the aisle by a tall, broad-shouldered old man who extended an enormous hand and introduced himself as Harvey Potts. He wore dirty long underwear, uneven suspenders, and khaki pants baggy enough to be mistaken for a woman's skirt. The closer he came, the bigger he got, and he smelled overwhelmingly of chewing tobacco. "Mornin'," he said, shaking and shaking her hand.

"Mornin'," she said, unwittingly imitating his country inflection in trying to be friendly. "I'm Maddie Cameron." His hand felt like cracked vinyl.

"How's yer drive?"

"Not too bad," she said. "We're very glad to be here."

"Well, darlin', we're glad to have ya."

To escape him gracefully, she moved toward the large organ console she saw back in the right corner. He came with her. "Do you need anyone to accompany the hymns?" she asked, wanting something to do—a place to sit by herself, where she could feel justified in sitting alone.

"No," he said. "That thing ain't worth nothin'. It's an old theater organ somebody dumped here five, six years ago. The women keep it around fer looks."

"Nobody ever plays it?"

"Nope. No pipes. Half the stops are busted."

"You sing *a capella* then?"

"Beg yer pardon?"

"You don't use any instruments—piano or anything?"

"Nope. Folks thought with the organ we wouldn't need a piano. The weather gets to 'em anyway."

Of course, Maddie thought, shivering in the draft. There *was* weather in this sanctuary. On a closer look at the organ, she understood why nobody ever bothered to try to restore it. The selection of workable stops included a tuba, a military drum roll, a vox humana, a broken window, a doorbell, bagpipes, and jingle bells.

"We used to have music," Harvey said as he escorted her to a front row center seat. "But the people started fightin' over it fer somethin' to do. Some folks wanted to do fancy opry stuff like John Peterson, and the rest of us wanted to stick to the tried and true. Do you know 'Railroad to Heaven'?"

"No, I don't."

" 'I Walked Today Where Jesus Walked'? 'Jesus Saviour, Pilot Me'?"

"I've heard of them," she said, lying. She had heard of John Peterson. The children's choir in her church in Pittsburgh had done one of his sentimental cantatas for Easter.

Harvey left her to greet other worshipers who were straggling in. In a few minutes, Nate opened the service with the Call to Worship. She was glad to be in the front pew, the better to communicate how well he was preaching by a set of signs and facial expressions they had mutually agreed-upon. If his voice level was good and he was coming across well, she would assume a look of rapt attention. If he was too loud or overly dramatic, she would knit her brow and look displeased. If he was wandering from the point completely, she would lower her eyes and not look at him at all.

But this morning she found it hard to pay attention. She tried to concentrate on what he was saying, but felt overwhelmingly drowsy. She read the inscriptions on the inside of the hymnbook three times, and then, to keep awake, let her imagination match his standard Calls to Worship with appropriate Pottsfield organ responses. "Now hear the word of the Lord!" Military drum roll. "Behold, I stand at the door and knock." Doorbell. "Make a joyful noise unto the Lord!" Sickly, exhaling bagpipes. "Let him who is without sin cast the first stone." Broken window. Fixing her attention on the Last Supper, a part of her felt like breaking out into loud guffaws. If one could back away and see it all objectively, it was riotously funny, wasn't it? She dug her right thumbnail into her left wrist to sober up.

Nate prayed the Prayer of Confession, and all heads went down. She took a moment to look behind her at the twenty-five to thirty odd souls gathered in attendance. They were a shabby-looking lot—many old women with round faces and puffy red hands folded in their laps. There were only four or five men, a few dull-eyed, leaning children, and one infant. The clothes of every one of them were shapeless and colorless, and she felt the ridiculous irrelevance of her perfect dress. It didn't matter how she looked. But yes it did, she reconsidered. If this church was like the others, they would look over every inch of her after the service.

On cue from Nate, they thumbed through coverless hymnbooks—copyright 1859—in search of the first hymn. It was a good old fundamentalist favorite, "Beyond the Sunset." When the time came to sing, she resolved not to take a superior attitude, but to stand and sing with enthusiasm. She did, and was surprised at the volume of sound behind her. They sang loud if not in any particular key. Halfway through the second verse, however, she felt an unsettling sense of conspicuousness. She was being looked at. She could sense it as palpably as if twenty-five guns were pointed at her. She cast a quick, sidelong glance behind her and realized she was the only one besides Nate who was standing up. Was it the tradition in this church to sing hymns sitting down? No wonder Nate was looking at her with such an imbecilic half-smile.

She could feel her face turning red. The back of her neck tightened. This was it, she thought. It was all part of the initiation—trial by exposure. She didn't need Nate's murdered syntax to embarrass her. She could manage to embarrass herself quite well. But what should she do for the rest of the hymn? Admit her awareness by sitting down in the middle of it? No. She decided to sing all six verses standing, and pretend she didn't know the situation. But she knew *they* knew *she* knew; and then for no particular reason, she thought of Katy and the seal imitations she had done in church twelve years ago to make her laugh. Katy would die laughing to see her now. "See where all that religion got you?" she would say. But then the weighty irritableness she had felt at dawn came back with double strength. It wasn't funny at all, really, unless one were looking in from outside. But she was inside. "Admit it," she addressed the cartoon Christ in the Last Supper. "I will never succeed as a minister's wife."

The congregation whined Amen to the hymn like a line of old vacuum cleaners. And just as she sat down, they all stood up to recite the Apostles' Creed. "For heaven's sake, why don't they have printed bulletins in these churches for visitors?" she rebuked Christ silently.

"Because they are too poor," came the obvious answer in a soft little Walt Disney voice. "Isn't this what you needed to know? Didn't you come to embrace the least of these my brethren?"

She couldn't sustain the conversation any further. The austerity of the ugly sanctuary, the ghostly whiteness of the landscape outside—not an inch of Romish stained glass in this

Protestant stronghold—the mockery of art on the wall, not to
mention the futile sophistication of Nate's sermon, all combined to fill her head with an almost disorienting pressure, like
a skull expanding within a skull. How could she ever conform
herself to a place—to a mentality—like this? What was the
bridge between Bach's *St. Matthew Passion* and "Railroad to
Heaven?" Between Paul Tillich and Harvey Potts?

She consulted her Timex; there was still a half hour to
go in the service.

"Let us worship God with our morning Offering," Nate
said, strong and clear. The Usher of the Day rose out of her
seat and ambled to the chancel on elephantine legs to receive
the offering plate—an aluminum pie pan—from his hands. She
was one of the heaviest women Maddie had ever seen, and
also tall, taller than Nate, and no doubt stronger. Her steel-
wool hair was tucked under a nylon stocking that served as a
cap, and she wore a pair of old men's dress shoes, cracked at
the toes. Maddie watched her with fascination. The slow de-
liberateness of her movements made this a very serious moment. She thrust the pie plate into the face of everyone in the
pews, not allowing it to be passed from person to person out
of her hands. Moving up and down, she looked each worshiper
in the eye, including Maddie, who put in two dollars, which
was more than anybody else. How she longed for the background of an offertory Bach chorale. Giving was grim business
here.

When the woman had finished collecting, she dug down
into the pocket of her full skirt, produced five nickels, and
dropped them into the pan making the most possible noise of
the event. Then she handed it back to Nate, ignoring his open
smile and nod of thanks.

Nate prayed the Prayer of Dedication. The congregation
rose, unaccountably, to sing the Doxology. Maddie rose with
them this time and realized she needed the outhouse again.

Her stomach cramps were back. But how could she possibly get there from this prominent place right in front of the pulpit—and right before the sermon? It would look as though she were walking out on him. As Nate moved from the lectern to the pulpit, a distance of barely seven feet, she could see the corner of the outhouse through the window to her left, and the cemetery beyond it. Potter's Field, she thought vaguely, where the poor-in-spirit are buried. And yet, wasn't there a difference between poor-in-spirit and impoverished-in-spirit? Could she live here if she had to? As Nate began to preach, she felt hostile toward him for underestimating the complexity of this congregation's simplicity—as well as the limitations of her kidneys. Fortunately the cramps were subsiding again.

He preached on. Everyone but Maddie and the infant were attentive. She rummaged in her purse for some peppermint Life Savers. Bert had said they could settle your stomach. But instead she found a bookmark one of the women from the Carbondale Presbyterian Church in Macon, Pennsylvania, had given her several weeks ago. "Are you saved?" she had asked, poking Maddie with a thin, crooked finger. "Are your sins in the Blood?" Then she'd handed her this limp satin bookmark with the Beatitudes printed on it, out of focus, and a picture of Jesus with long wavy hair and soulful blue eyes, a cocker-spaniel Christ. Maddie had thanked her politely. But now as she looked at it, purse-worn and garish, she fantasized about telling the old woman that, given a few years in the service of the Presbyterian church in Pottsfield, her blood would probably be crying out for sins she no longer had the energy or imagination to commit.

At last the sermon was over, and Nate gave the Benediction. His voice was gentle, shepherdly, wholly earnest. His ego is not mixed up in this, she noted admiringly; he truly feels what he is doing. She gathered herself together and prepared for the most challenging part of the morning—mingling

with the people, slowly but steadily smiling her way through
a maze of curious, now talkative parishioners, asking and answering questions. The transformation from solemn jury to
friends and neighbors in these churches always surprised her,
and most Sundays she took pleasure in talking to the older
ones who could tell her stories about local church history. But
this morning it was an overwhelming effort, intolerably forced.
She smiled and greeted everyone she passed as she made her
way to the vestibule, but the back of her head throbbed. If she
could just get outside into the open air, she would feel better.

Harvey stopped her at the archway. There was no getting
around him. He dragged her by the hand to the corner of the
vestibule, practically hugged her, then slid his huge fingers
underneath grease-stained suspenders and asked her how she
liked his church. A trickle of tobacco juice ran down his chin
as he talked. "I'm a retired farmer and telephone lineman, you
know," he said, "but I ain't retired from my church. No sir. I'm
Clerk o' Session."

"You are?" she said, surprised to hear there still was a
session of Elders here—nine actual men. Undoubtedly no
women.

"Just between you and me, young lady, I want to thank
ya fer standin' up when it come time to sing the Hymn o'
Proclamation. I been trying to get these folks to do that fer
years." He bent down close to her face. "They won't budge
outa their God-damned seats, pardon my French. That's the
trouble with the church nowadays. Too damn comfortable."

Maddie shivered violently in the vestibule cold. Yes, Lord,
the church was too comfortable.

"Yer boy'll make a good preacher," he went on. "He meant
what he said this mornin', whatever it was."

She laughed. "How long has Pottsfield been without a
full-time pastor?"

"Goin on 'leven years," he said proudly. "No offense, but
in my 'pinion, it's the hope of this place."

"The hope?"

"You betcha. That's why I come here. We got no preacher to do our prayin' for us, no budget to speak of. Nothin' fer us to fight over anymore. Future looks peaceful."

"Was there a lot of fighting before?"

"Hey," he said, his eyebrows narrowing, "we had a real famous preacher here once, back in the heyday. The Reverend Hiram Eleisha Jackson. Knew John Brown personally. Vida Jackson is his great, great granddaughter—that nice-looking stout lady over there."

Vida was lecturing Nate about something a mile a minute.

"This church give Reverend Jackson a lot of trouble, you see. He was one of the first to speak up against slavery, and they give him hell to pay. Vida's still seein' to it that we make it up."

Suddenly, as though struck with a thought, he narrowed his eyes and stepped back. "Wanna see the cold closet?" he said. Without waiting for an answer, he opened a narrow closet door off to their right, and there to Maddie's infinite joy was a small stainless steel toilet and sink. "You can thank Vida fer that," he said. "That's the Hiram Eleisha Jackson Memorial Facility. I was dead set against it. Pissin' can be done outdoors. But you go ahead and use it. It's nippy out there this mornin'."

With a genuine smile of gratitude, Maddie went into the closet and shut the door. It was pitch black, but she didn't care. The Reverend Jackson was still ministering to those in need. And then, as she sat down on the stainless steel seat, she understood why it was called the cold closet.

"What do ya think of the Last Supper?" Harvey called to her through the door.

"What?" she called, pretending not to understand, hurrying to finish. But she had heard very well what he asked. How honest could she be? "Well," she stammered, opening the door, "I . . ."

"Listen! If ya can't afford somethin' good, then don't buy

nothin'. Reverend Jackson was an art-lover, and somebody give that thing in his memory. Vida was against it. We agreed on that. How would you have voted on it?"

"I'd say I'm with you," she said, glad to be forthright.

He took her by the elbow to a side door. "You and yer boy oughta take a tramp over yonder," he pointed through the window. "My loved ones are lying out there. My daughter. My wife Pearl. Pearl weren't no bigger than you—had pretty brown hair and real dainty little feet. Nearly killed her to lose Ruthie." Suddenly tears were mingling with the tobacco juice, though he was unembarrassed by them.

"What happened to your daughter?" she asked.

"Died o' pneumonia when she was twelve. Maybe ya know what it's like to lose someone young like that."

Maddie nodded. She did.

As fast as his tears appeared, they disappeared. "But Pearl used to say it weren't a good idea to tell a thing over and over. Sometimes you can rub a thing in 'til ya rub it out. We got no preacher, as I mentioned, but we still collect good money every week, upwards o' fifteen, twenty bucks."

Maddie was beginning to enjoy Harvey in spite of herself. "Do you have any kind of mission program," she wondered, "any goal for the people to reach each year?"

"No program. But a little mission. Want to see the Deacons' Christmas project fer the kids in Pottsfield Hospital?"

He led her to a large closet with a padlock on it. From the pocket of his pants he produced a key and opened it. Inside were four shelves, deep and empty, except for three or four dried-up Bibles, a box of broken crayons, and two rolls of toilet tissue. On the floor was a paper shopping bag. Harvey pulled it out, opened it, and proudly revealed a jumble of about thirty-five giant candy canes, each with ten dimes taped to it and a little red ribbon. "We're gonna give these out on Christmas Eve," he said. "The kids go nuts over 'em."

Harvey watched her. "They're beautiful," she said. "Who did all the work?"

"Me and Pearl before she died, then Vida and Al and me over the summer, mostly. We do it every year. Last year the Deacons wanted to spend the thirty-five bucks on a plastic wreath to hang on the steeple. I said to hell with that."

"Are there so many sick children?" she asked, noting the number of canes.

"I give 'em out to the Sunday school kids too, if we have any. They'll all be sick sooner or later, I figure." And then, he dug down into the bag and picked the one with the nicest-looking bow. "This is fer you," he said, handing it to Maddie. "We can't pay yer boy, but we're grateful to ya fer comin all this way fer nothin'."

"It isn't for nothing," Maddie protested, not wanting to take it. But he wouldn't take it back. He locked up his shopping bag again—"to keep the secret," he winked—and escorted her back to Nate. "You come back here again," he said with a vigorous handshake. "It's real pretty here in the summertime. You could come fer lunch at my place when I get to makin' my fresh fruit pies again."

Maddie saw Nate just breaking free of a young woman with the baby. Vida, still hovering, was pressing a scrap of paper into his hand. Maddie greeted a few more people. Then after another round of nods and good-byes, suddenly the church was empty. She joined Nate as he was gathering up his papers at the lectern. He set out for the outhouse with a look of distraction.

"Nate!" she called. "There's a—"

"Can't wait," he said, and was at the outhouse in five strides.

He's human, she thought with satisfaction.

When he came back, she showed him the cold closet.

"Why didn't you say so?" he said with an uncharacteristic edge on his voice.

"Now don't you *scold* her," Harvey appeared at the door again out of nowhere. "I forgot—there's somethin' I ought to show ya before ya go. Come on."

He led them through the cemetery along what was probably a path under the snow to a small fenced-in plot. Here among a few new stones was Reverend Jackson's grave. The marker was a simple rectangle with his name, date of death, and one line of scripture: "Forgive us our sins."

"They run him outa town 'cause he was hiding slaves in the steeple," Harvey explained. "When his poor wife moved back to this territory after he died, the members decided to put that on his tombstone as a kind of apology. There's a coupla fools that still don't get it. They think he's beggin' forgiveness for himself. But most of the sheep finally knew their shame. It's our prayer to him. We're praying that he'll forgive us."

"What actually happened to him?" Nate said, bending down to brush off a dusting of snow.

"Couple o' pro-slavery Elders tried to make him back down on his stand. They told him Saint Paul himself once sent back a fugitive slave—that old argument. Know what he said to that? He gave 'em the same answer his friend John Brown gave the ministers that visited him in prison—'Then St. Paul ain't no better than you are.' They wanted his hide after that. Persecuted his family with rumors and rocks. Rumors and rocks. He never got another church. Broke his heart. Ain't the first time, of course. When they finally come to their senses, it was too late, except to bring his body back here and carve them words on the stone."

He moved on to a section of newer graves and uncovered a stone lamb from a drift. "This here's my daughter," he said. "Died at twelve, did I tell ya? Nearly killed Pearl 'cause she couldn't have no more kids. She wanted to adopt a little colored boy named Gabbie whose folks got killed on the traintracks

—drunk as skunks. But I said no. I had nothin' to offer him, I said. But I was just *embarrassed* to adopt him. I had Pearl to offer him. And I wouldn't do it." He moved on to Pearl's grave, still piled with dead funeral flowers and urns. "Sometimes you can feel a thing so long it makes you blind stupid."

Tears ran down both his cheeks. Nate put his hand on the old man's shoulder. "Well, I wanted to show ya," Harvey said, collecting himself after a few moments. "Come back here soon, like I said. I like both of ya."

"We will," Maddie said, knowing of course that they wouldn't. Nate would be long out of seminary before this church came up on his Association list again.

Harvey drove away in a pickup truck. Nate went back into the church to get his Bible, and they settled into the cold privacy of their own car.

"Well, it's over," Maddie sighed, feeling torn by conflicting emotions. Was she glad she didn't have to get involved with these people, or sorry that she couldn't?

"I wonder if Reverend Jackson haunts this place at night," she said as Nate ground the engine.

"What?" he said, not hearing.

"I doubt if John Brown's forgiven anybody. Do you think there's a curse on this place?"

"Maybe. The church has gone straight down ever since the Civil War."

But not entirely, she thought. Pearl Potts had wanted Gabbie.

"Do you know that every year this ragged little group gives a thousand dollars to send a Negro student to college?" Nate said, pulling out onto the road.

"How?"

"A couple of rich old women in town. They never darken the door of the church, Vida says, but they pay their insurance to their Lord."

"Something smells in here," Maddie said, detecting a sour odor coming from somewhere.

Nate pointed to the Bible thrown on the back seat, the precious Revised Standard Version his father had given him with all the notes and underlinings in it. "I held Vida's colicky granddaughter for a few minutes. She was so proud of her. The kid threw up all over the book of Jeremiah."

She laughed out loud. "Is it salvageable?"

"I don't know. How do you launder a book of prophecy?"

She could see he was upset about the Bible. He was gripping the steering wheel with both hands. "For what it's worth, you preached well," she said. "Harvey didn't have the faintest idea what you were talking about, but he perceived your sincerity."

"Great," he said. "Want to stop and get something to eat?"

"Sure. I'd like to see the town. It must be pretty big to support a hospital."

Once they were back on the main road, his grip on the wheel relaxed. "What were you and Vida talking about so long?" she asked, smelling the Bible all the way from the back seat.

"Oh, the usual stuff. There's a lot of sickness, marital problems. Three cases of cancer, two teenagers who've been vandalizing the cemetery. A few members are meeting once a month to discuss current events, especially what's going on in civil rights. And Vida wanted me to see her brother in the hospital on our way back. He's a diabetic—has a gangrenous foot. They're taking off half his leg in the morning, and he's not taking it well at all."

"Neither would I."

He handed her the scrap of paper. "Here are six more people she wanted me to see 'if I had time.' All in bad shape. I'm not supposed to do hospital calling on these trips, Mad. They need to yoke with another church and get a pastor."

"I think Harvey thinks he's it," she said.

"I can tell you something about Harvey," he said with a

smile. "He was a widower at Thanksgiving, and Vida's already dying to take care of him. She and a few other women looked in on him after the funeral, a few weeks after Pearl was gone. She told me he'd outfitted the corners of every room with giant coffee cans and extra ones strategically placed beside sofas and chairs, so that no matter where he's sitting, he can spit out his plug without having to get up. In the middle of a conversation, he'll spit off to one side or the other or over his shoulder. A loud splash indicates perfect accuracy. And he never changes the water until—"

"All right," she said, "I get the picture."

"Vida says his place is falling apart. He cries all day."

"He wants us to come for lunch sometime."

"At your peril. Pearl was a great cook and canner, and now Harvey tries to bake pies like she used to and gives them to the shut-ins. The crusts are like sheets of plywood, Vida says, and everybody knows to throw them away. He's also been trying to can pumpkins and squash, and everybody throws them away too. And in the morning after breakfast, he sits at his kitchen window and shoots rats with a twelve-gauge shotgun—"

"And roasts and eats them?" she finished the story.

"No. Just lets them rot among the garbage. Vida says his backyard looks and smells like the valley of dry bones. Nobody'll come near his place except Vida, once a week—if he lets her in."

"How old is he? He must be seventy."

"He's eighty-six, with no family but a sister-in-law who came in once after the funeral to take Pearl's engagement ring, jewelry, and china. She hasn't written him a postcard since. And he's got cancer of the colon. Just found out two weeks ago."

"Oh no," she said, feeling a pang of fondness and grief for him. Thank God for Vida.

They drove on in silence for a while. But after five miles,

there was no sign of a town, not even a road sign promising one. It was snowing again. Though the church was long out of sight, Maddie kept picturing it standing on the hill with its pathetic heart of locked-up candy in the closet. She wanted to go past it again for another look. Her satisfaction after these services was never complete, her feelings never clearly focused. She and Nate did the best they could, but it wasn't enough. Each service was too enormous an effort to really succeed anyway.

The snow came in little showers and gusts. As Nate slowed his driving, squinting to see the road through the fogging windshield, she watched the barbed-wire fence posts along the road go by with a lulling, monotonous regularity—Sunday after Sunday after Sunday. This is what it will be like, she thought. And she wanted to tell Nate how terrifying Pottsfield's valiant isolation seemed to her, and how meager its consolations. Those lonely sick people had attached themselves to him like—what? Like vampires. The twentieth-century church wasn't silver pipe organs or elevated pulpits. It was people, not artifacts. If one decided to give to them, it would have to be everything. A hundred percent.

Swirls of wind blew snow all over the road. The windows fogged and refogged as fast as Maddie could wipe them clear. "You better slow down," she said.

"We're going to have to skip lunch," he said. "It'll be a miracle if I find this hospital. I don't want to drive home in the dark in this weather."

"You're going to try to see all those people?" she asked, feeling suddenly passive and empty, not really hungry. She slouched down under a blanket and crossed her arms over her body. What should she do while he was at the hospital? Would the people want her to come in too, or would they prefer to see him alone?

There was a long silence between them. "You know," he said finally, as the odor of Jeremiah grew stronger, "they really ought to pay us something for doing this. At least the cost of a sandwich. None of the other guys in the Association do hospital calls. But how do you say no? I've got a systematic theology exam at eight o'clock in the morning. We'll be lucky if we get in by eight o'clock tonight. If I do the job right, there's no time left over for us, Maddie."

He feels it too, she thought. Resolved to try to cheer him up, she took Harvey's candy cane out of her purse and held it up. "We did get paid," she said. "Ten dimes, one ribbon, and a quarter pound of tooth decay."

Nate smiled at the cane with the shiny dimes taped all over it. "Not enough," he said, though appreciating the token.

Maybe you're right, she thought but did not say.

The snow was blinding now. They could hardly see the road at all. He slowed to a crawl and put his arm around her. "Don't mind me," he said, "I'm just hungry."

She unwrapped the candy cane, broke off a piece, and handed it to him. "Take. Eat," she said.

7

MOVING

In June, 1965, Bert rejoiced that at last there would be a great family festival. But from the moment she saw Maddie come down the aisle in her wedding gown, all she did was weep. Nate was interviewing for his first church in Welchburg, a small parish two hundred miles away. When Maddie told her she was moving to a declining industrial town in West Virginia, four hours away by car, she might as well have said she was going to the Arctic. "But are you *sure* about this?" Bert lamented. "I thought Nate would get a church in Pittsburgh. Now I'll never see you!"

But Maddie assured her she was excited and ready to move. She hadn't even been discouraged by the rust-and-litter atmosphere of Welchburg when Nate drove her down to see it, not to mention the green mildew stuck between the pages of the hymnals of the First Presbyterian Church. "What do you think?" he'd said, watching her closely.

"It's beautiful," she said, feeling challenged by the prospect of bringing new life to the congregation. All her education and growing up in the church had prepared her for this. She didn't expect it to be easy.

But six weeks after moving into the tiny manse on a busy intersection of highways (a Stop-and-Go and Virgil's Used Cars across the street), Nate was wondering if it wasn't too easy after all. "I have too much time," he said with some embarrassment as he came home for lunch one rainy afternoon in August and stayed two hours. "I've written my sermon, done my hospital calling, and taken care of the leaky toilet in the church basement. Now what?"

They sat on the couch and tried to figure out what he should do.

"Call on delinquent members?" she suggested.

"Only in the evenings," he said. "The husbands aren't home in the afternoons."

"Doesn't anybody stop in for counseling?"

"Not yet. They don't really know me well enough—or else I'm too inexperienced for them."

"Community affairs?"

The telephone rang. After a few moments' conversation, Nate rejoined her on the couch. "Well," he said with a smile more of perplexity than enthusiasm, "I have my first professional community function to perform."

"What?" she asked, glad of the timing of the call.

"I've been asked to dedicate the new flagpole at the firehouse—which means offer a prayer—Tuesday morning at ten."

She thought about how to react. "Oh," she said brightly.

He leaned back and looked at the ceiling. "What do you pray for a flagpole, Mad?" And then he broke out laughing. "Dear Lord, protect this nice new shiny pole from lightning and rain."

"Dear Lord," she joined in, "protect this pole from pigeons nesting at the top."

"Dear Lord," he concluded, "give me the words for what I'm really going to say next Tuesday."

He went back to his office and gave it his best. On Tuesday, the nodding, appreciative heads of the few local dignitaries who attended the dedication reassured him that he had done a fine job.

But the next week, he found something more challenging to do with his extra time. In going through the church rolls, he discovered that a sizable number of the 350 listed members of the church had either moved away years ago or could only be located in the cemetery up the highway. It was time somebody cleaned up the records, he told Maddie. With the Session's rather half-hearted approval, he plunged into the long, tedious work.

By the time he finished, the flattering 350 membership was reduced to a lean, less flattering, but real 249. But even after he explained to the Session that the weeded-out roll meant the church would pay less in their annual per capita assessment to General Assembly—and the budget was strained anyhow—many of the Elders were insulted by the reduction of numbers. "I know we're a bigger church than 249," old Al Kaufman said, puffing a cigar, staring at Nate as though either his math or his motives were way off.

At the Congregational meeting at the end of the year when the reduced numbers were published in the annual reports perused by all, Maddie overheard a woman sitting behind her whisper to two of her friends, "Look how the membership has dropped since Reverend Hart came! They're leaving in droves."

In fact, Maddie wanted to tell them, the membership was now 281. They were thirty-two members stronger, all of them active, involved, and best of all, alive.

But Maddie was too happy to worry about anything. She was three months pregnant.

When her daughter, Merrill, was born, she looked up at Maddie in the delivery room with the gravity of a fully formed spirit, as if to say: "How do you do, Mother? Here I am." And

Maddie found motherhood an astonishing and unexpected solution—hormonal, if not philosophical—to many of her old griefs and present tensions in the church. She had the remarkable power to add people to the family. "I want lots of kids," she told Nate the day they brought Merrill home from the hospital. "Five or six or seven."

"Maybe two or three," he laughed.

At a salary of six thousand dollars a year, from time to time over that summer, at the end of a tight pay period, he dressed up in blue jeans and a red bandana, drove into unknown neighborhoods, and sold plums and cherries picked from the fruit trees in their backyard. Maddie harvested the rhubarb that the former minister's wife had planted and sold pies. More than once she had to fill Merrill's bottle with tomato soup because she ran out of milk money before payday. But she half-enjoyed the austerity.

"It's fun," she wrote to her mother in September. Nate could preach "Go sell all that thou hast" without too much hypocrisy or guilt.

But in October, she wrote more confidingly to Esther that sometimes she felt discouraged. The church budget was stretched so tight, Nate had to tactfully decline a token raise for the second year in a row. And the congregation was not responding as well as he'd hoped. The membership consisted mostly of poor farmers and laid-off factory workers, a few high school teachers, and one doctor, all ruled over by a council of the gray-haired all-male pillars of the church that made up Nate's Session. Very few of them worried about the actual content of their religion. Rummage sales and fire-hall suppers were the social focus. (Ironically, sometimes Maddie felt she'd been more in tune with the remote little congregation of Pottsfield three years ago than with her own present flock.) She told Esther she wondered why Presbytery hadn't given Nate any warnings about it. Granted, graduates just out of seminary assumed they'd be hired by small or foundering churches that couldn't afford more experienced men. But Nate was finding many of these people to be chronically contentious and tradition-bound on every current issue. Sometimes it seemed that most of what seminary had taught him was irrelevant. Most Sunday mornings, he was so nervous before the worship service, he threw up right before he put on his preaching robe —no more big breakfasts. He began to accept vomiting as part of the normal priestly ritual. After a while, Maddie wished he could settle for something less than liturgical and sermonic perfection in the crafting of the services, since many of the people didn't seem to know the difference between Christology and cosmetology.

"I think they want a friendly mixer," Maddie told him after church one wintry Sunday afternoon when the response to his sermon had been apathetic. "Someone to baptize, marry, and bury them, and to teach their children that every word in the Bible is the literal truth."

"But I don't even believe that," he said dejectedly, pushing his untouched lunch out of the way.

Maddie knew he wouldn't pretend he believed it either, even to keep peace. It hadn't taken some of the older members long to see that he had no healthy guile in him.

"It's a hard time for all the churches," he said. "You have to work where God calls you, sympathetic to local customs and prejudices, but faithful to the uncompromising call for redemption."

"Yes," she agreed.

But from her own experience, she wondered how one could redeem a church entrenched in prejudice and tradition —or even a single soul—without breaking it? And if they broke the church, where would their salary come from?

The next Sunday, Nate preached a long sermon on the racial tensions in Selma, Alabama, quoting from Martin Luther

King's "Letter from Birmingham Jail." After the service the Clerk
of Session, rolled-up-sleeved, backslapping Jack Cunningham,
took him aside. "I think the solution is to castrate every damn
nigger that commits a crime," he said confidentially.

Nate thought he was joking. When it became clear that
he wasn't, he said, "I don't believe that's the feeling of the
majority of this congregation, Jack. Times are changing."

The Clerk smiled. "You're young, Reverend. The Session
will rally to support you when you fall on your face the first
couple of times."

Nate told Maddie he had felt the incredible compulsion
to say "Thanks."

Month by month, he began to grasp that at least half of
the congregation *did* agree with the Clerk. And he was feeling
a growing constraint of diplomacy bearing on his sermon writing. After suggesting from the pulpit that Jesus's miracle of the
five loaves and two fishes could be interpreted in more than
one way, two families left the church, and a number of those
remaining were incensed by his "liberal naïveté."

She and Nate *were* naive, Maddie realized.

But she assured Esther in her letters that, as beginners,
both she and Nate had a healthy instinct for survival. From
their experience in the Preaching Association, they had a fair
knowledge of what they were up against, even if they didn't
always anticipate the crises. Three of Nate's classmates from
seminary had already left the ministry, they had heard. By
comparison, they were doing well.

Then one Sunday morning Maddie competed with Nate
for the bathroom to throw up. Overjoyed when the doctor
confirmed she'd have another baby before Merrill was twenty
months old, Maddie drove home to Pittsburgh for a brief celebration.

On the way, over the car radio, she heard that Martin
Luther King had been assassinated.

                              *   *   *

"But are you happy?" Bert asked Maddie with a knitted
brow on the evening before she was to drive back to Welchburg. They were sitting in her mother's living room, the celebration party over, everyone scattered—her father and
Grandaddy taking Essy home, Ginny doing dishes in the
kitchen, Esther and her youngest sister Lynne giving Merrill a
bath upstairs. Maddie sensed that Bert had been wanting to
get her alone for a private conversation ever since she arrived
two days ago. She realized now she hadn't even had time to
see Bert's house, which she wanted to.

She pondered Bert's question. "John Cope, the executive
Presbyter, told Nate that Welchburg is 'a good initiation,' " she
answered. "His 'baptism by fire.' "

She hesitated to say that a few months ago the benign
Dr. Cope had put a paternal arm around Nate's shoulders and
said he approved of his taking on Welchburg because he was
"so bright and strong and could break the bones of its outmoded
traditions." He had neglected to warn Nate that this could be
a reciprocal process—bone for bone, fracture for fracture.

Bert smiled encouragingly. But independent of her smile,
Maddie saw that her eyes studied her sharply, like a snowy
owl flying over tundra scanning for hidden movement.

"They expect me to come to all the molasses-making and
quilt-stitching events," Maddie laughed. "I don't particularly fit
in there, but I'm learning to, for Nate's sake. Most of the women
are nice."

She didn't say that in her striving to please everybody,
she was feeling more and more tense and growing overly sensitive to criticism. But why say it? The important thing was
that with her help Nate was accomplishing a great deal. A
Board of Deacons had been established to call on shut-ins. The
Boy Scout troop was revived. Maddie had formed a children's
choir and led an adult discussion class on the Vietnam war

controversy. Nate had set up a food pantry for the families of
the unemployed workers. As she recalled from her conversation
with the cartoon Christ in the electric Last Supper at Pottsfield,
this was what the job required—ministry at a hundred percent
investment. She and Nate had a vast reserve of bones that
could bend very far without breaking.

But thank God she had a family to return to and visit, she
thought, sinking back into her mother's couch—a place where
she could abandon the role and be herself.

"Have you made any friends?" Bert asked.

"A few. But it's risky. Most of the women expect me to
be orthodox. Since I'm not, I have to be careful about what I
say. Children and recipes are safe subjects." She didn't mention
her latest suspicion—that a lot of the livelier women avoided
inviting her to anything more down-to-earth than a prayer
meeting over tea and cookies for fear she would cramp their
secular style. Nate was having the same difficulty in making
friends. People kept them at such a respectful distance.

"Surely at least one," Bert said, searching her face anxiously.

There was an awkward silence between them.

"I'm a Sunday school teacher," Maddie volunteered, "youth
counselor, organist, and on Saturdays I mow the church lawn.
The church is right next door to the manse. Sometimes the
women come in on mission luncheon days to use my oven.
And Mrs. Gilchrist, who lives across the intersection, watches
me with binoculars."

"Oh *no*," Bert said, horrified.

"You have to keep your sense of humor."

"Since when are you the organist?"

"The elderly woman who used to play the old Hammond
organ retired two months ago. No one else jumped for the job
since there's no salary. Strictly volunteer."

"A Hammond!" Bert cried contemptuously. "That's a piece
of machinery, not a musical instrument."

"I know. I bought a how-to manual to learn how to operate the thing. 'Pull out bars #3, #9, and #27 one-fourth inch, #11 and #8 half an inch, #16 and #5 one inch,' and so on. After thirty-seven separate adjustments, you might get a sound faintly resembling a bent eight-foot flute. I turned off the tremolo and alienated at least half the congregation. But I can't stand the skating-rink sound. I *won't* stand it."

"Well," Bert said, after a long pause, "at least you're putting some of your musical training to use."

"I belong to two of the Circles in the Women's Association." Maddie sighed, finding herself unable to stop telling Bert things now that she had gotten started. "Imagine listening to twenty-five women talk for two and a half hours about how to make carrot cake and apple butter, while assembling a hundred and twenty-five Christmas ornaments out of Styrofoam, pink sequins, and purple felt."

"Oh, I can imagine," she said with a weak smile. After a long pause she asked, "Do you write any poems?"

Maddie shook her head. "I do enjoy going with Nate on hospital calls. That's the best way to get to know people. Some of them are wonderful characters—hidden veins of gold. And I like the choir work. I've been offered the position of senior choir director. The old director used to conduct with stiff flat palms"—Maddie held up her hands to demonstrate—"jabbing at the choir with karate chops like this, beating out the eighth notes, sixteenth notes, everything. His wife refused to come to the services, she was so embarrassed by him. Thank God he quit when I turned off the tremolo." As an afterthought, she added, "With Merrill to take care of, there's not much time for writing poems."

"I don't believe it. You must *take* the time. Don't do what I did and throw *all* your time into other things."

"I help Nate revise sermons. Every week, we get at least two calls from members denouncing him as a heretic. But no one has set the manse on fire yet. Do you know that actually happened to a minister in Kentucky?" She paused and looked into the cold fireplace, away from Bert's penetrating gaze. She realized she'd been biting her nails. "It worries me how much Nate is hurt by some of the calls."

"I think I'd worry if he weren't hurt," she said quietly.

Maddie nodded.

There was another silence. Bert mused, looking down at her folded hands. And suddenly Maddie realized that for the first time in her life she felt nervous talking to her grandmother—as if she and Bert were playing a cat-and-mouse game. Was it pride that kept her from telling her the full extent of the conflicts she was feeling? She wanted to tell her how she was refining her talents for acting and evasion equally with her talents for choir directing and sermon editing—that it was a cat-and-mouse game with the congregation too. But she was afraid. Against what Bert would insist was her unchangeable Cameron nature, she was presenting herself to the people of Welchburg as perpetually cheerful, naturally optimistic, and full of faith, a friend to the poor and the needy at any hour of the day and night. Like Nate, she was always open, always deferring to parishioners. But she wasn't like Nate. She wondered if in time she might grow into the perfect minister's wife she was trying to be. Or if that was hopeless, might she forget how buried she really was, and year by year grow remote from her own—and Bert's—recognition?

No, she assured herself and Bert. Floating on a marital and maternal cloud of physical contentment, she was sure she could meet the requirements of the congregation. After the pain of losing Deane and Katy, the healthiest thing she had ever done was, like Deane, to deliberately choose another life and follow it. It was right to leave the town, the family, and the past behind.

Besides, the next church would be better.

*   *   *

In February of 1969, Nate accepted a second call.

At eight months pregnant, Maddie packed everything up and moved to Michigan. Though the Hadleyburg Presbyterian Church was farther away from Pittsburgh, its facilities were impressive—a big sanctuary, a gymnasium, and a new Christian education wing. The organ, a Baldwin electric, was no prize, but better than the Hammond. To Maddie's relief, the choir director was excellent and grateful for a supportive pastor. The new manse was two blocks away from the church, in need of paint, but surrounded with beautiful old locust and wild cherry trees.

She gave birth to a second daughter, Kate, and then, two years later, to a son, Nathan, in the Hadleyburg General Hospital. The women in the church generously showered her with baby clothes and toys. When not busy at a meeting or calling on prospective members (she often thought back to the afternoon in Welchburg when he hadn't known what to do with himself), Nate helped her fold diapers and bathe the babies.

As his reputation as a controversial preacher spread across town, the membership changed, and sometimes she worried about it. A number of the oldest parishioners left. But new ones joined, and after two years, there was strong cumulative growth. The choir director even managed to persuade the Worship and Music Committee to fund a special Christmas performance of Vivaldi's *Gloria* with chamber orchestra. Though a few committee members grumbled about "priorities," Nate reminded them that mission giving was up twenty-five percent, and they said nothing more.

With or without the babies, Maddie attended all the church and Presbytery functions for women. She often wished she had a mother or sister, any relative close by she could call on at a moment's notice for free babysitting without a feeling of obligation or imposition. But then the problem was unexpectedly solved by one of the local teenagers volunteering to babysit for free on a regular basis. Her alcoholic father sometimes threw vacuum cleaners at her, she explained, and she was glad to get out of his way in the evenings. Maddie paid her generously. She was an excellent sitter, and in time, provided a wealth of valuable information about the community.

"I'd never let Joanne Scholes babysit your kids," she told Nate the first week, among other bits of casually dropped information. "She poses for dirty pictures. And Dwight Zedtwitz sells grass by the pound. And don't let Merrill play down by the big water pipe. That's where all the kids get high and make out."

Hadleyburg was not paradise.

Then, in September of 1972, Nate organized a tour of the Holy Land for thirty members of the church. Maddie could go for free if he recruited twenty more people, the tour agency said. He tried but couldn't.

To pass the time while he was away, Maddie decided to go home to Pittsburgh for a long-postponed visit. Esther's letters had been keeping her up-to-date on how everyone was, what they were all doing. Though the bone and cartilage in Bert's knees had deteriorated so badly by now the doctor was talking about a wheelchair, she struggled to maintain the charm, if not the cleanliness, of the old house. When Maddie wrote to tell Bert she was coming for a two-week visit, Esther said at first she cried for joy, then fell into a frenzy of anxious activity. For weeks, she strained to shake the dirt out of all the throw rugs and beat five years of dust out of the bedroom drapes with a broom. She filled the two huge clay pots Grandaddy had brought back from Mexico with red geraniums for the porch, and arranged bouquets of bittersweet on either side of the fireplace. Deane's old globe was polished to a shine; the Mason and Hamlin was tuned.

When at last Maddie knocked on her door, with Merrill

and Kate clinging to her side and chubby nineteen-month-old
Nathan in her arms, Bert welcomed her like an international
celebrity of infinite fame and interest. After hugs and exclamations all around, Grandaddy took charge of all three children
while Bert conducted her on a grand tour of the house. "It
looks as beautiful as always," Maddie said over and over to
please her.

And yet, as she looked into the map room, into her father's
old bedroom, and then into Deane's room, she felt a vague
uneasiness—a little like a movie actress returning to the old
Shakespearean theater where she had gotten her start. Or perhaps, she thought again, like an exile sneaking back for a look
at her native land.

She recalled a note that Deane had written in the margin
of one of the photograph albums she had at home, a paraphrase
of something Einstein once said about how planets and comets
want to go straight, but can't. The sun curves them back and
back. Their motion is real enough, but their progress is illusory.
"What time does Grand Central Station stop at the train?"
Deane had underlined at the bottom of the page.

Had she made any progress in her years away?

She commented enthusiastically about everything in the
house—how lovely—how I remember this—how pretty that
looks there—until Bert was at last satisfied. Grandaddy laughed
as Merrill and Kate poked into the nooks and corners of the
old house like little squirrels set loose in a museum with no
glass cases over the exhibits, afraid to touch, but finding the
antiques and heirlooms irresistible.

But seeing Bert's kitchen had the strongest effect on
Maddie—a subtle revelation of her grandparents' decline into
old age since she had moved away. All the little cleansing and
maintenance actions were falling behind. The turquoise and
yellow linoleum floor that Bert still referred to as "new" was
turning up in the corners. Rubber shelf-mats couldn't cover the

rust patches in the bottoms of the enameled cupboards. The turquoise potholders that used to lift twenty-five pound turkeys out of the oven were flat and washed colorless. Merrill was fascinated by the four-legged refrigerator, pushed back against a wall in the alcove by the cellar stairs where it squatted like an old peasant woman—fat, boxy, its era long past. (Esther said the things Bert kept in the refrigerator reminded her of the displays of artificial eggs and oatmeal in the museum's section of "Foods Around the World.") The inside of the oven was as black as pitch. Maddie thought it looked as though it hadn't been cleaned in all the years since Deane had disappeared.

How much she missed Bert and Grandaddy, she realized now, seeing how the house had changed, how it and they were undeniably aging. How much of their lives she was missing. She wondered if Deane had ever felt like this when he came home to visit.

In the living room that evening, as Maddie and her sisters sat around Bert's fireplace and reminisced, Grandaddy taught Maddie a game he often played with Esther and Lynne called "What if?" As Bert excused herself to make a tray of trolley cakes and ginger ale, he asked each of them in turn, "What if you could have anything in this room to keep for the rest of your life? What if you had one minute to choose the thing you would most like to inherit? What would it be?" Maddie played the game happily, just like old times. After some thought, sixteen-year-old Lynne chose a copper cauldron in the corner that Bert had filled with pussy willows two springs ago. Esther wavered between a delicately etched pewter coffeepot and the crystal chandelier that hung over the entranceway, circles within circles of prisms that still shone in the lamplight despite layers of dust. Merrill, almost six years old —old enough to play, Grandaddy said—picked the Mason and Hamlin grand piano.

But Maddie had a harder time choosing. Leaning back in the easy chair by the old game cupboard, she wanted it all. More than that, she wanted a year of evenings just like this.

"What if?" was more than a game. Grandaddy meant the question to reveal something about each of them. What is your taste? he wanted to know. What do you consider beautiful today? And also, though unspoken to Maddie, the question both he and Bert wanted to ask: How have you changed since you left us?

Not at all, she wanted to tell them. Despite all the relative ground covered, the train was back at the station—or vice versa. A part of her wondered if the house hadn't traveled farther than she had. She felt vaguer, yet more contained than the day she had left home—contracted somehow, as if the growing pains of the past six years had been mixed with the cramps of a subtle atrophy.

Under pressure to play the game, Maddie made her choice: the rose-globed brass hurricane lamp that stood on the piano. It was Bert's most treasured heirloom, inherited from her own grandmother. The knobbed globe was as deep as rose could get without giving way to purple or red, just barely restrained from either extreme, its glow as concentrated as the light from the old stained-glass windows in her home church. But unlike the blue of the crucifixion window which, when she was a little girl, had made her feel pensive and solemn, now as she lay back in the easy chair and stared at the lamp, the rose made her feel serene, temporarily absolved of all responsibility and role-playing—like that little girl again. How many times had she sat here after Christmas or Thanksgiving dinners and looked into the recessed alcove where the lamp shone mirrored in the polished piano lid? She had blissfully given way to it many times. All her worries about school or Katy's nosebleeds had melted into a mute appreciation of the exactly present moment. She didn't even worry about Deane when she was in that chair, because she felt him present as he had always been, back in his own room, at work upstairs. Nothing could ever get his spirit out of that room. And nothing could keep him in it.

Now, as her own daughter, Merrill, climbed up on Bert's piano bench and picked out a tune, Maddie mused that the lamp gave off light in the Biblical sense, confounding the darkness, overwhelming it with a wider, deeper affirmation. For the first time in a long while, she altogether relaxed.

I am home, her spirit affirmed emphatically. She neither affirmed nor denied how much less at home she felt in the temporary house back in Hadleyburg. Tonight, she hardly thought of it at all.

A few days before Nate was due home from the Holy Land and Maddie was to return to Hadleyburg, at Bert's urging Maddie and Esther went with her on a shopping spree to the new Monroeville Mall. Bert loved the mall. Esther said she'd been gravitating toward it over the past year for its buying and selling energy, and despite her weak legs, would drag Howdy up and down the crowded thoroughfares until her knees gave out, then collapse into a wheel chair and let him or Essy push her from store to store. She would buy extravagantly, three or four pairs of the same shoe, a favorite style of purse in every color, as though preparing for a hundred years of future. "I'm getting tired, Bertie," Grandaddy would say after hours of this. But stimulated by the light and color, she had unlimited stamina. "Oh, please, Howdy!" she would plead for a little more time.

But today, with Maddie and Esther present to march up and down the aisles with her, Grandaddy spent most of the shopping spree on a bench in the center aisle of the mall, watching everyone go by. As Bert hobbled after a salesclerk to try on a new dress, Maddie commented to Esther how straight and thin Grandaddy looked—like the Buckingham guard Bert had always wanted.

"He's on a health kick," Esther said. "Or that's what he says. Every morning he gets up at four-thirty and scrubs all the floors so she won't worry about the dirt."

"Why doesn't she hire a cleaning woman?"

"Because she's so supernaturally stubborn," Esther said, making Maddie smile. Esther reminded her so much of Aunt Essy. "She can't stand strangers in her house—says they are 'a weight' on her. So to keep her from fretting about the mess, he does all the heavy work before she gets up. She doesn't even know he does it."

"But he looks fit—all tan, the military posture."

"He bought a sunlamp after Bert told him he had the aluminum pallor of Hamlet's father's ghost."

Maddie laughed.

"He boasts that he's never felt better—that he could swim the river if he wanted to. But Essy thinks it's a big show. She says his hands shake when he holds a coffee cup."

"I bet he could swim it," Maddie said, watching him jump up to help a woman who had dropped her packages.

"Bert envies his legs. She sends him out on scores of errands to the bakery or supermarket to take advantage of sales on Fig Newtons or toilet tissue. Essy thinks he's crazy to indulge her. But Bert says he's never happier than when he's out in the car on the road."

Maybe Bert was right, Maddie judged. Over the past weeks, she had seen how eagerly he responded to any suggestion to get out the car and bring in some treat from the outside. And Bert's eyes would light up at the simplest offering.

When the shopping trip was over, Esther went home to help babysit for Merrill, Kate, and Nathan, and Maddie helped Grandaddy carry in Bert's packages. Bert was in high spirits and asked her to stay for supper.

But once inside the door, Grandaddy lost control of his stack of boxes and spilled them all over the living-room floor —high-heeled shoes, a dress for Lynne, a pair of long black velvet gloves, cardboard and tissue everywhere. He burst out laughing. He'd been experiencing a sluggishness in his movements lately, he said—a tendency to drop his keys, to spill his coffee—which struck him as hilariously funny.

"Howdy!" Bert said, struggling to pick up the packages. "What is *wrong* with you?"

"No, Bertie," he said, pulling her up. "I'll get these. You go make supper. Maddie must be starving."

Maddie noted rings of white inside the tan around his eyes. She told him to rest in his chair and read the paper while she gathered up the packages and stacked them on the dining-room table.

But he couldn't concentrate on the news just then. Instead, he followed her to the kitchen, put his arms around Bert at the sink, and held her tightly. "What good am I?" he said, winking at Maddie. "I'm surrounded with artistry and expertise, and I can't do nuttin'!"

"Well," Bert said, struggling to open a can of tomato soup with an object that looked like an artifact from an archeological dig, "you could help set the table. We're having tomato soup and crackers and cheese—and hot tea. It's chilly for September, don't you think?"

He took cups and saucers from the cupboard. One of the cups slipped out of his hand and fell to the floor. He picked it up and dropped it again. He grinned at Maddie with a look of utter stupefication. "Look at me. Did you ever see anything like this?"

Bert shook her head and said he'd be more help to her if he went back to the living room and read maps.

He left. Maddie heard him adjust the creaky piano bench. He sat down to improvise. He still loved to make up "wind chime melodies," as he called them, played once, then forgotten. This, along with his claimed ability to swim the river at a moment's notice (Bert said stirring the soup), were his most recent claims to fame.

But he had difficulty playing. "My right hand wants to play faster than my left," he called out to them. The music stopped.

Ten minutes later, Bert called him for supper.

Four days later, when Maddie told Nate what happened next, she had a hard time remembering the sequence of things. She remembered hearing a cry, then Bert bending over Grandaddy on locked, splayed legs, shaking his shoulders with all her might. She was screaming, "Wake up, Howdy! Howdy! Wake up!" and striking his face brutally again and again. Maddie thought she'd lost her mind.

But then she saw there was no response from Grandaddy. No reddening of the skin where Bert slapped him. No movement at all.

What was happening? Maddie had wondered stupidly, staring from the kitchen.

Bert fell over him in an embrace, weeping hysterically, cradling the face she had just struck. It couldn't be Grandaddy, Maddie protested logically. It was Bert who suffered so many illnesses. It couldn't be him.

Bert turned to her, her eyes red as blood. "Telephone the ambulance," she croaked, looking as though she hardly knew who Maddie was.

Maddie stood paralyzed. She backed into the kitchen in confusion—saw the cooling soup, the crackers neatly arranged around Grandaddy's bowl. His cup of tea—lukewarm.

She moved into the dining room toward the telephone like an uncoordinated child, holding on, touching the chairs, the table, trying not to look to the right where Bert lay over Grandaddy, but unable not to look. She saw everything in the room at once. His open eyes. Her closed ones.

Who had turned on the rose lamp? she wondered, feeling more than seeing its rose glow over everything. *He* had, of course, when he played the piano. Its light seemed stuck in the thick air, hanging like gun-smoke.

Bert's sobbing rode on the smoke—rhythmic, repeating
—the old ram's bell in the wastes. What will happen to her
now? Maddie thought fearfully, picking up the phone with
trembling fingers. Now it was a house for one. In the kitchen,
in the dining room, in the map room upstairs, everything was
cooling to lukewarm, to cold, the rose light paling to blue—
having to give way.

She dialed the operator and called for an ambulance. Then
putting down the phone, she looked past Bert and Grandaddy
to the picture window. What if Deane came home now? it
occurred to her.

But no. They were beyond his power to set things right.

That night, the doctor put Bert to bed and told Willy not
to expect her to make an appearance at the funeral home. She
was physically and emotionally unable. "Oh, my poor, poor
Howdy!" she moaned, twisting in the bed.

Willy made the funeral arrangements. Ginny and Essy
greeted the people at the door during calling hours. Hundreds
of people who had known and loved Grandaddy from his
salesman days came to pay their respects. Willy said he hadn't
known there would be so many.

For three days Bert took sleeping pills around the clock,
but couldn't sleep. She refused to be a witness to Howdy's
death, she told Essy. She wouldn't see the cosmetic glow of
the embalmed body, the hard black line of his lips set in glued
repose, his gentle eyes clamped shut.

Ginny changed the bed linen and brought in meals. Maddie, Esther, and Lynne cleaned the house for the funeral supper.
Maddie found Valiums and Seconals hidden in flowerpots, between seat cushions, on windowsills behind the curtains, under
throw rugs. Had Grandaddy known how far her addiction had
gone?

On the last night of the viewing, after all the visitors had left the funeral home, Essy, who couldn't stop crying, told Willy that for once in their lives they must overrule Bert. "She doesn't know what she's doing. She'll never forgive us when she realizes Howdy is in the ground and she didn't even go to his funeral."

Willy said no, it was useless. He'd seen her like this before.

But Essy insisted. Why not bring Bert to the home right now? she suggested—under cover of darkness, when no one else was there. She ought to be given the chance to do what she could never do with Deane—to say good-bye.

Willy wavered. "What do you think, Maddie?" he said at last, acknowledging her closeness to Bert and, by inference, his distance. His asking of her opinion touched her.

"I'll help you, Dad," Esther volunteered, approving of the idea. "We can each take an arm."

"Essy's right," Maddie said.

"Don't even tell her where she's going," Essy urged.

But when Essy roused Bert from her half-conscious stupor and told her she had to get up and get dressed, Bert knew. "It will be private, Bertha," Essy assured her. "Nobody there but us. It's indecent to lie here and not see your own husband."

Bert looked up at her as though she were crazy. "*I cannot!*" she cried, wrestling her arm free of Essy's clutch.

Then she saw Maddie standing at the foot of the bed, and Esther and Lynne at the doorway.

"Why not just let her wear her robe and slippers?" Maddie said to Essy, feeling sick at this necessary violation of Bert's will. She searched through her closet and pulled out a long black velvet robe. "Look, Bert," she said with a smile, "here is your prettiest robe. Grandaddy loved it."

Bert looked at her as if to ask, Are you a part of this?

But matter-of-fact Esther, not so impressed with her grandmother's resistance, slipped her cold blue toes into black velvet slippers. "Oh no, no," Bert murmured as Esther knelt at her feet, reaching out weakly to stop her. But Esther did not look up or stop.

Willy took one arm, Esther the other, and they lifted her to her feet, but her legs wouldn't support her. She sagged passively as Maddie struggled to put her robe on her. Then Willy picked her up in his arms to carry her downstairs. She screamed in protest. "Wait! Maddie, make him wait! Wait one minute!"

Willy put her down and backed away, shaking his head.

"Come here, Maddie," Bert ordered. "Help me to my dressing table."

Her grandmother felt like a dead weight, but Maddie helped her as well as she could. Bert sat down hard in front of her mirror and looked into it with squinting eyes. "Oh my God, look!" she cried. "Look! I can't possibly see Howdy like this!"

"It's after calling hours, Mother," Willy said. "*No* one will be there."

"Maddie, help me find my rouge," she whimpered, ignoring him. "Where's my lipstick? September Rose, the one with the missing top." She rummaged ruthlessly through twenty tubes of lipstick, most of them with missing tops, through tangled hairnets, rhinestone pins with lost stones, pencil stubs, shredded Kleenexes. "Oh, where *is* it?" she cried in anguish. "Maddie!"

"Bertha, it isn't necessary!" Essy said, losing control.

"Yes it is!" she beat the table with her fist. "*It is!*"

Maddie found the lipstick. Bert wound it up out of the tube and broke it off applying it roughly, with stiff fingers. Then she applied dark red rouge, rubbing it hard into her hollow cheeks. Then a thick layer of powder. She turned to Maddie.

"Maddie, tell me the truth," she sobbed. "Do I look all right?"

Maddie removed the excess lipstick with a Kleenex. In Bert's bottom drawer, she found a comb and combed her damp hair out of her eyes, then took the black velvet hat off the right mirror-post where Bert had hung it, and pinned it in place. She pulled the ragged shreds of veil down over Bert's inflamed eyes. "There," Maddie said. "You look beautiful." In fact, her grandmother looked like an amusement park horror.

Now Bert permitted Willy to pick her up in his arms and carry her to the car. "It's dark," she repeated over and over. "I'm grateful that it's dark."

At the funeral home, in the empty, dimly-lit room where Grandaddy was, Willy set Bert on her feet and balanced her like a rag doll. After a moment, to everyone's surprise, she found the will to stand on her own. He and Essy led her slowly to the casket. She panted, "Oh," with each step.

Maddie, Esther, and Lynne stood back and watched her look at Grandaddy at last. Her grief was insupportable. She took two stiff steps toward the casket under her own power, then collapsed over its side, calling out his name with abandon.

"Oh, my Howdy," she wept, embracing the body, not caring who saw her now.

Then she bent down and kissed him on the forehead. The lipstick left the mark of the kiss, which Maddie was glad of. (It was still there the next day at the funeral service when they closed the casket.) Everyone wept but her father, who stood alone by himself, overseeing, controlling, responsible for everyone, everything now.

After five more minutes, he and Esther led Bert back to the door. But halfway, her strength failed her, and she dragged her feet. Willy picked her up again.

"Where is my son?" Bert called as he carried her past Maddie to the hallway.

"He's right there," Maddie said loudly, regretting the stoical look on her father's face. "He's holding you."

Maddie didn't follow them. Like two magnetic fields of the same charge, she couldn't bring herself to come any closer to Bert just now. Esther and Lynne went out to help get Bert into the car.

Dearest Grandaddy, Maddie thought, looking back at the casket, all inanimate and silent in the shadow: How much weaker we already are.

Back home in Hadleyburg, when the congregation found out about her grandfather's death, there were kind expressions of sympathy, a myriad of condolences. But none of the members had known him, so they meant less to Maddie than the senders might have imagined. After all the emotional intensity of the past week, she felt moody, senselessly irritable, and subtly pressured to react to the loss of her grandfather not as a close granddaughter but as a representative model of Christian grief, of Christian fortitude and submission.

As time went on, Maddie didn't feel like talking or listening to anyone. For weeks, she couldn't get the memory of Bert slapping Grandaddy's dead face out of her mind. Her mother sent her articles from magazines on "how to beat the blues," new recipes, and surprisingly, in a Happy Halloween card, a quote from Nietzsche: "That which does not kill me makes me stronger." Where on earth had she gotten that?

Then, two months after Nate got back from the Holy Land, there was trouble brewing in the church. A small contingent of members were renewing the fight over the alleged wasting of the congregation's money on a chamber orchestra for the *Gloria*. "Vivaldi isn't spiritual enough," one of the Elders said, to Maddie's bewilderment. Why couldn't Maddie accompany it all on the organ and spend the money on something more practical, like new robes for the bell choir? But to her relief, in November, the majority of the Worship and Music Committee voted to keep the orchestra; and on the third Sunday in Advent, the church was packed for the performance. As she sang the opening chorus with the choir, she felt she could re-believe in everything if there were enough good music. *Real* music—oboes, cellos, tympani. But the defeated members who had opposed the orchestra did not forget the incident. And after Christmas, the choir director started talking about leaving to work in another church where the music budget was more realistic.

A week later, Nate was approached by three Session members who recommended that he spend fewer nights at home with his family and more nights out "beating the bushes for new members." Some of the long-established members were complaining that they hadn't been called on in months. Surely two or three nights a week at home were enough.

Maddie wanted to ask these critics, who were all men, if they knew what it was like to care for three small children all day long, practice the organ, cook supper, and then care for them all evening too. But of course she didn't. Nate did more calling "to calm the waters," and she spent four or five evenings a week alone, reading to Merrill and Kate, writing letters to Esther, and practicing Handel's *Creation* for the combined choir festival in February. If it weren't for the music, she wrote to Esther, she would lose her mind.

Despite her mother's predictions that the loss of Grandaddy would kill Bert, it didn't. Esther wrote that she was struggling to recover, taking part in family gatherings again with weak, deliberate smiles, and begging to be taken on shopping trips to the mall. It amazed Maddie how faithfully she continued in her role as loving grandmother to her, and great-grandmother to her children, even as Nate's Presbytery involvements and commitments allowed for no visits home. What was it like to have weekends free? she wondered, sinking into

moods of fatigue and self-pity when Nate got home late two
or three nights in a row.

They rode the Liturgical Year like a merry-go-round.

In 1974, after five years in Hadleyburg, Nate accepted a
third call—to the large but declining church of North Hebron,
in the Gobegic iron district near the border of Wisconsin.
Against a growing inertia that slowed down the ritual of packing and unpacking, Maddie moved her family into the new
manse, this one an eighty-year-old white frame, built like a
fortress, but maintained like a barn. Bert still wrote long half-
decipherable letters in three colors of ink, with double and
triple underlinings, full of meandering sentences of inquiry and
concern that ran off the page and into Maddie's imagination.
"I *rely* on your sympathy and understanding," she wrote, "since
only *you* know what it is like to lose your home—as *I* have
lost mine with Howdy."

But as she settled into the new church, the new house,
the new town, a stranger to everything again, week by week
Maddie began to be glad to be at a distance from Bert and the
family. Something was strangely wrong with her. The back of
her head hurt constantly, she had no appetite, and she felt
drowsy all the time, as if she had the flu. But there was no fever.
When she slept, she had nightmares full of blurred garish colors
and violent high-speed motion that made her jerk awake in a
state of panic. She began to dwell obsessively on the painfulness
of the passing of time. "Time is slowing down," she tried to
explain to Nate when, for the fourth afternoon in a row, he
came home from work and found her half-asleep on the living-
room couch, no supper ready, the children watching television
passively. "I can't stay awake for longer than an hour," she
drawled in apology.

"Tie my shoe, Mom," Nathan whined at her side, having
hovered around her all day long like a lion cub around the
lethargic body of its old dying grandmother.

"I can't," Maddie mustered the energy to say, barely opening her eyes to look at him. She pointed at Nate to tie the
shoe to save herself the effort of even forming the words.

"You've got to go to the doctor, Mad," Nate said. "The
church secretary says it might be your thyroid. Or some kind
of anemia."

With dread, Maddie thought of Katy's leukemia. What
had her symptoms been? She couldn't remember.

"I'm learning to peel potatoes," Merrill said to her father,
showing him a sink full of thick peels and potatoes reduced
to the size of golf balls. "I'm making supper. And Kate won't
help."

Kate sat in front of the television sullenly, her thumb in
her mouth, saying nothing. Yesterday, Maddie had taken the
sheets off Kate's bed and hadn't had the energy to put clean
ones back on. Indignant, Kate had slept on the bare mattress
huddled under a quilt all night long, wet both mattress and
quilt, then climbed in with her mother to get warm. Feeling
the shudders of her daughter's damp body as she curled into
hers, Maddie had felt both comforted and guilty as she held
Kate close. Then Kate had looked at her with bewilderment
as a flood of tears streamed down her mother's face. "Mommy,
what's wrong?" she said, staring at her with grave gray-blue
eyes in the morning light.

"I don't know, dove," Maddie said, wanting to get up and
put clean dry clothes on her daughter, to air her bed and the
house and put everything in order. Instead she pulled Kate
closer to her, back into the well of sleep.

After a week, Maddie felt better for a while and was able
to drag through her work. But then she felt worse, and at last,
full of dull dread, went to the doctor. Not knowing her or any
of her family's history, Dr. Cunnard put her through a long
series of laboratory tests, eliminating, to his and Maddie's bewilderment, every possible physical illness. He could not muster a diagnosis until Maddie mentioned the nightmares she was

having, which were growing more and more frightening every
night. His head turned as she said it, and he looked at her as
though really seeing her for the first time. "It may be clinical
depression," he said. "You may be emotionally, not physically
ill, Madeleine. Many women fall prey to it at your age. It can
last three to six months, maybe even a year."

"A year?" she said, thinking he couldn't be serious. "What
kind of illness lasts for a year?"

"There's no way of telling. We'll just watch you for a while
and see how it goes."

She left his office in a state of shock, as though a partition
had gone up between her and the whole rest of the normal
world. She found herself reacting to the diagnosis both with
relief—this was the truth at least, she was sure—but also with
a feeling of terrible humiliation. Depression was failure—an
inability to cope. How could Nate tell the congregation that
his wife was emotionally ill? How could she tell her own family?

She decided she would not tell the congregation. How
many of them would react with anything but confusion, or
misunderstanding?

Over the next two endless months (Nate hired a part-
time housekeeper—he told the congregation she had a severe
case of mononucleosis), Maddie came to believe that she was
worse off than Bert. Even though she had perfectly good legs,
it was she, not Bert, who was crippled. Week by week, the
paralysis and fear inside her taught her that grief could damage
as well as toughen a mind and heart. Nietzsche to the contrary,
one did not necessarily become stronger because one wasn't
altogether killed by something. In a moment's time, without
warning, normal sorrow could shift into something else and
take a person beyond a point of no return—scramble the brain's
chemistry until neither religion nor logic had any relevance.
And after that, it was all masquerade, all cosmetics. The rest
of one's life must be spent aping life, keeping other people

from finding out you were undone, defective, indifferent to the
suspense of life.

But was it sorrow causing her illness? She thought back
to the day Deane had taken her to the zoo and she had been
worried by the small circle of the tiger's pacing in his cage.
She felt as though she had traded places with that muscularly
overendowed cat—too strong, too undomesticated somehow
to endure the circumference of its safe, contained life. But that
was flattery, she told herself, too weak to lift her own arm. "I
am sick, and I can't explain it even to myself!" she burst out at
Nate as the depression slid into its fourth blank month.

"What can I do?" he said, wanting to help, but excluded,
like everyone else, from experience of this thing.

"Am I the only woman in the world who's had this happen
to her?" she demanded, feeling alternately passive and enraged,
hopeless and desperately afraid.

"If there's anyone else in the congregation suffering from
it, he or she, like you, probably doesn't want to talk about it,"
he said, and reached out to hold her. But fearful of the exhausting demands of sex, she pulled away.

Some mornings, always the worst time, she fantasized
about killing herself to be rid of the agonizing sense of the
slow, slower passing of time, and of her terror that she was no
longer capable of living her own life. She felt possessed. For
the first time, she could understand why people in the Middle
Ages believed in demons.

In the evenings, when she felt a little better, she got out
Deane's old photograph albums and pored over them for as
long as she could hold up her head. He had taken off from
Tigvariak Island in May of 1950, in the confident expectation
of arriving at a destination. In a sense, everyone took off from
such a point. Somehow, crippled as she was, Bert, amazingly,
still believed she might arrive there—and held on to life in
hopes of it. But in depression, Maddie couldn't remember a

time when she ever expected to do anything but crash. The only suspense was where and when. The only living emotion was fear—who would she take *with* her? She went along in her life for the inescapable ride.

Though Bert still sent poems to her for criticism, she put off answering for fear of revealing her own state of mind. What baffled her most was how Bert's passions could remain so unblunted by her grief. She never gave in to resignation. She kept caring, kept fighting to come back, taking life and death seriously—as though, Maddie thought in her darkest, inmost self, anything really mattered.

Deane and Katy had died too soon, her own grief murmured in a tedious monotone. But some slipped connection in her brain's circuitry said: *So what?* In the twinkling of an eye, everyone would be gone anyway. Everyone was a wind chime melody. Everything passed into nothing. Fate could reach out a careless or calculating hand—what did it matter which?—and snatch one of her own children away while her back was turned over a row of sunny marigolds in the garden. To recover from that knowledge was useless—perhaps even mocking. She saw through the glass darkly, but perfectly clearly. It wasn't, as Deane had taught her, that *some* things got away. Sooner or later, everything in the world got away, and there was nothing anyone could do about it. It wasn't worth the effort it took to believe or hope for anything else. Grandaddy's game of "What if?" was meaningless. The things she most wanted to have from the house in Pittsburgh couldn't be inherited. And she couldn't pass them on to her children.

Some nights she lay awake beside Nate and thought obsessively of the lions and the Arab in the museum case, caught in a state of perpetual, stopped motion that trapped the observer into a state of permanent indecision. Her sister Katy had dismissed the whole dilemma in bed one night a month before she died: "Of course you can't decide who wins, stupid! Nobody wins until somebody moves."

Now Maddie wept in agreement dryly—with no tears. Of course that's what was wrong with her. She was encased and couldn't move. She could do nothing to heal herself.

But then, after four and a half months, Dr. Cunnard decided to try an antidepressant drug on her called Limbatrol. It worked for some women, he said, for whom chronic anxiety accompanied depression—perhaps even somehow caused it.

She drove herself to the drugstore in a burst of irrational energy, stemming from the hope that there was medicine for this illness. It could be made to go away. Why had Dr. Cunnard waited so long to try it? Had he any idea on earth what she had been feeling?

She took the smooth little blue pills with desperate faith.

Miraculously, in less than a week, she was on her way up, her frozen circulation thawing out, her energy and willpower coming back with a force she hadn't felt in over a year. Euphoric, she dismissed the housekeeper and retook charge of her household. She cleaned out drawers, closets, and cupboards, rearranging, redecorating, repossessing. On the evening of the seventh day of her medication, Nathan stepped into his bedroom and smiled with surprise: for the first evening in months, the covers on his bed were neatly straightened and turned down, a favorite book lay on his pillow for a bedtime story, and a new, voraciously hungry Venus Flytrap stood where his old dead one had been. "You're back," he said to her, hiding his face with embarrassment as she hugged him, showing for the first time how much he had missed her.

"Yes I am," she said, blinking back tears that came with wonderful, free spontaneity twenty-four hours a day in a gushing reembracing of life and all its burdens.

"Could you sew my gym shorts?" he asked, as they grinned at each other.

She sewed everything torn, mended everything broken, cooked turkeys, baked cookies, attended church and Presbytery functions, and filled and refilled her prescription for Limbatrol.

(She admitted to herself that among its other revelations, depression had suggested to her her own moral limitations, she would lie, cheat, and steal for these pills, if she had to.)

But after a while, her renewed energy led to another consideration: What did this sudden turnaround mean? What did it mean that her state of mind—her whole philosophy of life—could be chemically altered so easily? Which was her right mind? Which perspective was true?

She didn't care to pursue the question.

With children to care for, a husband who needed her, the question was meaningless. Whether the train or Grand Central Station actually moved didn't matter. She would prefer to accept an artificially induced energy and soar with it than to lie in a deadly genuine calm while everything flew around her. If other depressions came in the future, Dr. Cunnard assured her, the medicine would make them manageable. If the prescription stopped working, she could always try another. She could keep moving, or seeming to move, indefinitely.

Fine, she told him. Good enough.

Three years later, after breaking her leg trying to crawl up the stairs, Bert went into a nursing home against her will, assured by Maddie's father that it was only temporary, until she gained her strength back again. But she saw through the lie and cursed him as a "traitorous serpent."

She never knew exactly when the decision was made to sell her house. "Get rid of it," Willy had said to the auctioneer, resolved to wash his hands of the whole deteriorating mess against Maddie's and her mother's protests to salvage the heirlooms. Frantically, Maddie had driven home and gone through the house the day before the auction to gather a few of the treasures for herself, including Bert's music case full of poems and the rose lamp. As things had turned out, it occurred to her, Grandaddy hadn't willed her the lamp. She had simply taken it.

Bert couldn't live long, her father predicted. Her strength was failing. But as Maddie placed the rose lamp in the shadowy hallway of the manse in North Hebron, she disagreed. Bert had faith. She had unfinished business to settle—Deane to wait for. She could live very long.

Then, over the next three years, descending into a second and a third depression, Maddie learned that the power of the lamp hadn't resided in itself, but in its location on the piano in Bert and Grandaddy's house, a silent witness to Deane's and her father's childhoods, to Katy's and her own, to Bert's grief, and Grandaddy's sustaining strength and humor. It did not look the same in its new location in this temporary house. ("Will we still live here in three years, Mom?" Merrill had asked when her friends started talking about what middle school they would like to go to.) And so in Maddie's mind, it remained in its old place, in the original house, on the Mason and Hamlin piano that was now sold off, as a lovely, radiant exception to the incessant blue.

Once she owned it, it never shone that way again.

8

CRACKS IN
THE ICE

....
....
....
....

Nate wanted Kate to decide. "She doesn't have to come if she doesn't want to," he said diplomatically, looking for the song sheets Maddie had typed for the carol-singing at the Hinckley County Nursing Home. "I just don't want her staying home all night watching television."

"Merrill and Nathan are going," Maddie told ten-year-old Kate, who, named after her Aunt Katy and like her in nature, lay stretched out on the couch with her arms folded tightly across her chest. "It would be a good chance for you to see what kind of work your dad does out there. Please come."

"I'm *not* going to watch television," Kate said. "I'm going to draw. I'm making a new movie."

Kate's movies consisted of piles of sheets of tablet paper, each sheet with a hastily-sketched scene of drama on it featuring elongated stick figures flying on missions of fantastic adventure—long-haired ladies riding winged dolphins or swans in search of stolen babies or long-lost keys. As hard as Maddie tried to figure them out, the plots were indecipherable. More than anything else, Kate wanted to be an artist. But she simply couldn't draw. Nate wondered how she could have such a compulsion for it with so little talent. Yet she practiced in solitude for hours every day and had amassed a whole suitcaseful of movies. Maddie thought maybe it was the storytelling rather than the drawing that drove her on. Sometimes she asked Kate to narrate the stories to her sheet by sheet, but it didn't help much with the understanding.

"Did you call Mae Burson about the cookie plates?" Nate asked distractedly, opening and closing the drawers in his desk three times. "You draw every day, Kate. Remember what I said in the sermon last Sunday? Sometimes you have to give to others who have no way of giving to you."

"Dad," twelve-year-old Merrill said, looking at herself in the mirror over the hearth, "don't *ever* talk about the sermon in our real life."

"Everyone's bringing a dozen," Maddie said in response to his question. "I made three dozen extra gingerbread boys."

"Anatomically correct?" Merrill smirked, referring to the "help" her brother had given Maddie, making his batch with excessive physical detail.

"Have you seen a slip of paper with names and addresses on it?" Nate said. "All the people in my prospective members' class . . . ? I've got to get that letter of class dates out. I *can't* have lost that slip." He slammed the last drawer.

Yes he could have, Maddie sighed. If one were dying, the best person to have close by was Nate. But as the church of North Hebron grew, and the Session dragged its feet on hiring an assistant pastor, he was less and less of an organizer. "Do you feel all right, Kate?" she asked as her daughter folded her arms tighter over her stomach.

"I want to stay *home*. You know why."

Maddie knew. Kate had inherited not only Katy's name but her weak stomach as well. If anything, hers was worse. Over the past year, just watching the sun go down at night

could set off nausea. Sometimes at two o'clock in the morning
when Maddie got up to go to the bathroom, she'd find Kate
backed into a corner beside the toilet waiting to throw up for
the second or third time. She'd smile up at Maddie, embarrassed
at the absurdity of a weakness that was becoming a way of
life. But then she'd get up and go to school the next morning
as if nothing had happened, and forget all about it until the
next night. The doctor had prescribed medicine for relieving
the painful cramps. Her malady was "typical of nervous children," he said. (Where had Maddie heard that before?) She
must either grow out of it or learn to control it.

Fortunately, Kate got better just knowing the medicine
was available. But she hardly ever took it after hearing Grandma
Ginny tell her mother about Bert's growing addiction to sleeping pills, amphetamines, and tranquilizers. Instead, Kate resolved to try to control it by avoiding distressful situations.
Maddie was amazed at the elaborate preventions she devised
for avoiding relapses. She kept an inflexible schedule at school,
came home and did her homework, worked on ten or fifteen
new scenes for a movie until supper time, watched two situation
comedies on television, covered her parakeets at eight o'clock,
read a *Ranger Rick* nature magazine in bed, then turned her
lights out at nine-thirty. The magazine seemed to calm her
more than anything. She was becoming an amateur ornithologist—obsessed with trumpeter swans, Great Blue Herons,
owls, pelicans, even the pigeons in the backyard. Maddie had
done everything she could to encourage her, and was delighted
to hear her rattle on about native habitats and patterns of
migration. When they had lived in Hadleyburg, Kate had
dragged a bushel basket of sticks and hay up into the branches
of a mulberry tree and sat in it for two hours "to get the feel
of being an eagle." She loved that tree, hiding up in its branches
and eating the berries like a little bear cub. In fact, having to
leave Hadleyburg had started the stomach upsets. Now not

even the prospect of a peregrine falcon could get her outside at night past nine-thirty. If she wasn't asleep by ten, she told her mother, she would start "thinking" and risk being sick all night long.

"We'll be back by nine-thirty," Maddie promised her now. "Maybe sooner."

"There's probably a sitcom she wants to see tonight," Nate said irritably, still upset about the lost list.

"There is *not*," Kate said, insulted by the suggestion.

Nate sat down beside her. "Katie, all I'm asking is that you come with the choir to the county home to sing Christmas carols for the old people. Is that so scary? They need Mom to play the piano, and they love to see children. Most of their grandchildren live far away, just like you do from your grandparents. I've asked other people to bring their kids too. You won't be the only ones."

"Wanna bet?" Merrill said, applying styling mousse and a curling iron to her hair. Yet Maddie knew gratefully that Merrill could be counted on. She would complain all the way, but be cheerful with the old people when she got there. Thank God for Merrill, solid as a rock, like Nate—or as Nate usually was when not caught up in the accelerated activities of Lent or Advent.

"Why is it always *us* that has to go?" Kate said.

"Because you have good voices," Maddie said. "You've sung in youth choirs since you were born, practically."

"No. It's because we're the minister's kids," Merrill said.

"No. It's because I want you there," Nate said, squeezing Kate's hand. "I don't expect you to run right out there for the fun of it. They need you to come. Your face will cheer up Rudy and Hazel Latterman and poor old Renzy Thompson. I've told them so much about your bird-watching, Kate. There's a small lake out behind the home, and they say a couple of blue herons fly in there late every afternoon."

"Really?" she said, her interest perking up. She had never seen a real blue heron, Great or otherwise. "It will be dark when we get there. I won't be able to see them."

"There's a full moon," Maddie said. "You might."

Kate was persuaded to go. As Nate told her more about some of the poor people who lived there, her sympathy, which was as full and ready for others as it was for herself, became aroused. She began to see the goodness and nobility of her going. "Maybe I can make a movie about the herons," she said to Maddie, fully expecting to see them now.

The night was glowing with fog when they set out. The road that wound through the woods to the isolated home was slick with a thin layer of ice, no new snow to dig into, and the air was saturated with moisture. "The air looks like skim milk," Merrill said, fascinated, looking out of all the windows.

"It looks more like Halloween than Christmas," Kate said uneasily as Nate pulled into the gravel parking lot behind an enormous old cattle barn.

"Did you know this was an entirely self-sufficient facility in the fifties?" Nate said. "They grew their own vegetables, milked their own cows, raised their own poultry. But then the government said the residents were being 'exploited' for their work. So now they have no work to do, hardly ever get outside on the grounds, and have to buy all their food at prices higher than they can afford. They're going bankrupt. All that's left is a small herd of dairy cows."

"There aren't any Christmas lights," Nathan said, disappointed at the unfestive look of the place. The home floated like a great dark ship on a cloud, or like a haunted house.

"They're running on a shoestring budget," Nate said. "Only the poorest people end up here, when there's nowhere else to go."

"Are you sure they know we're coming?" Maddie asked,

seeing only one lamp burning through a first-floor window. She heard cars of other choir members pull into the parking lot behind them.

"Yep," Nate said. "The recreation hall's on the other side. There won't be many residents, so don't be disappointed. We'll be lucky if ten or fifteen come down from their rooms."

They went up wide, broken steps into a dark-paneled foyer. A nurse took their coats, all but Nathan's, who held on to his for security, and led them to the recreation room. Maddie stared at the paint peeling off the walls, at the scuffed wooden floors and exposed water pipes and heating ducts. In spite of Nate's warnings, this wasn't what she had expected at all. In Hadleyburg, the old folks' home had been furnished with marble-topped antiques and crystal chandeliers. Here the furniture consisted of old church pews that looked as though they'd served as park benches for ten years before being dropped off here. "I can't believe this," she whispered to Nate. "I had no idea it was this bad."

"You're on the edge of real rural poverty," he said. "This is an old county home. There's no Presbyterian home for sixty-five miles. I've been trying to tell you."

Maddie felt a twinge of guilt. She used to accompany Nate on many of his hospital and nursing-home calls to get to know the parishioners. But after the first depression, she had stopped doing it. In fact, she didn't want to do it at all anymore.

Nathan giggled as the first few floppy-slippered residents shuffled into the recreation room, one on a walker, another in a shabby sport coat and shawl. To Maddie's surprise, they were mostly old men, hairless, toothless, one missing an arm, bundled in layers of sweaters and flannel shirts buttoned tightly up to their chins. They sat down on the pews at spaced intervals like riders on a bus to a tiresomely predictable destination, and looked over the choir members who, arranging themselves in three rows, put on cheerful Christmas faces and smiled back like actors. "Are some of these old people crazy?" Merrill whispered to her father.

"They've lost their marbles a little," Nate explained to all three children, "but they're good people. Renzy can play the banjo like nobody's business." Maddie noticed that Merrill was smiling nicely too by now.

Uncomfortable at being stared at, Nathan stifled another giggle by pulling his coat up over his face. He turned it around until his right sleeve stuck out like an elephant's trunk, then peered out of the hole under the arm at an old woman who was taking a coughing fit. Nate reached out and gripped his shoulder. "Enough," he said sternly.

Then Maddie caught a look of emergency from Kate, a split-second question, "Mom what am I *doing* here? Why did you make me *come?*"

Be tough, Maddie communicated back. Think of *Christmas,* not of *yourself.*

She took her place at the piano and set up her music. It wasn't easy, since the piano was on wheels and rolled away from her at the slightest pressure on the pedal. In the course of the evening, she guessed she and the piano would move a considerable distance from their starting point.

Nate placed the children in the second row of the choir, then waited for a slow-moving latecomer to find a place to sit. "I'm glad to see you here, Gladys," he said warmly as she took a place close to him. "Can we begin by singing 'O Come, All Ye Faithful'?"

No one assented or objected, and Maddie played the introduction. About a third of the keys didn't play. But accustomed to this, she knew by the end of the introduction where to substitute and compensate an octave higher or lower to keep a steady melodic line. At least this was better than the piano at the Juvenile Detention Center, where three keys in a row had had the same pitch.

Nobody sang but the choir.

Merrill nudged her father to remember the song sheets. She passed them out for him, setting them on the seats beside the people who didn't reach out to take them.

They sang "Deck the Halls" next. Nobody even looked at the sheets. Most of the old people sat or leaned expressionlessly in their places—a dozing, bored audience, not participants.

A nurse who stood in the corner raised her hand and suggested "Jingle Bells."

"Oh yes," Nate said smiling, as though recalling something. "Where's Manny Hooty?" he asked, looking around at the faces.

A tiny old man with suspenders and no teeth stood up and grinned. "Here I am, Rev'rend." He waved at Nate like a little boy.

Maddie caught a glimpse of Kate staring at Manny, then at the crèche figures on the big warped mantel, so old and worn as to be indistinguishable from one another. Maddie couldn't tell a lamb from a donkey, or for that matter, from the baby Jesus. Someone had substituted three tin soldiers for the Wise Men—probably lost over the years. Or maybe the Magi hadn't arrived here yet. The tinsel behind the crèche looked as though it went back to the Reformation, gray and coiled like a dusty old snakeskin.

A few of the old women joined in the first verse of "Jingle Bells," but Manny Hooty (could that be his real name?) gave it his best. He stood and sang the second verse, then kept on going at Nate's urging through the third and the fourth verse. "He knows it all, keep playing," Nate whispered to Maddie as the old gentleman continued on tunelessly but lustily all by himself, verse after verse. By the fifth verse, Nathan got into the spirit of it and started singing any words at all. The choir began to clap and hum along. When it was over, the old man asked to do it again, which they did. To Maddie's relief, this time almost everyone in the room joined in to sing or clap or at least wave a thick-socked foot in time with the music.

Manny asked to do it yet again, but the old man next to him told him to shut up and sit down and give someone else a chance.

"That's Archie Sliker, his best friend," Nate told Maddie. "They're inseparable. Manuel Josephus Hooty saved his life in World War One."

After the carol-sing, the nurse asked Nate if the choir would mind walking up and down the halls upstairs and singing to the residents who couldn't get down to the recreation room.

"Of course," Nate said, seeking out and shaking the hands of each one of the old people who were getting up stiffly from their places. He knew almost everyone by name, Maddie noted, as well as all about their illnesses and lost or distant families.

The old woman who had taken a coughing fit hugged him, then took another one. "You take Ada back to her room," he said to the nurse. "We'll find our way."

Familiar with the halls, he led the choir up a dark side stairway and down a chilly corridor toward a turquoise blue hurricane lamp that burned at the far end. Obviously, the place had been well built and beautifully furnished at one time. The remains of an Oriental rug ran the length of the hallway, but the color and pattern were worn out, and clumps of rotted fringe lay all over the place.

"Something smells!" Nathan said, holding his nose.

"Shh," Maddie said, also aware of the strong sour-sweet stench of urine and disinfectant.

The choir crowded into the last room on the right. Merrill, Kate, and Nathan were pushed to the front (except for a thirteen-month-old baby, they were the only children), and everyone sang "O Little Town of Bethlehem." But there was no acknowledgment from the skeletal old woman who sat tied to her wheelchair. Her glazed eyes stared at them in unrecognition. When Merrill put a small plate of cookies on her lap, she raised a stiff hand, dropped it on the plate, and the cookies fell on the floor.

"This is Martha McKinney," Nate said, picking them up as if nothing had happened, introducing her to Kate, Merrill, and Nathan. "She used to be an art teacher at the high school. Some of her work is on the walls downstairs. Fifteen years ago, she gave the money to buy a new pipe organ at the church."

After another verse of the carol, the choir filtered out. But Kate stayed behind, and Maddie watched her observe her father bend down on his knees, hold Martha's arm, and whisper something into her ear. The old woman's eyes closed, and her hands, which had been clutching the wheelchair tightly, relaxed and fell limp. Nate prayed with her, kissed her forehead, then put the cookies on the stand beside her bed. For a moment there was the ghost of a smile on her lips, which faltered when he left the room.

In the next room, there were two more old women, both blind. The choir sang "It Came Upon the Midnight Clear," and the smaller woman waved her arms aimlessly with pleasure, staring sideways at nothing. Then, to Maddie's amazement, she burst into tears when Nate told her he had brought his wife and children to see her as he promised. Reaching out a bony hand, she felt for them in the air, found Nathan's arm and stroked it eagerly. He pulled back at first. But then seeing how weak she was, too frail to do him any harm, he came forward and let her pull him to her. Then in a spontaneous gesture, he put his arms around her neck and hugged her. God bless Nathan, Maddie smiled at Nate—impulsive, wide-open Nathan.

"Oh, how sweet," the old woman crooned, a yellowish fluid draining with tears from her eyes. "How beautiful you all are," she said, seeking Merrill's outstretched hand next. Kate held back, behind Maddie.

In the next room, a curled-up old man lay on a tousled bed. There was an overpowering odor of vomit, and the nurse told the choir to pass by. Nate went in alone. It was Renzy, he told Maddie, going in. He was dying.

"I have to go to the bathroom," Kate said, tugging on Maddie's arm as they waited for him to come back out. "Where is it?"

"I don't know," Maddie said, looking up and down the hallway.

"I have to go right *now*," she said a minute later with a desperate look. Nate emerged from the room.

"It's down that corridor," he said, pointing in the direction of a dim, offshooting hallway. "Mad, you'll see an old yellow raincoat on the radiator to your right when you go in. Put it on her before she sits down."

"What?" Maddie said, as Kate tugged at her.

"The pipes leak over the toilet."

"You're kidding."

Halfway to the bathroom, Kate stopped, flushed pink, and changed direction. "I'm going to throw up, Mom," she said. "I have to go outside."

"But it's just a little farther—"

"No! If I get outside, maybe I won't."

Maddie ran behind her now, back past the baffled faces of the choir members, down the stairs, and out the nearest door into a silent, spacious field of stubble and mist, with the lake barely visible beyond. "This isn't the door we came in," Maddie said, trying to orient herself. "Where's the parking lot?"

Kate broke away and ran into the field. Then she dropped to her knees and began to vomit. Her body arched stiffly.

Maddie got down beside her and held her forehead to save her neck muscles. "Go ahead, baby. It's okay."

She threw up her supper, what little she had eaten. But the retching continued.

"Almost done?" Maddie asked, holding Kate's hair out of her eyes as she began to tremble. "What set it off?"

Saliva poured out of her mouth, and tears ran streaming down her cheeks. "I don't know!" she said between gasps for breath.

Maddie held her tightly, and at last the vomiting and shaking subsided. "Okay?"

"No!"

"Let's go back inside before you freeze."

"No!"

"But it's warm inside."

Kate rested limply in her arms, shaking her head no, no, no.

Maddie held her close and shivered. There was the back of the barn. The parking lot must be on the other side.

"I'm *not moving*," Kate said, reading her thoughts.

Maddie reconsidered. "C'mon," she said. "Let's go to the car. We can turn on the heater and listen to the radio until Dad is finished."

"No!" she insisted. "If I move, I'll throw up again. Mom, I know how this *works*."

The trembling began again. She looked at Maddie with moonlight reflected in huge black pupils. "Something's *wrong* with me," she said.

Maddie felt a twist of fear and memory in her own stomach. She thought of the night her sister Katy came home from the Tenebrae service and took a tantrum after vomiting and throwing her shoes against the door.

"It's nerves, Katie," she said calmly, stating the obvious. "I didn't know the home was going to be this run-down. These people need—"

Kate burst out in a fury of rage. "I don't ever want to get the way they are!" She squeezed her eyes shut like two little clenched fists. "Not ever!"

"You won't," Maddie soothed her. "These are the most unfortunate ones who have no family or savings or anything to—"

"Who knows what it will be like when I'm old, Mom?" she interrupted. "You'll be dead. Maybe everyone in my whole family will be dead or far away. You can't *tell* me what it will be like."

Maddie was silent. Of course she couldn't. Just like her namesake, this Kate spared herself no possible truth.

A fog-magnified moon had risen over the wooded hills and shone in eerie shafts on the frozen pond. So, Maddie thought, surveying it: Christmas in Transylvania. "Look," she said lightly to change the focus of Kate's attention. "It's beautiful out here—the misty hills, the moon, the trees. I bet there are blue herons over there beyond those trees."

"It's horrible!" she said, looking only for a moment at the moon over her shoulder and across at the lake. Then turning her head to the side, she let out a scream, not of anger but immediate fear. "Mom, look!"

Maddie looked in the direction Kate was looking. Through the fog, two, three, then four pairs of eyes became visible. The field they were standing in was full of cows. They were surrounded by them. One of them was not more than ten feet away, standing as silent and motionless as a crèche animal.

"He's mad, I bet," Kate said, shuddering.

"He doesn't look mad to me," Maddie said, not sure. The cow was huge.

Kate frowned. "This is *his* field, and I've made a big Christmas barf in it. I never should have gone out. I knew it. I should be at home. Oh, I wish I were home!"

In a moment, she was overtaken by another fit of vomiting, this one harder than the first.

"Won't you let me take you back inside?" Maddie pleaded between the convulsions. "The nurse can help you."

"No!" she panted, looking up at the cow through blurred eyes to make sure it wasn't moving.

She was shaking uncontrollably now. Her lips looked navy blue in the moonlight. Not knowing what else to do, Maddie opened her suit jacket and took her inside, holding her so tightly she didn't have the space to tremble. "Stop it, now," she said firmly. "These cows will think you're crazy."

"I *am* crazy!"

"No you're not. You just feel things very strongly. Are you warm?"

"No!"

"Are you warm-*er*?"

"Ye—yes."

If only Nate would hurry, Maddie wished. But she knew he wouldn't. He would talk with each and every resident, take time to pray and joke and reassure them, more than was necessary. She prayed he would hurry anyway—divine intervention this time, Lord, just once for us? Then she prayed for a blue heron to appear and take Kate's mind off her stomach.

No heron appeared.

As Kate's shaking subsided again, they sat down on the brittle stalks of weeds. Maddie rocked her back and forth, listening to the fog drip from the trees. She heard the ice on the lake crack at regular intervals, as though someone were walking across it, east to west. She looked up. No one.

She thought of Deane, long lost on the ice thirty years ago.

"It's a ghost," Kate said, as though reading her thoughts.

"Maybe," Maddie said softly. Then, feeling Kate's steady breathing again, she stood up. "I don't care what you say, Kate. We're going to the car. You're freezing."

Too weak to protest, Kate gave in. Not wanting to walk through the cows, Maddie took a long, roundabout way toward the ghostly lake, stopped to look and listen a moment, then went up the path to the barn, and finally around to the parking lot. They got in the front seat of the car. Then she realized she didn't have the keys to start it. Nate did. She couldn't turn on the heater or the radio, and she couldn't leave Kate to go inside to get them.

Then for no reason at all, Kate leaned out the car door and started to retch again. This time Maddie felt torn between sympathy and anger. "Why am I *like* this?" Kate gulped in between efforts to bring up what wasn't there, her face contorting with the pain of her stomach cramps. Saliva ran out of her mouth in a stream, and she couldn't get her breath. "Mom!" she cried, clutching Maddie, close to panic.

Why hadn't she brought Kate's medicine? Maddie reproached herself. From experience, she knew that once her cramps progressed this far, they couldn't be stopped by anything but her falling asleep. Somehow Maddie had to help her turn her mind off so she could relax. Kate had to be made to detach from everything she was feeling—to let go.

Against her frantic protests at being moved, Maddie put her in the back seat and laid her out full-length on her stomach, talking calmly the whole time, ignoring the almost continuous dry retching. She massaged her back and neck. "It's all right," she said. "Your Aunt Katy used to have spells like this."

"Aunt Katy died!"

"Not because of this. She grew out of it. Your feelings are making you sick because they're exaggerated, that's all. There's nothing wrong with you at all."

"I want to go home!"

"You can't yet. For now, home is right here, in your Dad's car."

Maddie remembered an old army blanket Nate had stashed under the seat after the last campout with the youth group. She found it and spread it over Kate's back, then lay down lightly on top of her, embracing her whole body at once. She talked nonstop, drawing Kate's mind away from the images of the nursing home.

"My nerves make me sick too sometimes. And I'm as

healthy as a horse. Only when it happens to me, it hits my head instead of my stomach. You know those blue pills I take every so often?"

Kate nodded, her shuddering coming in rhythmic waves now, subsiding, rising, subsiding.

"They're not just for headaches. They're to help settle me down when my nerves go bonkers—just like yours do some-times."

"That's not as bad as *this*," she moaned, tears streaming onto the car seat. Good, Maddie thought. Real tears would help drain it off.

"Oh, yes it is. It's worse than you think. Sometimes I don't think I can get out of bed in the mornings. I feel like I have wax in my veins, or like a robot has his steel fingers around the back of my neck."

"You do?"

"Everybody's afraid of getting old and sick and dying, you know, Kate."

"But what if a person dies too soon—like Katy?" Her eyebrows narrowed in anger. "Besides, that's *not* what made me sick."

"What else then? Tell me what else."

Kate hesitated. She had a proud private streak in her that resisted confessing strong feelings. "That old lady who hugged Nathan reminded me of Bert," she said, "and how she hated that place Grandpa put her in."

Surprised, Maddie thought of the one time last summer when she'd taken the kids to visit Bert in the nursing home in Pittsburgh. Bert had greeted them bravely in her new despised wheelchair, dressed in a turquoise chiffon negligee that mocked rather than flattered her emaciated features. None of them had seen her since she had fallen down the stairs, when her right leg had cracked under her weight and wouldn't heal properly. That was when Willy had decided to move her straight from the hospital to the nursing home. (Trying to keep up the house was killing her, he had said, though Maddie knew it also gave her the will to live.) Desperate to see the great-grandchildren, she had begged Maddie to take a week off and bring them home. When at last they came, she had held out a curled bony hand to Kate (her favorite great-grandchild, there was no doubt) and smiled broadly, revealing yellow crooked teeth stained with lipstick. Frightened, Kate had backed away. Seeing the look on her face, Bert had been crushed and burst into tears. "I am a *horror!*" she cried to Maddie, after trying so hard to look presentable. "Why must you and Nate live so *far* away?" And then she lashed out at her son for bringing her to that hellish place, calling him a "serpent" and a "rat" for divesting her of her rightful property. In fact, Maddie knew her father had moved heaven and earth to get Bert the brightest, airiest room in the best home in Pittsburgh. But it didn't matter. It wasn't *her* home. She hated its impersonality and coldness, its ideals of efficiency and relentless routine.

"Yes," Maddie answered Kate honestly now. "She reminded me of Bert too, the way she conducted the music."

"It's no use living if you end up like that," Kate said fiercely.

"Oh no?" Maddie said. "Bert wouldn't say that. Remember the poem she sent you last year for your birthday?" Confused about the occasion, Bert had sent Kate a homemade valentine raggedly cut out of a piece of red foil wrapping paper. On it she had pasted a copy of "To a Very Little Girl" as her gift, the sonnet she had written to Maddie when she was seven. "Watch Katie," she had scribbled in a note to Maddie. "*She is in the line. Blue in the blood. Thank God, but watch her. Don't give* her too much freedom to explore too soon *lest she be overwhelmed.*" How lucid she could still be, Maddie had thought—still persisting in her own definition of blue blood: blessing and curse, from her own mother to her, to Deane, to Maddie, to Kate.

"Yes," Kate said, recalling the valentine.

"Remember the line about the sword?" Maddie continued. "She said you wear a sword. And I know it's true. You're a fighter. You fight every night when the sun goes down and most of the time you win. You're going to be strong because of this illness, Kate. You can look at that spooky moon and tell it it's nothing, just a piece of rock, that it has no power over you. That's what your Great-uncle Deane would have said."

"The one who crashed in the plane?"

Maddie nodded.

Kate turned over and looked out the window at the moon. "I think about him sometimes, Mom," she said. "I look at all the neat stuff he gave you."

"He told me once about a creature called a Snowy Owl."

"I know Snowy Owls. They live in the Arctic."

Maddie could feel warmth coming back into Kate's body as she lay still, her heart beating more slowly. She looked like a baby to Maddie, her eyes dreamy and drowsy.

"He would have loved you if he'd known you," Maddie said. "He felt all the things you feel, but he knew how to keep those feelings under control—how to fight, even when he was completely alone, in places much colder and darker than that cow field."

"Did he take medicine?"

"In a way. He learned from the Eskimos something like what the Indians call Big Medicine—a lot of knowledge mixed with a little real magic. He taught me that even though the Snowy Owl is small and weak-looking, it's just a disguise. It's not helpless. It can make a home on the ice. And it doesn't barf at Christmas just because it will get old someday."

"We should throw our medicine away then?" Kate asked, closing her eyes in exhaustion.

Maddie hesitated, wishing she could deny her intermittent dependence on it. "Yes. We should. When we're tough enough."

"I came out here to see a blue heron," Kate sighed, "and all I saw was a bunch of cows."

Maddie smiled, stroking her hair. "Well, that's Christmas for you. The Wise Men came all that way to see the Lord of the Universe, and all they saw was a wrinkly little kid."

Now Maddie felt glad to be outside, away from the choir and the cookies. "You'll see a heron someday. Sometime Dad can bring you out here in the early evening, just the two of you."

"Bet we won't," Kate whispered barely audibly. "He's always working." She fell into a doze.

No, they probably wouldn't, Maddie conceded. Nate had so little time for such things. She was braced for the ordeal of Christmas. Tomorrow, Grandma Hart's plane would be in. And now, against the advice she'd just given her daughter, Maddie thought how wonderful it would be to spend one Christmas at home with her own family again. But Nate's mother was alone and resisted people's kindness as aggressively as Nate embraced it. Ever since his birth, she'd also been susceptible to clinical depression, but of a different kind from Maddie's, making her slow-witted and nasty to other people. She had no other children or family besides Nate, no friends left, and no one to invite her for Christmas if Maddie didn't. But she was so cantankerous, Maddie couldn't invite anyone else along with her.

At least the children were learning tolerance—how to love the unlovable. They'd been entertaining Grandma at Christmas for twelve years.

Overcome with tiredness, she put her head beside Kate's and rested her hand on the soft silkiness of her cheek. "O, cheek like a swan," the line of the exquisite Good Friday anthem occurred to her.

Hearing the ice on the lake crack again, this time west to east, she thought once more of Deane. Were there ever ghosts? Then gradually she relaxed, and fell asleep.

* * *

It was snowing up, sideways, and down. The unpredicted storm slammed gusts of wind against the house, and she loved it.

At the sink, Maddie swallowed her maintenance dose of Limbatrol—the tension headaches were always worse when Nate's mother came. Then she went upstairs to make sure the kids were all really sleeping. Nathan was an expert faker on Christmas Eve, with bedclothes tangled convincingly, mouth open, regular breathing.

She checked Kate and Merrill first, kissed them, picked up their socks and underwear, and pulled up their covers. She lingered over Nathan a moment, who wasn't faking, soft and warm in the fuzzy red "bunny suit" Grandpa Willy had sent in the mail. The muscles in her neck and shoulders ached as she bent over to kiss him in the semidarkness. She wished she could give in to the dark, lie down beside him, and sleep Christmas Eve, 1979, away.

But Santa Claus must be over the Yukon by now, she could hear her father saying. There was magic to perform.

At least the early service at the church was over. The sermon she and Nate had worked on until two in the morning had gotten a good response. A few people hadn't liked using T. S. Eliot's "Journey of the Magi" as a co-text with the Gospel of Matthew, but some of them had. (The sermon ought to be viewed as an art form, she remembered telling Nate on one of their first dates in the seminary cafeteria—perfectly crafted, focusing the general human heart at the free expense of tedious orthodoxy. One must leave nothing up to the Spirit in the writing, but everything in the delivery.) She glanced at the clock: twelve forty-five A.M. Nate was probably preaching the midnight service right now. As usual on Christmas Eve, she was alone in the house with her children and her eighty-two-year-old mother-in-law, Grace, who, Nate said, after giv-

ing birth to him when she was forty-five, had never been quite
sane since. She was now slumped and snoring in the den.
Maddie decided she had better get started decorating the tree.

She considered putting some carols on the stereo, but
didn't want to wake Grace. So she lit candles for herself in the
foyer and living room, and one tall red one in the center living-
room window. ("To light the wandering Christ-child home,"
Bert had told Essy, when she had dispensed with all other
decorations in her house after Deane disappeared.) "For Grandaddy, for Katy, for Deane," Maddie said aloud now as she lit
the candle: *In memoriam.*

She congratulated herself on her good spirits, considering
how much she still missed Esther and Lynne, her parents, and
everyone at home. Esther had written on her Christmas card
that Lynne had no idea what she wanted to do with her life,
and liked to talk in bed all night long. Maddie would give
anything to have Lynne come spend Christmas with her, to
sit in robe and slippers, eat cookies, and help her stuff the
stockings or set up the train. But North Hebron was too far
to drive in the unpredictable weather, and undoubtedly
Grandma would be jealous of Maddie's attention to anyone
else, and show it in no uncertain terms. So Christmases together
were out.

Right now Maddie's family was probably gathered in her
mother's kitchen, still dressed up from church (how wonderful
to go to church and come home, and that be all of it), laughing
and having a wonderful time. They would call her tomorrow
and thank her for all the gifts she'd sent, and tell her how
much she was missed. But she was here now, listening to the
faint hiss of the candles burning in the high-ceilinged manse,
and to the pipes, probably freezing in the cellar, clanking like
the chains of Jacob Marley. She was on her own to make
Christmas Present for her family, and for herself. She hated it.
She loved it.

At the window, she took pleasure in the motion and smoky
light of the snowstorm and felt a momentary defiant exultation,
a glorying in aloneness—though a self-pitying voice insinuated
a word and said that at least Mary and Joseph had each other
on the first Christmas Eve. Where was her husband? Where
were her friends? She admitted that especially at Christmas
she felt hidden away from the real world by the church—
provided with all the necessities and many genuine kindnesses
so she and Nate could be on call at all times, like spiritual
mistresses, at the whim of any one of a thousand members.
Both he and she were responsible for representing a Christian
perspective on modern life; but what that perspective actually
was, not many members agreed on. If she made friends in
the church, she worried that she could unwittingly make ene-
mies for Nate by the expression of one carelessly uncensored
opinion.

Given her own eccentricities and unorthodoxies, she
hardly expressed any significant opinions outside the house
anymore. How bland and unreadable she must seem to the
parishioners. But above all, she couldn't stand being subject to
their conflicting judgments about her. She had come to prefer
loneliness to risking new friendships that might end in a church
member's shocked disillusion. She had learned that even if she
and Nate did become close friends with a few church members,
other members would fault them for showing "favoritism."

She preferred isolation, she told herself.

But it wasn't utter isolation. There was something between
her and the night, the bluish snow and her aching head. Cold,
darkness, exile—joy born *here* against all the weight of circum-
stance. She could understand what Deane meant when he said
that his walks across the tundra had left him frozen, exhausted,
and exhilarated. A part of him reveled in the long Arctic night;
he felt a connection to the distant past in that utter darkness,
and also the sense of a presence—a latent presence—that he
couldn't feel in the light.

Or was this just a new depression descending, muddling her emotion with an artificial high before the crash? Was it rationalization? And yet, some of her rationalizations coincided with those of Bert's favorite poets and theologians. All the interesting ones were dark and a little crazy. The truth about life, about oneself, was, like the face of God, hazardous to confront. It could make you sick—and then the sickness deepened your grasp of it—as if Holy Ground could only be reached through the primordial chaos.

She liked to test her strength against her knowledge. She believed she'd learned to do what she told Kate to do last week at the county home: to stare down the bone-white magnified moon as if it were nothing. She thought of the stone pelican over the arched entrance to the church at home where she had first understood Bonhoeffer's revelation: The God who is with us is the God who forsakes us. The best theologians all resorted to poetry in the end. The prose of their systematic theologies cracked under them like thin ice. The starving mother pelican let her starving chicks consume her own body when the winter was too long. The strength had to come from her, not from God, in her isolation.

Her thoughts became more and more disjointed as she pressed her nose to the glass and watched the storm. In the back of her mind, a billion bits of information floated in disconnection.

But then all of a sudden two came together. Where were the trash bags? What day was this?

The kids had been hearing so much mockery of Santa Claus in school and on television lately, she'd been trying to mystify them with little signs and magic tricks to keep them wondering, as her father used to do. For the past three Christmases, cynical Merrill had led a house search for hidden presents to prove to Nathan there was no sleigh or reindeer, and last year she had found half of them. But this year, Maddie had hidden all their gifts—candy, stocking stuffers, even the tree and village decorations—in trash bags in the garage, stashed in heaps among the real trash. For a week, all three kids had walked past them a hundred times, looking for the stash in cupboards, in the car trunk, in closets and under beds. "See?" trusting Nathan had said to Merrill, vindicated in his faith when she hadn't found anything. Even wily Kate had looked at Maddie wonderingly. Maddie had shrugged and pretended a wistful sort of regret. "Your Dad and I can't afford very much this year. Santa will have to do most of it."

But in the chaos of Grandma Hart and choir rehearsals, deacons' food baskets and Sunday school pageants (she had quit her job as organist, but been called back when the new organist had gone to Oregon for the holidays), she had forgotten to tell Nate about her strategy. And yesterday had been trash collection day. With a panicked feeling now, she remembered watching him carry out the bags, not thinking at all. "No," she said aloud, her eyes wide, realizing what had happened. "Please no."

Her face grew hot. It couldn't have happened. In a momentary rush of irrational hope, she ran to the garage to look. But the bags were gone. Every one. All her gifts for Grandma and Nate, the candy canes and tinsel and three oversized anatomically correct gingerbread boys, the intricate Swiss-made models for the village under the tree that had taken Nate six nights to put together after the kids were in bed, everything wrapped with poems on the tags. "It can't be," she protested, overwhelmed with helpless anger and panic.

In the matter of a few moments, the pressure points in her skull turned up their volume to high. She sat down on the floor, held her enormous head in her hands, then massaged the two main trigger points hard, around and around. They hurt so much, she felt nauseated when she pressed them in. How could she have been so stupid? How could she set up the train without the switches, or decorate the balsam? Even the fresh pine branches and holly she'd gathered from the grounds of Christmas tree lots around town had gone into a trash bag. "No," she repeated, grieving for Nathan's red scooter, the dollhouse furniture Essy had sent from Pittsburgh, Merrill's new dress, Kate's stuffed trumpeter swan with the baby zipped inside it. "How could I do such a—"

"Madeleine!" Grandma called out in a hoarse voice from the den. "Where are you?"

Oh, Maddie thought. *Not now.*

"Madeleine!" she called again. "What time is it?"

Maddie rose. Somehow she would have to get this obese, sour-tempered old woman up the stairs and into bed. "It's one o'clock," she shouted back, feeling a guilty repulsion for her mother-in-law's physical and mental torpidity. Nate had said she'd been an unhappy person even when she wasn't depressed, obsessed with punctual dinner hours, full of envy of anyone happier than herself. At first, Maddie had been sure love and patience could win her over in time. But she'd been wrong. Grace (the irony of her name never failed to strike Maddie) kept her long fingernails filed to a sharp point, her hair perfectly coiffed and netted, and considered that sufficient justification for other people's love—for heaven itself. To irritate Nate, she still called black people "coons" in front of the children.

"A.M. or P.M.?" Grace demanded.

Come now, Maddie thought, not answering. Look out the window.

Entering the den, Maddie forced a smile and closed the drapes to keep out the cold drafts. She took momentary satisfaction from the narrow spray of snow the wind had forced through a crack in the glass onto the rug.

"Where's Nate?" Grace asked, pretending to be more confused than she really was, as Maddie held out her hand to help her. Ignoring the hand, she pulled an afghan Maddie's mother had made around her shoulders and huddled under it.

"Still at church. The weather's terrible. He won't be back for a long time. He'll probably have to drive some people home. It's time for you to go to bed now."

Grace grunted understanding and didn't move.

"Come on now," Maddie said, trying to be kind as she took hold of the old woman's slack, flabby arm and pulled her up. Grace made a face and strained excessively.

Maddie saw a large round stain on the cushion. Grace had wet herself again. "Never mind about it," she said. "I forgot to wake you at midnight to go to the bathroom. It's my fault."

She led her slowly through the dining room and to the stairs, knowing she hadn't forgotten to wake her at all. She had simply wanted to be alone when she lit the candles.

At the bottom of the stairs, Grace halted, dropped the afghan, and looked around as if her surroundings were suddenly interesting to her, a common tactic of procrastination. "Keep going now," Maddie said. "One step at a time. You have to get warm and dry."

"You know I have nothing to give you," she said coldly, fingering the dust on the newel post. "I can't shop. I brought a few little things in my suitcase for the children."

That may be all they get, Maddie thought, the pain of the lost trash bags stabbing at her again.

Upstairs, she helped Grace undress—layers of long yellow undershirts, a baggy slip, an ancient straitjacket corset—then washed her underwear, and got her into a pair of Nate's large flannel pajamas for warmth. She gave her her depression and high blood pressure pills.

"Thank you, Madeleine," she said formally as she sat down on the edge of her bed. "Shouldn't I be packing to go home soon?"

The question was a reproach—another tactic. "You have another whole week yet," Maddie said pleasantly, as though looking forward to it. Nate was letting her stay two weeks this time. Grace wanted to move in with them.

"You still have work to do tonight, I guess," she said, accepting but not approving of all Maddie's duties. "You over-do. Always doing and doing."

"Would you like me to leave your tree lights on?" Maddie asked. She had decorated a small Scotch pine in Grace's room for atmosphere, against Nate's advice that it was a waste of time. Perhaps he was right. She seemed incapable of en-joying it.

"I don't care anything about it," she said dully, not even looking in its direction.

May depression never take me this far, Maddie thought with dread. It would be better to be dead.

As Maddie tucked her in, she thought back to the Christ-mas when she and Nate had gotten engaged, the only Christ-mas Eve they had spent in Pittsburgh at her mother's house. Nate had been amazed at the huge tree, the train and village under the tree, the decorations and merrymaking. "Christmas was a roast chicken and a pine cone when I was growing up in Washington," he laughed, taking it all in appreciatively. Then a few days later, they drove to Washington, D.C., for a New Year's celebration with his parents. The day after their arrival, Grace lashed out at Maddie for taking her son away "on the last Christmas I will ever see him." Baffled by such an assumption, Maddie said she intended to have her and Nate's father spend Christmas with them every year, that holidays were times for families to be together. And she had kept her word—every Christmas ever since. But it made no difference in Grace's attitude. After Nate's father—a gentle tired man who could abandon his wife only by dying—did die, she had gotten worse. For the kids, "Grandma" had become synony-mous with grouchy, grumpy, and begrudging.

Maddie went downstairs and tried to think clearly. What could she do about the presents? What could she make at the last minute? She sat in a chair facing the undecorated tree.

Nothing. There was nothing she could do.

Moments later, she heard Grandma's thick wedge heels clomping across the floor of the upstairs hall. She had gotten up and put on her shoes. Gritting her teeth, Maddie listened to her clomp slowly to the top of the stairs and pause.

"Is it time to get up?" she called down in a rasping voice. "The stairs are dark. How can I see to get down?"

She'll wake the kids, Maddie thought furiously. She ran to the bottom of the stairs. "Shh!" she whispered up. "You just went to bed. I told you, I'll wake you when it's time. Go back to bed."

Defiantly, Grace descended three steps to the small landing where Maddie had stacked empty boxes, wrapping, and ribbon to carry up to the attic. She looked at them with an expression of disorientation and distress—whether an act or for real, Maddie couldn't tell. "What are these things doing here?" she said at last, frowning. "Do you expect me to carry these down?" Before Maddie could answer, she had kicked at them with her fat purple foot and sent them spilling down the steps, the ribbon spools unwinding, tissue paper falling out all over the place.

Maddie stared up at her.

Grace turned and went back upstairs to her room.

Maddie gathered the boxes together, and, too tired to go upstairs all the way, put them back on the landing. Seeing that Grandma had shut her door, she went back to the living room to watch the snowstorm and try to calm down. Her heart was racing. She felt like putting her fist through the picture window.

"Damn the church," she heard herself say involuntarily. Where was Nate? She couldn't do it all alone year after year.

Then out of the blue, as she stared blankly at the drifts beyond the driveway, a thought occurred to her. Sometimes there *was* Grace. Without hat or coat, she ran outside down the front steps toward the curb beyond the stand of hemlock trees. She could barely see the outline of the trees in the blizzard. The cold was so sharp it made her cough, but she didn't care.

There was a mound on the other side of the hemlock. Piles of shoveled snow only? With her bare hands, she brushed away the powder, hoping against hope (a queer phrase—"hope against hope," she thought with the clear objectivity of a by-stander). There were the trash bags, exactly where Nate had stacked them. There had been no trash collection because of the snowstorm—*of course.*

She sank down in the snow as if it were a soft warm bed, laughing with relief, playing with it, eating it, unburying the bags one by one with renewed energy. She hugged the bags, garbage and gifts both. How could she have forgotten there was no collection yesterday? Her fingers were too stiff to undo the twist ties, and she couldn't tell which bags were which, so with a flood of adrenalin that made her perspire in the cold, she carried them into the kitchen two by two, delighting in her new strength and the gusts of wind that cut into her throat like knifeblades. The thermometer on the porch said 13 degrees below zero. Her fingertips were blue, and her nose ran down to her chin. But she felt nothing but surge after surge of thank-fulness. The God who forsakes us is the God who is with us, she laughed, opening her mouth to catch fat flakes of the falling snow.

Inside, the snow melted out of her hair and down her back. She made herself a cup of steaming tea to keep from getting chilled, drank a gulp of it, then sorted the frozen bags and carried the trash back outside. In record time, she put the lights on the tree, hung the ornaments and candy canes, and hauled Nate's ladder out of the garage to wire the star at the top. Next, she put the train layout together, minus the wiring which Nate would have to do tomorrow (at least it would *look* right in the morning). She constructed a temporary village, adding the new models, then filled the stockings to overflowing.

Feeling alternating waves of dizziness and euphoria, she arranged each child's stack of gifts as her father would have done, creating a mood of Christmas whimsy and magic with the various shapes and colors. She put Kate's unwrapped swan at the top of her pile of gifts; it looked out over the whole scene with glassy, penetrating black eyes, a red ribbon around its neck.

From the last trash bag, Maddie took the garlands of pine she'd gathered, and hung them over the mantel, on the piano, over the mirrors and archways, up the railing on the stairs. She set off each garland with a big, red velvet bow. With all the candles glowing, the mood was solemnly beautiful, medieval —definitely High Church. At three-forty, when she stepped back to the hallway to look and see what Nate would see when he came in the door, she was satisfied. It was all right.

But then, as she no longer needed it, her energy left her. Suddenly she didn't have the strength to stand up straight, let alone gather up the empty bags and throw them down the cellar. But she did it anyway. There mustn't be any evidence in the morning that anyone but Santa Claus had done this. Think, she thought, sinking weakly into the chair beside the tree: think what people must feel who have nothing to give their children year after year—nothing at all. That's why she packed all the food baskets at the church. That's why the cookies were baked. That's why they went caroling at the nursing home. For the ones who had nothing. She mustn't forget it.

What kind of Christmases had Grandma had when she was a child?

Then irresistibly she thanked God for giving her this insight, although she well knew God didn't play such games or administer such tests—or, in fact, didn't trouble Himself about trash collection schedules in Michigan. But then, she further thanked Him for not taking the test too far. It wasn't the presents she dreaded her children losing, but the faith that they would be there. Losing the faith too soon.

She began to shiver violently and realized her blue jeans were still wet up to her thighs. She got the afghan Grandma had dropped on the floor on her way up the stairs. It smelled faintly of urine, but she was so tired, she didn't care and wrapped herself up in it anyway.

She thought back to her childhood, when the spirit of Christmas had seemed so easy and spontaneous. She wanted to recreate that for her own children, and not let them see the expensive effort—without aunts, uncles, and grandparents to help bring it alive, make it real. Of course Grace was right about her overdoing. But her kids must never know she overdid to compensate for what was missing at the heart of everything for her. And now, looking around at it all, she had a nagging bitter sense, as she had last year, that this would be the last time she could bring it off.

Shaking off these thoughts, she wondered what time Nate would get home. She looked at the snow roaring sideways up the street. Nathan would be tearing open his presents in three hours. She sat down again, and felt as thin and taut as a stretched-out piece of wire, unable to move or relax. How could she cook the big turkey dinner tomorrow, be cheerful all day against Grandma's Scrooge-like gloom? It had happened before. Energy from nowhere. Making bricks without straw. She could always play cheer, if not joy.

Then all at once, the glowing room was devoid of everything but denied grief, welling up behind the partition of her will like the red hot wax in the candle in the window, testing for a place to spill over. The room was full of useless beauty. No one to see it but her.

No, she denied the denial angrily. Her doctor had warned her about the effects of prolonged exhaustion. She had to distract herself so she could fall asleep for what time she had

and not be overtaken by another depression. But how to distract
herself?

Nate came in at four-ten. "The roads are almost impass-
able," he called out from the hallway. "I probably should have
canceled the service."

He stamped around, snow in his hair and eyebrows, ice all
over his coat. "I parked at the bottom of the hill and had to walk
the rest of the way," he said, and then stopped to look into the
warm, glowing room—the candles lit, the tree trimmed, and
Maddie waking up from a doze in the chair with a stack of old
photograph albums half fallen out of her lap onto the floor.

He went to the chair to kiss her. She looked up, saw the
outline of him, snow-covered, against the Christmas tree light.
Disoriented, her eyes sparkled wildly as if at someone who had
come back from the dead. The recognition in her eyes made
him hesitate to tell her who he really was.

9

THE RAILING

The bed was not a bed. It was a point of no return, an end of resistance once and for all, every night. And it was all right to think of it that way, her psychiatrist Dr. Hazelett had said. If it helped, she could think of each night as an infinity of time for rest and reordering. The universe could expand to the limits of its energy, pause to measure its cumulative mass—"We are not enough," the atoms would say to one another objectively —then fall back into fifteen billion years of collapse, back to the black hole of the beginning. That's all Maddie wanted in this latest, worst depression. Not to have to participate. Not to be held accountable. To sleep spring of 1981 away.

The bed had an old mattress, which added to the problem. When she got under the covers at night, the soft motherliness of the mattress and pillows almost made her cry with relief. But she hadn't been able to produce tears for four months now. Nothing reached her. She was frozen.

She had told Dr. Hazelett her medicine wasn't working as well as it used to. It only kept the symptoms from getting worse.

"Depression is still something of a mystery," he'd replied, trying to allay her growing fears, "the common cold of psychiatry. It will let go like the others. Try to work through it."

But in such a slow-motion state, who could resist the comfort of the bed? In spite of the nailheads of pain up and down the back of her skull and neck, every position she assumed in the bed was languorously pleasurable. She felt cradled in her own weakness. It was a hundred times the force of gravity pulling her down into a well (a singularity, astronomers would call it?) of accelerated collapse.

But the next morning she had to get up again.

This morning, the fifth Thursday in Lent, the tension was turned up high and the argument already underway even before the alarm clock went off: I cannot; you can; I won't; you will. Feeling flat, two-dimensional, as uncoordinated as a mummy waking up in the museum unaware that it is wrapped, Maddie gathered her resolve, swung her legs over the side of the bed, and waited for the first wave of vertigo to subside.

The kids were already up, arguing about dental floss and clumps of toothpaste in the bathroom sink. Still very young at almost nine, Nathan was too scatterbrained to dress himself sensibly or make breakfast without supervision. She couldn't let him go to school with his hair combed like Adolf Hitler, his jelly-dotted face unwiped, his sack lunch forgotten. Teachers knew which mothers got up with their children and which did not.

Irritably she tried to remember what else she had to do today. Nate's sermon had to be revised and typed for the Maundy Thursday Communion service tonight—he had no time. How was she going to stay awake through that service? The new organist had quit, and she was back on the job full-time. But how could she sit up straight at the organ console, turn pages, lead the choir in the responses?

She sat balanced on the edge of the bed like a skydiver

on the edge of a plane. She hadn't missed a Holy Week communion in fifteen years of Nate's ministry. What would proper
Agnes Gibson say if Maddie lay down on the pew in the middle
of the sermon and fell asleep?

What else to do? Music to transpose for the Junior Choir
anthem for Easter Sunday, Kate's skirt to hem, an adult Sunday
school lesson to prepare, candy to buy for abused children at
the Women's Shelter, as well as for Nathan, Merrill, and Kate,
and a fact sheet to type up on where Presbyterian mission
money was going. ("We're supporting terrorists!" Belva Minot
had protested over the phone yesterday. "I read in *Newsweek*
that our denomination is subsidizing literacy programs in Central America taught by Cuban communists! Not another cent,
Mrs. Hart, from me.")

But first, there was the laundry bin to reckon with. And
the undusted furniture downstairs. Floors. Walls. The argument
inside her head resumed: I cannot; you will; I refuse; you have
no choice.

Dr. Hazelett had lately tried to put it in flattering terms
for her: Depression was failed energy and failed morale versus
ruthless conscientiousness and perfectionist determination.
Complimentary, in a way. He said she would have to fight it
out minute by minute, day by day, since modern psychiatry
knew better how to deal with violent psychotics than depressed
women. Nobody really understood it completely, except to
assure her that sometimes drugs helped, and that it did no good
at all to surrender to the deadly fatigue. Somewhere in her
past or in her own psyche, there was an explanation—or perhaps it was a genetic predisposition?

Perhaps, she agreed. But knowing that, *then* what? In the
meantime, she had to keep on functioning as if she were fine,
running under water without slowing down. (She remembered
the Eskimo analogy of "swimming through rock" she'd heard
from Deane when she was a child—perfect.) She didn't dare

lie in that motherly bed for as long as she wanted to, like a child safe within the walls of her father's house. But that was exactly it: wall to wall to wall to wall. Not a square inch of open or unknown space in the days, weeks, months ahead, she thought.

But it wasn't a thought. It was a physical sensation of utter dread.

"I'm up," she said, poking Nate, who was trying hard to stay alseep beside her. He still looked like a boy when he slept, even now at thirty-nine years old, hung over from a budget committee meeting the night before. He had come in at eleven o'clock, thrown his pens, notes, tie, and keys on the desk, said "No raise," and collapsed on the couch and fallen asleep. "Better get up," Maddie prodded him now, her mouth dry as a puppet's. "Nursing home service at nine."

"After you in the bathroom," he mumbled, eyes closed.

She braced herself and stood up. The blood drained in a rush from her head. For ten or fifteen seconds, objects disappeared, then gradually reappeared first in black-and-white, then in color. She turned on the lamp and the overhead light. She'd replaced all the sixty-watt lightbulbs in the house with hundred-watt bulbs, but they still didn't seem to put out enough light.

She tied on a robe and looked at herself in the mirror. Always surprised at how relatively normal she appeared, she noted the dark circles under her eyes, the lank hair, the sickly sallow complexion—a bona fide gink, Grandaddy, she laughed; but at least no wrinkled, stooped, pock-covered crone. Not the thing she felt she was.

In the bathroom, she brushed her teeth hard to get rid of the acrid taste in her mouth, but the mint lasted only a moment. Nathan stood beside her beltless, shoeless, giving all his attention to a complicated Tinkertoy windmill. Stiffly, she brushed his hair and adjusted the mismatched buttons on his sweater. "Get your cowboy boots on," she said. "It's almost seven-thirty."

"They feel prickly inside," he said, knitting his silky brown eyebrows. She could smell the physical health of him, was proud of it, envied it.

"Why, Nathan?"

"I don't know."

"Put them on anyway. Your tennis shoes are covered with mud. What about your fish?"

He shook his head. He loved his three goldfish—a gift from Grandma Ginny—but not enough to remember to feed them regularly. Lately Maddie had forgotten too. One of them was sick, swimming at a list. Golda, Frank, and Myrrtal, named after the gifts of the Magi, would probably be dead by Easter.

Maddie called downstairs to Merrill to set out lunch bags and milk money on the counter. Merrill yelled something back. Kate complained from her bedroom that she had to have a report on volcanoes on Monday and couldn't find her library book on Mount Saint Helens anywhere. And where had her mother hidden her *plain* white kneesocks? Her demanding tone grated on Maddie's nerves.

"I don't know where your library book is," she answered unsympathetically. "Your kneesocks are still in the bin. Wear your other socks."

"I *hate* my other socks," she said, catching her mother's irritable mood and giving it back to her.

I hate all socks, Maddie thought. I hate all socks that I don't wear on my own feet.

Kate and Nathan went downstairs, and Nate locked himself in the bathroom against their return. Maddie moved from room to room, pushing through air, picking up toys and pajamas, pieces, parts, cores of this, crumbs of that. She bent over the clothes bin. There were socks in balls, brown-stained underpants (why must Nathan still wait so long to go to the bathroom?), dirty handkerchiefs stuffed in pants pockets, Kate's gravel "fossils" falling out of her Girl Scout uniform, Merrill's expensive new wool skirt thrown in with the rest—and at the bottom, a rolled-up towel someone had used to wipe up cat vomit. Dizzily, she loaded it all into a basket, trying not to inhale the foul mildew odor of the bin itself. "This is disguzz-ding!" Kate had reproached her about the mildew a week ago, mimicking her mother's obsessive frustration with disorder.

Maddie took down the home-visitation communion kit from the top shelf of the hall closet—Nate would need it at the nursing home and probably forget it—balanced it on top of the overflowing laundry and started down the stairs. She staggered past the railing and bannisters to the landing where, exhausted and out of breath, she stopped to rest.

A flash of panic shot through her that backed her up against the wall. She'd had another nightmare last night. Just now, going past the railing and bannisters, she remembered it. In the dream, she had all her strength and energy back—was almost musclebound with strength, and she had been beating on an attic railing over a stairway just like this one with a heavy club, so hard she thought either the club or the railing would break in two. Her whole body had shaken with the fury of the blows; her mouth had actually foamed. But instead of the railing or club splitting, she herself had split in two, or rather become two of herself. One of her continued to beat on the railing furiously while the other stood apart, watching. Strangely, her consciousness was entirely in the watcher, and she saw the eyes of the beater begin to change, grow larger and larger, become segmented and bright yellow, then start to spin around and around like the spiral of Kate's pinwheel, faster and faster, the eyes of a devil whose capacity for rage and hatred was out of control—free. The watcher backed away in horror.

She tried to escape. But there were no stairs beneath the railing. Someone had filled them in with concrete. She was contained in an airless attic space that was all shadows and angles, dark reds and oranges, ceilings too low, tiny window frames with no glass in them, only more wall. Then out of the shadows, swimming in air, appeared Nathan's fish, enormously bloated and sick. They began circling her, the muddy color of river carp, making unpredictable twists and turns in an effort to stay upright, disappearing into the shadows, then floating out again. They brushed her body and sucked at her face and arms with soft starving mouths, too weak to bite. Nothing seemed more horrifying to her than the deranged, listless aggression of their physical condition. She beat at them. They fell immediately, hitting the floor like torn-open sacks of garbage.

Then the watcher turned and faced the railing beater again. She saw through the skin to its tangled and disjointed skeleton, a tangle of bones linked at odd joints and impossible angles. Recoiling in recognition, she backed away. This is *myself*, she understood, recalling the Eskimo legend Deane had taught her when she was Nathan's age: the *tupilaq* is *me*, grown evil with anger. Beyond anger. Nothing sacrificed, nothing she was denying about herself to spare Nate's reputation or to spare herself the parishioners' judgments, nothing she had renounced for appearance's sake, nothing that had been taken from her or lost, with or without her consent—none, none of it was forgiven or forgotten. It was all stored here, filed away and preserved in this Upper Room. Everything was waiting for judgment day—wound for wound, burning for burning.

She gasped as the laundry basket tipped over on the landing, spilling communion cups and dirty underwear down the stairs. Her hands were sweating. She could smell herself through her robe.

"Are you okay?" Nate called from the bathroom.

"Yeah," she called sharply, appalled that her brain could have kept such records—that she was so madly, miserably begrudging.

But maybe it wasn't true, she grasped at a denial. Dr. Hazelett said there would be nightmares, even when she was on medication, especially when she was going in or coming out of depression. It was all part of the scrambled brain chemistry.

Trembling, she gathered up the laundry, put the communion kit back together, and carried the basket to the kitchen. Merrill and Kate were finishing bowls of cereal, crushing stray flakes underfoot. Nathan was making a piece of toast, dripping honey between the cracks in the table. His chubby cheeks and hands still looked like a baby's. Big as he was, she wished she could keep him home from school today and hold him close to her in the rocking chair all morning long.

"Something's in my boots," he said, tugging at them with sticky fingers. He took off his right cowboy boot, turned it upside down and emptied a shower of pulverized leaves and dirt on the kitchen floor. "I guess that's from the fort," he smiled apologetically, referring to the half-decayed mound of last year's leaves behind the garage. Maddie imagined herself lying blissfully under it like a tulip bulb, undisturbed all winter long.

"Couldn't you empty that outside?" she said.

"There's no school tomorrow," Kate said matter-of-factly.

With moist hands, Maddie poured Nathan a glass of milk, almost dropping the waxed carton. "They're giving you Good Friday off this year?" she said, surprised.

"No," Kate said. "A makeup conference day. The snow canceled the real one."

"You're supposed to see my teacher from eight-thirty to nine," Merrill said.

"Mine is at eleven," said Kate, carrying her bowl to the sink.

"That means your spelling test is today then, Nathan," Maddie said, worried that he hadn't gone over his words with her since Monday. "Do you know them?"

"Not while I'm eating, Mom," Nathan protested, rolling his eyes—which meant no, he hadn't studied.

"Spell 'leopard,' " she insisted, trying to recall the list that he'd probably lost by now. He had no sense for words. His teacher had suggested getting him a tutor with training in learning disabilities.

"L-e-p . . ." He paused, engrossed in something on the cereal box.

"No. Remember how I said to think of it? *Lee-o-pard.* Try it. Do you know you had a great uncle who was once the spelling champion of the whole state of Pennsylvania and got a gold—"

"You *have* to pick me up at exactly two-thirty today," Kate interrupted. "I have to do grocery shopping for the Brownie cookout. I said you'd drive five girls to Camp Redwing on Saturday. Okay?"

"You should have asked me first," Maddie said, heavy-headed, breathless. Her cheeks felt glowing. Her neck muscles ached. "You know I don't feel well, and your Dad and I want to work on the Easter Sunday sermon on Saturday. Doesn't your leader know it's Holy Week?"

"Mom," Kate said with rolling eyes, "a lot of people think church is no big deal. Mrs. Farber gave me the list of stuff. All the other mothers are helping."

"Where's the list?" she demanded.

Kate paused. "Somewhere."

Maddie looked at the clock. "Get your coats on."

She put their lunches into their school bags and set out three pairs of gloves, three stocking caps.

"I don't need a hat," Merrill said. "It's warm."

"It's cold, Merrill. Thirty-nine degrees."

"I don't want to mess up my hair. None of the other girls wear hats. They're stupid."

Meaning that hats—like umbrellas, sweaters, scarves, and boots—were uncool. Warmth was square this year. "But you get sore throats all the time. You don't always have to go along with the crowd."

"Mom," Merrill said, disgustedly. "I don't take drugs or

*any*thing. I shouldn't have to wear a hat if I don't want to. I refuse."

Not taking drugs absolved Merrill and her friends from resisting any number of other temptations. It was the ultimate justification these days. "And when you're sick again," Maddie said, "can I refuse to pay the doctor bills?"

"Isn't it neat how fast your eyeballs move?" Nathan said, studying himself in the kitchen mirror, his coat hanging off his shoulders.

"Just get out the door," Maddie said, pressure growing physically inside her. She had never felt more indifferent to the wonder of anything than at this moment. Only a frantic desire to get rid of her children.

"You *have* to find my library book, Mom," Kate said as she opened the front door. "And the grocery list. *Please.*"

Nathan followed, babbling about a science experiment he intended to try after school with ginger ale and floating raisins. Merrill next, without the hat, who paused guiltily, then leaned up and gave Maddie the softest of good-bye kisses.

"It's okay, Mom," she said. "I'll help Kate with the shopping."

Maddie closed the door behind her and found herself responding to Merrill's act of unexpected sympathy in extreme, overreacting to the strong emotion unaccountably breaking through her depressed composure—her dead dullness. Merrill's soft cheek had utterly disarmed her. She could not go back to the kitchen.

Taking a deep breath, she went into the living room, looked out each window, then sat down at the piano and listlessly sorted through the kids' stacks of music. Merrill's and Kate's lessons were the day after tomorrow. They hadn't practiced. Nate had been too busy to help them, and Maddie had forgotten.

Where was her own music? Not all small rooms were

terrifying, she knew, thinking over the nightmare again. She remembered the tiny practice cabins at Lake Chautauqua where she'd spent two of her high-school summers at Bert and Grandaddy's expense. They had been rustic, clean-swept little rooms with nothing in them but a piano, a bench, and warm stripes of sunlight slanting through the curtainless windows onto the keyboard and floor. She leafed through Bert's old Schnabel edition of Beethoven now and found a piece of sheet music inside, her original copy of "At the Cry of the First Bird." The wonderful minister—what was his name? Rutke?—had introduced her to it long ago in the first Tenebrae service she'd ever heard. As an adolescent of Merrill's age, she'd been deeply moved by the drama of Golgotha from the mother's point of view. *"It was like the parting of day from night,"* Mary sang, watching her son die. Unspeakable sacrifices for unredeemable acts—who cared? *"O cheek like a swan."* Oh nightmare, oh daymare of sacrifice—for what? For what on earth?

Maddie gave up trying to sort out the music. She couldn't play half of it anymore. And Nate was still in the house. In coming out of other depressions (Was she coming out? She refused to ask, tired of the question), she'd learned to be wary of inroads like Merrill's kiss, or even the power of an old piece of music she hadn't heard for a long time. Her illness could give way like a cracked dam. One minor perforation could trigger an instantaneous crumbling, a bursting forth of feeling so frighteningly excessive it could shock her husband and children, even as it relieved her. No. She didn't trust it. They must never see the railing-beater.

But sitting at the piano, playing nothing, she imagined the beater set loose, beating on the laundry bin, the pulpit, the washing machine, the baptismal font, the ironing board, the communion table, the stove, the wedding kneeler, the furniture—beating everything in the house and in the church to a million pieces. What would her mother and father say, or

her sisters, or Bert and Essy, if Nate called and described
cracked-up Maddie beating up everything in sight?

She noticed how dirty the piano keys were—Nathan's
mud, Kate's peanut butter, a penny wedged between C and C
sharp. The C sharp wouldn't play. She went to the kitchen
and returned with a damp cloth and began wiping and polish-
ing. It wasn't the lack of privacy she resented, she tried to
explain to Aunt Essy in her last letter, or the fishbowl exposure
of her marriage, or even the "dimity convictions" (she liked
Emily Dickinson's description of her father's parishioners) of
hundreds of members with hundreds of preconceptions about
who she was and what she ought to believe. She knew there
were some wonderful people in the congregation. It was the
subtle isolation, the unrelieved propriety and repetition of her
days. In a melodramatic gesture, she had framed her Phi Beta
Kappa certificate over the kitchen sink to symbolize what had
gone down the drain, a little joke on herself over the macaroni-
and-cheese pans. Yet, refuting any oversimplification of things,
she argued that life was repetition for everyone, for every living
thing, male and female, Christian and non-Christian, for pulses
pulsating and blood circulating and lungs breathing and comets
orbiting and dust settling on the *Well Tempered Clavier* she dusted
yesterday and the day before and the day before. She never
played Bach anymore; she only dusted him, as Bert used to do.

But the question was, *What* was repeated?

She halted the argument and went back to work. She
carried the laundry down to the cellar and sorted it into piles,
separating the white things from the colored. All housewifely
acts were symbolic, she proposed a new argument. Nate's
profession, difficult at best in the twentieth century, and hers
as a wife and mother, had over the years sorted them both out
precisely: the white things on the surface, the muted, acceptable pastels directly beneath them, and all the deep colors and
rough textures selected out and put away in a mock-hope chest

in that frightening attic. (Like Kate, she was becoming scatterbrained; she couldn't remember everything she'd put away
in that chest. But the railing-beater knew. Undoubtedly she
counted the store like a miser every day.)

Somehow Nate had fared better than she had. He was
still human, still what he seemed to be to people who knew
and loved him. Wasn't he? But she was nothing *but* surface—
a wonder of artificial sincerity, impersonal sympathy, theoret-
ical love. In the beginning, Nate had doubted himself, and she
had bolstered his confidence, coaching him on how to write
strong sermons and use his affecting voice to its powerful
advantage. But now that he was capable of writing them himself, he had so little time. The needs of the congregation and
Presybtery fragmented him if he tried to do it all perfectly—
which he relentlessly did—and he relied more and more on
commentaries and bland "sermon helps" for inspiration. Or on
her. Thank God for that. It was the only work she really
enjoyed. Otherwise she had become a Cheshire-cat Christian,
smiling, smiling into a shadow. She didn't even read much
anymore, only again and again the illustrated astronomy books
that Deane had packed away in her father's attic over thirty
years ago. She could understand Deane's early passion for it
when he'd been forced to listen to the preaching of old Reverend Stark every Sunday. The vastness of the Milky Way
minimized the importance of the time he was wasting there;
the limitlessness of space could stir even the most repressed
imagination. Meanwhile, red socks in this pile, white socks in
that pile.

Was it Kafka, she tried to remember as she poured in the
bleach, who had said that a great book could function like an
axe for the frozen sea within us? That's why she didn't read.
Surely Kafka had been talking about surface ice, the tiredness
and defensiveness in Nate, not the pack ice, the mile-down,
subsurface Arctic hardening in her. If Kafka should happen to

be born female in the next life, he ought to be warned to leave
the frozen undersea alone. If the ice were melted, there would
be nothing left to stand on. Unlike the Antarctic, the Arctic
had no continent beneath it. It was nothing but ice.

She went back upstairs to the kitchen and made coffee
for Nate, setting out cream and sugar, the drinking mug that
had belonged to his father. A moment later, he was in the
kitchen, energetic with the expectancy of going out, conser-
vatively dressed (not too rich, not too poor, since both could
be judged as affectations), just right for the old women who
would nod and dream through his weekly nursing home service.
There were exceptions to the nodding, of course. Halfway
through last Thursday's sermon, a gaunt old woman had stood
up, pointed a long finger at him and shouted, "Shut up and sit
down, we've heard all this crap before!" Embarrassed, the nurse
had whispered to him that the woman was stone-deaf, and he
shouldn't take it personally. But Nate started to laugh and
couldn't stop. Unable to sober up after her refreshing directness
(he wished he could tell her she was right, that most sermons
these days *were* crap), he had to apologize and let the rest of
the service go. The story had made Maddie laugh too—laugh
hard—for the first time in weeks.

"Any better?" he asked gently now, resting his hand on
her shoulder.

"Maybe a little." She turned away, not wanting him to
look at her for too long.

He poured his own coffee. "Anything I can do to help? I
have to take the car all day."

She shook her head. "Could you bring home McDonald's
for supper?"

"How about if I make sandwiches when I come home?
We're low on funds."

"Okay," she sighed, thinking of the messes Nate's cooking
made. But it didn't matter. Nobody ate very much before an
evening service anyway.

He drank his coffee standing up, staring out the window. "Do you think it would help to increase the dosage?" he said at last.

"Dr. Hazelett renewed it at the same level," she said. "He gave me a choice. I decided to stay where I am."

"It's been almost five months this time, Mad. You're losing weight."

She said nothing. Lately even Merrill had been encouraging her to take more pills. They needed her back on the job, cooking supper, deodorizing the bin, keeping drawers full of folded kneesocks.

"Can you make it to the Tenebrae tonight?" he asked, not meaning to add pressure, but preferring her at the organ to anyone else. She could be counted on to create the right mood, no indiscretions.

"I don't know," she said, surprised to hear herself say it. "You might call Mary Ann Abel to stand by. She knows the responses."

"It's your service, Mad," he said, turning to look at her. "Darkness compounded."

She nodded. Three years ago, she and Nate had cut down a tree and built a rough wooden cross just like the one she remembered from her childhood. She'd gone to the overgrown Catholic cemetery across town and woven a crown of thorns out of the wickedest-looking wild briars growing among the graves. In this latest church, it was her job every Maundy Thursday to remove the white draping from the chancel railing and replace it with black. She hated that railing with its effeminate pleated skirt. But it pleased her to hear Nate read the Seven Last Words of Christ without any sentimentality or droning piety, just as Reverend Rutke used to. His voice rang strong and true, as, one more time, two by two, the candles went out, and all the protections, doctrines, consolations, and illusions fell away.

"I'll try to come," she said, wanting, not wanting to go.

"Got to get going," he said, rejecting her offer of breakfast.

"What's your schedule?" she asked, cleaning up Nathan's milk and honey mess. I should call this table Canaan, she laughed weakly to herself; this is the land flowing with it.

"Four people to see in the hospital, a revised bulletin to write for Sunday, a Human Relations Committee meeting at noon, Elders to line up to serve Communion tonight, a Ministerial agenda to—"

"No lunch then?" she asked, relieved.

"No."

Reassuring him of what he wanted to know but didn't ask, she said, "I'll go over the sermon this afternoon. Don't worry. It'll be ready."

He hugged her. "The opening is pretty rough. I only had two hours to put it together. I don't know if the idea is heresy or not. It gets harder to tell anymore."

She smiled. "I know."

"You're a saint, depressed or not."

"Oh no," she said, leaning heavily against him for a few resting moments. He smelled good, and she breathed deeply. She wanted to breathe him in, to curl up in the imperturbable solidity of his spirit.

"What can I do?" he asked one more time.

"Nothing. Just . . ." She hesitated.

"What?"

She just wanted—wished—she could *explain* to him. She thought of a line she'd read in an article on modern American literature several years ago, about the depressed, negative spirit that must pervade all twentieth-century art: "Now we see through a glass darkly; there is no then." That was what depression felt like. There is no then.

He looked down at her quizzically. She said nothing. He let go of her and put on his coat. As much as he sympathized, he couldn't understand, and both he and she knew it. No one could understand who hadn't felt it. She handed him the communion kit.

"I put the bread in, but we don't have any grape juice," she said.

"I'll stop off at the church," he said, looking inside. "Did I tell you the latest about the august Reverend Haymaker?"

Haymaker was the new president of the Ministerium, a fat, blustery little man who decided he didn't like Nate even before he met him.

"When he takes communion to shut-ins, he doesn't take along any bread or wine. He appropriates whatever's available. He bragged at lunch yesterday about using old Margaret Lacy's prune juice and Keebler Fudge Cremes."

"You're kidding," Maddie said. What was happening to the Protestant Church? The Body of Christ, baked by elves.

"What about the railing?" he asked, pausing at the door.

"What?"

"The railing. Where did you put the black cloth last year? I couldn't find it."

"You mean at the church . . . ?"

"The black draperies. Where are they?"

"I think I left them in the sacristy. The crown of thorns is there too."

He blew her a kiss. "Don't worry. I'll set it up exactly as you do. It will be perfect. As Haymaker would say, 'There won't be a dry eye in the house.'"

He left. Maddie went to the sink, annoyed by his last words. She ran water so hot it sent up clouds of steam, and she breathed them in in lieu of anyone's spirit. "Not a dry eye in the house." Of course Nate meant nothing but disdain by the phrase, she knew, contradicting her annoyance. No offense at all. But no, how could he even quote such a thing? She felt herself growing passionately angry. Haymaker was crude and manipulative, a pompous, common ecclesiastical type. She had

seen him mock his own parishioners at a Christmas party this
year, mimicking the way they walked or talked. She'd heard
him preach only once, but had been so offended by his mixing
up of a shallow, happy-faced Christianity with pop psychology
and his own puffed-up ego, she'd wanted, just once in her life,
to walk out conspicuously. Thinking of him now penetrated
her dull surface as much as Merrill's kiss had, but this time like
the sticking of a pin into a hairline fracture in her skull.

She finished cleaning up the kitchen. That done, she made
the beds clumsily, in a wave of dizziness. But she was so bothered by the wrinkles she left, she made all the beds again,
surprised she had the energy to do it. She then reordered
Nathan's bookshelves, straightened shoes in everyone's closets,
lined up magazines and papers on desks and tables. (Who cares
that I do this? Who cares if the books are geometrically aligned
with the corners of the table?) Yet relentlessly her eyes saw
the configurations of ordinary objects not as a housewife, but
as a painter or sculptor. She couldn't leave Kate's pink fuzzy
slippers lying on the gold throw rug. The colors were wrong
together, and the perfect rectangle of the rug's woven pattern
was ruined. I'm crazy, she thought, kicking the slippers under
the bed. Then, in the living room, it infuriated her that for the
third day in a row, Nathan had left four garish Burger King
balloons lying on the floor. On an impulse, she took a ballpoint
pen from Nate's desk and stabbed all four of them. She stuffed
the remains down deep in the wastebasket. Nathan wouldn't
even notice they were gone.

She did the sweeping and vacuuming next. In this huge
old manse the church had provided for her and Nate, the third
such house they'd lived in and tried to be grateful for, dust,
dirt, debris—fallout from the Big Bang, Merrill called it—
collected everywhere. It aggregated. It incorporated. Added to
this was the microscopic litter of five people coming and
going—lint balls, paint flecks, hem threads, tracked-in mud, spit-

out fingernails, pulverized Cheerios, ends of envelopes torn off and dropped. Who could attend to the removal of these minutiae day after day and not go crazy? What nightmares would Einstein have had if circumstances of gender had landed him in an old house where his life's work was to shepherd fuzzballs year after year after year? Sure, she thought. Me and Einstein.

But it had baffled and even frightened her lately that in spite of all her housekeeping, the scrubbing, mending, patching, repairing, and artistic decorating (she had striven for an atmosphere roughly equivalent to the Smithsonian), despite all this, she could never really see a room whole anymore—only its flaws, its litter. She never really lived in a manse. She was indeed only its keeper. And she was also the one kept. Her unmarried feminist friends in town had warned her about this. One of them, a successful lawyer, had recently converted from the Episcopal faith to a sophisticated new goddess-theology (maybe not so sophisticated, Maddie thought after reading its thin credo), and given Maddie stacks of articles to read about her oppression. She had read them obsessively for a time. They assured her of the hopelessness of any faithful wife and mother and housekeeper salvaging herself in the reactionary 1980s.

And yet, sometimes, late at night when she was reading astronomy, deep in concentration on black holes or rotating pulsars, she might happen to look up from her book—as if from the reaches of outer space—without anticipating what she would see, and be totally surprised, utterly astonished by the beauty of the room before her. There was color, design, and warmth here—including the scattered toys. There was passionate investment, thriftless and real. From the perspective of all those lifeless stars and barren planets, this was paradise. Perhaps that's what her children saw all the time. That was why Kate, who helped her the least, would bring her friends into the house to take "tours," to see the murals she and Maddie had painted on the basement walls, the Martian and lunar globes Nate had brought back from the Air and Space Museum, the bookshelf display of Eskimo art her uncle Deane had given her, the nudes she and Nathan had sculpted out of marshmallow-rice-crispy treats, or the *monstera* plant Nate had brought home from a funeral and she'd nurtured all the way up the fourteen-foot ceiling. The work took its toll. But was it—wasn't it worth it?

Who could answer the question if she couldn't?

The cleaning done, she searched the cupboards for something to eat. She felt hungrier today, and, now that she was moving, a little lighter. But the food in the cupboard looked good until she actually brought it to her mouth. She chose crackers, cheese, an apple, held them in her hand, then put them back. She went back to the living room and decided to tackle Nate's clumsy, earnest sermon, the only work that could still totally absorb her when she was in depression. After all these years, she could still lose herself in the line and curve of the words. This time it was a sermon on the circumstances of chosen rather than required sacrifice. Was Calvary prophesied, or not? What was decided in the Garden of Gethsemane, Nate asked? A token compliance to a prewritten script, or real consent bled out of Jesus of Nazareth's human will like water out of a stone? As usual, she began to play with some half-radical implications in her mind, but was careful to be subtle and metaphorical in the sermon, sensitive to conservative nerves. (It was the conservatives that wielded the sharpest weapons, she'd learned; their orthodoxy could be vicious.) Above all, she wanted to appeal to the common heart, beyond all dogmas. This Easter season, for some reason, Jesus's resurrection scars had fascinated her and Nate. Jesus did not rise from the tomb whole, Nate wrote at the top of the second page. It would have been easy for the Gospel writers to claim that He had walked out of the tomb spotless, perfectly restored; but they

didn't. *He* didn't. "Think of it," she imagined herself preaching
in an oversized black robe from Nate's pulpit. "The wounds"
—and an unexpected flash of tears blurred her eyes for an instant,
reflexively reabsorbed—*"the wounds are permanent.* Christ is risen
with his scars. The hurt we do is forever. The marks are forever.
There can be forgiveness, and there can be recovery. But
never—not even for Christ, not even *by* Christ—can there be
any unwounding. Christ is risen, *with his scars.* Alleluia."
    It was a beautiful sermon, rough or not. From the second
page on, she hardly changed anything at all.

    It was two hours past lunchtime when she finished typing
up the mission lists, but she wasn't hungry. Overwhelmed with
fatigue, despite Dr. Hazelett's advice to resist it when she could,
she lay down on the living-room couch to sleep. But after ten
minutes the telephone rang. She jumped up, her heart pounding, breathless. But by the time she picked up the receiver, she
was able to assume a calm, answering-service voice. It was Viola
Campbell, wanting to know if there should be ice cubes in the
water glasses for the communicants' class breakfast Sunday
morning. The church freezer had broken down, and it would
require advance planning. Maddie said yes, of course, it would
be nice if there were ice cubes, she would bring some herself.
And then, out of habit, knowing it would take at least the next
half hour of her time, she asked lonely old Viola how she was.
She listened, sympathizing with polished, professional agape,
as Viola talked for forty-five minutes.
    By the time Viola hung up, there was no time left for a nap.
Maddie took out her notebooks for her adult book-discussion
Sunday school class and began to organize a comparative study
of the book of *Job* and Archibald MacLeish's play *J.B.* There
had been some rumblings lately from a few of the members
about her choice of books—that *J.B.* was "humanistic" and
"defeatist." She couldn't concentrate as she struggled to say

what she wanted to say in words that wouldn't give offense to anyone or be misunderstood. She felt tired to the point of nausea. "I will get it done," she said aloud to wake herself up.

But that is the trouble, she conceded, throwing down her pen. Why couldn't she just not do it? Why not just stop? What difference would it make in the orbit of the earth? The peculiar thing was that she had never completely lost patience with the church's demands on her. (She recalled a snickering comment made at Nate's installation service in their second parish—"She teaches, she plays the organ, she directs children's choirs. We're getting two, but we only have to pay one!") She never lost patience with Nate's faithful, often draining devotion to the church, nor with her children's natural selfishness. These were facts, laid at the foundation. She lost patience only with her own limitations. That was the fact she couldn't accept. Last month, she tried to explain to Dr. Hazelett how sometimes she would deliberately work herself into a state of unrelieved exhaustion as a kind of mystical defense against disaster. (If one were already broken by experience, why would Fate strike again? Fate didn't have to exact a sacrifice from this latest generation to teach her her place.)

There was even a privileged knowledge that came from depletion, she told him. It kept the demons of the world— metaphorical, of course—at bay. (He looked at her for once, almost admiringly, as though she really were crazy.) She admitted she spent herself lavishly, experimentally, without any thrift at all. But there was a peculiar exhilaration to it. Old Dr. Mallinger, the orthodox Jew who had delivered ten-pound Nathan, had understood. Maddie was small-boned, and the birth had been complicated—"The gate's not opening," he had whispered in her ear in the delivery room when the baby had gotten stuck in the birth canal and for a moment he simply hadn't known what to do. Despite her agony, she couldn't be put under an anesthetic, he said. He had to know exactly what she was feeling, moment by moment, if she wanted her baby born alive, undamaged. "Sometimes it must be this way," he said to her, looking down with steady eyes, steel forceps in his hand, estimating her stamina. And she struggled to form the words: *I know.*

She had driven herself, she told Hazelett, as if she were a Christian magician's cup, pouring out an endless supply of blood.

But wasn't this what all these descents into depression meant? he responded. The reality was, there had to be an end to the perfect sacrifice. She couldn't be that crucified thing that she and Nate had been preaching all these years. The depressions weren't merely bad moods. They were total shutdowns—her body's declaration of neutrality in a war her spirit could not win. In time her nervous system simply wouldn't support the war anymore.

Yes, she nodded. But knowing that, *then* what?

She put the class notes aside. Absurd work. She listened to the silence of the empty house, not home, one of a succession of houses, churches, strange places she'd tried to make home for her family. There was never ownership. Just upkeep. What had Nate said he wanted when he asked her to marry him— "a visionary who can scrub floors"? Now he had a floor-scrubber who had hallucinations.

But what to do? What changes could she make short of ripping out all the confining and protective railings in her life, the beauty and safety uprooted along with the drudgery and ugliness—perhaps the security of her children traded for her own recovered mental health? Would that cure her?

She gave up on doing any work, and chose one of the new records from Nate's stacks—his one financial indulgence —Vangelis's *Heaven and Hell.* Expansive, haunting, outerspace music, he'd told her—infinite distance and duration translated into sound. She hadn't listened to it, though he'd urged her to

many times. (Why listen when there was no emotion to spare
or to risk?) But she listened now, lying down on the floor, then
rolling under the roof of the dining-room table. We aren't
meant to stay here forever, the music communicated at once.
Perhaps we won't even be bottled up in one life-form and bound
to one solar system forever. There are other systems, other
forms. We've just barely crawled out of the oceans. The glaciers
are still melting. We're a little lower than the angels—and just
recently shut out of the simian community on the African
savannahs. No wonder there are illnesses, nightmares.

The tonic chord of the music's theme came back on itself
again and again in endless, almost tedious repetition, seeming
to get nowhere, until suddenly, it was somewhere beyond,
having spun itself through and still spinning. Modulation, she
thought—like a mutation in evolution. She took a deep breath
and held it, reaching up to push against the lid of the table
over her head.

Then, as she half-dreaded, half-hoped, the music bored
into her containment like the pen into Nathan's balloons. She
shivered, felt hot, looked around at the table legs as if she were
an animal escaped from the zoo, unfamiliar with the simplest
everyday objects. How nice to see these table legs—their
graceful walnut curves. She was thawing again, certainly. There
was no doubt. After almost five months, tables and chairs were
not anything but objects, not shapes of entrapment or symbols
of anything. Inside, Kafka was hacking away.

Alone in the house and in the music, she gave up resistance
to resistance and began pouring out sounds of feeling that had
no coherence even to her, primitive sounds of subconscious
emotion, exclamations of strain, unintelligible confusion, questions and answers for which there was no conscious vocabulary.
She rocked back and forth like a sleeper tossing in a dream.
Sooner or later, at the bottom of every descent, a chemical
change would take place in her brain, Dr. Hazelett had ex-

plained; after an indefinite holding out, the balance would restore itself somehow. Neurotransmitters would fire again. She would begin to wake up.

Now words came to her, the senseless perfect recall of something she'd read yesterday, or was it twenty-five years ago? "Being in a metabolic icebox can protect the brain and other vital organs from deterioration far longer than the four to six minutes they would have at normal temperatures. *Hypothermia victims are never dead until they are warm and dead, and must never be abandoned.*" They were from her mother's medical dictionary, notes on what happens to the human body when it freezes. Ironically, the effects of freezing could protect the brain from the very process of freezing, at least for a while. Perhaps that's what depression did—protected her from something worse.

She laughed. Streams of tears soaked into the freshly vacuumed rug. As the music neared its climax, as always at the beginning of emotional melting, she found herself addressing someone, as if there were an intimate witness to the moment, had always been since the first hour of her life. He—It—had withdrawn farther and farther from her sense of Him, drawing her on. I know You, she croaked through her constricted throat, in recognition. As soon as I am well again, You will tighten the screws even tighter.

By the time the children came home from school, Maddie was quiet, functioning. She looked at Nathan's school papers and helped with Kate's practicing. At five o'clock, she ironed an outfit for each child to wear to the Tenebrae service. But her head ached, and Merrill pointed out that her hands were shaking. Maddie said she might be coming down with the flu.

Nate came home late, nervous about the service, worried about the events of the afternoon. Yola Madigan had phoned to offer criticism and threaten to decrease her pledge since

Nate refused to use the King James translation of the Bible in all of his Scripture readings. Later, Elder Tucker Swift had barged into his office to lecture him on his insensitivity to the Sunday morning ushers who were offended that he hadn't asked them to usher for the Tenebrae. Why had Nate asked teenagers—boys *and* girls—to usher instead? Teenagers had never ushered before. This was the same man, Nate told Maddie, who six months ago had complained about the lack of "program" for the young people of the church.

He'd forgotten about his offer to make supper, and Maddie didn't remind him. She got out cans of tuna and tomato soup.

"I had to pick a Prayer of Confession out of a book," he said frustratedly, proofreading the bulletin for tonight's service. "A transient showed up at the office at two o'clock and poured out his life story for forty-five minutes, leading up to a plea for a bus ticket to Memphis and ten bucks. The discretionary fund's gone, so I had to give it to him out of my own pocket."

They were already low on funds, he had said this morning. Now how low? This was the third time this month he'd done this. All the transients in town ended up at his door sooner or later, some of them two or three times, knowing he never turned anyone away. A few were getting quite professional at storytelling.

"And Yola's gathering a small contingent together to 'have my ministry investigated' by Presbytery."

"What?" Maddie said, terrified at the casual inclusion of this bit of news.

"Don't worry," he said. "It's fear—fear of my opposition to the creationists, to prayer in the schools, to cushions in the pews—everything. It's all coming to a head. Most of the people stand behind me, but I wish the retired Executive Presbyter were back. This new guy doesn't know me at all." He put the bulletin down and added another automatic, "Don't worry."

"Maybe it will be good," Maddie said evenly, sick to her

stomach. "It will get the charismatics out of hiding." But, she thought, with a surge of anger, *why can't they ever just leave him alone?* Why can't they let a minister do his work without continually setting themselves up as an overseeing superior court?

He hurriedly looked over the stack of mail she'd laid out for him on the counter. "Can you come tonight?" he asked without looking up.

She hesitated, stirring the soup. She pictured herself at the organ, the choir behind her in the dark, the cross casting its huge shadow in the same high place on the sanctuary wall.

"No, I can't, Nate," she said, astounded to hear it said. "Not this time."

He looked up, not altogether astounded. "Are you sure?"

"I have a sore throat," she lied, offering him a sandwich. "I want to go to bed early so I'm not sick for Sunday."

"It's okay," he said, taking half a sandwich. "Mary said she could fill in. I called her."

Maddie was sorry for him. Mary played the same Prelude and Postlude every time she substituted. "I started crying this afternoon," she said. "The thing's letting go."

He looked at her closely, as though trying to see through her eyes to verify it. "You don't mind missing communion?"

She smiled. "No."

He nodded.

She called the kids in for supper. "You'd better go over the sermon a couple of times, Nate," she said. "It's a little different than it was."

"Of course," he said.

"But it's good. It was good before I touched it."

He took an envelope out of his breast pocket and handed it to her. "I was going to save this for Easter," he said, with a strange, painfully tender look that touched her. "But maybe now is better. Happy Good Friday."

"What's this?" she looked up, afraid of more bad news.

"Last month I took the liberty of sending the sermon you wrote when I had the flu—for Epiphany?—to *Contemporary Ministry*. They accepted it, Mad. It'll be in next December's issue—the featured contribution. They're going to pay you for it."

Maddie opened it, read it. She sat down and read it again.

"Congratulations," he said, obviously delighted at her speechless pleasure. "I apologize for having to tell them it was a joint effort. It will be published under both our names since they don't usually accept stuff from obscure housewives without a single course in systematic theology. But needless to say, you get the money."

"You did the research," she said. "I just wrote it. Who cares?"

But a thousand miles beneath the surface, the railing-beater would care, she knew. She'd stayed up till four o'clock in the morning to write that sermon so Nate could sleep, and she'd been proud of it. "I can't believe it," she said, shaking her head. She could hardly wait to write and tell Bert.

"Hey, Mom, look at this," Nathan interrupted, looking up from the mangled remains of an orange she'd put on his plate. He grinned broadly. Where his teeth should have been was a big wedge of yellow orange peel. "This is my church smile," he mumbled through the peel.

Merrill and Kate broke out laughing. Nate joined them. Almost choking, Nathan spit it out, giggling hilariously at his own joke.

At quarter to seven, Maddie lined them up for inspection. She knew by now that preachers' kids—PKs as they were called at school, to Kate's fury—were watched as closely as preachers' wives. Their clothes were clean, their hair combed. But there were bulges in Nathan's pockets.

"What are they?" Maddie asked.

"Nothing."

"They're action figures," Kate said.

"I need these," Nathan protested as he pulled several plastic Star Wars grotesques out of his pocket—"from the bar scene," he explained, as though that were sufficient justification. "There's nothing to do in the service."

"You're supposed to listen," Merrill said. "You're old enough to understand some of it, baby."

"I don't understand *any* of it," Kate lied, to make a point of her new preadolescent indifference to church, "but I don't need to take toys to church."

But Kate had her imagination to take with her, Maddie thought, suppressing a smile. All she needed was a pencil and a bulletin to write on, and she could create her own action figures.

"*I* understand it," Merrill said piously. "I like the candles and black cloth all over the place. All the gold junk's gone. It's like a Halloween service."

Nate shook his head at the questionable theology of his children as he came into the kitchen with their coats. "Come on," he said. "It's time to go."

"Did you find my volcano book?" Kate asked Maddie.

"No," Maddie said firmly. "Did you?"

"You've got to find it," she begged. "And I still have to go shopping. Why didn't you pick me up after school? Merrill said she'd help and then forgot all about it."

"Come *now*," Nate demanded, gathering prayer-sheets, sermon, notes, books, and papers together at his desk. "Get in the car. Nathan, I'll let you help out in the nursery this time since Mom isn't coming."

"You're not coming?" Kate said, astonished, just now noticing that her mother wasn't dressed. "Why not?"

"She doesn't feel well," Nate answered from the door. "Come right now, Kate! I have a hundred things to do before the service. Two Elders canceled out."

Maddie waved Kate and Merrill to go and pushed loitering
Nathan, action figures and all, after them. She waved to them
as they drove away, then closed the door. She closed her eyes
and leaned against it.

For the second time that day, she was alone in the house.
She was hungry, she realized, but too restless to focus on fixing
something to eat. Happy about the sermon to be published—
that was it—a good restlessness, coupled with the realization
that the news had come on the first occasion of her refusing
to go to church. She felt guilty for sending the kids with Nate
without her, but also excitement, and something else too—a
kind of spurt of discharged subsurface energy, the direct opposite of the overwhelming fatigue of depression. She wanted
to sit down and write a hundred more sermons right now.

She went to the kitchen. Half-hardened tomato soup
spills, bits of tuna on the floor, orange seeds, mayonnaise, butter,
breadcrumbs. Not now, she resolved. She wouldn't do that
either. One more disciple, one more discipline falling away.

Instead she went into the living room, sat down with an
afghan over her, and began to sort through the books and
magazines on the coffee table. Three unread issues of *Natural
History*. The new *Smithsonian*. And there, on the bottom, under
Nate's latest issue of *Christianity and Crisis* was Kate's lost book.
As usual, Kate had given it up for lost before she'd even looked
for it. Nothing like her great-grandmother, Bert.

Maddie picked the book up and admired the color photograph of lovely, snow-veiled Mount Saint Helens as it had
looked twenty-four hours before the eruption. How quietly,
how completely it had contained itself, even fifteen minutes
before. Who living there could have imagined the pressure
building underneath?

She curled up with the book and leafed through the color-
plates, looking at all the Befores and Afters. Who was the
original Saint? she wondered. She daydreamed about devel-

oping the event into a sermon—the mountain, the saint, lying
in wait, peacefully in her place. A feminist sermon it would
be, she guessed, about pressures and impositions building up
slowly, imperceptibly, then the first deep-down buckling of
stone foundations, the inaudible crumbling of inner parti-
tions, the collapsing of supports and bursting of ceilings, the
forcing upward of the molten cone. Ominous roars and ground-
shakings would disrupt the lovely Eden morning, and then all
at once the mountain would blow itself to kingdom come,
scorching and decimating life in all directions. Every green
thing rooted in her side would die. Nothing that had lived
protected in her shadow would survive.

As she looked at the devastation pictured in the book,
the vast gray wasteland that resulted, she concluded that such
eruptions could not be afforded often.

Maddie put down the book, tired, neutral, altogether
quiet. She felt like a mouse that had been carried around in
the mouth of a cat all day, now finally put down and left, not
too badly injured after all. She stretched out on the living-
room floor and fell asleep as fast, as deeply, as someone lapsing
into a coma.

Two and a half hours later, she was awakened by Nate
and the children coming in noisily from the service. "Are you
okay?" Nate asked, bending over her.

"Uh-huh," she said groggily. "What time is it?"

"Nine-thirty."

"I slept the whole time," she yawned, unbelieving—right
through the crucifixion. "How was the service?"

"Light attendance, as usual on Maundy Thursday. But they
liked the sermon. There were several requests for copies. And
there were some tears. 'Not a dry eye—' "

She gave him a warning look.

He smiled and produced a brown paper bag.

"What's this?" she asked dubiously. "The tears?" She no-

ticed his fingers were swollen, as they often were after a difficult
service. He smelled of "pp," as Kate called it—pulpit perspiration. Yola Madigan had undoubtedly been there.

"We had several loaves of Gertrude Grunwald's homemade
communion bread left over. She thought you might like to
have them since you weren't feeling well. She said to tell you
she missed you at the organ."

Maddie pictured white-haired Gertrude, the stern elderly
German lady who was Nate's staunchest ally, as strong and
straight-backed at eighty as most people were at twenty.

"Three loaves, my love, just for you," he said, holding out
the bag, smiling deep into her eyes. "Take. Eat."

She opened the bag. "Oh," she said. The rich wheat-and-
honey aroma was the best thing she'd ever smelled. She hadn't
eaten anything all day, it occurred to her, and her stomach
growled loudly. She picked up the first small loaf, as soft and
firm as a newborn baby, with a thick golden crust. "God bless
Gertrude," she said.

"She makes the most Christlike bread in the world," Nate
said quietly, watching her.

Maddie broke off a large chunk. "There's something pro-
fane about this," she laughed, feeling herself at the center of
all Nate's attention at this moment and embarrassed by it. She
took a bite. "I feel like a spiritual glutton."

"Sometimes special needs, special mercies," he said.

Nathan came in from the kitchen with half a banana
sticking out of his mouth. "Mom! You didn't clean up the mess
in the kitchen," he said, delighted to report it.

"Were you good at church?" Maddie asked.

"No," Merrill said, following him to Maddie's side on the
floor. "He said the 'sh—' word to Mrs. Swift."

"Oh no," Maddie groaned. Anybody but Mrs. Swift, president of the Women's Association. "Nathan," she said sternly,
"you know better than that. I think you'd better march straight
upstairs and get ready for bed."

"Okay," he said, unbowed and cheerful. "But wait." From
his coat pocket, he pulled out a flat disk of blue clay. "Look
what I made in nursery. Mrs. Jackson made me help all the
little kids make one, then she said I could make one too."

It was his handprint, five fingers spread out and pressed
into the clay, like he used to make in kindergarten. As he held
it up, it reminded her of something, but she couldn't think
what.

"It's nice, Nathan," she said, as he fit his hand into it, "but
you still have to go upstairs."

"Can I have some of your bread?" Kate asked, lying down
and pressing herself close against Maddie. "Church was spooky
without you. It was so dark, I couldn't draw." To Merrill's
disdain, Kate put her thumb in her mouth and said she had a
stomachache.

Maddie stroked her cheek. "Bet I can cure it," she said,
and pulled the volcano book out from under the afghan.

"I'm saved!" Kate shouted, jumping up. "Oh Mom, I'm
saved!"

"Well, that's one out of three," Nate said, unloading his
pockets at the desk.

Kate kissed Maddie passionately.

"Can I have some bread too?" Merrill asked, handing her
mother the bulletin from the service.

"Leave your mother alone," Nate said firmly. "You'll catch
her germs. Besides, she needs the bread for herself."

"If you bring me the butter," Maddie said to Merrill, "I'll
give you a hunk."

All three children gathered around her, and she dispensed
a little supper full of happy, chattering communion. Then in
a few minutes, Nate herded them all upstairs. She could hear
him lecturing Nathan about language, the sound of running
bathwater in the background. Without being asked, tired as
he was, he was taking care of them tonight. She wondered
greedily if he would clean up the kitchen too? Fold the laundry?

Pack the lunches for school tomorrow—no, no need. No school tomorrow.

She lay back against the arm of the couch under the afghan and ate more bread, listening to the clashes and conflicts above her. Before Nathan was out of the tub, she had devoured another loaf.

Nate might be hungry too. She saved him the third loaf.

What kind of nightmares did Jesus have when he was lying in the tomb, she wondered, studying the plaster cracks on the ceiling? After such an afternoon, what did he dream about on Friday night and all day Saturday?

"He descended into Hell," she said aloud, quoting from the antiquated Apostles' Creed, one of those unpreachable texts that pastors rarely chose. The Harrowing of Hell—when He threw open the gates and let out all the good lost ones who didn't belong there—of which she guessed there were many.

She picked up Nathan's handprint and traced the lines of the splayed fingers. Where to display it? He liked all his artwork prominently featured so that everyone could admire it for months.

She went to the shelves of Eskimo art and blew on the dust. It had been a long time since she'd looked at these things closely. She put the handprint between the old mask and the piece of driftwood Deane had given her when she was Nathan's age.

Then the similarity struck her. Except for the number of digits, the size and proportion of the handprint exactly matched those of the Raven-god's footprint. This was the echo in the back of her mind when Nathan first handed it to her: the footprint of the Eskimo god, the sign of His presence in the reality of His absence.

She wanted to go upstairs and kiss Nathan good-night despite what he'd said to Mrs. Swift, to gather him and Kate and Merrill around her as a miser gathers his hoard.

10

I O N A M U T

"Why do you still take medicine after your depression's over?" Kate asked, staring at the plate of fruit Maddie had cut up for her. "I can't eat this piece of banana."

Maddie swallowed her pill like a blue M & M, smooth, easy. "To keep it from coming back," she answered Kate's question. "Dr. Hazelett said it might help even things out." For nine months after that strangely intense night of thawing a year ago, she'd felt good and strong. Had it been something in Gertrude's bread? A mild depression had descended after Christmas and lasted until Lent, beginning to lift two weeks ago when her father had called with the news about Bert's stroke. Somehow, despite the burden of that news, Maddie had steadily recovered. She felt poised and quiet in herself, hoping against hope to see Bert again.

"So you take drugs all the time now?" Kate said, feeling superior to her mother since she'd thrown her own medicine for stomach cramps away. "I can't eat this banana," she repeated. "It's looking at me."

She held it up for Maddie to see. Where the knife had

sliced through, there was a little face formed out of the seeds with a definite expression of elfin defiance. Kate and the banana stared at one another.

"Eat it," Maddie said. "We'll be late for the Lenten dinner. If you're too nervous to eat at the church, you have to eat here."

Lent, 1982, was approaching its fourth Sunday.

Maddie worked on what seemed like the hundredth covered dish she'd prepared in the last few years—"enough to feed twelve," the bulletin said this time, as though for the Last Supper. But there was never a last supper. In January, Nate had accepted a new call, this time to the First Presbyterian Church of Burton in southwestern Ohio. Although glad to be nearer Pittsburgh, Maddie was having a hard time adjusting to the warmer climate—in the upper seventies for the past three days. And she still couldn't find anything in her new kitchen. Where was the plastic wrap for the covered dish? I myself am a covered dish, she sighed over the pale quartered chicken breasts and thighs arranged on a bed of rice. Eat me, Lord. I take no preparation.

"How's Bert?" Kate asked, seeing her great-grandmother's last letter to Maddie lying on the counter.

"Losing ground. The doctor doesn't know where her will comes from."

Essy had told Maddie over the phone last week that Bert's will to live came from her fear of death and judgment. But Maddie didn't think so. Over the past year she had been amazed at how valiantly Bert had fought the battle to retain her personality against old age, to keep her senses sharp with words as her only weapons, until the stroke finally took away what powers remained to her. "Oh, that my words were now written! Oh, that they were printed in a book!" she had scrawled in a letter to Maddie a month ago, quoting from *Job*. Bert had sensed that her memory and imagination were confused, but didn't

know how to straighten them out. Yesterday could be twenty
years ago; the present hardly existed at all since she hated the
nursing home so much.

"When did Bert write this?" Kate asked, taking the letter
off the counter. "May I read it?"

"Two days before the stroke," Maddie said distractedly,
"to thank us for the Easter card we sent. I'm glad I sent it early."

Kate read the letter aloud:

"Dearest Maddie and all,

I thought Easter was over for me *forever*, but now
has come your beautiful card with the gentle rabbit
on it with its *rebuking* eyes. Shall I ever return any
creature's joyous glance? I somehow have gotten my
nightgown on *inside out* for I *feel* it rather than *see* it.

I feel like an egg that has been dipped into too
many colors in an attempt to arrive at loveliness
only to be discarded because it is lying *alone* on the
kitchen table, chosen for *no one's basket*.

I wish you weren't *so far away*. But it is a risk
to complain about distance. There is a contingency
of trouble that is just an ironic dream. As Robert
Frost said, as though for me and Grandaddy, 'We
all have so much unfinished business.' *I guess there is
no right time to go, and often no right time to stay*. I know
you understand. I cannot limp to the phone anymore
if anyone should *ever* ring. All I have is prayer for
help.

A long time ago, Deane used to say, 'Never
abandon a mineshaft until you have gone fifty feet
farther.' (The halls here are dark tunnels.) How I
hate it. I WILL NOT STAY! Tell your father.

How I love you and Nate and the dear children.

Can you send more photographs of them, of Kate especially—her smile! I *recognize* all the children. Each one. We are one family, *near and far.*

> With *sincere affection,*
>
> Your loving grandmother"

Hearing it read in her daughter's voice, Maddie was moved again by the letter's full-heartedness and miraculous earnestness. If I were in Bert's condition, she thought, I'd die without a word or a sound, utterly untraceable in my disappearance. Not the merest wish to be witnessed or watched by the people for whom life is still real, healing still possible.

Wait for me, she prayed silently to God and to Bert. Wait until I get there.

But how could Bert wait? Her kidneys were failing, her mother said over the telephone this morning. Sensation in her left side was hopelessly gone. She was being fed intravenously. The doctor said it could be only a few more days at most. And Maddie was so deeply involved in the season at church— dinners, meetings, study groups, rehearsals for Brahms' *Requiem,* children's choir processions for Palm Sunday—she couldn't possibly leave until after Easter Sunday, still two and a half weeks away. The ties of the season were unbreakable.

"Snap out of it, Mom," Kate said, as though responsible for keeping her mother on the emotional straight and narrow since she herself was doing so well lately. (Her strategy, Maddie had deduced, was to make light of the serious issues and get deeply involved with the trivial ones, such as—as she turned back to the banana face now—the present question: to eat or not to eat.)

Kate knew the dilemma was ridiculous. Since the night over a year ago when she'd vomited in the cow pasture at the

Hinckley County Home in North Hebron, she and Maddie had had many discussions about wasted feelings and useless worries. Although she still took her "pukepan" to bed at night, her stomachaches were fewer and far between. A week ago, she decided to "get off drugs" altogether and flushed her pills down the toilet.

But Kate still considered herself "different," and was in senseless sympathy with everything in the world that happened to have gotten itself created, whether animal, vegetable, or mineral—with the possible exception of human beings, who lately didn't much interest her. But as Bert had predicted, special powers came with these eccentricities, and Kate was beginning to enjoy them. She could approach and pick up skittish butterflies when no one else could get near them. She'd hold up her arm and balance them on the tip of her elbow as if they were trained pets, "far enough away from my eyes to feel safe," she told jealous Nathan. She could nurse injured birds or run-over squirrels back to life after Nate had warned her it was hopeless. Kate understood hopeless perfectly well—as a given, the place you had to start.

Maddie watched her examine the other pieces of fruit on her plate for more faces. Kate's sympathies were painful, they were so undiscriminating—except where people were concerned. Her great-grandmother was dying, Kate accepted; that was the way it had to be. Better not get emotionally involved since it was inevitable. "Just eat your banana," Maddie said as Kate sat licking the face tentatively. "It's all right."

Kate considered it. She ate a piece of orange instead.

Stifling a smile, Maddie recalled the plague of seventeen-year locusts last May when all the neighborhood kids had swatted the infested trees with brooms, or picked off the newly hatched cicadas and thrown them down on the sidewalk so hard they could hear them pop. The boy next door had brought out a magnifying glass and concentrated sunlight on the bodies of the smaller ones until they exploded. Kate had watched him do that once. Then she got Maddie's broom and swatted the back of his head with it. Though Maddie had no love for the droning insects and had to remove them by shovelfuls from around the base of the trees in the backyard, Kate was utterly absorbed by the pure whiteness of the females as they worked to free themselves from their hard shells on the tree bark. She spent whole afternoons gently assisting them break free of their seventeen-year prisons.

But lately Maddie worried that Kate was withdrawing into an exclusive, self-feeding privacy that her brother and sister resented, taking on a protective shell of her own. Kate knew by now she wasn't going to be a great artist, but she continued to make movies for hours in isolation, letting no one see what she drew. She practiced the piano doggedly despite a lack of coordination that made every piece twice as hard for her to learn as it had been for Merrill. But once Kate mastered a piece, she'd play with such will and intensity that Maddie, with a housecleaning rag in her hand, would get caught up in it and have to stop and listen. But as soon as Kate realized she was being listened to, she'd switch over to her scales, or stop playing altogether.

Maddie thought of the dancing worms in her old aquarium; Kate had Katy's temperament, but not the specialized artistic talent. Maddie didn't know if she should be sorry or relieved.

Merrill was feeling especially shut out by Kate lately. On Ash Wednesday, still in the fatigue of depression, Maddie had lain under the dining-room table to listen to Vaughan Williams's *The Lark Ascending*—its lovely flights against gravity. Kate had joined her, curling up close and tight, sharing the emotional release of the little bird's victory. "What are you crying for?" Merrill had said, passing by, hearing Kate's sniffs. "I thought you liked that music!"

"That's *why*, stupid," Kate had answered. "Don't you understand *anything?*"

Of course Merrill understood it. But for her, as for her grandfather Willy, emotion was often too embarrassingly intense to risk showing. Like him, and perhaps like her mother too, Merrill kept her feelings contained.

Of the three children, Nathan seemed the most blithely immune to emotional extremes. Last month, when a baby rabbit was mauled by a cat and died despite all Kate could do for it, she'd run out of the house in a fury, abandoning the corpse as a personal failure. Nathan had been upset too, for about fifteen minutes. Then he told Maddie something ought to be done for it—a funeral service. The rabbit's death should be honored with a ceremony. So he dug a hole by a holly tree. Watching from a neighbor's yard, sulking by the fence, Kate yelled over that she wanted nothing to do with it. What was the use? But she moved closer as Nathan wrapped the bundle of torn fur in a handkerchief and positioned Maddie and Merrill around the gravesite. "Someone should say something," he said, solemn as a minister. "Like Dad does at the cemetery."

"Go ahead," Maddie said, encouragingly. "You do it."

Nathan paused to think, and it occurred to her that in all their years of grieving, the family had never done this for Deane. They had never held a memorial service for him, since Bert had never conceded he wasn't coming home. She noted Kate's eyes peering around the corner of the house now, saying no, I do not consent to this death.

Not knowing what to say, Nathan made a salute and recited the Pledge of Allegiance.

"That's not a prayer," Merrill laughed, superior to it all. "Mom, he is *such* an idiot."

But Nathan finished the pledge, dropped the rabbit in the hole, and filled it up with dirt. "Poor bunny," he said, and then, after a brief stare at the ground, went into the neighbor's driveway to shoot some baskets.

In a few days he forgot all about it. But for a month afterward, Kate tended the grave as if the President of the United States were buried there. No wonder Kate was Bert's favorite, Maddie had thought, watching from the kitchen window. That evening, she decided to give her daughter a lesson on the Eskimo mask displayed in the living room, explaining what Deane had taught her, that some things got away from people—health, youth, a loved pet, tomorrow night's supper. (She did not tell her the experience of the vanishing Christ she'd had when she was Merrill's age, when the mask had actually spoken and said that plenty of things got away from God too. She had never been able to remember the last words the emaciated Christ had told her, the forgotten compensation or comfort—whatever it was.) Listening gravely, looking at the mask with new respect, Kate said she could see the rightness of the Eskimo lesson for the hunters of the world; they shouldn't get all the game. But not for salvagers like herself who only wanted to throw some of the washed-up losses of life back into the ocean for another chance. If they got washed up or hurt through no fault of their own, they deserved to be saved, she argued. Not even one should get away. "Well, we wish that were true," Maddie said, unable to refute her logically.

As Maddie slid the chicken-and-rice casserole into the oven and prepared to make filling for two lemon pies, Kate still sat at the table in a funk of indecision about the banana. Merrill sauntered in, dressed in blue jeans and a torn sweatshirt. "I don't want to go to the Lenten dinner," she said routinely. "I have too much homework."

I don't want to go either, Maddie thought, and I have no better work to do.

"That means she wants to talk to Lance Meyer on the phone all night without you being here," Kate said.

"Shut up," Merrill said.

Maddie looked at her sternly. Compared to the casually obscene language she'd heard from the kids at the open-house at school last month, she knew her kids were angels, and she wanted to keep it that way. "After the supper," she said, "there's going to be a short film instead of a speaker. It won't be long."

"We already saw it in Sunday school," Merrill said. "A whole bunch of Ethiopians sitting outside little broken-down shacks, walking down dusty roads, and everybody goody-goody for Jesus—as if we should all just pack up and go there and carry water buckets with grins on our faces. Yuk."

"Missionaries do good work," Maddie said automatically, "for people who don't have chicken and rice."

"Oh, I know," Merrill said listlessly, draping herself over the counter and looking into the lemon froth Maddie was stirring. "I just can't stand the way some of those women at the church talk about them. Mrs. Jackson keeps gushing in Sunday school about our 'Christian obligation.' "

"I hate all missionaries," Kate said, eating the banana, logic triumphing.

"What will the church do when everybody *does* have chicken and rice?" Merrill pressed. "What are Christians sup-posed to do then?"

"That's easy to ask with Jordache jeans on your behind and two pies in the oven," Maddie answered. "Weren't you the one that couldn't settle for jeans with a Sears label?"

Merrill nodded begrudgingly.

But in fact, the same question had occurred to Maddie lately. There were ways of starving to death other than those the activist church was addressing. But she added, for a positive note, "I used to look forward to Lenten dinners when I was growing up. There wasn't as much tension in the churches then. But there also wasn't much social awareness. Now congregations have to confront important issues like racism, sexism—"

"And homosexualism," Kate snickered at Merrill, who, not in the mood, didn't laugh back.

"Homosexuality," Merrill said with a condescending roll of her eyes. "*Gayness.*"

Maddie could see she was losing her audience. "Just try to be good tonight," she said. "Only two more Lenten dinners left. And then we can go to Pittsburgh and see Grandma and Grandpa."

After a silence, Kate stood up and flared with anger, "How can I be good all the time and have any of the kids here really get to know me? The kids in North Hebron were finally getting to know who I really was, and then we moved again. Nobody can be as good as we are and be real."

"Speak for yourself," Maddie replied softly. (How well both her daughters were picking up on her own hypocrisy.)

Merrill pushed her mother aside and took over the stirring. "How do you keep from getting mad, Mom, when people like Harry Munson, who pretends to be Dad's friend, spreads rumors about him and works behind his back to get rid of him? Harry hates communism, and now he hates Dad for teaching a class in nuclear dismemberment—whatever it was."

"Nuclear disarmament."

How did Merrill know so much of what was going on? Most of the time her kids seemed oblivious to her and Nate's discussions about church matters. But they were getting too old to protect. She supposed it would become harder and harder to convince them that some of the church's problems weren't endemic—like dust in Ethiopia. "Your father doesn't much care for communism either," she said firmly.

"Becky's dad is an Episcopalian minister," Kate said, referring to her new friend at school. "Somebody threw a snuffbox through their living-room window on the first Sunday in Lent because her dad said women ought to be priests."

"I admire him," Maddie said. "But we're supposed to always try to forgive and understand people."

"They don't always try to forgive and understand *us*," Merrill shot back. "Just think what would happen if I got pregnant or something, or—"

"Merrill," Maddie said, "don't—"

"Just *what if?*" she continued. "What if you decided to become a Hindu? Or what if *Dad* ever did anything wrong? Would they understand and forgive *him?*"

Maddie thought of the gentle "What if" game Grandaddy used to play with her and her sisters. She was sorry her children played this one instead. "Of course they would," she said reassuringly. "That's what the church is all about. Now why don't you go upstairs and get dressed?"

"Some people act like everything wrong in the world is our fault," Merrill said, carelessly slopping the lemon filling into the pie crusts Maddie had made that morning.

"Take it easy," she said irritably. "I want them to look nice."

"Oh, who cares?" Merrill said. Both she and Kate frowned and left the kitchen.

There was fault everywhere, Maddie conceded. And at that moment it felt like it was all hers. Her daughters were so close to the church, all they could see was its flawed inner workings. Never the grand conception.

What was the grand conception?

She rinsed Kate's fruit plate and looked at herself in the mirror over the sink: face calm, impassive. Lent, 1982, is interminable, she sighed. I want to go home. I want to be at Bert's bedside. But then she resolved to be more careful, to deprive herself of any expression of frustration that might prejudice her children against the church before they knew what it really was.

What was it?

Nate and Nathan burst into the kitchen noisily through

the back door, back from a volleyball game with the newly
formed Youth Club at church. Nathan was high with excitement. "Guess what, Mom?" he said, eyeing the pies.

"What?" she said, checking the clock. Not much time left.
"Nathan, could you hand me six eggs out of the refrigerator?"

"I saw a real bum at the church," he said, not hearing.
"This real old raggedy man came to the door of the kitchen
when my team was getting drinks of water—"

"A transient," Nate said, getting the eggs for her. "One of
the worst I've ever seen."

"I mean he was a *real* bum," Nathan said. "He had on this
scummy old brown raincoat and carried a bottle in a paper bag
and everything. His tennis shoes had high tops, and he tied
them *around* his ankles with his shoelaces instead of lacing them
in his shoes, and his face had big purple marks all over it. And
you should have seen his *teeth*. He said the minister down the
street was a God-damned-son-of—"

"Never mind," Nate said firmly. "I gave him five bucks and
a ride to the Salvation Army. But they were filled up and
wouldn't take him."

No, Maddie communicated to Nate sharply: not here. I
don't do that anymore.

"Don't worry," he smiled. "I found a shelter over on Grant
Street that took him—fleas and all."

"I've got to feed my flytrap," Nathan said, grabbing the
flyswatter out of the cupboard and bouncing out of the kitchen.

"What did Nathan really think of him?" Maddie asked
Nate after he'd gone, worried about the lasting effects such a
person might have on her impressionable son.

Nate laughed. "He wanted his autograph."

Lent dragged on into the fifth week. Willy called to say
that Bert had a second stroke, was bleeding from the rectum,
and was breathing steadily but shallowly. Maddie apologized

again for not being able to come home, but her father said it was too soon, meaning, logically, that she shouldn't come until it was too late. Bert was in and out of semiconsciousness, never fully awake. And who would take Maddie's children's choirs (they were behind in their cantata), host the Lenten study group, or play the organ for the adult choir rehearsals? ("To visit her always-ailing grandmother?" she could hear Hettie Barnett whispering to Fred Barnett if she went to Pittsburgh. "She's so tied to that family of hers!") I do not own my own life, Maddie thought resignedly as she hung up the phone.

Sympathetic to Maddie's worry about Bert, her next-door neighbor—the mother of the boy Kate had swatted with the broom—brought over a big coconut-covered cake in the shape of an Easter bunny. Maddie loved it; the giver wasn't a self-conscious church member extending kindness to the pastor's wife, but just a good neighbor concerned for another person. As an experiment, Nathan fed one of the pieces of coconut to his flytrap, pestering Maddie and his sisters to help him pick a name for it. "I want the *perfect* name," he said, bringing the plant to the supper table. Kate suggested Godzilla or Hydra. Merrill suggested Napoleon. Nathan shook his head no. They were stupid names—not right.

The next day, Maddie hunted out the old crown of thorns from the cellar for yet another Tenebrae service next Friday night; it seemed that Jesus was always being born or dying, sermon after sermon, year after year—and just lately, Nate was looking tireder, older to her, and a little stooped in the shoulders, as Reverend Rutke used to look when she was fourteen years old. Yesterday he'd walked old blind Mary Gurney up and down the street for an hour and loved the conversation with her. Some of the work he did was what he'd expected to do in the ministry, he told Maddie when he stopped in at lunch. But then, back at the office, a note was waiting that another one of the local service organizations wanted him to

give the Invocation and Benediction at a fundraising dinner
Thursday night, which meant sitting through the entire evening's agenda instead of going shopping with Maddie for stuff-
ings for the kids' Easter baskets. And the printer needed help
getting out the church newspaper—Maddie's book review was
too long again. And regarding the choir rehearsal the night
before when someone had broken into the vestibule and stolen
all the singers' wallets and purses, wealthy Mrs. Horn (the gold
chains around her neck could support a small family in Ethiopia
for a year, Nate had said) was threatening to take the amount
she'd lost out of her church pledge and urging other singers
to do the same. "The church has no security," she said. "Right,"
Nate had told Maddie after walking home in a wet spring
snow. He said he felt preached out, that he had no idea what
he was going to say for Palm Sunday.

When Palm Sunday came, Maddie's Junior Choir sang,
and Nate preached an adequate sermon, leaning heavily on
"pulpit helps." She could tell that most of it wasn't his voice.
Instead of listening, halfway through, her mind wandered back
to when Bert first went into the nursing home in 1976. Her
doctor had predicted that she probably wasn't going to relin-
quish her own life with any less of a struggle than she'd given
up anyone else's, and he'd been right. Two years later, when
Bert finally realized that her house and Grandaddy's car had
been sold along with everything else (except for what Maddie
and Ginny had salvaged), she cursed Willy week after week
for depriving her of her possessions, of her very dignity. "I
have no transportation!" she complained to Essy, as full of life
and will for the future as ever. But then, in desperate need of
her son's affection, she blocked out the knowledge that the
house was gone, and began to think in terms of making an
escape to it. If she could get back to her house, she wrote
Maddie, she could get well and resume her old life.

Actually, she had spent most of her days in a wheelchair.

Esther wrote that she worked for hours trying to undo the cloth tie around her waist that held her securely in her chair, only to collapse on the floor as soon as she put any weight on her ruined legs. Too helpless to get up, she would scream for Molly, the old black nurse who liked her, to come help her, cursing her son anew for putting her in this place. But Molly had gotten to know Willy well over the past years and told Bert again and again what a fine son she had. The next day, Bert would forget all about it.

Essy came to see her every other evening. Receiving her as though she hadn't seen her in a year, Bert would tell her that snakes crawled around her room at night and that rats were served to her on breakfast trays. The nursing staff was rough, she wept; they scolded her; they had no *affection* for her. Some of them even mocked her, inviting her to participate in children's recreations and kindergarten amusements. But she refused to shake a broken tambourine in their dreadful little band, she informed Essy. She would not paint a ceramic dog or sit in a circle and play a C sharp bell when a musically ignorant band director pointed at her and said "Play." No, she wrote to Maddie in long, anguished letters, she would neither *Play* nor *Stay*. She was going to get out. She was going home. "I can't understand the women here," she wrote at the end of a long, convoluted Christmas letter in 1979. "They have so little sense of family or past. Nobody is tied to anything or remembers anyone with *nostalgic* pleasure and pain. It is so strange to me—apples without cores."

Then last fall, Maddie heard from her mother that Bert had actually tried to crawl out of the home. On a warm September night, she had decided to act on a long-harbored plan of escape: to call a taxi, to crawl down the corridors in the middle of the night, right under the noses of the nurses at their station, to the front door, and to make her escape out to the street and ride away. Silently, at two A.M., painfully, she slid out of bed, crawled into the hallway, and looked both ways. No nurses. No one at all on duty at the moment. Nothing but silence and a long lighted runway to freedom. Exhilarated, almost at the door, she decided that perhaps her legs could support her if she willed them to. She wanted to walk out of the place with her head held high so the taxi driver wouldn't think she was doing anything wrong. But after a few steps, her right knee cracked to the side, she went down hard, and her body slid into a jammed-up position in the corner. Molly heard her fall from a nearby room and came running. She found her looking up from the floor with panicked eyes. "Mrs. Cameron," Molly said, "what happened? Where were you going?"

"I'm going home," Bert sobbed, recovering her determination when she saw who it was. "You help me."

"You can't," Molly said, dragging her out of the corner by the shoulders. "You are seven miles away."

"I've called a taxi. My son stole my car. I have no transportation. I'm going to buy a new car I can drive myself. *You* could buy it for me and drive me out to the country . . ."

Molly cradled her. "No," she said softly. "I can't do that."

"*Why not?*" Bert pleaded. "I'm a grown woman. I have property. I raised two sons in my house—model sons."

"Tell me about your sons," Molly said, motioning to another nurse to call an ambulance for Bert's twisted leg. "I know Willy. He's a wonderful man. Vice President of his company by now, isn't he?"

"Oh," Bert sighed, "he was the sweetest, gentlest-spirited little boy . . ."

"Tell me about your other son," Molly said, rocking back and forth. "What is his name?"

"Who are you?" Bert said, agitated by the question. Then losing consciousness, "Do I know you. . . ?"

After that, the doctor ordered more tranquilizers and mood elevators. In her better moments, Bert would reminisce with Essy and Willy and Ginny about all the happy times they'd spent together. She'd ask for books to read, and Essy brought them, though Molly said she didn't read them, only held them in her lap from the time she got into her chair in the morning until she went to bed at night. But in her worst moods, she still begged Willy to take her home before it was too late. "I can't endure the loneliness," she would plead, clutching his arm. "The white sheets and walls, the linoleum, the chrome railings and fixtures and bars!"

"They want everything to be clean and bright," Ginny said, having gotten permission to decorate Bert's windowsills with artificial geraniums since real plants were not allowed. Bert said through tears that she tried to enjoy them.

Maddie wrote that maybe Willy ought to bring in some of Bert's flow-blue china and antiques to personalize the room. But Essy said no. Bert would take it as a sign that her household wasn't intact, that everything was not in its place exactly as she'd left it. Besides, the home said it would not be held responsible.

In January, Lynne had called Maddie to say she was worried about her father's spirits as much as Bert's. On a recent visit, in an effort to cheer Bert up, he'd praised the decor of the home—the Oriental rugs in the lobby, the cheerful print draperies in the dining room, the watercolors on the walls of the hallways. But renewed rage had spurted out of Bert's eyes in tears that streaked the rouge she still rubbed into the hollows of her cheeks. "You are a liar!" she reproached him. "You have stolen my car! You have abandoned me! When have you ever cared for rugs or draperies?" As logically as Willy dismissed her words as the effects of age and illness, Lynne could see how hurt he was by them. That day he had whispered to Essy, "*I* should have been the one who died," and hardly said anything

at all during the next few visits—just stood against the wall
or looked out the window while Ginny and Essy did all the
talking.

What was worse, Lynne said, he was gravitating toward
the comforts of Essy's religious fundamentalism, interpreting
everything that happened as according to a Divine Plan; all a
good person could do was accept, be unfailingly strong, perform all duties with unquestioning faith, and endure the Mystery until Judgment Day. He attended to every task with a
driving, perfectionist control, Lynne said. No loose ends. Nothing left to chance. And no mercy for those who doubted or
weakened.

No tolerance for ambivalence, Maddie remembered
Deane saying about him thirty years ago. And now he was
surrounded with it.

"It's as though all the sun in the world had gone out,"
Bert wrote to Maddie from the home, "and there was only the
moon left to light night *and* day." Could Maddie imagine the
horror of immobility in a place where no one knew her? she
demanded.

Yes, Maddie wrote back, thinking about her depressions
in the last two parishes. She could well imagine.

"My hair is white," Bert confessed in the next letter. "They
refuse to let me dye it for fear of inflaming my eyes. The very
idea!"

Worried that Bert would try to do something foolish again
in her will to escape, Essy counseled her at every visit to be
patient. "It takes time to make new friends," she said, knowing
that, even in good times, Bert might know a person for five
years before she revealed a single confidence.

"Friends!" Bert laughed scornfully. "There are no friends
in a place like this. There's no time. You know that! If only I
could get out, I could live again. I *know* I could."

More and more in sympathy with her loneliness, not feel-

ing physically well herself, Essy promised Bert she would
write a letter to her every day from now on, in addition to her
visits. That way Bert would have a certain daily contact with
someone who loved her and knew her—something she could
count on.

"Oh, would you?" Bert had leaped at the suggestion. "Do
you *promise?*"

Essy promised. And she kept her promise, day after day,
month after month.

After the Palm Sunday service, Maddie went home in a
strangely hopeful mood. Easter was only a week away. Maybe
by some miracle Bert would live to see her again after all.

"What should I name my flytrap?" Nathan asked everyone
again around the lunch table.

"Who would want to name a plant?" Merrill said, sick of
the subject.

"Maybe it should have something to do with its appetite,"
Maddie said, "a mythological name."

"How about Pier Rana?" Kate said. "Get it? Piranha? Or
Zambesi. That's the name of a shark in South Africa that eats
people."

"No," Nathan said, dissatisfied. "I want a name with—"

The phone rang. It was Grandma Ginny, Merrill said,
handing her mother the receiver.

Maddie's stomach tightened. First, her mother wished
them all a happy Palm Sunday. Then she reported that
the doctor had ordered antibiotics for Bert. Her lungs were
filling up with fluid. He doubted she would get through the
night.

Feeling a sense of finality after hanging up the phone,
Maddie sat on the living-room couch and went through all
Bert's letters one by one. The last one she looked at had come
in early March, just six weeks ago, a disoriented, late thank-

you for a Christmas box Nate and Maddie had sent in December with stamps, pens, poems, and a few handmade gifts from the children. Reading it again, Maddie found it surprisingly long and expressive:

Dearest Maddie, Nate, and the three little
    darlings I had hoped to *happily* know,

First I must thank you for the box of LOVELINESS you have sent me and apologize for the box of NOTHINGNESS I give in return. I am just getting over the flu and *not* getting over losing Howdy.

Your mother called me and said why don't I stop grieving and invite her and *her* mother and Essy over for a card party. Why don't we ever have parties anymore? she asked. We don't. It's true. You know I can't walk, but I said I would try. So I cleaned painfully *for three days*, put out my best pink satin bedspreads, bought fresh strawberries, an orange coconut cake with beautiful *pink, green, yellow*, and *white* rose decorations on it. I got out my prettiest dishes, and the Spode Tower—shining blue after I washed all the years of dust off them. I dragged up early, for my grief is just too much to bear, and the telephone rang. It was your mother telling me that Willy had decided to drive them all down to the Campground for a weekend. I said Oh! Don't say you're not coming!

I sent Christmas cards, but I must have misunderstood, for Essy said they were all upside down. I opened one card with a large colored picture of Jesus at the Last Supper, and it read: ANOTHER SOLITARY PERSON. I wept and wept. It is so insulting to be here, Madeleine. Can't you convince

your father to release me? His heart has hardened.
I don't know how it has happened. I WILL NOT
STAY. The other people here get more cards, and
one of the women THREW a card at me and said,
You thought you were better than we were, but it
didn't turn out that way, did it?

I have no transportation, your father has sold
my car. I was ready to learn to drive it if only he
would have taught me! My son! I should have
learned these things earlier. I thought it was a safe-
guard to put things in his hands. Mama lived to her
last day in her own house, surrounded by her children *who all lived* and who *loved her*. I miss my mother.
I never heard of such a thing in our family. A false-
hood, a compounded lie! And now my dreadful cys-
titis again. They are so rough with a catheter. Except
for Molly. Molly has *breeding*, you know. It was immediately apparent. I have fallen and my eyes are
poor since the blow to my head. Imagine not being
able to *read*. I am starving. I can't eat chocolate and
salads and cheese, as you know, and they bring it
every day.

Essy brings me books, just to have them in my
lap under my hand. And she writes *every day* so I
shall have something coming in the mail as the other
women do. She is a very good sister even if she
does think I am damned.

And you, my dear Maddie, are *very good* with
your young family. This was meant to be a happy
letter. Love your children.

Good-bye *everybody*, and please remember—
THANK you. Remember, dear Maddie, what I used
to repeat to you when you were small and close
to me?

I she went oh! am she gone?
Have her left I all alone?
Will her never come to we?
Would I never go to she?
It cannot was!

It's funny how its downright WRONGNESS
makes it RIGHT. *It cannot was.* When will I see you
again? Surely I could never have been as happy as
I suffer the memory of now—? Did I write this? I
cannot remember.

And from that I'll try to grab the brass ring and
get off—

Thank you and love, *sadly,*

Your loving grandmother

Maddie read the letter through twice, fighting back tears.
Then Kate joined her on the couch and helped her put the
pile of letters in chronological order. She read the one Maddie
had just read.

When she finished, she put her head in Maddie's lap and
stayed there, not making a move or sound for a long time.
Nathan came into the room, loudly announcing that at last he
had chosen a name for his plant.

"What?" Maddie said, trying to show interest. "Maybe you
ought to name it Bert?" she suggested impulsively, thinking of
Bert's voracious appetite for life.

Nathan looked at her as though she were crazy. "Who
would name a Venus flytrap after their grandmother?"

"Well, maybe not," she reconsidered.

"Stan," he said enthusiastically. "Its name is Stan."

Kate sat up, looked at him, and then at her mother.
"Stan?"

"Yeah," he said. "Isn't that perfect?"

"But it doesn't mean anything," Kate said, unable to believe it. "I suggested Zambesi, and you picked Stan?"

"I don't want it to mean anything," he said. "I just like it."

So he wouldn't see her laugh, Maddie pulled Nathan toward her past her face for a hug. Where on earth had *he* come from? she communicated to Kate.

Love your children, Bert had said in her letter. I do, Maddie thought, as Nathan returned the hug and she and Kate exchanged grins behind his back. I do.

The night of the *Requiem* performance, four guest choirs joined Maddie's choir, along with an orchestra and a brilliant guest conductor. As Maddie sang alto, she thought that the text of the *Requiem* was perfect for Bert, who was still dying, still alive. How she would have appreciated the words: "They that sow in tears shall reap in joy . . ."

She sang hoarsely, unable to decide between listening to the performance and participating in it. The orchestra was small, but good. She looked out over the congregation at so many familiar faces at such a distance, and felt a longing pain to be one of them, to really love them. She wished even one of them knew Bert.

The next day was Good Friday. She helped Nate set up for the Tenebrae service, which she had missed for the first time last year. She noticed that several spiders had taken up residence in the crown of thorns. There was a fine little network of webs all through it. Thinking of Kate and the locusts, she let the spiders stay.

That evening, when the service began, she gave herself over to it unreservedly, as she used to when Katy was alive. Nate preached a short, passionate, entirely original sermon. Jesus died completely and utterly, he said, as every other person dies. He had no protections or immunities or divine anesthetics.

Anyone who didn't believe that was a heretic or a dreaming fool.

Amen, Nate, Maddie cheered silently from her place. Wait for me, Bert, she prayed, habitually by now.

Saturday night, her father called to say Bert's condition was terrible, but unchanging. Maddie's mother would have supper waiting for them tomorrow night no matter what time they got in. (Dear Mother, Maddie thought, anticipating the homemade soup—how much she wanted to see her.) Don't race, her father warned, cautioning her about fog, deer jumping out across the highway, drunken holiday drivers. (Did people get drunk on Easter? Maddie smiled as she hung up the phone after promising they would be careful. For someone sold on the Divine Plan, he seemed mightily concerned about safety.)

On Easter morning, the kids' baskets were lost between the sunrise service and two later services. The warm humidity of these latter weeks of Lent was persisting with a vengeance. By the second service the sanctuary was hot and sweet-smelling with a hundred and twenty-five potted lilies and ferns. Blaring brass proclaimed resurrection, mostly on key. Maddie's choirs, forty children tripping over choir robes and lilies, filed up the steps of the chancel and sang three memorized anthems well —but for Maddie, as if out of a tunnel half a world away. Her ears hummed. Her hands shook as she conducted. Then one overheated child leaned out over the first-row pew and threw up a colorful mass of half-digested jelly beans. Maddie was thankful to see Kate's look of "No problem, Mom, I'm used to this," as she ran to get paper towels to clean it up and thirty-nine children snickered through the Offertory. Someone left Nate a one-pound chocolate rocket ship on his desk. Nathan claimed it as his reward for sitting through two services.

After church, Nate called a brief Session meeting to ask permission formally to leave for several days. ("Why aren't we entitled to weekends as a matter of course?" Maddie asked, frustrated with the further delay.) Nate packed the car, and they drove seven straight hours to Pittsburgh.

When they arrived, Esther and Lynne welcomed them joyfully. Maddie's mother sat them down to delicious home-made bread and vegetable soup. Her father hugged and kissed each child, throwing Nathan around until he was black and blue. Watching, Maddie remembered how Deane used to roughhouse with her like that long ago.

"Rest tonight," her mother said, looking at her closely. "You're exhausted. Go see Bert in the morning. It won't make any difference."

"Nothing's changed," her father said. "Her heart is weaker and weaker, but still steady as a rock. It's almost horrible how she holds out."

Maddie nodded. Yes, and No.

While Nate and her father discussed holiday traffic, she went upstairs to look around. For a moment, she stepped into each of the bedrooms. She felt Katy's presence—or rather, could still feel her absence in the house. On an impulse, she went up to the attic. Breathless and dizzy at the top of the stairs, she realized that, in the rush, she'd forgotten her pre-scription for depression. She looked around hurriedly, into the back room where she used to paint and write poems for Bert, into the middle room where she and Katy had made Legion, the Prince of Darkness, and into the corner where the mask had fallen off the broken lampstand. The lampstand was still there. Stimulated by memory, she tried once more to recall what the Christ-mask had said to her in her dream that had been so comforting. But she couldn't. She looked into the cupboards where Deane's boxes were stored. They were gone.

"I want to go see Bert tonight," she told Nate when she came downstairs, feeling a strange urgency and anxiety. "Bring your Bible. You can read her favorite passages. I know them."

"She won't hear it," her father said, grabbing his jacket,

glad to go, Maddie noted with surprise. "She doesn't see or hear anything."

"Sometimes they can hear through a coma," Nate said. "I don't know how it happens, but it does."

Nate helped Maddie on with her sweater and held her tight against him for a moment.

No, she felt, not wanting to be touched or reached. Not yet.

They drove to the nursing home. It was dark, cooling off. Maddie could see grape hyacinths and daffodils along the entrance walkway, bleached white under the outdoor spotlights. Inside it was dim and quiet, not such a terrible place, she thought objectively, unless one had to live there. The halls *were* tunnel-like—long, beige, and lined their entire length with pastel watercolors of generic farms and cities in chrome frames.

Maddie dreaded turning the corner to Bert's room. When she did, she was shocked, not by the horror of her appearance, but by the change in it. Bert looked as though she'd been burned in a furnace to a pure-white powdery ash. No cosmetics, no dyed hair; just the smooth white skin and spread-out snowy hair of an old woman almost weightless, utterly colorless. A dim fluorescent tube over her bed lit her face like moonlight. Then Maddie saw where all her color was. At the foot of her bed, hanging down from a chrome bar, was a clear plastic bag slowly filling up with purple blood. It looked like a pillow, soft and plump. Bert was literally draining away, dissolving into liquid. But she was still alive. What did it take to kill her? Maddie wondered—to finally defeat her will? And where, she wanted to know, were Bert's sources of resistance?

Bert's eyes were open but unfocused, her brow "as moist as an athlete's in the middle of an Olympic competition," Nate whispered behind her. She was tied down. But her right forearm was free and in constant motion, going restlessly back and forth, back and forth. Her lips moved in an effort to form words.

"I thought you said she couldn't talk," Maddie said to her father, who stood back against the far wall, familiar with it all, shut in, shut out.

"She talks in her sleep," he said. "Rambling—the same syllables over and over. Sometimes I think she's remembering things from the past, old conversations. But it's all nonsense. She's more restless tonight. I've told her every day you were coming. Maybe she senses you're here."

Yes, Maddie hoped, approaching the bed.

"Happy Easter, Bert," Nate said softly, and pulled up a chair close to her head. Maddie chose a passage from the Old Testament first—*Job*. Nate read with earnest, unpretentious diction: " 'Oh that my words were now written! Oh that they were printed in a book! Oh that with an iron pen and lead they were graven in the rock forever . . .' "

Tears blurred Maddie's vision. She turned so that her father couldn't see her.

Nate read from Ecclesiastes: " 'Say not, Why were the former days better than these? Who knows the interpretation of a thing?' "

Bert knew these verses by heart. She had known Ecclesiastes inside and out: " 'What is crooked cannot be made straight,' " Nate read (Maddie thought of Bert's poor crooked legs), " 'and what is lacking cannot be numbered . . . Like fish which are taken in an evil net, and like birds which are caught in a snare, so the sons of men are snared at an evil time, when it suddenly falls upon them. There is an evil which I have seen under the sun, as it were an error proceeding from the ruler . . .' "

That was Bert's whole contention, Maddie thought—that in letting Deane go, the Ruler had made an error. She moved to the side of Bert's bed so she could look into her vacant eyes. There was a faraway, unreachable distress in them. Nate turned back to *Job* and read, half from memory, in a slow, comforting cadence. (How many funerals had he done that she hadn't

attended? How many bedside scenes just like this had he pre-
sided over? When had he learned to do this so well? She gave
in to the plain comfort and authority of his voice.) " 'In truth
I have no help in me,' " he read, " 'and my resource is driven
from me. Teach me, and I will be silent; make me understand
how I have erred. How forceful are honest words! I am allotted
months of emptiness, and nights of misery are apportioned
to me.' "

He turned the page. " 'If a man die, shall he live again?' "

If a son die, will he be restored? Maddie paraphrased. For
a moment, Bert's swinging hand stopped in motion. But as Nate
stopped reading, the restless motion began again. Nate looked
at Maddie. He thought Bert could hear. He continued: " 'My
spirit is broken: where then is my hope? Who will see my
hope? I call aloud, but there is no justice. He has walled up
my way, so that I cannot pass, and he has set darkness upon
my path. He breaks me down on every side, and I am gone
. . . Have pity on me, have pity on me, O you my friends, for
the hand of God has touched me!' "

Nate drew closer to Bert's ear. " 'But I know that my Re-
deemer liveth, and at last he will stand upon the earth; and
after my skin has been thus destroyed, then from my flesh I
shall see God, whom I shall see on my side.' "

He is reading for me as well as Bert, Maddie sensed, tugged
at by the familiar affirmation, heard in so many services over
the years.

Now he read from the New Testament: " 'Come unto me,
all ye that labor and are heavy-laden . . .' " And again there was
a brief pause in the motion of Bert's arm. As Nate continued
to read and pray with her, Maddie looked over at her father
against the wall, standing resignedly like one who had brought
in the shaman and then retired, believing, but not participating.
He was awkward with suffering, so steeled in himself against
weakness.

Nate finished. He prayed a prayer for Bert. Her hand resumed its motion.

Then with an authority she didn't know she had, Maddie asked Nate and her father if they would leave for a few minutes so she could be alone with Bert. To her surprise, her father agreed immediately, as if he had expected it.

They went out into the hall, and Maddie shut the door behind them. She came back to Bert's bed and stared at her with a clarity she wasn't capable of when the two men were in the room. Bert would have understood that.

"Bert," she said gently but firmly, as though trying to wake one of her children from sleep. "It's Maddie. Can you hear me?" She touched her arm, smoothed the damp strands of white hair. "Do you know who I am?"

No.

"Bert," she called louder, trying to place her face exactly in the line of her empty stare. "I've come home for Easter to see you."

Bert's brow knit slightly—a familiar response. Was it random? Had she heard her voice? Her eyes took on the slightest expression of confusion, not recognition, as though she'd been interrupted in her concentration by a call from a great distance from an uncertain direction. The murmuring began again. Maddie bent down closer to listen. It was incoherent, just vowels. "Eh . . . ? O . . . Eh . . . ? O . . ."

What was it? A question and answer?

That was all she said, over and over. She was debating with herself about something, Maddie guessed. But with each conclusion in the debate, the question arose again, and she was all the more undecided and unsatisfied. Whatever the question was, the indecision occupied her whole body.

What can I do when she can't hear me?

There was nothing else to do but join her in the debate. And so, together they shared the bed and tried to decide:

Yes . . . ? No . . . Was that it? Wondering Yes about something
and deciding No, but asking again and again. But Bert's face
showed a deeper distress as Maddie formed the words with
her. It wasn't helping.

Then unrestrainedly, out of frustration, Maddie took Bert's
hand and stopped its motion, held it tightly to her cheek and
cried over it, wanting Bert to feel her tears if she couldn't see
or hear them—to feel her mourning.

Bert responded—but in complete perplexity. Who was
weeping? Who was there? And then all at once she wrestled
with Maddie to get her hand free. Maddie let it go. She couldn't
hold it.

That was the problem: Bert couldn't see. She didn't know
who held her by the hand—too tightly. Perhaps she'd
wrenched it free so she could hold it out again to whoever the
child was who was crying and needed comforting. So, very
gently, less possessively, Maddie took hold of her hand again,
let it go, lightly caught it again, not to bind the least part of
her that could still move, but instead to move with her.

As their hands went back and forth, she spoke unreservedly to Bert as though everything were audible and visible:
told her how much she would miss her, and how much she
had learned from her about paradox and beauty—Beauty's massive sandal set on stone (no less overwhelming than depression
on the grass-blades, Maddie knew)—and about the common
family sadness, the blueness for which there was no cure, and
none wanted.

Maddie was sure Bert's eyes strained to focus on her, but
it was from too great a distance. She couldn't travel it. Yet she
was distracted for a moment from her anxiety.

But not for long. The debate resumed. "Eh . . . ? O . . .
Yes . . . ? No . . ."

What else could Maddie say?

She knew perfectly well what she hadn't yet said. But her
father and Grandaddy and Essy wouldn't approve. Maybe even

Bert wouldn't approve. But now, in an effort to reach her, Maddie spoke what she most felt: that the answer was probably No. No to the recovery of health and youth and beauty and pleasure—if one were lucky enough to have ever had them. No to the recovery of sons and daughters who condensed out of nowhere, then could be lost again into the air in a moment.

No, Deane would never come home.

No, Katy would not live. Talent buried in the ground. The failure of the parable.

No, Grandaddy would never have his soup and crackers in his own kitchen. Not here, not anywhere.

No, blue herons would not appear when they were needed, nor raven-gods.

No, justice would not prevail. The crooked could not be made straight.

No, words spoken in anger and petty vindictive actions could not be taken back. The dead would not rise in time for us to ask their forgiveness—if they needed to be asked.

No, Essy's faith would not save her from the whirlwind. Her own health failing, she was suffering Bert's decline along with her, more than she would have imagined.

Maddie paused. But there were other No's.

No, mourning for a loved one was not to be abandoned simply because a length of time had passed. The meaning of a loss did not diminish with the mere failure of a survivor's memory. "Blessed are those who mourn, for they will be comforted"—not comforted by a gradual forgetting of the reason for mourning, but by eternal companionship in it. Christ's own.

No, Deane had not been mortally wounded by what he found in his suitcase. He had understood his mother and loved her. Perhaps he had not been hurt by anything but chance. But somehow his mother and father had made him strong enough to risk chance. He had been fully prepared for the possibility of No.

And No, Katy had not died a helpless victim. She had

understood better than Maddie how to solve the problem of the lion and the Arab: nobody wins until somebody moves. Submission to God was not to be understood as passivity or a failure of will.

And one Yes.

Like Deane and like Bert, Maddie hoped, if not believed, that Yes and No might one day come together. She didn't know how or when, whether God would do it by weaning the earth from His active concern, strategically forsaking it era by era; or by intervening in selected times and places forever, Grace when it was least expected. There was no denying that in the present era many things got away. God himself sustained losses. There were holes in His hands.

Then with the clarity of a child who remembers it's Christmas Day at the first moment of consciousness in the morning, Maddie suddenly clearly recalled the words of the message from the skeleton-Christ—actually the *single* word she'd forgotten, or refused to remember for so long. It was Eskimo (had she heard it from Deane?)—only four syllables—*Ionamut*, meaning "No help for it." If something gets away, one must let it go, the Inuit say. It is right to let it go. It falls into a different sort of gravity. Let it go. Yes, or No, there is no help for it.

Maddie brushed tears out of her eyes roughly. They were an encumbrance. She wanted to see Bert clearly. I am Eskimo, she meant to say: *Ionamut*. There is no help for death. Do not mourn the not-to-be-mourned.

But then, in her imagination, she heard Bert talking back to her. "Why are you crying then, Maddie?" she asked with her old sternness, head at a slant, brow knitted.

Because for a long time now, she answered, there will be no bridge between us, between Yes and No, no bridge of words. No letters. No poems. Nothing.

"I know," Bert would answer. "I am no Eskimo. Perhaps no Christian either."

"No," Maddie explained, tears streaming into Bert's palm, "I don't mean that wherever you're going with this death, there's nothing to mourn. Only that wherever it is, Deane and Katy and Grandaddy are already there. That's all. And I'll be there as fast as the Eskimos say '*Peechook!* All gone!' And we'll see that the words that bubble up from that 'Icarian Sea' from Deane are love and thanks and forgiveness . . ."

Without Bert's giving any dramatic sign or change, something happened between them. Maddie felt suddenly both lighter and heavier, as though weight had been redistributed in her, or as if some kind of formal dismissal—or transfer—of responsibility had taken place. A suspense or cause for anxiety was removed. And yet she felt that an added grief had been given to her. Bert could never abandon her grief. She could be free of it to die only by bequeathing it to someone else who would take it up for her, who would stand by, in case Deane should come back. Maddie accepted it. "I love you, Bert," she said. "The hairs on his head were numbered"—believing it whether she believed it or not.

Then she gave Bert's arm back to her. Soon, it resumed its restless swinging back and forth, the rhythm of simple action, a gesture against powerlessness, without words.

Maddie backed away feeling foolishly young, insubstantial, barely present in the room compared to Bert, who was all spirit now. She was not qualified for what she had just done. And yet, because of depression, perhaps she was more qualified than she might have been. Where was her purse? What else should she do?

Nothing. Only back away from the bed and look at Bert alive from this great distance for the last time.

But she felt dissatisfied.

What else could she do on Bert's behalf? She bowed her head and prayed to the No: *let her go.* Let her get away. Beyond that, Maddie couldn't concentrate. Everything had already been prayed for Bert in the *Requiem* on Good Friday: " 'Now Lord,

O, what do I wait for?' " the choir had sung. " 'Yes, I will comfort
you, says the Lord, as one whom his own mother comforteth.' "

Was there such comfort? Yes. She was here. Be comforted,
grandmother.

Maddie wondered for a moment what the hospital did
with her grandmother's blood when the pillow was full. She
heard more of the text of the *Requiem* in her head: " 'O my God,
I am poured out like water ... Consider my frailty, O Lord
that I must perish ... And he answered, Lo, I unfold before
you a mystery: Blessed are the dead.' "

She slung her purse over her shoulder and went to the
door, not sure whether to go or stay. She looked back once
at the head turned away from her, paused, then went out to
find Nate and her father. There was a latent excitement about
her father when he saw her, a sense that everything was almost
over, which struck her as sadder than Bert's dying.

At dawn next morning, Easter Monday, the hospital called
Willy to say that Bert was dead. He woke Ginny, Nate, Maddie,
and her sister, then called Essy.

Maddie stared out of the bedroom window in her old
room and listened to the birds singing. She felt physically good,
caught in a calm. Bert had waited for her to come home before
she gave up her fight, she was sure. Sometimes the No said
Yes when least expected. Kate, Merrill, and Nathan joined her
and Nate in the double bed. They lay together and talked
about Bert and Grandaddy for over an hour, as though it were
a holiday.

Nate ended the funeral service with the words of Paul:
"None of us lives to himself and none of us dies to himself. If
we live, we live to the Lord, and if we die, we die to the Lord;
so then, whether we live or whether we die, we are the Lord's."
Ginny, Essy, and Kate wept the most; Willy, Maddie, and
Merrill not at all.

Maddie had no difficulty until the closing of the casket when she had to say good-bye to the crooked hands. They held her old reading glasses (the mortician had put them on her face, but Essy had taken one look and said "No, oh *no*, put them in her hands this way!"), and also a handful of blue forget-me-nots, the state flower of Alaska, from her great-grandson, Nathan Deane, whose little-boy hands gently rested beside Maddie's on the edge of the lid. None of the children were frightened or repulsed by Bert's emaciated appearance. Kate was the most quiet, observing, thinking. At the funeral home, she had stood at Maddie's side, the whole time concentrating on Bert's right hand—should she touch it or not? She decided not to. Merrill had stood far back, her eyes red, but composed. She couldn't come any closer.

The lid was sealed. Good-bye, Maddie thought only. Good-bye.

They went to the cemetery. Before the committal service, Essy put a slip of paper into Nate's hand. "I found this yesterday among Bert's papers," she said. "I wanted you to read it at the funeral, but I forgot to give it to you. It's from a book called *White Dawn*, about the Eskimos and their beliefs. I guess it was Deane's. I don't know where she got it."

As they all gathered around the gravesite, Maddie was touched by Essy's desire to have something read besides Scripture for Bert's committal. After reading the "ashes to ashes, dust to dust," Nate read from the scrap of paper: "'And at that moment I seemed to be a part of the earth and a part of the sky, and it did not matter that my legs were twisted ... I dreamed that I could see my soul flying over the soft summer tundra, mirrored in a hundred lakes, and my soul was not like me. It was like some swift gorgeous bird with countless wings and many flashing colors.'"

Maddie wept and laughed. How Bert had suffered with no transportation.

When it was over, the cemetery attendants stood around waiting to lower the casket into the ground, but no one hurried to leave. It was a breezy spring day, the sunlight dazzling if one took one's eyes off the green ground. Kate sensed the lightness in the air and pointed out the birds in the trees to her grandmother. She picked a pink rose from one of the funeral baskets and put it on Grandaddy's grave, then another one for Aunt Katy's. Merrill was embarrassed by Nathan's cheerful chatting with the attendants and peering down over the edge of Bert's grave to see what was down there. Then bored with that, he danced around from grave to grave in this park-like place to find a gravestone with "Nathan" written on it. "He's not even crying," Merrill whispered to Maddie, baffled by his inability to be decently sad. "Why is he acting so happy?"

"Probably because we're all together here," Maddie said. "That's what Bert enjoyed the most too. I bet she'd be glad to see him jumping around here."

Willy told the attendants to go ahead and lower the casket in place. There was no reason why the family shouldn't see Bert to her final place.

Good, Maddie thought, at his decision.

Kate observed the lowering in solemn silence, and then Maddie was relieved to see her attention distracted by a bright red bird perched on a nearby tombstone.

"It's a scarlet tanager," she said excitedly, moving closer.

Still no one was ready to leave.

Nathan peered through the stained-glass windows of the mausoleums across from Bert's and Grandaddy's plots. "Look at this!" he called to his mother and then Grandpa Willy, who stood with his hands in his pockets nearby. Together they looked through the iron bars at the marble interiors—silent, colored sunlight slanting through smoky, enclosed air. "I don't like that," Nathan said. "I want to be dead outside like Uncle Deane."

"It doesn't matter, Nathan," Essy said, hobbling over to them on her newly acquired cane—short of breath, Maddie noticed. "We're all alive somewhere."

Essy turned to Maddie. "You know," she said forthrightly, holding her red nose with a Kleenex, "I've been a selfish person. I hope God will punish me here so he won't punish me hereafter. Maybe He is already."

"No, Essy," Maddie said emphatically.

"Oh, yes," she insisted, following her back to Bert's grave. "I waited so long to tell Bert something Deane wanted me to, until I *couldn't* tell her, and then—"

"Hey, Mom." Kate ran up breathlessly, interrupting. "What did the doctor say Bert finally died of? Dad wants to know what to write in his Bible."

"Another stroke," Essy said sadly, not minding the interruption, hugging Kate. She dropped what she'd been saying to Maddie and wandered off to join Ginny at the car.

"No, Kate," Maddie said when she was out of hearing. "Tell Dad to write she died of a decision."

Kate looked at her quizzically, then accepted it. "Okay."

Back at Bert's grave, as the caretakers rolled up the rug of artificial grass exposing the fine real grass underneath, Maddie thought of what Nate had read from Essy's scrap of paper. She pictured Bert's soul, free and flying over the summer tundra—all in bloom—searching every inch of surface and undersurface at the speed of light, finding in an instant what she had waited so long to find, gathering it up on her countless wings and flying up and up, home at last. Let her go, Maddie told herself, looking up at the blue sky overhead. Let them both go.

No, I can't quite, she qualified the resolution honestly. But I will try.

She watched her father and Nathan walk hand in hand from mausoleum to mausoleum. Nate shook hands with the caretakers, and came over to stand with her. He put his arm around her. "If we lived closer," she whispered, "Nathan would be good for Dad, and Dad for him—do you see?"

"Yes," he said. "I see."

How tired Nate was, she felt, leaning against him.

"We'll have to leave early tomorrow morning," he said.

"So soon?" she said, her voice flat, accepting.

"Vocation and Ministry Committee meeting. I'm the Chairman, and the new candidates are meeting with us tomorrow night. Two weddings Saturday. And I haven't even started the sermon."

She sighed, wanting, wishing simply and plainly, to be out of the church for a while. But how could she say so? She'd been breathing so freely for the past few days. She submitted to no one's judgments but her own. She could be who she was, walk in a cemetery where people from her own past were buried. The missing depression prescription hadn't entered her mind.

And last night, Esther had said she was getting engaged to be married. Maddie hadn't met her fiancé. To Esther's kids, Aunt Maddie and Uncle Nate would be Hallmark relatives: send a card so they won't think you've forgotten them. (But I *have* forgotten them!)

"I'm sorry," Nate said, pain in his eyes.

"It's okay," she said, pain in hers.

E P I L O G U E:
T H E   B L U E
H E R O N

It was January. Maddie jogged along the four-mile bike path
that followed the river, more like a drainage ditch since the
Army Corps of Engineers had rechanneled it to keep the town
from flooding every spring. Jogging would help ward off a re-
lapse of depression, Dr. Hazelett had said before she dismissed
him, or he her. Which had it been? On good terms, they had
both realized there was nothing more to say. She hadn't taken
Limbatrol since Bert's funeral eighteen months ago. Though
her tension headaches continued, she hadn't gone over the
edge.

At the familiar bend in the almost frozen river, she listened
for the ducks. The park lakes had frozen over three weeks ago,
but the river ice took longer because of the pollution, Nate
said. Recently, a small community of mallards had migrated to
the river to drink out of the narrowing channel of still running
water. What kept them from getting sick on it? Now, with
snow covering the brownish, mushy surface and rocky banks,
the river looked even less natural, more constructed. "Something's wrong with that river," Nathan had observed, riding his
bike along the path one day. "I bet there's poison in it."

The mallards were gone. Was it a sign? Maddie wondered. On the first Sunday of this new year, Nate had announced that he was taking a temporary leave of the ministry. He'd written a letter of explanation to the congregation. They had received it, and until the next Sunday, there had been an eerie silence. What would they think of him? Maddie had worried anxiously. For a week, it seemed like the whole town was talking around them. But as Bert had written in her letter, sometimes there is no right time to go and no right time to stay.

At first, many people in the congregation had been shocked, baffled, some bitterly disappointed in Nate—how could he desert his call? (How *can* we? Maddie thought with snow coming down, running, as she was called to, the second mile.) A few answered cynically that, if he could quit, he was meant to quit, and never had the call to begin with. Others were more sympathetic and blamed themselves for failing him. A few vocal ones blamed it all on Maddie.

But then the letters and cards started coming.

Not until now had she known how many people truly cared for them, how grateful they were for all the midnight vigils in homes and hospital rooms, for the counseling through marriages, divorces, family tragedies, for the picnics and family suppers and outings for youth groups, classes and committees, for renovation of the Christian education wing, the children's choirs. (But why was all this love—if it was love—so submerged until they left a church? Why were so many parishioners still so reluctant to accept them as people who liked to go out to dinner and a movie, had sexual ups and downs, sometimes yelled at their children too much?) A faction that had already been working to get Nate out of the pulpit—the "church arsonists," Maddie remembered the former pastor had called them—were rejoicing now. At last the way was clear for the next minister, they were saying among themselves. He would be the one they wanted. He would be the perfect pastor.

God help him, Maddie thought, running the third mile. God give him strength.

The evening after Nate made a preliminary announcement to the Session, Bill Moss, a wonderful old Elder, had called Nate to wish him Godspeed "as you step out into the secular dark." After hanging up the phone, Nate said that somehow that was the first time he felt he'd truly talked with Bill as an equal, man to man. It was as though some invisible barrier had been removed. And it felt not so much like coming down out of the clouds as rising up to sea level. The rest of that evening, the phone had been silent. For the first time in sixteen years, they felt a right to that silence. ("I should be out calling," Nate would normally be thinking, "I should be working on the budget," "I should be reading for the sermon," "I should be planning a Session retreat," I should be, should be, should be.)

To celebrate their ambivalent feelings, Maddie decided to light the ancient gas fireplace in the den of this fourth manse; it was similar to the one that had been in Bert's living room back in Pittsburgh. She and Nate stretched out in front of it, their hands under their heads. "These fireplaces are illegal now, you know," he said. "They emit carbon-monoxide fumes."

"Oh," Maddie said, moving closer to him, feeling both afraid of the future and full of excitement. "Well, that explains everything about my family. Now what about your mother?"

They laughed. They felt disoriented, expansive, like inmates turned out of a prison-monastery before serving their whole life sentences. Could they ever be anything but a minister and wife and not feel guilty for the rest of their lives? Part of her wanted to burrow underground like some tiny Arctic mammal until it all blew over and they were out of town. Another part of her wanted to take off her clothes and dance on the church roof. It seemed like the whole government of the world was changing. But at bottom, she felt God approved of the Harts moving out for a while. God said let them go.

Maddie ran the fourth mile. She was breathing hard against the cold and the pain in the back of her head: the old enemy, the Black Dog, Winston Churchill had called it. The solution was to run at it, to move, to keep outdistancing it.

She had told Nate that, in Columbus, where he'd found his new job as assistant administrator of a nursing home, she intended to look for a part-time job herself, maybe even at a college or university. She wanted to teach American literature, if they would let her: Jonathan Edwards—hounded out of his church—Thoreau, Frost, Emily Dickinson, Santayana, Melville, Poe, Hawthorne, and (forgive me, Bert) Walt Whitman. These authors were her religion. Or rather, what they wrote about God was what she had confirmed in her own life. If there had been a time when she admired the Reverend Arthur Dimmesdale and had gone out looking for his church, it was past. The best thing he'd ever done was love Hester. The worst thing was repent of it. His salvation in Christ was selfish— perhaps a little like Essy's old fundamentalist faith—claimed at the expense of other sinners.

It was snowing hard, beautiful thick snow, softening the surface of the five inches already packed hard on the path. No one else was running today. Not a sign of life in either direction. Could it really be over? she asked herself. Nate had said that Judy Muncy, the church treasurer, had cried when he told her his decision. "What is happening to the church when men like you leave it?" she had said. A good question, Maddie had thought. For as long as they could, they had given it everything they had. But they had never been free of the feeling that it wasn't enough, that in these times the church was a runaway train, and they hardly had the strength to keep it on the track, let alone determine its new direction.

Perhaps they had tried too hard, Essy had told her. Maybe Nate would go back.

Maybe, Maddie agreed. The universe was curved.

At the end of the path, she stopped to rest. Usually, she walked down the steep bank to stand at the water's edge and look at it. "What do you look for in that brackish water?" Nate had asked her when he jogged with her several times last summer. "Why are you drawn to it?"

"Because it moves," she had said. "It moves out of here."

She liked to watch it for at least a few minutes each day. But today, common sense said she shouldn't walk down the bank to the edge. Her shoes leaked. Her socks would get soaked tramping through the new snow.

She went down anyway.

And there, exactly there, looking at her, was a Great Blue Heron—three feet tall, standing like the slate blue of a summer evening against the frozen river. Its long reedy legs stood in the narrow channel of running water. Startled by her sudden appearance over the bank, it took off and circled the ice, gliding, as Deane had written long ago, "like a pterodactyl evolved into grace"; or, as she thought now, like a leathery carnivore turned into the silhouette of a master glassmaker's elongated blue bottle—perfection.

It can happen to us, Lord, she thought. Give us a few more million years.

The heron circled a second time, then returned to its original spot. She didn't move. It stood at ease, on guard, and so did she. But then she couldn't resist moving closer to get a better look at it. If only Kate were here. (She'd never believe a heron could possibly be here in this dirty river. But where else does Grace manifest itself? Nate would say.) The bird looked at her warily as she tested its tolerance of her. At ten feet, she overstepped the boundary. It stooped, jumped, and took off again, up into the blue-white air, immune to the cold, almost out of sight.

Let it go, Maddie thought, having learned her lesson. Let it go.

But every muscle in her body strained after it. Go *with* it, another voice in her said.

And so in her imagination she followed it, higher and higher, keeping its slow, rhythmic wings just barely in sight, not realizing or caring how high it was taking her, through blue-white, to dark blue, and then into black. She paused in the darkness, thinking that, like Icarus, she had flown too high. She turned and looked back.

The sight took her breath away. There, free and floating, was an exquisitely blue planet, flattered by its setting in utmost emptiness and dark. Its blueness was blinding bright, swirling scarves of cloud around its equator-waist like a seductive cosmic dancer. It was altogether beautiful. This was the color of invitation and refuge to any weary traveler in the cosmos, she thought dizzily—the Holy Ground of the solar system, the crystal ball of Yes/No. And no one knew its real destiny or even its real name—except Home. And perhaps, despite all the dire predictions she'd been hearing on television lately about nuclear winter and the projected decimation coming at the end of the arms race, there was nothing people could do to destroy it utterly. They could destroy themselves, certainly. If they were foolish enough to do that, then God would have to let them go. But life would come back again, out of the first blue-green algae that said Yes to the first seduction of returning warmth, up, all the way up to consciousness and government and art and religion—and maybe beyond religion, at last, to true faith. *Ionamut.* No help for it. Alleluia.

Maybe the blue whales should govern the next time, she laughed out loud—huge, benevolent, coming back in force after near extinction.

She turned away from the blue planet to look for the heron. But it was gone. And then, she imagined out of the corner of her eye, the first glint of Halley's comet roaring back from six thousand billion miles out, still a long way off, but well on its way home. By the time it gets here, she made a vow to herself, I will be finished with depression.

And then it occurred to her that, before the comet swung out again, for the first time in history scientists would know what it was made of, what was really at the core of its nucleus. That's what I am learning, she said. I will not go out into that darkness again without knowing why.

But how do I get down from here? she wondered, looking around at the suns and moons and stars—the sublime beauty —all around her.

"Mom," Nathan greeted her as she came up the front steps, "Don't get mad."

"What?" Maddie said, still panting from her jog home, feeling good, her headache gone.

"Nathan broke the Eskimo mask," Merrill said, looking as though she wanted to kill him. "He was dancing around pre-tending he was doing an Eskimo hunting ceremony or some-thing and ran into the coffee table. Look."

One of the hands with the holes had cracked off. It lay palm up on the floor in a gesture of helpless appeal.

Nathan cowered. Kate watched Maddie for her reaction.

Maddie picked up the hand and inspected the twisted end where it had snapped off. It couldn't be glued. She felt let down from the flight of the heron, back on the earth, the blue all scattered, diffused. But she could still feel how it had felt when she was flying.

Calmly she took off her coat, scarf, and ear muffs—and smiled at Nathan to relieve his anxiety. Let it go, a voice said. Let even this go. How could she be angry at Nathan for doing with the mask what the Eskimos intended—dancing, calling down the gods?

Looking at her children, lined up for judgment, she felt the cracked-off hand at the back of her neck, not like the vise-

grip of depression, but more like the "mystic Shape" in the
Elizabeth Browning sonnet Bert had read to her years ago.
"Guess now who holds Thee?" the voice of her uncle laughed
out of the hole in the hand.

    She remembered the answer: "Not Death, but Love."

    And joy, she added now: in lieu of justice. Merrill for
Deane, Kate for Katy, and Nathan—she reached out to give
his soft-cheeked, perplexed face a kiss—Nathan was pure
profit.

Credits continued from page iv

"On the Death of a Metaphysician," reprinted with
permission of Charles Scribner's Sons, an imprint of
Macmillan Publishing Company, from *Poems* by George
Santayana (New York: Scribner's, 1923).

Steve Donelan, "Blood, Sweat, and Chill," *Sierra*, January/
February 1985, Vol. 70, No. 1, p. 115, for his definition
of hypothermia and description of accompanying
symptoms.

Book of the Eskimos by Peter Freuchen, published by
Bramhall House, a division of Clarkson Potter, Inc., 1961,
by arrangement with The World Publishing Company, for
the Eskimo creation myth.

Rodgers Dean Hamilton, "The Tundra Primeval and a
Probable Frog" (unpublished), 1946, and for information
on the Dream Theater and the Bering Sea Fog in "The
Mask with Holes in Its Hands."

Bertha Lynwood Hamilton, for her poems "To a Very
Little Girl" and "Arctic Summer" (unpublished).

Kathryn Rice Letterman, for letters, photographs, and
family papers.

The Alaska Geographic Society, for maps and references
sent promptly upon request.

The Carnegie Museum of Natural History, Pittsburgh;
particularly "Polar World: The Wyckoff Hall of Arctic
Life."

Eileen Hale McLaughlin, for the phrase "blue nature,"
used by permission of her son and daughter.